ODY

TRILOGY

ODY

TRILOGY

FAIRY TALE

JORRI DUURSMA

atmosphere press

Published by Atmosphere Press

Cover design by Kevin Stone

Part I: Translated by Frank Little
Illustrations: Cees Deen

Part II : Translated by the author and verified by Jasmine Kane
Illustrations: Cees Deen

Part III: Translated by the author and verified by Jasmine Kane
Illustrations: Jorri Duursma

Atmospherepress.com

Part 1 of 3

ODY

I

My name is Ody, short for Odysseus. My mother gave me this hero's name because she thought I was so brave. But she should have called me Ignavus, which means "coward." That name would have fit me much better.

I don't have a father, and when I asked my mother why not, she would answer, "You don't have a father anymore. You haven't had one for a long time, a very long time."

Although my mother thought otherwise, I had always thought of myself as rather simple. I could read and write, but I hadn't learned much all the same.

It was my job to feed all the ducks in my village, including the mayor's flock. They were lovely animals, all of them. The ducks were called Annie, Ria, and Jacob, after the mayor's wife, his daughter, and himself. The ducks would see me coming in the distance early in the morning and begin to quack very loudly. This would wake up the mayor, who enjoyed sleeping in, and he would blame me for all the quacking.

"They're quacking because you don't give them enough to eat," he'd always shout angrily. "'You're keeping some of that food for yourself, aren't you, you little rascal."

The villagers were always grumbling and swearing. I didn't do that, though I really couldn't think of anything to grumble about, and I was too simple to think up nasty words. They also often spread mean tales about me, said that I treated the ducks badly and all sorts of other things which scandalized people. They shouted at me and called me names: Fisheyes, Duckbill, or Feedface. They said that I wasn't good enough to feed pigs, let alone the mayor's ducks. There was always somebody jeering at me or shouting nasty remarks and then running away laughing.

In the end, I couldn't bear it any longer, and I decided to leave my village and go looking for a more pleasant place to live.

"You're right, my child," said my mother when I told her of my decision. "Why stay here?" She didn't even seem to mind much!

I wrapped up my belongings in a handkerchief and tied it to a stick. Before leaving, I said goodbye to the ducks with pain in my heart and gave them all an extra helping of corn. My mother waved me goodbye with her handkerchief.

I chose to walk south along the sand track. Some of the villagers booed me for the last time instead of waving goodbye. But I controlled my temper and walked on without turning back.

The track was difficult to travel, and I soon grew tired and hungry. I wouldn't have minded eating a large slice of ham or something similar, but since everything had happened so fast and I had been so angry, I had forgotten to take along anything to eat.

In order to at least quench my thirst, I started to look for a stream. Luckily, I found one within a few minutes. I bent down and rinsed my hands in the cool water. Scooping some up, I swirled it around in my hands, sniffed at it, and then drank it up. I had seen the mayor do that once with wine in a crystal glass. The water was deliciously cool and refreshing.

I walked back to the road, and suddenly there stood a large, bearded man in a yellowish tunic in front of me. His face was the same yellowish color as the tunic, and he had long grey hair.

In a stern tone of voice, he asked, “What are you doing on my property? And what were you doing at my stream?” His voice was so deep that it shook the ground l was standing on and rattled my heart against my ribs.

I was scared stiff and trembled with fright. Only after I had gotten over the shock a little could I manage to stammer a few words: “Passerby ... I ... hungry ...” I stuttered. “Uh ... who are you, sir ...”

“Ha ha ha,” he laughed. “I’ve never heard such a weak excuse. Hungry! Ha ha ha!” In a serious tone, he resumed. “I am the brookbush troll, and you will be my dinner, even though you are a bit scraggy. Well, as I always say: Tasty pigs never grow fat.”

These words scared me so much that I was rooted to the ground. The brookbush troll slung me over his shoulder with a slap and strode with great steps straight through the shrubs and high grass to a cave far from the road. He set me down on a stone in the middle of the cave and then knelt down and began to rummage around in a corner.

This was just the moment I had been waiting for. All I had to do was stand up and run off. But no matter how hard I tried, I couldn’t get off of the stone. It felt as if I was glued to it.

The brookbush troll stood up with a huge cauldron and two knives in his hands. “I think I’ll eat you tomorrow,” he said, intently sharpening his knives. “But I shall start boiling the water now, so you won’t be cold in my pot tomorrow.”

He dragged everything outside, where I suppose he was lighting his fire. When he returned, he studied me thoughtfully for a long time. Then he turned around and laid down against the wall of the cave, falling asleep with a contented smile on his face.

Hours passed, so it seemed at least, and then suddenly, a miracle occurred. The stone I had been stuck to for so long released its grip on me. I scrambled off the stone in an instant, grabbed my belongings together, and crept quickly and silently out of the cave.

A scroll of paper lay on the ground in front of the entrance.

I grabbed it and ran off as fast as I could.

2

It took a long time to walk back to the track again. The brookbush troll had carried me for several hours the day before, but luckily, I had kept my wits about me, and even in the early dawn light, I could find my way back. As I reached the track, the sun began to rise. I sat down on the grass for a moment to catch my breath and think things over.

By now, the brookbush troll would be awake and probably furious, having discovered that I had escaped. No breakfast for him this morning!

For that matter, no breakfast for me, either. To take my mind off my grumbling stomach, I looked over the scroll which I had found by the cave entrance. It was a kind of parchment, a map of some area or other. It showed a stream, a few trees, and some houses. But I wasn't really interested in it right then, so I shoved the scroll into my handkerchief bundle and started off along the track again.

Despite my hunger, it promised to be a glorious day. There lay a village in the distance, not all that large from what I could see, but perhaps the people would have something for me to eat.

It took several hours before I reached the village. There was not a single soul to be seen on the streets; the whole place seemed deserted. It looked like I could forget about getting some food here. But my stomach growled like mad, and if I didn't find something to eat soon, I honestly wouldn't make it much further.

In desperation, I shouted at the top of my voice, "Hello! Hello ... Is anybody around? I'm sooo hungry!"

And suddenly, heads began to appear all over the place. Hundreds of heads. They popped out of rain barrels, attic windows, chimneys, and rain spouts. They eyed me gravely and seriously from top to toe, and slowly, wide smiles spread across their faces.

The people rushed up to me, offering all kinds of food: meat, ham, butter, cheese, and eggs. Then they led me to a tavern where I could sit down and eat in peace. These hospitable people were somewhat smaller than me, and they all wore the same clothing: blue trousers, a green sweater, and a yellow cap. They made me feel good, so good that I felt like staying a few days or perhaps even forever.

A man named Bloomy invited me to stay the night at his home. Like all the houses in the village, his house was made of wood and rather large. Having a very big house was certainly necessary since he was the father of twenty children.

In the evening, I was given the bed of one of the children who was away that night. It was a small bed, and I lay there, extremely uncomfortable, curled up like a ball with my nose against my knees. I dropped off to sleep for a while but woke up in the middle of the night. All my muscles had grown numb. As I lay there in the dark, I thought about the parchment. Would it come in handy for my trip? I had difficulty falling asleep, so I got out of bed, threw a blanket over my shoulders, and sat down by the fireplace.

One of the children in the row of beds also woke up and

came and sat down cautiously beside me. He was very shy, but after a while, he began asking questions. “Where are you going?”

“I’m headed for a village where I can live in peace without being yelled at and called names all the time.” I told him about my adventure with the brookbush troll, which made him feel more at ease.

“Do you still have the map?” he asked.

“Yes, but I don’t think it’s of much use to me,” I said. “I was just considering throwing it into the fire.”

“Oh, no! You mustn’t do that!” cried the boy, as if the map was something he was familiar with. “A large dragon lives near our village, and he wants to have this map very badly.”

“A dragon?” I asked, confused. “What does a dragon want with the map?”

“If you give him the map ...” He couldn’t finish this sentence because suddenly there was an enormous noise outside. I heard a stamping sound followed by screaming, at which point the boy who had been sitting listening so peacefully to my story grabbed hold of me, trembling with fear. I was trembling too, though not nearly as much as the day before when I met the brookbush troll. The noise grew much worse; enormously heavy footsteps crashed through the street.

The boy suddenly let go of me. He looked at me solemnly and said with a tone of command in his voice, “Quick, take the map and go outside. Put the map right in front of the dragon’s paw. Don’t let him see you. Be careful he doesn’t step on you.”

I obeyed him immediately, even though he was only six years old. My heart beating wildly, I grabbed the map, ran down the stairs, opened the door, and looked around. Smoke filled my eyes; there were houses burning all around me. People were rushing about with buckets of water. And then, a huge paw stopped right in front of the door.

It looked like a tree covered in scales. I didn't dare look up at the rest of the dragon; I was scared enough already. I sprang from the doorstep and laid the map right in front of the paw, desperately hoping that the dragon wouldn't step on me. Then I ran back inside, slamming the door behind me, and flew upstairs.

"It worked!" cried the boy, beside himself. "No one has ever dared to do such a thing. The dragon wants the map because it makes him the owner of the property of his enemy, the brookbush troll. He didn't dare steal the map himself, but he wanted us to do it for him. Every night he comes to burn a few houses and tread them to the ground until we fulfill his wish. It's over now, thanks to you!"

Amazed by my own courage, I crept back into bed, trembling all over. The heavy footsteps died out in the distance. Only the noise of people putting out fires and voices calling to each other remained. Did they realize they've been rescued from the dragon?

The next morning, I was awoken by children and adults laughing. They shouted with joy, hoisted me on their shoulders, and carried me outside. "Three cheers for our savior!" they all shouted.

The mayor gave a speech in the middle of the square. It was a tremendous feeling to be so praised, as he said, "And to show our gratitude, we offer you this ring. You will certainly find it useful when you cross the Precarious Mountains. We wish you a good trip. Well, that's all I've got to say."

And so, I left the village with all these happy people around me and a rusty old ring in my bundle. I wouldn't have minded staying a while longer, to be praised and spoiled even more, but the cheerful parade of people just carried me along, onto the road. I couldn't do anything else but go along with them.

3

The friendly villagers walked with me as far as a bridge just outside the village. I walked on alone again from there. It was a beautiful day. I was in such good spirits that I felt like jumping for joy. I couldn't help thinking about the mean, ungrateful people from my own village and knew for sure that I never wanted to have anything to do with them ever again. They were nothing like these kind villagers, who were so grateful. And hadn't I been awfully brave and daring! How nice the world could be now and then.

I walked on at a vigorous pace. The landscape began to change gradually. There were fewer trees now; the ground was very rocky and the air rather chilly, even though it was only midday. A high mountain range rose in the distance, its sharp peaks covered in snow. It was harder going now that the track began to climb more steeply. "*This road must go right over the mountains*," I thought.

After a few hours of walking, I became so cold that I pulled out my sweater from my bundle. The handkerchief was quite large, not a good-for-only-one-blow handkerchief. By now, there were absolutely no trees to be seen, although stacks of wood lay scattered here and there along the way.

I sat down on one of these stacks to rest and take a good look around. The mountains rose like giants nearby, and the grass along the slopes was the greenest as could be.

"Hey, fatso! Get off me! I've enough problems without you adding to them. Come on, get off!"

I jumped up, terrified. "Oh, I'm terribly sorry," I said. "I didn't realize I was sitting on you."

"Excuses," sneered the voice from the wood stack. "You were the one who sat down on top of me. You could have realized that this was my place."

"I don't understand," I said. "Who are you then? Do you live here?"

"Do I live here? Do I live here? What a question? Of course, I live here. Who else did you expect would live here?" replied the voice. "And as to who I am, if you don't even know that, then I shall beat you to death."

"Oh, how awful!" I said, dumbfounded. "Eh, eh ... pleased to have met you, but I really must be on my way now ..."

And I ran away as fast as my feet could carry me until I could no longer hear the voice. What a terrible monster must live in that wood stack; he even wanted to kill me. What a day! What a day! I began to wonder whether my life had really improved since I had left my village.

My feet were crying out for a rest. I was all in favor of that but first looked back to see if I was far enough away from the monster.

Up ahead lay another stack of wood, but I wasn't about to sit there for anything in the world; one never knows! So, I just sat on the ground and peered into my handkerchief to see what there was to eat. When I left that morning, I had grabbed something from Bloomy's table. And sure enough, I found an extremely small piece of cheese.

"How on earth is that possible?" I said out loud. "I'm sure

I only took a piece of bread, certainly not cheese."

"Oh, I'm very sorry. I think I've made a mistake. Here's your bread." said a small squeaky voice.

"Who—who—who said that?" I stuttered. My heart began to beat rapidly.

"Good lord! You've been carrying me with you all this time, ever since you started your journey. I'm your handkerchief, stupid!"

"I don't think I feel very well," I whimpered hoarsely, my nerves in shreds! "I must be going mad here. Help! ... Help! ..." I jumped up and began to run in search of a safe place somewhere, anywhere where nothing would talk back to me, certainly no handkerchiefs! My own handkerchief, no less! And definitely no wood stack!

"Hey! You ungrateful fellow! You've forgotten me! You can't just leave me here like this! It wasn't my idea to come here. Come back!" squeaked a voice behind me. The handkerchief had spread itself out, and, using two of its corners as legs, it was running after me.

"Oh, how awful! This is horrible," I kept sighing over and over again. I was so wound up that, at first, I didn't notice how the mountains began to bend over towards me. Only when the mountains began to laugh and tried to catch me did I notice them. I screamed at the top of my voice, "Oh, I'm scared! I'm so scared! Help ... Help! Please, somebody, save me! Won't anybody save me? Heeeelp!"

"Lie down! Lie down!" deep voices rang out from somewhere in the clouds. Since I couldn't think of anything better, I immediately did what the voices said. I lay flat on the ground with my face buried in my arms as much as possible. Slowly everything around me grew quiet; there was not a voice to be heard.

When I looked up, I saw three men dressed in large, loose rags standing before me. One of the three said in a deep voice,

"You asked for help, and we replied. Now you must thank us by giving us the ring."

I thought to myself for a minute before speaking. "You don't mean that old rusty thing that the mayor gave me?"

"Yes, that's it. We were sent to help you because you allowed yourself to become so ridiculously distressed over a bad-tempered woodworm, a talking handkerchief, and several other things trying to show off for you," said the men in chorus. "This is the region of the Precarious Mountains. Everything here is a bit topsy-turvy."

I walked with the men to where my handkerchief was lying. It appeared to be its normal self again. The ring was still inside the bundle, but it was no longer rusty. In fact, it gleamed like gold. I handed it over to the man in the middle and thanked all three for their help. They bowed stiffly and suddenly disappeared.

I examined my handkerchief thoroughly and was glad to find that it was my trusty old handkerchief again. The mountains seemed to be back to normal too.

I walked on with a relieved heart, glad that I had come through this adventure in one piece.

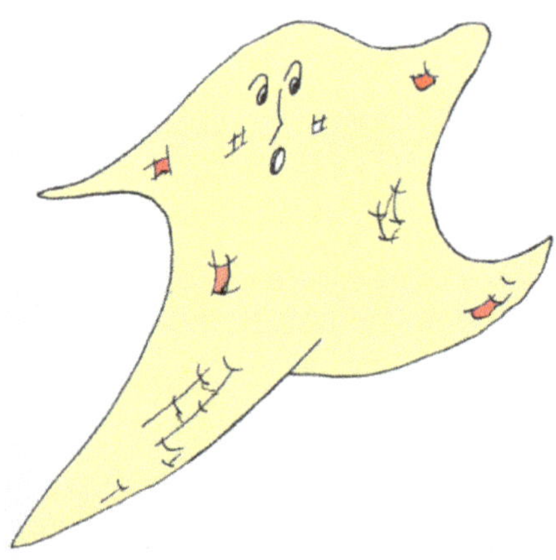

4

The road became less and less steep until, eventually, I found myself on a kind of plateau. Ginger Plateau, it said on a crooked sign right in the middle of the road.

"*That's a funny name*," I thought. "*I wonder what country I'm in now?*" My sense of direction said that I was still headed south. I was just guessing, of course, since I'd learned barely any geography. "*Oh, but what difference does it really make? What matters is that I find a decent place to live, where I won't be teased and insulted. After all, that was the purpose of my journey!*" So, free of care, I walked on.

At the edge of the plateau, there were mountains, and I could make out caves on the hillsides, large, gaping holes. It had already begun to grow dark, so I decided to find a warm and nice-looking cave in which to spend the night. It had been a rather tiring journey, and I could use a good night's sleep. There was one cave with pale pink curtains hanging in front of the entrance, fluttering softly in the wind. I walked up to it but could not see through the curtains. A strange place to find curtains, I thought. More what you'd expect to find behind a window.

I stepped inside cautiously, just in case there was anything wrong. To my surprise, the cave was very pleasantly furnished. Several lamps hung on the walls, giving off pink reflections. A Persian rug lay on the floor, and on a long table, laid out for a feast, were delicious-looking dishes. Duck with onion sauce, tomato pies, filled banana skins, and much, much more—too much to name them all. To top it off, in the middle of the table, there was a bottle of exquisite wine.

I invited myself to join the party, and needless to say, I wasn't about to refuse an offer like that. The food tasted even more delicious than it looked. I ate and drank to my heart's content. Within half an hour, I had eaten the plates clean. Then I looked around the room for a chair and sat down to relax and savor the delicious taste of the onion sauce in my mouth.

"Vas zee meal to your zatisfaction or deed my chef make some mistakes?" asked a strange voice right next to my ear. A rather elderly man was standing beside me. He looked at me kindly, certainly not an unfriendly type.

"Oh, yes, indeed! It was superb," I said contently.

"Excellent. I am glad to hear zat. You zee, eet's been so long since we've had any guests," said the man contentedly. "Kugelschreiber's the name. I have leeved here now for zeveral zenturies."

"Several centuries!" I said. "Then surely you must have known my grandfather Joe."

"Joe? My boy ... zat ees my chef! Yes, he ees a fine fellow, and he can zertainly cook too when he zets hees mind to eet."

"But that's incredible! Do you think I could see him?" I asked, overjoyed.

"Zee hem? No, no zat ees not possible. He zends all zis food from the Zeventh Heaven where he ees presently staying," said Kugelschreiber. "But I believe I have a portrait of zem lying around zomevere, from ven he vas still leeving on Earth." Kugelschreiber rummaged around in a chest and came up with a small discolored painting. It was a portrait of a man with a bushy beard, laughing eyes, and many wrinkles. He was neither fat nor thin, and his hands were as large as coal shovels. He somewhat closely resembled my mother.

"Yes, yes, he vas a chef all hees life, and he still is."

"Where is the Seventh Heaven actually?" I asked. Due to my limited education, I did not know where it was situated.

"Zee Zeventh Heaven ... Zat ees zee firmament ... Ach, zat ees a coincidence ... I vas just zearching for it!" the man cried out. "Vait a meenet ... come, stand here close to me, and hold on tight!"

He pushed a button on the wall, and immediately everything began to spin around and around. Within a few seconds, everything was once again dead-still, and I was standing in a room, the same one as before, I believe, but now full of pots and pans, glasses, bottles, and so on. The table still stood in the middle but was piled high with glass test tubes and flasks that contained brightly colored liquids, boiling, bubbling, and churning. There was also a large supply of feathers, pens, and notepads scattered about.

"I am a professor," declared Kugelschreiber. "I am momentarily busy researching ze heavens to determeen eets constituents, zat ees, vhat eat ees made of."

"Yet you don't know where it lies?" I asked, puzzled.

"Yes and no," was his reply. "I only know zat I must be enveeseble eef I vant to deescover eet, and zat I must try out zee formula veech I have developed to become eenveeseble. Look over here," he said, grabbing a notebook filled with all kinds of secret symbols, names, and signs. "I must only meex all zees zings togezer to make an enveeseble paste." He showed me the page, but I did not understand much of it.

"Two ounces of pepper, zree grams of cobwebs, nine feet of sand grains," he began to read off. "A peench of zalt, five paint boxes, and ..." Kugelschreiber was silent for a minute.

Then he threw together all the ingredients into a large pot and thought deeply. “I have no deectionary … I must have a deectionary!” he shrieked. He pushed the button again, and everything began to spin around. Tables and chairs flew through the air. I was barely able to stay on my feet since I hadn’t been given any time to prepare myself.

When everything settled into place again, we appeared to have landed in a bedroom. The professor ran directly to a bookcase and began frantically searching the shelves.

“Ah ha! Here eet ees!” he cried out joyfully. “Now vhat vas zat I must look up? … Ah yes, of course, a screep … yes, zat ees vhat I must look up.” He began to leaf through the dictionary until his finger stopped at the right word. “Screep means script,” he stammered. “Vas zat really vhat vas called for in zee receepee? But zat ees terreeble. I don’t ‘ave a screep.”

Distraught, he paced up and down until his eyes suddenly fell on me.

“Do you happen to have a screep?” he asked sweetly.

“No, I’m sorry, I don’t have a … uh … screep,” I said.

“Yah, yah. But do you zeenk you could vetch one for me?”

“I would like to oblige you, but I would really much prefer to go to sleep,” I said since I had no wish to spend another sleepless night.

“Good,” pronounced Kugelschreiber. “Zen first, you shall get zome zleep.” He pointed to one of the beds. “Tomorrow morning, vhen you avake, you veel find yourself outside, and zen you must emmeedeately go fetch ze screep for me.” I listened carefully, memorizing his instructions for the following day.

Then I got undressed and climbed into bed. It was a terrifically comfortable bed. The professor closed the pink curtains and got into the other bed, which stood next to mine.

“What a comfortable bed,” I remarked.

“Yah, your grandfather Joe provided eet,” he answered

matter-of-factly. I fell asleep immediately and dreamt about Joe.

The sun had not yet risen when I awoke the next morning, for the room was still rather dark. Nor was I lying outside as the professor had predicted. I was glad about that because the rocks would not have been very comfortable. The bed in which the professor should have been lying was empty. I sat straight up in bed and thought about the "screep" that the professor seemed to need so badly. Where would I ever find such a thing?

The professor came into the room dressed in a beautiful kimono embroidered with pure satin. "Yah, yah." he said. "Joe has made zis keemono for me ... hee ..." He seemed very pleased; the kimono must be brand new!

"Good morning, Professor," I said politely.

"Yes, to you too," replied Kugelschreiber. "Zo, I zee zat eet ees almost light out. We don't have breakfast today, but I vil get you some new clothes to put on before you leave." He went out through the door and returned within five minutes carrying a blue curtain. I stepped out of bed, and Kugelschreiber draped the curtain over me. It turned out to be a long and wide tunic that fit me well, at least according to the professor.

"And now to get to verk," he yelled. "Zer ees zo much to get done. To begeen weez, you must dreenk zees up." He handed me a cup filled with a deep pink liquid. I drank it up bravely, and immediately incredible things began to happen.

Everything began to spin around, just like the day before. But now it felt as though I was being lifted up by a giant hand. Finally, after what seemed like hours, I stood again on the ground. Soft ground, like a cloud, it was so soft. Someone, who looked exactly like good old Joe, stood before me.

"Is that really you, Joe," I asked, amazed.

"Yes, my boy!" his voice quavered, "I have brought you here. Professor Kugelschreiber knows nothing about this."

"My gosh, Joe," I said. "1 never realized that you had such large hands. It was you who carried me here, wasn't it?"

"It certainly was, my boy. You are permitted to enter the clouds. You are expected. You no longer need to bother about the 'screep.'"

"But I must at least thank the professor first for his hospitality?"

"No, that's not necessary; you are sure to run into him again. Come now, you must walk along this road." And with these words, Joe disappeared. So, I began to walk alone along the cloud-like road. It gave me a feather-light feeling as if I was walking on a trampoline.

I must have walked at least a mile or two when I came to a large door. A fat man in uniform stood before it. His nose was red, and his cheeks were blue. It looked to me as though he had had a bit too much wine to drink.

"Good morning, doorman," I said politely.

"Ah ... *hic*! You are expected ... *hic*! Walk on this way ... *hic*! ... ha ha ha ... " He seemed to be enjoying himself. He swung the door wide open for me, nearly knocking himself over in the process. A road lay before me. A sign stood at the side of the road with the words: CLOUD CENTRE.

5

The road on this side of the door gave less under my feet than the path on the other side had done. I had hardly walked more than a few paces when two very large soldiers, dressed in Chinese-like uniforms from around the 15th century, strode up to me. Without saying a word, they each took hold of one of my arms and raised me up off the ground, letting my feet dangle between them.

"Ahem ... do you mind telling me what's going on?" I coughed.

"Hmph!" replied the man to my right. They obviously were not interested in making conversation, so I decided not to waste my breath.

After I had hung between these two "giants" for quite a long time, we arrived at a palace built out of pure white marble. "Well, here we are. He lives here," said one of my carriers. And with this simple statement, he took hold of my collar, held me out at arm's length, and gave me a boot in the rear with his large foot. I landed on all fours at the steps to the palace door. The door opened, and a servant girl appeared.

"Is this the one?" the girl asked one of the men who had

just “delivered” me.

The man didn’t appear to have heard her, so she yelled in a loud voice, “Harry! Is this the one?”

“Yeeeesss!” Harry yelled back.

Satisfied, she pulled me inside, closed the door behind her, and turned towards me.

“That must have been a real experience, I bet ... “ said the girl, bending down towards me. “But the fun is not over yet. Oh, no!”

“Oh,” I said shyly.

The girl wore a blue dress with white polka dots and white lace. She had dark brown hair tied into a bun on top of her head. Her eyes were a beautiful color, dark blue with a tinge of green.

“First, I shall take you to him,” she said. I scrambled onto my feet and followed her through marble hallways and chambers full of rich decoration and furniture. Persian rugs lay everywhere, and the walls were inlaid with mother-of-pearl. We stopped in front of a large, intricately carved door with golden doorknobs. The girl went through the door, and I followed after her.

What I found before me was so impressive that I will never forget it as long as I live. It was a magnificent chamber. Sitting along the side walls were rows of ladies and gentlemen, exquisitely dressed. Their garments were fit only for royalty. The walls of the chamber were covered with gold leaf, and the curtains hanging in front of the windows were pure satin, glittering in a blaze of colors. The ceiling had been painted in soft, warm shades, with lovely cloud formations and people with wings.

In the middle of the room stood a throne strewn with velvet cushions and an animal skin. A young man with dark eyes and long blond hair sat on the throne. He wore a pure golden crown inlaid with numerous diamonds, emeralds, and rubies. The man had large white wings growing from his back but more splendid than those of the most beautiful swan I had ever seen. He wore a red cape decorated with gold brocade, and he carried a golden rod in his hand.

"Welcome," he said in a melodious voice. "I am the King of the Clouds. I have invited you to enter my kingdom because you will become my jester."

"Bow, dummy!" the girl whispered in my ear.

I bowed down. "I am sure that it is a great honor to be your jester, but I'm afraid I really must get back to Earth."

"Not so fast." the king continued calmly. "You must remain here because you cannot get away."

I was struck dumb. I looked around me at all the splendor. I wasn't accustomed to this tremendous wealth, nor could I imagine ever growing used to it.

"Let me put it to you this way," the King began again, now in a somewhat harder tone of voice. "You have a choice; either you become my jester, or you can go to hell."

"I ... I ... I guess I'll stay here," I answered.

"Now, it is your job to see to it that I remain in the clouds!" Then he clapped his hands, at which point two lackeys entered the room. "Get an outfit for this young man," the king ordered them. They left the chamber, walking backward and bowing, and soon returned still in the same bowing position but walking forwards, carrying a red suit covered with jingle bells.

"Put that on," the King commanded, pointing to the suit.

"Well, say 'Yes, Your Highness,'" one of the lackeys whispered in my ear.

"Um—yes, Your Highness," I said quickly. The suit was made from red flannel and fit me exactly.

"How does the suit please you?" the King asked.

"It fits perfectly," I said.

"Fine, I am glad to hear that. Joe made it. Do you know Joe?"

"Oh, yes, Your Highness. Joe is my grandfather and a very kind man. When I was younger, I used to visit him every Sunday."

"Really! You must tell later me more about Joe. Since you were such good friends with him, you must surely have some amusing stories to tell. But before you begin, go first with Lidia, who will show you your room."

Lidia was the girl who had brought me here. She nodded for me to follow her and led me through hundreds of passageways and chambers. Up a stairway, down another. I ran after her, panting, trying to keep up.

Finally, we arrived. Lidia opened a small door and motioned me to enter. The door closed after me and was locked. I could hear the key being removed from the lock.

"What nerve!" I mumbled to myself. The room was small and rather empty. A wardrobe, a bed, and a chair made up its furniture. Poems decorated a wall. One of them read:

A jester with a cart
and wood to devour,
the way to his wishes is in his power.
And another one read:
The first of April is the day.
Do not forget or miss your way.

I didn't bother with the poems anymore but turned my attention to the window. I opened it and looked out on a lovely park filled with beautiful trees and flowers. There was also a pond in which birds and children were wading.

There was a knock on the door. "Come on in if you've got a key!" I called out. Whoever it was apparently had a key because I could hear it turning in the lock, and Lidia came in.

"The king wants you to entertain him," she said. "Come along with me."

Once again, I followed her up and down stairways and through passageways and chambers. On the way, I managed to gasp out a question: “Who stayed in that room before me?”

“Oh ... a poet. He was always sick. He said he wanted to return to Earth. He wasn’t a very good poet either.”

We soon stood before the large door, and I entered the magnificent room alone. The beautifully dressed ladies and gentlemen were no longer present. There was just the king, alone on his throne.

“Amuse me,” he said.

“Um ... Wait a minute ... It’s been a long time since I’ve told a joke.”

“Hurry up, or I shall get angry!” threatened the King.

“Oh! Um, um ... yeah!” I began to recite:

Between the teeming shoals of cod,
Swam a large, bedraggled dog,
Proudly said the dog, fish swimming,
“Catfish take like ducks to water.
Anything a cat can do, I do better!”

How I ever came up with that one so quickly, I’ll never know. And it even rhymed!

”Hee, hee, hee, ha, ha, ha!” the King squeaked with pleasure. “I haven’t heard such a good one in a long time. Hee, hee, ha, ha, ho, ho!” I felt myself blush with pride.

“You can go away now,” the King said, with a somber look once again on his face.

I was taken aback by these sudden changes in his mood, but his tone of voice convinced me not to stand around thinking about it. I quickly left through the door, and on the other side, I ran into Lidia, who took me to my room again. I surely would have gotten lost if I had had to find it on my own. We went running and flying back.

"Sleep," said Lidia, as if I was her dog. So, I took off my jester's suit and put on the night clothes which were under the pillow. Then I crawled into bed. There was a teddy bear lying there too.

"Ha, ha!" I chuckled to myself. "That poet must have been fond of his childhood." Cuddling the bear in my arms, I fell asleep.

The next morning, I was awoken by a knock on the door. Without waiting for a reply, Lidia walked in carrying a broom and a duster.

"Aren't you awake yet?" she asked, surprised. "Everyone is responsible for cleaning their own room. Here is a broom and a rag. Go ahead."

"Oh, thank you," I said.

"And when you're through, go to the room left of yours. Breakfast is ready for you there," she continued. "See you there." She left, leaving the door unlocked.

I quickly pulled on my jester's suit. Then I grabbed the broom and began to sweep the tiled floor. With the duster, I removed a number of spider webs in the corners of the room. I opened the window and noticed that the weather was splendid.

Just as I was about to leave the room, I saw that the poems on the wall were also dusty. There was no point in leaving a job half done, I thought. So, I stood on the bed and pulled a poem off of the wall. Another piece of paper, which had been hanging behind the one in my hand, fluttered to the floor. I picked it up, it contained a poem too:

A cart for a jester stands in the stable.
The wood to be digested
Can be divested from the king's shoe.

This obviously had something to do with the poem which

I had read the day before when I arrived. But what it meant was beyond me. I hung the poems neatly on the wall and stepped off my bed. Of course, then I had to make the bed again.

In the course of all this, I had worked up a good appetite and was looking forward to a hearty breakfast. So, I went in search of it. Lidia was in the next room, buttering bread.

"What do you want to drink with your breakfast?" she asked when she saw me. I felt like having tea and said so.

"Whaaat did you say? Tea? Ha ... Ha! Whatever made you say that? You really are turning into quite a jester. Ha, ha. We only drink heavenly water here, carbonated or uncarbonated."

"Oh, excuse me! Well, then make it heavenly water, carbonated." I had no idea what I had just ordered.

Then Lidia asked, "Do you prefer fish or grapes on your bread?"

"Um ... fish, please," I answered. I began to look less and less forward to the breakfast as I saw it being prepared. By the time Lidia set it before me, I had lost my appetite completely.

"Here you are. Eat it up; it'll make you grow strong!" The pieces of bread with what she called fish stuck between them were not exactly what I would have called tasty. Hard as a rock; just flour and water. And the fish consisted entirely of scales. The least unpleasant part of the whole meal was the heavenly water, though that tasted like ditch water. But I had to swallow every last bit under Lidia's watchful gaze.

"The King is fond of acrobats," she began to explain. "Especially acrobats on horses. In a little while, you must do your best to make him laugh by performing some tricks. Do you understand?"

I felt pretty scared. "*Gulp* ... y—y—yes ... *gulp*." I never had been much good with horses, let alone having to perform tricks on them! Oh, lord, what a nightmare this was turning into.

Lidia took me to the stables. The first horses I saw were beautiful light grey stallions with curly manes and tails which danced in the wind. They had slender, graceful legs and lovely blue eyes. To one side, there stood a cart and pony. Lidia said it belonged to the king. I was hoping that I would get to ride one of these beautiful grey stallions; they appeared to be friendly and gentle. But to my horror, she brought me to a wild-looking animal, which eyed me angrily.

"This is your horse. Let me help you to mount him. If you say 'hoo,' then he will run very hard, and if you say 'haa,' then he will stop."

I climbed up onto the horse's back. It was just my bad luck that he hadn't even been saddled. "Oh, well," I sighed. "I'll just have to try it this way." Without any warning, Lidia gave the horse a slap on his rear and called out, "hoo." The animal flew out of the stable at a breathtaking speed and galloped straight towards the grassy fields which I had seen from my window. The king and all the dignified ladies and gentlemen were seated in garden chairs around the field.

As I appeared on stage, everyone began to applaud. I had great difficulty just holding on tight. The result was that I made the craziest capers, whether I wanted to or not.

"Hooo!" I cried out in fear. "Help!" But my cry had the opposite effect that I wanted, and the horse galloped even faster.

"Ha haa!" the king shrieked. The horse stopped dead, me hanging on to just his mane.

"*Whew!*" I thought. "*At least that's over.*"

"Hoo, hoo!" cried the king. "I cannot laugh anymore! Hoo, hoo!"

And off shot the horse as straight as an arrow, which made the King laugh again, and the horse stop again. The king cried, the horse took off, the king laughed, the horse stopped, and so on and so on. I soon grew weary and sick of the whole thing.

The wild brute finally appeared to have had enough and slowed down to a walk, at which point I fell forward onto his neck, unconscious.

When I came to, I was lying in bed. Lidia was sitting next to me. “That was fun, wasn’t it?” she said excitedly. “Oh, boy, I laughed so hard. I can’t remember when I’ve laughed so much. Ha, ha, ha!” She got up and went out of the room, leaving the door this time unlocked. Slowly, I began to think straight again. I knew for certain that I had to get back to Earth. Perhaps the poems could help me escape? And what a coincidence! Today was the first of April.

That was the date I mustn’t forget. One of the poems mentioned a jester. Could that be me? And he needed a cart ... Well, there was a cart in the stable! Did I really need to get a piece of wood from the king’s shoe? Ah, but everything seemed to point towards a possible escape, I concluded. The poet had probably found this way and used it! He wrote about “the road of his wishes.” Could that be the way back to Earth?

The poems started to make sense to me. And now that Lidia had left the door unlocked, here was my chance to look for a way out. I crept out of bed and wished for my own clothes. Perhaps there was something I could wear in the wardrobe. I hadn’t even taken a look in there yet.

To my delight, my very own familiar clothes were hanging there. Surely, I had left everything at Kugelschreiber’s. Even my handkerchief bundle was there. I felt so much better in my own clothes. Then I walked to the stables, pretending I had business there, but I didn’t run into anyone anyway. The pony and cart still stood there! And in front of the pony lay a golden shoe with a broken heel, a heel of wood!

“*Wood to eat*,” I thought. “*That’s what I have to take with me.*”

I grasped the reins and rode out of the stable. The pony seemed to know where he had to go, which was lucky since I hadn't the faintest idea. The pony took a road I recognized, the one on which I had come, which led to the large gateway. The guard was gone! We rode along the cloud path until the pony suddenly stopped.

Joe stood in front of us. He looked at me with a pleased expression on his face and said, "I see you were able to escape. Give the pony the piece of wood to eat. He likes it." I picked up the heel and noticed that something had been written on it in chalk. It said: "Good luck! Lidia." The pony munched it up with great pleasure and then turned back towards the palace.

Joe said, "My boy, you've been very brave. Take this priceless document. Read it thoroughly when you get back to Earth."

"Why, thank you, grandfather," I said, eyeing the document curiously. "Goodbye!" I called out as I started down the road. Joe waved after me.

The road began to resemble more and more a solid track, until finally, I was standing back on Earth. All right, I had come through that in one piece! "Now for the document Joe gave me," I said to myself. It read as follows:

> THIS DOCUMENT DOES HEREBY GRANT TO THE OWNER ETERNAL LIFE.
> ANYONE WHO STEALS IT FROM
> THE RIGHTFUL OWNER
> SHALL PERISH.
> THE OWNER OR THIEF
> WHO BURNS THIS DOCUMENT
> SHALL BE STRUCK DOWN ON THE SPOT.
> Deathday Appointer, Joe.

"Good old Joe," I said to myself. I shoved the document into the bottom of my bundle.

6

I was standing in the middle of a beautiful landscape filled with flowers and greenery. The grass stood so high that the stems of the flowers were no longer visible, just the reds, blues, pinks, purples, and all the other colors of the petals. What a sight to behold. This was the kind of place where cats lazed in the grass or hid behind the flowers and waited for their prey. I decided to do just what a cat would do, nestle down in the grass but with a blade in my mouth. It was lovely to lie there. The long grass closed above me, making a snug little covering. As you could expect after such an adventure as I had just had, I fell fast asleep in no time.

It was dusk when I awoke. The sky had turned a purple-blue color. The flowers had already closed up for the night. It was quiet everywhere. The thousands of bees that I had heard earlier buzzing to and fro were no longer around. The silence was not alarming; on the contrary, it was very peaceful. The purple-blue sky was soothing.

Suddenly, as if by magic, a small figure appeared in the distance. It danced from one blade of grass to the other, as if it was as light as air, while it sang in a girl's delicate voice. It sounded beautiful! The little creature seemed to be heading in my direction. The closer it got, the lovelier it appeared to be. It was an elf-like girl dressed in a fluttering light-blue dress. She had gleaming black hair covered with red flowers, and she sang without stopping, accompanying herself on a harp that she carried. I stood very still until she stood before me.

She said, “You are welcome here; please, follow me ♫.” She spoke in singsong, high and clear. Then she took me by the hand and pulled me through the long grass. She could walk on the tips of the blades of grass, but I almost fell to the ground with just about every step, breaking off many leaves from the flowers like a heavy animal. After much stumbling, we arrived at her house— a small tree, with the emphasis on “small.” It certainly wouldn’t hold my weight if I climbed into it, I feared.

“Take a seat on one of these leaves ♪,” she said. Not wishing to offend her, I started to sit down on the largest leaf I could find. “Oh, no, not in the bedroom ♪,” she sang. “Come, sit over here ♫.” She pointed to another leaf.

I slowly let myself down onto the leaf—slowly, slowly ... yes ... yes! I sat. To my relief, the leaf did not break off.

“Let me introduce myself. I am Toodle Hidoo, but you may call me Toodle ♪! “

“I am Ody, but you can call me O! Say, where am I actually?”

Toodle replied, “In The Land of the Elves, the most beautiful land in the world. Surely you are familiar with it, The Land. The Land lies east of A Land, do you follow me ♪?”

“Of course. The Land next to A Land,” I said, trying to look clever.

“Are you hungry ♫?”

“Yes. Oh, yes, indeed. It has been a long time since I ate anything decent,” I answered. My mouth watered at the thought of roast chicken and apple sauce.

“Fine, then I shall prepare something for you in the kitchen ♪.”

Toodle sprang onto another leaf, where she plucked off something. I couldn't see what it was, but it didn't take long before she returned with a four-leaf clover. Different colored food lay on each leaf: blue, white, black, and yellow. She offered me the "plate" and then sat down next to me.

I first ate the yellow ... mmmm ... that tasted very good. I asked rather impolitely with my mouth full, "Mmmm ... munch ... what is this? ... *Gulp.*"

"Oh, that is caterpillar porridge, freshly made ♪."

"*Cough* ... *cough*," I choked. At the thought of eating a caterpillar, my appetite disappeared in a trice.

"Um ... say ... I'm not very hungry anymore, but it was delicious. Thank you," I said politely.

"Oh, do you want to go to bed now ♪?" Toodle asked kindly.

"No, that's really not necessary. You see, I had just woken up before I met you," I explained.

"Aha, then you can take the night watch. To guard against caterpillar thieves, you see ♪."

"Oh, that'll be fine," I said and took up my post like a proud watch dog who must protect his master. Toodle went, or I should say leaped, to the bedroom and covered herself with flowers.

Night soon fell. Only the crickets could be heard. "I shall take a night walk," I said to myself and jumped off the leaf. "*I can leave my 'baggage' here*," I thought. "*After all, there's nothing worth stealing.*"

I started walking eastward towards an enormous tree. On each side of the tree, a stripe had been painted on the ground with the word: Frontier. All sorts of posters had been tacked onto the trunk, displaying various messages: "Hip, hip, hooray!" and "Away with you!" I couldn't read anymore since it was dark. I was curious, though, and wanted very much to know what was written there. Therefore, I whistled together some fireflies to produce some light for me so that I could read all the posters.

"*Bzzzz* ..." they hummed. Thousands of flies flew to the tree, giving off more than enough light for me to read by. Most of the posters were written in a strange alphabet which I didn't understand, but there was one that was very clear. It read:

On account of having stolen caterpillars and
other livestock,
the above-mentioned person
has been sentenced to mortality.
The above-mentioned shall die
at the age of 104.
The convicted shall never again
obtain immortality.
Elves, let this be a warning to you!
Never steal livestock!
The Elf Court of Justice

I was suddenly very alarmed as I thought of Toodle, who was innocently sleeping and therefore unable to guard her caterpillars, having entrusted me with that task. And here I was neglecting my duties. Yet I just wanted to see who the "above-mentioned" was. I stretched my neck as high as I could. To my great dismay, I read: Toodle Hidoo.

"Oh, how awful ..." I said, terribly shaken.

I ran as hard as I could back to Toodle's house. Jumping onto the leaf, I found Toodle busily searching through my belongings. She pulled out a piece of paper and began to run away as quickly as she could, springing from one leaf to another like a feather.

I checked my bundle to see what she had taken and realized immediately what it was. She had stolen the document which Joe had given me, granting me eternal life.

I yelled after Toodle, "Stop, Toodle! Don't do such a stupid thing! Give the paper back to me, or it will only turn out the worse for you." But she didn't listen and disappeared into the darkness.

I was in complete despair from fatigue and sadness, as well as from my own stupidity. It was too dark to chase after Toodle, so I climbed into a larger tree and picked out a sturdy branch to serve as my bed. I fell asleep but had bad dreams. I dreamt that, as a result of my stupidity and indifference, I was prosecuted and Toodle hanged.

My own loud screams woke me up. The sun had already risen, and everything was covered with a heavy mist. The only thing I could think about was finding Toodle before anything bad happened to her. I jumped off my branch to the ground, where the mist reached up to my knees.

I first called out in every direction, “Toodle! Too ... dle!” An echo called back: “oodle! oo ... dle.” I called again, “Where are you?” And again, the echo: “... are you?”

As I expected, there was no reply, no reply at all, no “Here I am, and I want to give you your parchment back.”

So, I decided to head south, the direction in which she had disappeared. I couldn’t tell whether I was walking on a road or on grass. I just kept walking on, until suddenly I heard voices, or was it the echo of voices, perhaps an hour’s walk behind me.

The voices said, “Where could Toodle be? We must find her quickly because, today, she must die.”

“*Oh, no!*” I thought. I was about to faint from fright. I wasn’t the only one looking for Toodle. Perhaps they were policemen or the Grim Reaper. At any rate, whoever they were, it was bad news for Toodle. I had to find her before the fellows behind did. So, I put my best foot forward and hurried onwards.

After running for about an hour, the mist began to lift, and everything became clear. It also became easier to walk. I saw a similar large tree in the distance, another boundary marker. That’s where I had to head for. On the tree was written “Frontier between The Land and A Land.” I stepped across the border.

A voice sounded from somewhere in the tree branches: “Hey, you! Stop! Have you got transit papers?” I peered up through the branches. A brown owl stared at me with large, angry eyes.

"Uh ... well, actually ... no," I said shyly and blushed.

"Oh. All right. You may pass," said the owl.

"*That's strange*," I thought. "*Well. It must be me.*" A thought suddenly occurred to me. Toodle certainly had no transit papers either. Perhaps she had crossed over at this point, too.

"Um ... Mister Owl, excuse me, but could you tell me whether an elf crossed over here yesterday evening?"

"Heh? What a stupid question. There must have been well over one hundred elves who passed by here yesterday evening," he replied.

"Oh, but I'm only interested in Toodle. Did Toodle cross over here?"

"Toodle? Let me think ... yes, I believe so. She had a piece of paper with her!" the owl called out. "Is that the elf you mean?"

"Yes, yes! She's the one. Thank you very much, Mr. Owl."

"Oh, it was nothing. Just please get on your way now. My eyelids are getting rather heavy."

Relieved to know that I was at least on the right track, I went on. I really had to hurry because I could hear the voices behind me getting closer.

"Hup, two, three, four. Hup, two, three, four. Come on, men. Keep up the spirit." I took to walking in their rhythm, receiving encouragement from behind. Up above my head, birds were flying to and fro, singing and chirping loudly. A gigantic bird stood on the path in front of me. I asked him if he had seen Toodle.

"Certainly. I just brought her to the other side. Not a very heavy load to carry, I might add," the bird replied. "Would you like to cross over to the other side, too, by any chance?"

"The other side of what?"

"The other side of the mountains, of course!"

"Yes, that would be fine. But I can't pay you."

"Well, then you can pay me on your return flight."

"But I don't want to return! I want to find Toodle!"

"Nonsense!" said the bird. "Everyone wants to return. It is very unsafe behind the mountains." I climbed onto the bird's back, and he took off from the ground, flapping his wings vigorously.

"You're certainly heavier than my last passenger!" he grumbled.

"I'm sorry! I'd like to ask you something, if I may. What kind of land is this?"

"A Land is the land of the birds."

"You mean to tell me that only birds live here?"

"My lord! You really are sharp. What else did you expect to find here?"

I didn't ask anything else since the bird obviously didn't like being disturbed in his work. A beautiful but rather empty landscape passed under me. There was not a living soul to be seen on the ground, in contrast to being up in the air; here, it was very busy. Birds flew everywhere in all shapes and sizes.

Boom!!! The bird on which I was sitting had collided with another.

"Can't you watch where you're going?"

"Don't you know the rules of flying?"

"I happened to have the right of way!"

"Oh, really! And what about paying for the dent in my beak?"

"Don't hold your breath on that one. You earn more than I do."

"That may be true, but my bank has just been robbed."

"Oh, yeah? And my egg has just recently hatched." And so on and so forth. I became sick and tired of the whole stupid argument and only wished to move on.

I kicked my bird in the side. “Ow!” he cried out. “What do you think you’re doing?”

The bird which had collided with us said, “Yeah, who do you think you are, kicking my colleague?”

“I ... um ...” I said timidly. After all, the birds were much larger than I. Behind me, the bird commotion was getting louder. “*Caw, caw, caw*” and “*Fuuut, fuuut, fuuut*” and “*Beo, beo*” and “*chirp, chirp*”.

“Got to be moving along now. They’re getting impatient behind me,” said my pilot.

“Okay. I’ll send you the money for damages done. Regards to your wife and kids.”

“Will do. Bye!” And everyone peacefully flew further apart.

After flying for a quarter of an hour, the mountains came into view. The air traffic grew less and less.

“Here you go. I’ll leave you off here,” said the bird as he slowly descended. He set me off just on the other side of the mountains.

“Thank you very much for your kindness,” I said politely.

“Kindness! You don’t think I’m doing this for nothing, do you?”

I ran away as fast as I could, trying to avoid another argument with him. Behind me, I heard him shouting insults: “Brat! Monkey face! Blockhead! Pig’s Ear! You, nothing ...” I’ve been called a lot of things in my life, but nothing like this. As I got farther away, the shouting grew fainter. I certainly didn’t want to go back to that place again, no matter what.

1 had been set down on a flat piece of land covered in fresh green grass and flowers in all colors of the rainbow. Well-groomed cows with large bells dangling from their necks grazed among them. It was a peaceful landscape, especially compared to where I had just come from. As I walked, I kept wondering why no one lived there. Looking back, I saw my pilot bird landing with a new load. It was the group of men

who were also looking for Toodle!

"Go away! Go away!" voices called from around me.

"*Oh, sure,*" I thought. But I said, "Because you are looking for Toodle too; of course, you want me to go away! I wouldn't dream of it. I'm staying right where I am."

"We aren't looking for Toodle. We are the spirits of the grasses."

"Ha, ha. Ha." I laughed, not believing a word of it. "You can't fool me." And I walked defiantly onwards. To my surprise, I suddenly realized that I was no longer making progress. The grass under me disappeared, leaving nothing in its place. Just a vast emptiness. I plunged down into a deep pit and hit bottom with a hard thud. I didn't understand what had happened at all. One moment, I was standing on solid grassland, and the next moment ... nothing. I looked up and saw the grass growing quickly back into place again, closing off the pit with a green roof.

"So. Were you looking for me ♫?" a small voice sang out behind me.

"Toodle!" I cried in surprise, turning around to face her. "Toodle, you must give me the document you stole immediately."

"Perhaps I would if I had it, but someone took it away from me, the scoundrel ♪!" Toodle replied.

"How on earth did that happen," I asked.

"Well, it all began like this ♫," Toodle began to tell her story. "When I was born, my parents were very poor. They could just scrape by. They always dreamed of me owning a large flock of caterpillars and never needing to work ♫. When I was a bit older, around eighty years old or so, I stole a flock of caterpillars, but somebody discovered it and sued me. The Elf Court of Justice sentenced me to mortality, and ... *sniffle* ... *sniffle* ... I have to die at the youthful age of one hundred and four years. You came along just in time with your document, which could've granted me immortality ... So, I stole it ♪. I knew you wouldn't like that, so I ran away. But I was also running away to avoid the policemen who were going to kill me today. You see, it's my hundred and fourth birthday today."

"Oh, happy birthday!" I said politely and shook her hand.

Toodle continued with her story: "I met a bird who offered to fly me across the mountains ♪. We were already on the other side when he demanded payment. He grabbed the document from me as payment, and I didn't know what else I could do than walk on ♪. I didn't let myself be scared by the spirits of the grasses, and that is how I ended up in this pit, just like you ♪."

"You mean, the spirits of the grasses really exist? I thought that was just a trick of those policemen."

"Oh, yes, they really do exist. That's why no one wants to stay here ♪," replied Toodle.

Five dull thuds sounded next to us. The policemen had also fallen into the pit.

"Ah, there she is, men!" cried the largest of the five. "Grab her!" All five dashed towards her at once.

In a flash, Toodle pulled out a small sort of weapon from under her dress, put it in her mouth, and blew on it. Soap bubbles streamed out, which she blew right in the policemen's eyes. They obviously hadn't expected this and cried out in pain and anger. I myself was as scared as a frightened mouse. It didn't occur to me to help this "damsel in distress." I watched the fight from a corner with sweat on my brow. As it turned out, the policemen weren't interested in me.

Toodle blew as hard as she could until all the policemen, crying and wiping their eyes, yelled out, "We give up!" These words gave me back my courage. I helped Toodle tie up all the men with elf rope, which she happened to have with her. I searched through our prisoners' clothes, and in the pocket of the leader, I found the document Toodle had stolen from me.

"Where did you get this?" I asked him.

"That was the change from the bird which flew us here," he answered.

I was very glad to have it back. I had not been very helpful in the fight, so I wanted to make up for it now. So, I made a few changes to the document and handed it to Toodle. She was very surprised and happy and thanked me kindly.

The document now read:

> THIS DOCUMENT DOES HEREBY
> GRANT TO THE OWNER ETERNAL LIFE.
> ANYONE WHO STEALS IT
> FROM THE RIGHTFUL OWNER SHALL not PERISH.
> THE OWNER OR THIEF
> WHO BURNS THIS DOCUMENT
> SHALL not BE STRUCK DOWN ON THE SPOT.
> Deathday Appointer, Joe

"I am so grateful ... O ♫," said Toodle.

"Well, I didn't really have much use for it anyway," I replied shyly.

Meanwhile, the grass had disappeared above us, and cows were peering down at us instead.

"Mooo! We've eaten the grass away from here, and we can now haul you out. Mooo!" said the cows. Two of them thrust their tails into the pit. Toodle and I each grabbed one and were pulled out.

"Thank you very much ♫," said Toodle, once we were again above ground.

"Yes, me too," I said. The grass immediately grew over the opening. Nothing could be seen of the pit. "Oh, dear. And the policemen?" I asked.

"Mooo! We shall haul them out tonight," lowed the cows. "We aren't hungry right now."

I said goodbye to Toodle and shook her hand. She turned back to The Land, and I continued on my journey.

7

The view ahead was now very different from the grazing cows. It was something completely new for me because in the distance lay the sea. Never before had I seen a real sea. It looked as though the whole surface had been strewn with pearls that twinkled in the sunlight, and the water was so blue, so very blue. I liked the look of it a lot. I could see a small fisherman's village near the seashore, sleeping peacefully in the afternoon sun. The only movement was a few fishing nets waving in the wind.

I headed quickly towards the village. As I approached, I noticed the houses were all painted white like snow and had flat roofs. A large round hat was leaning against each house, with a pair of shoes sticking out from underneath. The hats seemed to be baking in the sun; at least it sounded that way: "*Zzzzz.*" I walked along the very clean but deserted streets. Houses lined each side, but their doors and shutters were shut tight, as if to prevent the sun1ight from entering.

Finally, I reached the seashore. It had a rocky coast with a pebbly beach. I saw just one pier, only one boat, and one man. The man, who looked like a fisherman, was busy hauling a net full of fish out of the water and dumping the unwilling fish into the boat.

I hesitated a moment, trying to make up my mind on what to do. Should I spend a few days here, or should I continue immediately on my journey? I decided to cross over the sea anyway. I strolled down the pier and tapped friendlily but firmly on the fisherman's shoulder.

He turned his brown face towards me and asked, "What can l do for you, señor?" He looked around thirty or forty years old and had a very friendly voice.

"I would like to cross the sea, sir," I replied.

"Oh, that is fine, amigo. Step aboard," said the man without hesitation. I stepped in with one foot and shoved the fish aside with the other. Then I waited to see what the man did next. He pulled out a sail from under the mass of fish and hoisted it. Then he cast off, and away we sailed. The boat was not very big, but it was stable and fast. The tanned man sat at the helm, although most of the time, he didn't even hold onto the tiller. Nevertheless, the boat kept on the right course. The sail fluttered in the almost windless air. I had to admit that I didn't understand how he managed it.

"Why don't you hold onto the tiller?" I asked.

"Oh," said the man. "We have sailed this route often enough before, you see." I didn't see it at all and wasn't sure whether to take this as a joke or not. At any rate, I decided not to worry about it and took to enjoying the splendid sunset. It turned the sea into a golden platter, and later when the moon rose, everything changed into silver.

"My gosh, the sea is so beautiful," I sighed. The fisherman nodded his head. He didn't have much to do and therefore began to tell stories about the sea and its inhabitants.

"Once upon a time, there lived a large fish in the depths of the sea. He was so shy that he always hid himself in a cave. He didn't dare let anyone see him because then he would blush very red. One day, another fish swam into the cave. It was a small yellow fish, and it swam in through a crack. 'Won't you come out?' asked the little fish. 'I want to play with you.' 'Wh—wh—what do you mean?' the big fish stuttered nervously, his gills turning a bright red. The small fish didn't have much patience and elbowed the larger one in its side until he finally left the cave. The little fish then threw him a ball made from rolled-up seaweed. The large fish enjoyed the game very much until a few curious fish swam up to watch. That was too much for him. He became as red as a lobster and crept quickly into a shell. With the help of a few starfish, the others were able to open up the shell. The large fish closed his eyes tight and thought, 'I'm not here; I'm not here.' The small yellow fish felt sorry for him and thought up a plan. 'We shall paint you completely red with a special coral paint. Then no one shall ever see you blush again, and you need no longer be shy.' That's exactly what they did, and from that day on, the big fish played with the others. There was also once ..."

I didn't hear anymore because, at that point, I dozed off to sleep.

The next morning when I awoke, the man was preparing baked fish. To my surprise, all the other fish had disappeared.

"*Had that man secretly eaten them all up while I was asleep?*" I wondered. He offered me a baked fish, which I eagerly ate. He also took one for himself.

"What happened to all the other fish?" I asked.

"Oh," said the man. "They are gone. After all, the boat has to eat too, amigo." I didn't have time to ask anything more since we had arrived at a sandy coast.

The fisherman beached the boat and let me out. As the boat turned around, I saw, to my surprise, three sharks harnessed in front. So that was how he kept up speed! I paled at the thought that I had slept without care while I could have served as dinner for the sharks. At that moment, the fisherman stepped into the shallow water next to me.

“I guess I owe you something for the crossing,” I said.

“Oh no,” said the man. “That’s not necessary at all. We’ll see each other again, sometime.”

“I wouldn’t be so sure of that if I were you. You see, I don’t expect I’ll be coming back this way ever again.”

The man knitted his eyebrows but spoke again in a friendly tone. “You just gave me an idea. Tell me, what is your name?”

“I am called Ody, sir.”

“Ody, eh? Okay, we shall see each other again around 1492. Does that mean anything to you?”

“No, I’m afraid not. Nor can I promise that I’ll be there.”

“Oh, you’ll be there,” the man assured me. He got back into his boat again and gave the sharks the reins.

“1492,” I mumbled. “Hmm, that really doesn’t mean anything to me at all.”

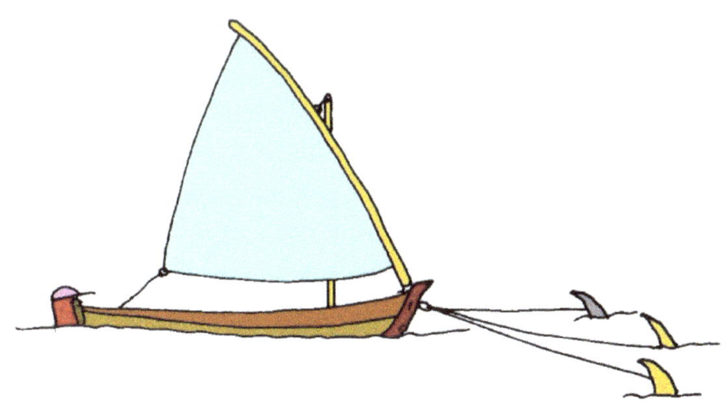

8

An enormous sandy desert stretched out in front of me. I felt no bigger than a fly, so small and insignificant. The sun shone sharply in the sky, which was as blue as the sea. There wasn't anything green in sight; everything was dry and barren. I started walking, but my surroundings did not change in the slightest. The sand seemed to go on forever.

The sun beat down on my sweating forehead, and my tongue, which was as dry as a cork, hung half out of my mouth. Yearning for water, I shuffled onwards, leaving the tracks of my sluggish feet in the sand. My head slumped down on my chest, and my hands dragged along the ground.

At one point, I looked up and saw something wonderful. A large white castle built completely out of marble rose in the distance. Lovely music poured out of the windows—sounds of harps and female voices. The castle had a high facade and rounded roofs. It was very broad with left and right wings. The windows were rather small and had the same shape as the facade. I stumbled forward, trying to walk straight toward the entrance.

I soon stood before a marble doorway and knocked three

times. The double doors opened immediately, and I found myself looking into a large hall, also made out of pure, white marble. A pile of colorful cushions made from white, blue, red, and yellow satins lay in the middle of the room. A woman with long black hair was sitting on these cushions; her hair contrasted beautifully with the whiteness of her complexion. She had light skin and a pretty face. All around her lay, or should I say stood, harps strumming out melodies by themselves. Before her lay sheets of music singing songs.

After I had taken in all there was to see in this unusual room, I asked, "Do you perhaps have a glass of water for me?" It was very quiet for a while; it was as if the woman on the cushions had to think about my question.

"Yes, I do," she finally replied, and without wasting another breath, she snapped her fingers at one of the harps, which immediately stopped playing and left the room. The woman remained silent until the harp returned, carrying a golden tray upon which a delicious-looking glass of water stood.

"Drink," she said. I didn't wait to be asked a second time; I drank in large gulps. The glass filled itself up again so I could drink some more. This went on until I had had my fill of water.

"I am really very grateful, Lady ... um ... um ..."

"My name is Ramses," said Lady Ramses. "Would you like to spend the night here, honored sir?" she asked.

"Well, actually, I should be moving on."

"You would do better to travel early in the morning while it is still cool outside," the lady explained.

"Oh, I see. Well then, I'd be happy to accept your invitation. I would really like to go to bed immediately. I'm very tired after such a long trip through the desert."

"Yes, I can imagine!" She snapped her fingers again, and another harp stopped playing. He took me by the arm and led me out of the chamber. The harp brought me to a blue room containing a bed made ready with satin sheets. Light-blue transparent curtains hung around the bed to keep out the mosquitoes. The sight of all this was almost enough to make me fall asleep. The harp left the room, closing the door behind it. Brushing the curtains aside, I climbed into the bed which gave underneath me. I snuggled under the covers and soon fell fast asleep.

When I awoke the next morning, a large jug filled with water was waiting, and a wash basin had already been made ready for me to use. I washed myself thoroughly, got dressed, and left the room. A harp was waiting for me in the hallway outside of my room and led me back to the large hall where a table had been set for breakfast. I sat down on a marble chair and ate off a marble plate with a marble knife and fork. I drank out of a marble cup. The breakfast itself wasn't made of marble; it was very nourishing! It consisted of a flat, brown cake and a red-colored drink, which tasted like strawberries and cream. Just as I was finishing, Lady Ramses entered.

I wiped off my mouth, stood up, and said, "I wish to thank you sincerely for the manner in which you have received me. You've been very good to me."

"I am glad. Now you can continue further," said Lady Ramses. Under the guidance of a harp, I was led outside. The doors closed slowly behind me, and *poof* ... *zzzttt* ... the castle disappeared!

The sun was still very low on the horizon, and renewed, I set off on my journey again. The extremely friendly way I had been received at the castle really made me feel good. I had only walked a short distance when an enormous structure arose in front of me. It was built completely out of large stone blocks, and its base was very wide; it grew smaller as it rose, ending in a point at the top. It resembled a gigantic triangle. I had a great urge to climb it; well, why not? I had the time, and besides, I was very curious.

It turned out to be a relatively simple climb because there were crevices between the blocks large enough to give me a foothold. Nevertheless, it was over a thousand steps to the top, which turned out to be a large opening. I hadn't expected to find a gaping hole staring back at me. I stuck my head inside to see what there was to see. But before I knew what was happening, I was falling head over heels downward. I landed with a crash on my head, and everything went dark for a long time.

When I finally came to, I had a tremendous headache and was quite dizzy. The hole through which I had fallen was so far away that it wasn't even visible from where I lay. Slowly, I sat up and began to crawl around on all fours in the darkness. I crawled further and further, until, to my great horror, I came upon a hand ... an arm ... a whole body! In view of its size, I guessed it was a man, but of course, in the dark, I couldn't see his face. However, I did feel that he had a beard. The body felt warm, so he couldn't be dead. I slapped his cheeks gently to bring him back to consciousness.

He began to groan and whispered, "Where am I?"

"Here, with me," I replied.

"Oh," the man whispered. "There should be a pocket torch lying around here somewhere. Surely, I had one with me."

"A what?" I didn't know what he meant.

"My pocket torch. You know, a light which runs on batteries," explained the man.

"Battery's?" I asked.

"No, batteries!" he corrected me. "Goodness, fellow, which century do you come from. Surely, you've heard of pocket torches and batteries before?"

"I was born in 1750, and I have never heard of these things before," I said.

"What did you say? 1750? But ... that's impossible ... it's 1981," exclaimed the man, barely able to contain himself.

"No, no, it's not!" I cried back. "I've just come from outside, and there it was 1750!"

"Oh, dear!" said the man. "Well, let's not argue about what year it is. Please just find my pocket torch for me."

I felt around in the darkness and finally came upon what turned out to be this object he was looking for. He took it from me, sat up, and turned the thing on. A bright white light shone in my eyes. Then he shone the light on his own face, so I could see what he looked like. He had red hair, a red beard, and brown eyes. His skin was somewhat wrinkled. Funny, he was the spitting image of a great-uncle of mine, great-uncle Flip.

I asked him what his name was. "Plif," he said. Naturally, he asked me my name, too. Then he took my hand, and together we walked through all sorts of passageways. I could now make out everything around me. Characters and figures had been painted on the walls. We came across a skeleton leaning against one wall that seemed to glare at us with its hollow eye sockets. After a while, we reached a kind of doorway behind which a new passageway began. Directly to the right of the opening stood a mummy, supported by two poles sticking out of the wall. Torches hung above it, and by some miracle, they were still burning. Apparently, there was no lack of oxygen.

Plif drew the conclusion that this was the burial chamber of an Egyptian Pharaoh. The torches must have been lit when the Pharaoh was placed here, he concluded. They had been burning ever since then; therefore, there must be an opening somewhere so that oxygen could enter. Otherwise, the torches couldn't burn. It was strange that the fuel had not yet been used up.

The mummy on the wall began to move and said, "*Mmmm ... mmmm ...*"

Plif jumped at this noise and quickly stood behind me. He looked anxiously over my shoulder and stuttered. "The mum—

mum—mummy moved!"

"*Mmmm*! *Mmmm*!" the mummy repeated.

"I think he wants to get out of all the sheets. I wouldn't like being wrapped up like that either," I said. I slowly approached the mummy and carefully felt the sheets.

"*Mmm, mmm*," he said again. This time I was the one who jumped back, but then I approached him again. I pulled him away from the wall and laid him on the ground. Then I searched for the beginning of the cloth that shrouded him and began to unroll the figure. Plif watched wide-eyed.

After unrolling for a long time, a man appeared. He had brown skin and wore a red-black skirt. His face was greenish with a black goatee. Later on, it turned out that the green color was due to the speed with which I had unrolled him.

"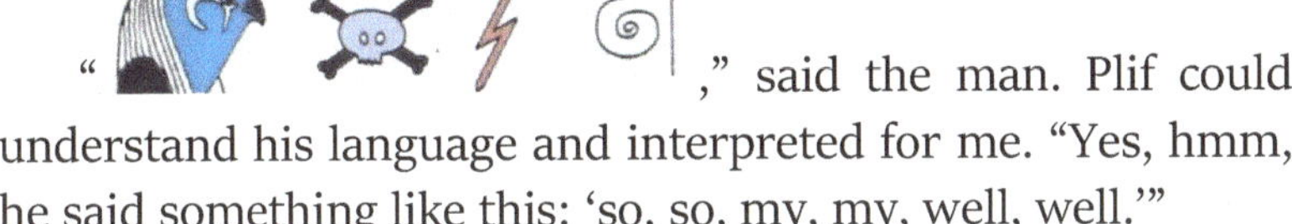," said the man. Plif could understand his language and interpreted for me. "Yes, hmm, he said something like this: 'so, so, my, my, well, well.'"

The man stood up and said: " ." Plif explained, "I am Pharaoh Ramses." I immediately thought of Lady Ramses.

"I, PHARAOH RAMSES, order you to lead ME out of the pyramid," the Pharaoh continued. He could speak our language as well, it seemed, so Plif didn't need to translate anymore.

"But we don't know the way out of here," said Plif.

"You got in here, didn't you?" the Pharaoh said. "I know the way. I entered the pyramid too, but I remember the way out. Besides, I had this pyramid built."

"How come you are still alive? Mummies are dead, aren't they?" I asked.

"Ah, I can explain that. A few weeks ago, I became very ill. I had all the doctors from Thebes come look at ME, but none of them could diagnose MY illness. I could no longer keep MY eyes open or speak. Therefore, I appeared to be dead. However, I could hear. It so happened that yesterday, a famous doctor visited ME. His name is Petro. Petro realized I could hear and explained his plan to ME. I would be considered dead and therefore be buried. Mummification of MY stiff body would do no harm; on the contrary, it wouldn't differ all that much from the manner in which he had planned on treating ME. I could hear and feel MYSELF being buried this morning. And the next thing I heard was your voices and felt you roll ME out of that cloth—it could have been done more gently—but at any rate, I am now cured!"

"May I ask you something?" asked Plif. "What year was it when you died?"

"It was 1600," said the Pharaoh.

"Oh," groaned Plif. "In the Egyptian calendar, that is equivalent to 1250 B.C. in ours!"

"Now I'm really confused! What year is it now? Is it 1250 B.C., 1750, or 1981?" I exclaimed, somewhat wound up. Plif could give me no answer.

The Pharaoh nodded for us to follow him, and we passed through innumerable passages. He opened many secret doors, and sometimes we had to take ten steps to the right, three forward, or fifty steps to the left in order to avoid being caught in booby traps. Finally, after what felt like an endless journey, we came to a massive wall with a large hole closed off by an enormous boulder.

"What a shame!" Ramses groaned. "MY men have just closed off the pyramid, and now we shall be stuck here for centuries."

"Couldn't we try calling to your men? Perhaps they will still hear us," murmured Plif.

"No. Not a single sound can penetrate these walls," replied the Pharaoh.

“Perhaps we can try scraping out the cement if it is still soft and then work the boulder loose,” I suggested.

“Yes, that’s a very good idea!” cried Plif, and he diligently began to scrape away the cement with a small stone. I quickly followed his example while the Pharaoh merely sat down and watched us.

“I’m not accustomed to manual work. I have you for that purpose,” he proclaimed. Plif nearly blew up at this remark; I could only just keep him from wringing the Pharaoh’s neck.

Slowly but surely, after a lot of hard work, the boulder began to shift, and we started to work it loose, using a pole that we found by accident. I was searching for another sturdy stick, but because I didn’t know where the booby traps were hidden, *bang*! *Boom*! I managed to get myself trapped in a wooden cage. The cage was made from poles and rope. I called to Plif for help, and he loosened one of the ropes which held the poles together. Not only could I then get out of the cage, but we also had our lever pole. Shoving the pole under the stone, we began to work it loose.

Finally, we succeeded in rolling the boulder half a yard forward, just enough for us to squeeze out. We said goodbye to each other before leaving. Plif planned to return to 1981 and write a book about the pyramid. Pharaoh Ramses was returning to his wife, Lady Ramses, and their marble castle.

“MY wife would have enjoyed meeting you, but if you insist on immediately carrying on further, I shall give you MY consent,” said the Pharaoh, not knowing that I had already met Lady Ramses the very day he was being buried.

We went outside. It was terrific to see the sky again, but when I looked at Plif and the Pharaoh, they had disappeared in a cloud of sand. It was as if the pyramid itself had also disappeared in the same way. The wind started blowing very hard, bringing a sandstorm along with it. It grew worse and worse, finally blowing so hard that it nearly ripped my clothes from my body. If I hadn't thrown myself down on the ground and curled up like a ball, I surely would have lost my clothes. I kept trying to shake the sand off me, but it was hopeless. When the storm finally stopped, a large heap of sand lay over me. I shook it off just like a dog shaking off water and rubbed the sand out of my eyes. Then I searched for my "baggage" and walked onwards.

9

I hadn't walked all that far before the sandy desert changed into clay ground, and more plant life appeared along the roadside. I even came across small fields every once in a while. There was a small river flowing between the fields, and boats made from papyrus were tied up at the banks. There wasn't anyone in sight. I stopped and gazed down the river and then decided to take one of the boats to travel further.

Choosing one that was fastened to a pier, I climbed in, unfastened the ropes, and started rowing upriver. There didn't seem to be any dangerous currents, which made rowing easy. After I had rowed along for several hours, my surroundings began to change. The fields were replaced by thick forest. The water had also turned muddier, and the reeds along the shallow sides were abundant. I had grown rather tired, so I lodged the boat among the reeds. I investigated the contents of the boat. There were all sorts of things: spears, rope, dried meat, and water. The water was in a large white can with a drinking spout. I helped myself to the water and dried meat.

Since I still wanted to find a quiet and safe place to spend the night, I untied the boat and paddled contentedly further.

Suddenly, I saw behind me a large number of crocodiles swimming noiselessly towards me and looking very hungry. I didn't feel much like serving as their dinner, so I started rowing very fast, as fast as I could. But the crocodiles were catching up to me. The only thing I could think of was to throw them the leftover dried meat and distract them away from me. And indeed! It worked perfectly. They all began eating the meat, which gave me a chance to slow down.

Now I no longer had anything left to eat for myself, so it seemed a good idea to try catching some fish for later. After all, I did have spears in the boat. I rowed further and further.

Suddenly, I heard branches breaking and the crackling of dried leaves. An arrow whizzed by my face. Another quickly followed. By the third one, a large man jumped out from behind the trees, armed with a bow and arrows. He drew the bow, and this time the arrow landed—ow!—right in my right arm.

When I came to, I was tied to a pole. The arrow had been removed from my arm, which was now completely without feeling. My whole sleeve was red, and I could make out a deep wound underneath. It was still bleeding and hadn't been treated at all. Reed huts stood around me. A brown-colored man came out of one of them. He had a bone sticking through his nose and rings hanging from his ear. A sneering mask sat on top of his head, and he carried a spear in his hand.

Raising the spear above his head, he cried out, "Woah!" A mass of people immediately came out of the reed huts. They all had the same brown skin.

Together, they all cried out, "Woah!" One of them had a drum upon which he began to pound. "*Boom, boom, boom, boom, boom.*" With each *boom*, the tension grew greater.

The chanting now changed to "Away with him. He chased away our head!" I didn't understand what they were talking about at all. I couldn't remember chasing away a head.

Now the leader approached me. He raised his spear to stab me ... but then he froze at a sudden, deafening roar. It wasn't a noise made by wild animals; it was clearly coming from a human throat. The leader dropped his spear in fright, and all the village people began running around in panic.

They screamed out, "The Chief, the Supreme Chief of the Crocodiles is coming!" The noise grew even more deafening as it grew closer, and all the people kneeled down on the ground to receive the Supreme Chief.

A long procession came out from between two of the huts. Two crocodiles were at the head, and four more followed behind them, carrying a sedan chair upon their shoulders. I couldn't make out who sat inside. The chair was followed by at least fifty crocodiles in parade. The village folk bowed down low, their leader included. The four crocodiles set the chair on the ground, and a very strange figure stepped out. It was dressed in crocodile leather; on its head was a crocodile head, and it wore crocodile tails twisted around its ankles. Even its shoes and belt were made from the crocodile hide. There was an angry look on the figure's face; with his eyebrows raised and his mouth screwed up in a grimace, he gazed around. His skin was lighter than that of the other man.

Taking large self-assured steps, he approached the leader in the sneering mask, ordered him to rise, and then talked with him for a few minutes, all the while pointing towards me. The rest of the villagers rose along with their leader. Meanwhile, my heart was beating so hard I could feel it in my throat, and my mouth was dry. The leader bowed again and walked towards me together with the Supreme Chief. He had a large knife in his hand. He walked behind me and cut the ropes loose. The Supreme Chief seized my left arm, led me to the sedan chair, and helped me climb in next to him.

The procession started up again, and we were soon out of the village. In the swinging chair, I tried to ask my fellow traveler some questions. However, as soon as he noticed this, he laid his hand over my mouth to silence me. The coach stopped soon afterward. The man beside me stepped out and helped me down too. I still wasn't all that steady on my feet.

We had stopped in a savannah. There were few trees or bushes to be seen. A few reed huts stood in a circle. The man took me by the hand and brought me to the largest of the huts, where he sat me down on a stool. Then he stood in the doorway and began to cry out in the deafening howl again. He closed the door and shuttered the windows carefully. He removed his crocodile outfit and sat down in a chair opposite me. I could now see his face clearly, and I really couldn't believe what I saw. Sitting in front of me was Professor Kugelschreiber!

"Professor Kugelschreiber!" I cried out joyfully.

"Yes, zat is me!" Kugelschreiber said. "I am very pleased to see you again. But let me first explain a few zings. As far as zat ozher business vent, I found a screep, but I didn't end up going to zee firmament. I received an assignment from a friend to go to Africa, vhere I vould learn much more about zee heavens. For my own safety, I chose to present myself to zee natives as zee Chief of zee crocodiles, and zeese brown-skinned people believed me. In zis manner, I can do all kinds of research anyvhere I vant wizout being attacked. I also tamed zee crocodiles vith a magic formula. Since I don't like nosy faces vhere I am verking, I have zee crocodiles chase away all strangers, vhich is very effective. Zeese brown skins feed zee crocodiles zemselves, but you, idiot, fed zem yourself, and zen zey didn't appear for zeir daily meal. Zo, zhey believe zhat you chased away zhe head crocodile. Zhey took you as a prisoner and vanted to kill you. I heard about it and came as quickly as I could. I had to rush to save you. Ah, but I now see zat you have been vounded. Let me take care of zat emmee-deately. By zee vay, zee door and shutters are closed zo zat zee brown skins do not overhear us speaking. Ozhervise, zey vill kill boths of us."

"And I thought you were going to kill me. Thank you so much for saving my life!" I exclaimed.

Kugelschreiber attended to my arm using a salve and herbs. While he was busy doing that, I told him all about what had happened to me. The incident with the King of Clouds and the document granting me eternal life interested him in particular.

"I am glad you have been in zhe clouds. But let me finish my story. I have begun an investigation on sorts of tea."

"Tea? What use is that?" I asked.

"It appears zat tea pozesses extraordinary powers, and I plan to find out vhat exactly zhey are. But you must get some rest. You surely could use some sleep." He offered me a very comfortable bed, exactly like the one I had slept in Kugelschreiber's cave.

"I bet Joe made this," I remarked.

"Yes, zhat is right. How did you know?"

"Oh, just a wild guess."

Kugelschreiber also lay down. Outside, the crickets chirped loudly. It was a peaceful noise. I asked Kugelschreiber where he got his enormous voice from.

"Ah, my boy. Drinks vill do vonders, don't you agree? Besides, a Supreme Chief must be able to perform somezing!" We soon fell asleep.

The next morning there had been crackers with marmalade and cheese, a boiled egg, and tea made ready for me. There were two chairs by the table over one of which hung some clothes. They weren't my own clothing which seemed to have been taken away. I stepped out of bed and pulled on the new outfit, which consisted of a pair of crocodile shoes, a loose white shirt with wide sleeves and narrow cuffs, dark-blue cotton trousers, and a dark-blue felt hat. It was a very comfortable outfit, and it fit me well. I began my breakfast. It tasted delicious.

Kugelschreiber came in from outside in a rush. He exclaimed, "You haven't tried my tea yet. Drink, eat up. Eet is vunder tea."

"Good morning, Professor Kugelschreiber. I'll drink it up immediately. Tell me, where have you been?"

"I am coming from zhe village. I visit zhe village every day. How do you like your clozes? Joe made zhem."

"They are very nice and fit me well," I said. "By the way, I've got the feeling back in my right arm, and the wound no longer hurts."

Kugelschreiber nodded. He sat down at the table and lit a pipe that he had pulled out from under the leather skins that he wore. He began to puff slowly at first and then harder and harder until he was completely enveloped in a cloud of smoke. He seemed to be concentrating deeply. He knitted his eyebrows and blinked his eyes nervously several times. He finally finished his pipe, having, in the meantime, nearly knocked me out with all the smoke.

Then he began to speak in a serious tone, more seriously than I had ever heard him speak before. "You must leave here as quickly as possible. Vhile I vas in zhe village zhis morning, I ran into zhe leader. He said zhat he vanted to see you. Zhey assume zhat you have been killed by me, and now zhey want to have your remains. Zhat is custom here. If zhe Supreme Chief has killed someone, zhen he must deliver zhe dead body to zhe villagers. Vhen zhey realize zhat you are still alive, zhey will kill both you ànd me. Zherefore, you must get out of here. Zhe ocean is not far from here. Zhere is a boat vaiting for you vith vhichs you can cross to zhe ozser side. Zhe boats of zhe brown-skins are not very strong. Zhey vill never be able to catch up wiz you and take you prisoner. I vill say zhat you escaped and zhat you are much too dangerous to be used as an offering. As long as zhey don't see you again, zhey vill have to believe me. I have an appointment at twelve o'clock. Zhen, I must hand you over. Zhat gives you zhree hours' head start to get avay. The crocodiles come at midday to eat, so you must go on your own."

I was scared and disappointed. I had just run into a friend, and now he wanted to send me away. But I had no other choice than to listen to the professor. I packed my belongings together and stepped outside the hut. Kugelschreiber pointed me in the right direction, and off I went in search of the ocean. The cluster of huts gradually disappeared from sight behind me. I still had lots of time since the sun hadn't yet reached its high point in the sky. In other words, it wasn't yet noon. I reached the sea after an hour's walk.

A row of boats lay along the beach. I had no idea which one was meant for me since they all looked the same. I slowly walked from one boat to the next until I came upon one which was named Ody.

This must be it, I thought. The boat looked like a raft made from bamboo poles bent and bound together. Both the mast and rudder were also made from bamboo. A yellowish cotton sail, mats, blankets, and dried fruit were scattered on the bottom of the boat.

I pushed the small boat into the water and climbed in. Then I raised the sail, took hold of the tiller, and slowly sailed away. The farther away from shore I got, the faster we went. The clear water raced past me. The water was so clear that I could see to the bottom, even where it was very deep. It was a fantastic sight; the whole seabed was covered with the most beautiful plants and corals, white and red in color. Thousands of magnificently colored fish swam among the coral in the most beautiful colors imaginable. Before I had left Kugelschreiber, he had suggested that I head west, and so I followed his advice closely.

I was on the open sea; the coastline grew further and further away. Meanwhile, the wind had strengthened and now cut right through my loose shirt, which fluttered in the wind. I pulled a blanket around my shoulders to avoid getting chilled. That was much better.

I had sailed for several hours when I noticed small boats approaching in the distance. They were clearly the villagers, so I tried sailing as fast as possible. However, my pursuers didn't give up easily. They kept after me as long as they could, but after a while, they were forced to turn back. They had all become seasick and hung weakly over the sides of the boats.

I had to admit that it was blowing quite hard, but luckily, I wasn't seasick. I guess the dried fruit helped to keep down the nausea. Finally, all the boats with the seasick pursuers had turned back, and I was safe!

I continued sailing for many hours. The sea grew calmer, and the sun began to set. The wind finally stopped altogether, and the surface of the sea turned into a mirror. My boat was no longer making any progress. There was nothing I could do but wait until the wind began to blow again, so I laid a mat out on the bottom of the boat and lay down, covering myself with a blanket.

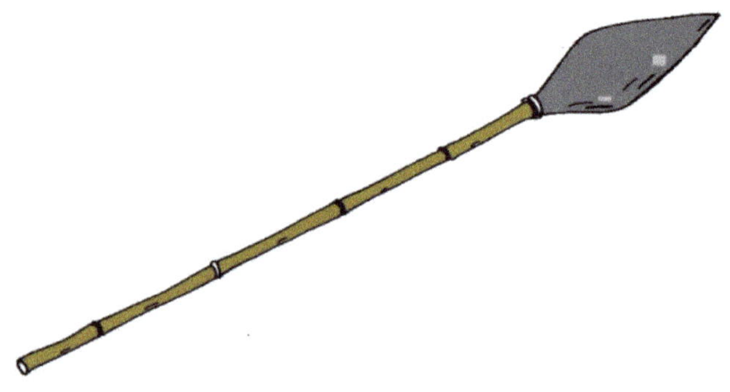

10

It was almost dark by the time I awoke. I must have slept for a long time because the surface of the water was no longer so still as when I had laid down. The waves were growing by the minute, rocking the boat like a cradle. Finally, the wind was blowing so hard that my sail tore. It hung in tatters in the water. By now, the waves were mountainous, and my boat and all its contents were being slung high into the air.

I tried my best to keep the boat upright, but it wasn't easy. Standing up straight in the middle of the boat, one leg on each side, I spread my arms wide to maintain balance. Of course, I realized that I wouldn't be able to keep that up for very long. Tons of water were spilling over the sides and into the boat, and waves were breaking over my head. I was thoroughly soaked and dead tired, and only with the greatest effort could I keep standing. My new clothes hung like rags on my body.

Suddenly, there came a huge wave which knocked me flat onto the bottom of the boat. I tried to get up, but the ropes holding the bamboo poles together began to break one after the other. I knew that the next wave would doom my boat, so

I took the precaution of securing myself to one of the poles. Clasping the bamboo pole in my arms, I waited for the next wave to break over the boat. I didn't have to wait long; it was here already! My boat fell to pieces, and I was flung high into the air. My hands had become so numb, they could no longer hold onto the bamboo pole; it slipped out of my grasp. I landed on top of a large wave and slid into the deep trough. Another wave washed over me, nearly knocking me out. I only had a hazy vision of what was happening. Slowly but surely, I sank deeper into the water, as if it was a bed of clouds. Then everything grew black.

It seemed like ages before I opened my eyes. "*I must be dead now*," I thought. Though I didn't feel any different than when I was alive.

A high ceiling made of shiny polished stone stretched above my head. In fact, the same material was all around me. I hadn't the faintest idea where I was, nor whether or not I was dreaming it all. I pinched myself hard in the nose to be sure. It hurt, so it couldn't be a dream, and I was still alive.

I heard footsteps approaching from the distance, footsteps belonging to someone who must have gone swimming with his shoes on. The squishing, squashing footsteps kept coming closer. I would have moved heaven and earth to stop me from falling into another dangerous adventure.

And, sure enough! The heavens and earth began to move! The ceiling above me slid away; only the backside remained attached to the wall as if on a hinge. I thought I could see light shining through the opening and pressed my eyes tightly shut. But the footsteps were by now so close that I could have touched the person just by sticking out my hand.

A light shone in my eyes. I opened them a crack. I don't know why exactly, but I heaved a sigh of relief when I saw that the figure standing before me resembled a fish. He was mainly red and had yellow fins. He carried a lantern with one fin, out of which a strange light shone. It was red, but when I looked more closely, it appeared to be blue, then green or yellow, or sometimes just plain white.

The red fish opened his mouth and said, "*Blurp* ... Blody, blome blith ble blo Bleptune; Ble blants blo blee blou." I sat up straight and scratched behind my ear, puzzled.

The fish gestured with his head, said, "Blome blith ble blow," and headed back to the opening through which he had arrived. Hoping he had something for me to eat, I followed him. We entered a long dark passageway which the fish illuminated with his lantern. I turned back to look at my room and saw that it was a shell, a gigantic shell, which slowly closed. There was no return now.

The tunnel was long; it rose and sometimes descended. Finally, I saw a beam of light in the far distance, which I assumed to be the end of this passageway. When we left the darkness, the fish extinguished his lantern and motioned for me to walk ahead of him. He had led me to a small room; the walls were completely covered in seaweed. I sat down and waited to see what would happen.

After a short while, a second door opened, and there stood the red fish again.

"Why did you leave me here alone?" I asked the fish.

"Blat blo blou blean? Bli blidn't bleave blou blere blalone; blou blean blhe blish blith ble blantern!" Once again, I hadn't received a decent answer. I shrugged my shoulders, thinking that it was useless asking this fish anything since he kept avoiding the questions.

"Blome blith ble. Bleptune blants blo blee blou."

The fish motioned for me to follow him, which I did. We left the room together and entered a wide, well-lit passage that led to another door. The fish walked ahead, stuck his head into the room, mumbled something, and then turned towards me.

"Bleptune blis bleady blo bleceive blou." He pushed me

impatiently through the door and closed it behind me. I turned to ask him not to leave me alone again, but I realized I wouldn't get a decent answer anyway.

The room he had pushed me into had a low ceiling, but it was very large. The walls, ceiling, and floor were completely covered in writing. I bent down to read what was written there and saw that the words were in my own language. Words such as cat, dog, rat, and nut were written quite legibly all over the place. Some had been crossed out with red ink, and some had corrections. There were no recognizable sentences, just individual words written in different hands.

I stood up and saw a large man sitting in a chair made from shells. He had a long beard of seaweed, and he wore a garment made from shredded sails.

"Have you read it all?" He asked.

"Um, actually, I've only read a few words. I just came in," I replied.

"Of course, of course. You haven't had much time."

I was surprised that he spoke my language. "Who are you?" I asked. "And what happened to me? What do you want from me?"

"Ah," said the man, "let me explain. I am Neptune of the Sea. You are probably wondering why I am wearing your sail. Well, that is quite simple. Since there is no material for clothing on the sea bottom, I must make do with the sails from wrecked ships. In this way, I have at least one new outfit per week. I have my own designers. Perhaps I might show you my collection. There really is no such thing as a perfect garment, but I do know ahead of time what I'll be getting." Neptune pulled on a bell cord, and the red fish with the yellow fins entered carrying a portfolio.

"Look," said Neptune, "this is a design using a sheet from a ship that will come along this way someday." He showed me a white piece of paper with the word TITANIC written in gold letters.

"Very pretty," I said.

"Oh, but now we've drifted from the subject. I was going to explain what happened to you. You were sleeping when we received your signal and—"

I interrupted him to ask, "What do you mean 'my signal?'"

"Ah, my dear boy, don't you even know what ... Well, while you sleep, you think. And that thinking produces a vibration which we receive here and can interpret with the help of the dreamometer. It tells us exactly what you are thinking and indeed everything that you know, not that you're aware of it. Let me show you what I'm talking about."

He rang again for the fish, who now came in carrying a machine. Neptune put it on his lap and said, "Now, concentrate deeply on what you most desire at this moment. Close your eyes, and don't think of anything else besides your chosen subject."

I closed my eyes and concentrated until I heard, "Okay. That is enough. You can open your eyes now. The machine is working on it. Yes, yes. Take a look ..."

Very slowly, wheels began to turn, which caused a fishbone filled with ink to move about on a piece of paper. Forms appeared on the paper. First a long one, then a short one, followed by a short curly squiggle. I could see the letters o, f, o, and d. Then the f moved to the front: f-o-o-d. I was amazed; food was indeed the only thing I was thinking of.

"Let me see what we can do for you. While we are waiting—oh, here it comes already."

The fish brought my dinner into the room, and I began to eat immediately. It tasted delicious, dried seaweed with shrimps.

"Very satisfactory thought processes," said Neptune. "Perhaps you didn't even realize that you have thought processes, and very fine ones, too. Rated between clever and very clever. Down inside you, there is an extremely knowledgeable intelligence, though you yourself know very little to almost nothing.

The dreamometer measures how much this intelligence of yours knows. From our research, you appear to be a master of languages. Yet because you are unaware of it, this great talent goes to waste. In short, you are two beings in one. We would like to borrow your intelligence for a while if that's all right with you. Just for a few days, or maybe even one day, is enough. Afterward, we will return it to you immediately. We, well, at least the fish have a speech deficiency which we believe your intelligence can help to correct. The fish, you see, only possess one being. Do you follow me?"

I mumbled, "*Scrunch*, umh, bot beally."

Neptune continued, "Well, let me go on. In a few moments, we will turn you inside out. Your smart side will then be exposed, and you shall give the fish speech lessons. I taught them how to write myself. Since we have very little paper, we use the walls and ceilings for that purpose. The fishes' speech defect is the following: they preface or replace the first one or two letters of every word with 'bl.' For example, instead of saying 'cat,' 'dog,' 'rat,' and 'nut,' they say 'blat, blog, blat, blut.' Do you understand?"

Before I had time to answer him, he said, "Fine, let's get started." Neptune opened a door and led me into another room which was papered with shells. A bed of seaweed stood in the middle.

"Lie down and go to sleep. We can only turn you inside out if you are sleeping. We do that with the help of a contratometer, which works in the following manner—"

"Oh, um, I believe you," I said. "You really don't have to explain it. Let's not get into how a con—con—contrometer works; just get started," I said, in the hope of avoiding another long explanation.

"Okay. Lie down then and sleep ... sleep ... sleep." My eyes slowly shut, and I fell into a deep sleep.

When I awoke, I felt like a totally different person. I wasn't in the least bit tired, and I felt much wiser. Neptune offered me a hand and helped me to get up.

"So, Ody. Please follow me and teach the fish how to speak well. I have not been successful in that task." Neptune and I returned to the room with all the writing, where he led me to his very own chair made from shells. An enormous school of fish stood before me, every one of them red with yellow fins. So, it hadn't been the same fish all that time, after all!

Neptune stood next to me and called to the gathering, "This is Ody. He is here to teach you all to speak properly. Please welcome him!"

Thunderous applause filled the classroom, and they cheered, "Blip, blip, blooray! Blip, blip, blooray! Blong blive Blody!" Neptune put a finger to his mouth and bade the fish to quiet down. Then he took a seat on the ground.

I stood up, coughed, and began, "Fish!" I stopped, surprised at my own voice. It sounded so deep and warm, the voice of a wise, elderly gentleman. "Fish," I said again. "Please repeat after me: COME HERE."

The crowd cried out enthusiastically, "Blom blere!"

"No, no," I said, "c-ome h-ere!"

"Cobl heebl."

"C-O-M-E H-E-R-E!"

"Come here!" the crowd cried out. I looked at them happily, full of surprise, while Neptune nodded.

"I knew you could do it," he said.

"Now say after me, 'Now, go away.'"

"Blow, blo blaway."

"No." I said, "Now—go—away."

"Now, go away," they yelled out. They were so pleased with themselves that they repeated the sentences over and over again.

"Now let's try the alphabet: A, B, C, D ..."

"Bla, ble, ble, ble ..." I sighed heavily and repeated the letters again. The fish said them after me, and this time they succeeded in saying most of them properly.

I continued the lesson by teaching them sentences like "Hello Ody. Hello Neptune. Hello everyone." And, "We are good; Ody is good, and so is Neptune."

When I had given a full day's lesson, Neptune dismissed the class. He turned to me and said, "You have done your work well. You must be rather tired now." He led me back to the bed of seaweed to turn me right-side-out again with his contratometer.

Neptune was still standing next to me when I awoke.

"You are back to your old self again," he said.

I asked, "Did I sleep long?"

"Oh yes, you have slept a good deal of the day. It's late. Let's smell ..." He stuck his nose up and inhaled deeply.

"To be precise, it is 1492 hours."

Somewhere deep inside me, something began to niggle me. I suddenly felt an uncontrollable urge to get away from here as quickly as possible. Just like that, for no reason at all.

I grabbed Neptune's hand and shook it vigorously. "I'm terribly sorry, but I really have got to be on my way." Neptune looked at me sideways but didn't attempt to stop me.

"Then I shall call the class together so that you can say goodbye," he said. I soon stood again in front of a very full classroom.

I called out, "I want to thank you from the bottom of my heart for your warm reception. It was a pleasure to be able to work with you, but it is late now, and—" Flashes shot through my head, and I kept hearing these words: *It is 1492. It is 1492.*

I cut my speech short. "Well, that is that. I'm off now." And I rushed away. I ran up dark corridors and down lit passageways, not knowing the way to the exit. Behind me, I could hear footsteps coming after me. The fish didn't want to let go of me yet, but I felt such an urge to get away that I grabbed an ax and hacked a hole in the wall. I climbed through as quick as lightning and was suddenly completely surrounded by the sea.

Behind me, I could still hear a vague chanting: "Come back. Come back!" And then everything was quiet.

I eventually reached the surface, where I drifted in the water. I don't know how long I lay there, but suddenly I felt someone take hold of me. He tied a rope around my body and hoisted me out of the water. Then I was laid down again, and the rope was removed.

II

I was lying looking up at a low wooden ceiling. The bed I was in was high up. I threw the blankets off and carefully lowered myself from the bed. The room was extremely small, and it moved up and down. The door opened, and a large man entered the room carrying a map in his hand.

"Ahoy there, mate!" he called out good-naturedly. "Did you sleep well in my bunk? We saw you bobbing around there in the water and thought, 'Aw, let's haul the poor fellow aboard. Perhaps he's still alive.' And indeed! Allow me to introduce myself. I am Harry the Helmsman, and you are?"

"I am Ody, sir," I replied shyly.

"Ah ... the Ody? Then the captain is expecting you. When you leave the cabin, turn right. It's the first door you come to. But let's first find you some decent clothing. It wouldn't be appropriate to appear before the captain in those rags. Here you are. Try on these things." He threw a shirt and trousers, which he had pulled out of a closet for me. The clothing was strange and old-fashioned; the shirt was striped, and the trousers were like knee-breeches. They looked like they came out of the 15th century.

"Go along now. The captain should be eating his breakfast. With a little luck, maybe you can join him." I closed the door after me as I left, turned right, and knocked on the first door I came to.

"Come in!" a male voice called out. A very elegantly dressed man sat at a table. This cabin was also built from wood. Paintings of sailboats hung on the walls.

"Ah ha! There you are. Right on time," the man at the table said. "I told you you'd be here. You must be rather hungry. Will you join me; how about an egg?"

I gazed at the man questioningly and replied, "Yes, please. I am very fond of eggs. But who are you? Do I know you? And what do you mean by 'right on time?'"

"Take a seat, my boy." He pushed a chair towards me, handed me an egg, and continued, "Let me explain. Perhaps you will remember that, before you started through the desert, you crossed a sea in a boat pulled by sharks, which I personally steered. I asked you your name. You are Ody, aren't you? I bade you goodbye and said that I would see you again in 1492. You said that you weren't sure whether or not you would be there, but you can see for yourself. You are exactly on time. It is now 1492."

I thought for a minute, and it all came back.

"And who are you?" I asked.

"Oh," said the man in a mysterious tone, "I am Columbus." For a minute, I thought I understood everything, but that moment of clarity vanished quickly. I couldn't quite grasp what he meant by what he had just said.

"*Oh, well,*" I thought. "*At least I am safe now. There's no risk of being thrown into the sea.*"

Columbus began to tell me about himself and his past. How he used to earn his living by ferrying boats over, as he put it. And how he later received a royal warrant to sail around the world and discover new lands.

"Well," he sighed deeply. "I don't know what will become of me, but I am sure that the world is round and not flat. We shall sail as long as it takes to reach the edge of the world or until we return to the place of our departure," he declared.

Meanwhile, I had finished my egg and Columbus his. He offered to show me around the boat and let me see everything, from the cabin boys' hut to the officers' mess to the top of the mast where the crow's nest hung. Sailors climbed up and down the mast, adjusting the sails. One of them was a girl.

In the evening, all the sailors sat in a circle on deck and played musical instruments. The girl sang and danced in the middle. She told scary tales about sea monsters and dragons, which felt so real that I shook like a straw in the wind when I heard them.

I slept in the captain's cabin at night. We became closer and closer friends as the days passed and as he learned more about all of my experiences. He trusted me a lot; if there was a problem on board, he would ask my advice. We discussed the matter at length, and I would give him my opinion. He'd believe me immediately without a trace of doubt. In this way, we traveled together for many days.

One October day, something happened that threw us all into a commotion. Columbus and I were standing on deck when someone suddenly yelled out from the crow's nest, "Land in sight! Land in sight!" Columbus quickly grabbed a telescope. A long, thin coastline stretched out ahead of us. It looked like an empty and hostile place. Columbus asked me if I had any idea what country it could be. I concentrated deeply for a while and came to the conclusion that it must be the Indies. He personally thought that he had discovered America, but since he always believed me, he too assumed it was the Indies.

"You are always right, anyway," he said. "I shall record in my logbook that we have discovered the Indies."

We stepped ashore the very same day. I stretched my legs, glad to be on solid ground again. Columbus and his crew remained on land for a few days but then decided to turn back home to bring news of their discovery.

I decided to stay behind and continue on my journey. Columbus was sad when he heard of my decision because he would have liked to have introduced me to the royal family. We said goodbye this time as good friends. I wished him and his men a good trip back and waved them farewell with a handkerchief.

12

I kept on waving until the ship disappeared out of sight. Then I turned my back to the sea. Now I had the feeling that centuries separated the present moment from my encounter with Columbus. Yes, I was quite sure of that; it had happened centuries ago. I let out a deep sigh and slowly began climbing the steep cliff which rose before me. The rocks were flat and slippery and seemed to go on forever.

After hours, I reached a plateau; it was very extensive and flat. Rounded, weathered mountains stood in the far distance. The climb had taken a lot of energy, and I was now exhausted. I longed for a warm, friendly house. Halfway across the plateau, I stopped and gazed all around me. There wasn't a sign of life to be seen anywhere. The area was barren, and the soil appeared washed away, exposing the rocks.

Suddenly, something caught the corner of my eye. Far in the distance, I could make out a pole with what looked like wooden arrows nailed to the top. The pole was painted red, green, and several other bright colors. The object fascinated me. It had a strange attraction; I couldn't pull my eyes away. I was more and more curious; what was it? A totem pole, perhaps?

I hurried towards the object, and as I got closer, it started to look like a sign. Finally, standing in front of it, I read, to my surprise, the word "BARBER" painted in red and green paint. Underneath, an arrow pointed to the left. I raised my eyebrows as I inspected the sign from top to bottom, left and right, back and front. On the back, I found another puzzle: Over 1000 thumbs were drawn there.

"*What on earth does that mean?*" I wondered. In order to satisfy my curiosity, I decided to follow the sign to the barber. I felt my hair; it was far too long.

"*Well,*" I thought, "*I could use a shampoo and haircut.*"

I hadn't walked far before the path turned off to the right, taking me along with it. It was heading towards a forest. "Is that where the barber is?" I asked myself. I hesitated a moment, wondering if I dared enter the woods. But I walked on.

I had hardly set foot in the woods when I heard lazy, sluggish voices call out, "Heeelllooo," in a high tone. The voices seemed to come from the treetops, but they didn't frighten me since they sounded warm and friendly. They didn't seem to mean any harm. I walked onwards, following the arrows along the path. They led me to the left and then to the right, and sometimes in circles. The deeper I walked into the woods, the darker it became. Then I noticed a flickering light far away. I headed towards it, but just before I got to it, I heard a rustling in the trees, so I hid behind a thick tree trunk.

Before me lay a clearing where the trees had been chopped down. The light came from a campfire burning in front of a small log cabin. A small fellow with black wavy hair and a pointed beard ran out of the cabin. He cried, "Where is he, then? Where is he?" He glanced up at the trees whose leaves began to rustle again. "Oh," said the little man. "Is he over there?" He pointed straight at my hiding place and walked directly towards me.

"Come on out!" he called to me. "I am the barber, funny, hee! Well, that's why you came, isn't it?" I slowly stood up, like a boy who had just played a trick on his mother and had now been caught. The fellow laughed contentedly and nodded for me to follow him. "Come along. We'll get started immediately!" he said and headed for the fire. I followed behind.

He stood before the fire, snapped his fingers, and called out, "Chair!" A wooden chair flew out of the hot fire and landed gently on the ground. My mouth dropped open. He snapped his fingers again, called out, "Table!" And, just like the chair, a wooden table flew out of the fire and landed on the ground.

"Take a seat," said the little man, gesturing to the chair. I sat down, expecting it to be on the warm side. After all, it had just come out of the fire. But to my surprise, it was not in the least bit warm. On the contrary, it was ice-cold.

"I am Ody," I said in the hope of learning his name in return.

"I know," the man replied but didn't tell me his name. He wore a white cape, shirt, and pants. From under his cape, he pulled out a pair of scissors, which glittered in the light from the flames.

"I've waited years for this opportunity," he said softly, grinning to himself. He picked up a few locks of my hair and cut, catching the hair deftly in his cape. And so, he continued to cut and cut and cut. When he was finally finished, he produced a mirror from under his cape and handed it to me.

I was looking forward to seeing my new face, but when I looked in the mirror, I saw a horrible sight, literally and figuratively. I turned the mirror over to see if this was some sort of joke, but there was no ugly picture pasted to the back. I looked at myself in the mirror with horror. My hair had been cut very short, so short that it stood straight up on end.

"You are not a good barber," I said, looking at my prickly

head with disgust.

"Indeed, I'm not," the fellow agreed, dancing joyously in circles.

"But this is worse than horrible," I cried out, pointing at my almost bald head.

"Oh, but I needed your hair," he replied. "You should be grateful that I left anything growing." I didn't know whether I was supposed to be happy or sad at this remark of his.

"Whatever do you need my hair for?" I asked.

The man looked at me thoughtfully, then sighed and said, "Well, I suppose I owe you an explanation. Come inside where we can sit down and talk in peace." He skipped happily into the cabin. I followed after him. He lit an oil lamp that hung above the table.

Then he began to tell his story: "I am a magician. The forest which wished you hello as you entered is bewitched. That barber's sign is a lure for people with long hair, such as yourself. The trees told me where you were hiding, so I could obtain your hair. I needed your hair badly because, you see, I can only produce wooden objects out of the fire since I only have wood to burn. It has always been my greatest dream to have my own small violin. The problem was I didn't have strings or hair for the bow. I could only make the wooden parts. But now I have the hair I need to make my violin."

Timidly, I asked him, "But why didn't you use your own hair?"

He looked at me, astonished. "What an idea! That would be a waste, don't you agree? No, no, this way is much better. Tomorrow, I shall make my violin. It will be very special." His eyes sparkled, and he grew enthusiastic at just the thought.

"The wood for the fire will come from all the different types found in the whole world. I have cultivated them all here in this forest. Now let me explain why I want to burn all these kinds of wood together. The answer lies in the word 'hetero-genius.' As I'm sure you already know, the word means 'many-sided.' When one splits it into syllables, one can form 'het' and 'genious.' 'Het' comes from heat or hot, and 'genious' is better spelled as 'genius.' Obviously, one must be a genius like me to turn many-sided things into magical power with heat. I have chosen wood as my many-sided object since it is most readily available. And my violin will be magical. As soon as I begin to play—I used to take lessons when I was younger—the music will enchant all who hear it. They won't be able to stand still but will dance around merrily. You see," he concluded, "I enjoy being surrounded by happy people."

Everything was now quite clear to me: the "heeellooo" when I entered the woods, the chair and table that came out of the fire, everything ...

"I would like you to stay here tonight so that you can witness the birth of my violin tomorrow," said the magician. These words sounded like music in my ears; after all, I needed a comfortable place to spend the night. He conjured two beds from the fire and had them land in the room. Then he took mattresses, pillows, and sheets from a closet and made both beds. I lay there very comfortably and fell asleep immediately.

I awoke with the sun shining on my face. I stepped out of bed, washed my face in a bowl of water that I found on the table, and got dressed. I didn't need to comb my hair. Then, I sat down at the table and ate the bread which had been laid out.

The magician wasn't in his bed, so I assumed he was outside. I found him squatting in front of a pile of wood. As I approached, the trees began to rustle. The magician looked up immediately and said, "Ah, there you are. I was just about to start the fire."

I stood next to him and watched as he rubbed two sticks together. The pile of wood contained many different types of trees. On top of the pile lay my hair which he had so rigorously cut off the day before. He stood up with a burning stick in his hand and threw it on top of the pile. Gently, he pushed me backward.

"Be careful. The flames can shoot out far," he warned. Slowly but surely, the branches began to burn.

"We can begin in a few minutes," said the magician, his eyes twinkling. And indeed, it didn't take long before the pile of wood was ablaze. "Violin, violon, violoniere!" the magician cried out, dancing around the fire.

Then he ceremoniously took off his cape, snapped his fingers, and said, "A violin and a bow!" At this command, the flames flared up high and turned various colors: first green, then yellow, red, blue, purple, white, black, and finally brown. There was a rumble, and suddenly a tiny, delicate violin and bow flew out of the flames and into the waiting arms of the magician. He was in ecstasy and caressed the violin lovingly. The fire was now out, leaving nothing more than ash.

The magician was so happy that he wanted to try out his violin immediately. He clenched the instrument between his chin and shoulder, tuned it up, and raised the bow in the air. And he began to play. It was beautiful, so lovely that my mouth fell open. The music from the little violin was smooth and pure. It was a delight to hear.

And then something strange began to happen; my feet began to dance. I had to dance, whether I wanted to or not: two steps to the left, three to the right, a leap into the air, a pirouette, and many other dance steps. The magician watched me cheerfully over his violin. As a final number, he chose an extra fast melody. My feet shot out from under me, barely under control, and then I sprang high into the air.

Just as I soared to my highest point, the magician stopped playing. The result was that I fell like a stone. The magician saw me falling, raced into the house, and returned at the same speed with two mattresses. Anticipating the spot where I was falling, he threw the mattresses down. And just in the nick of time. I landed with a thud less than a second later.

"I'm sorry about that. I should have chosen a more appropriate moment to stop," the magician apologized.

"Oh, it doesn't matter," I replied, rubbing my bruises. "I'm just glad that you thought of the mattresses in time."

"The violin plays wonderfully, don't you agree? I am terribly pleased with it," the little man squealed with delight.

"All that because of my hair. If I hadn't come along, you still wouldn't have it," I pointed out.

The magician scratched behind his ear. "Yes, yes, you're right. I suppose you deserve a reward. Let me think a moment; what would be appropriate?" He wrinkled his forehead in concentration, and then his face lit up. "I know the perfect thing," he cried out, elated. He put his fingers to his mouth and whistled. Between the trees, a beautiful white horse appeared. The creature walked up to the magician and bowed its head.

Pointing at me with his finger, the magician addressed the horse, "This is your new master." The horse came towards me and snorted. Using his head, he pointed to his back.

"That means you should mount," the magician explained.

I could hardly believe that this horse was meant for me and me alone. He was pearl-white; even his mane and tail were white. A magnificent red cloth with an embroidered gold edge lay over his back. The horse eyed me earnestly with golden eyes; he seemed almost human and looked at me as if he completely understood me.

"Come, come, don't waste time. I'll help you mount," said the magician. I was lifted into the air and set down gently on the animal's back. "You can command him to do anything you wish by whispering in his right ear. Whether he will listen or not is another matter. He eats and drinks what he likes, and what more you need to know about him, you shall discover soon enough, I'm sure," the magician said, chuckling. "Well,

get along now."

I whispered in the horse's right ear that I wanted to leave the forest and continue my journey. He slowly began to walk. He turned his head for one last glance at the magician. I waved goodbye, and we were off.

I was so happy with the horse. I no longer needed to walk, and if I encountered danger, I now had a means of getting away quickly. While we rode, I thought about a name for the animal. But I couldn't think of a name that really suited him.

So, I asked the horse, "Can you talk?"

The horse shook his head. Well then, there was no point

in asking him his name. I decided to call him “Sseus.” We would be Ody and Sseus, together Odysseus.

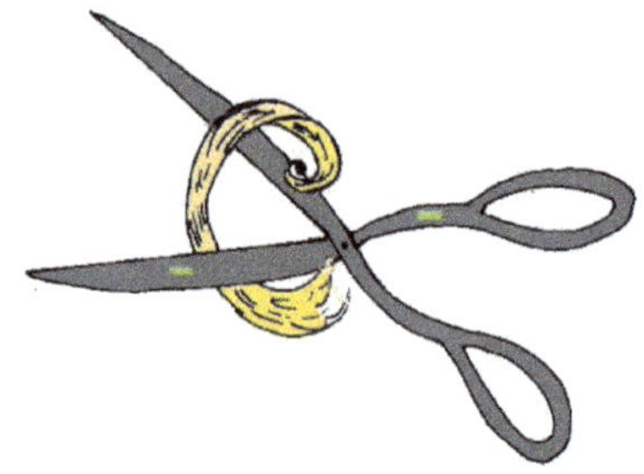

13

Sseus obviously knew the road like the back of his hoof, for we quickly came to the edge of the forest. In front of us lay a barren sandy region bordered by high cliffs which rose like giants towards the heavens. Nothing grew, only a blade of grass here and there. Sseus kept on walking in a straight line; he seemed to know exactly where he was heading.

Suddenly, I heard a loud crashing and thundering. The horse pricked up his ears and looked up at the cliffs. I turned my head too and saw, to my surprise, large boulders falling down directly towards us. They would have squashed us easily, but Sseus didn't hesitate a moment. He took off at a gallop, whinnying fiercely.

"The giants are playing marbles," I said, shocked. Sseus only shook his head, chuckling. When the crashing stopped, I looked back to see if rocks were still falling. But what I saw was worse than falling rocks. A number of large horsemen dressed in black were galloping towards us. They were all dressed alike: a black hood, a black shirt, black trousers, and boots. And they each sat upon a large black horse.

I quickly turned my head towards Sseus and stammered,

"Ss—Ss—Sseus! We're being followed! We're being followed!" A shock went through the horse's body, and he began running even harder than before, as fast as his hooves could carry him. However, the black horsemen were catching up to us. Their horses were much larger than Sseus, and they took longer strides. Sseus was just a pony next to them.

"Faster, Sseus! Faster!" I cried. "They're overtaking us!" But it was too late.

Five black horsemen rode up on either side of us. One on our left threw a lasso over me and pulled it tightly around my middle. On the right, another followed his colleague's example, and so at the same time, they lifted me up. Sseus raced on from under me, leaving me dangling from the two tight ropes held by the horsemen.

"Stop, Sseus! Don't leave me here!" I cried out helplessly, but Sseus didn't slow down. On the contrary, he only ran even faster.

"Hey! We need that one too!" one of the horsemen shouted in a deep voice. "After him, men!" Two of the horses shot off after Sseus, but he was running so hard that the horsemen couldn't get any closer than his tail. One of them reached out his hand for the cloth on Sseus' back and succeeded in pulling it off. At that point, Sseus was nearly flying, and the other horses could no longer keep up.

The black horsemen turned around, and when they rejoined the group, they said to their leader, "Sorry, boss; he was a fast rascal, that one. We only managed to get this cloth from him." They handed Sseus' beautiful cloth to their leader.

"That is a lovely piece, men. Well done! You shall be rewarded for this. Let's return now with our loot."

With that, they all turned around. We must be heading for the place where they had just come from. While the men grabbed Sseus' cloth from each other and admired it, I swung to and fro between the earth and the sky. I had an extremely uncomfortable journey back to their hiding place.

As they rode, the horsemen sang false songs, like this one:

Whoops-a-daisy ... ta-rah-lend
We trot for many hours on end.
Hoopla, the color is in.
A feast! Yes, we shall soon begin.
Red and white, orange and blue,
Haul those colors, don't let them slip through ...

They sang rowdy songs all the way back. Many whoops-a-daisys and ta-rah-lends later, we came to a group of small wooden homes built in a neat little circle. I was flung roughly into one of the houses and landed on a wooden floor. The door was slammed shut and bolted. It was very dark in the hut, and there were no windows to let in any light. Piles of hay were strewn over the floor.

I made myself as comfortable as possible by squatting on one of the little heaps while I thought on Sseus. He had abandoned me just when I needed him most. On the other hand, I could sympathize with him; after all, why should he risk his life for an Ody?

"I'll just have to get out of this one myself, like always," I sighed out loud.

"Yes, me too," a voice groaned out of the darkness behind me.

"Who—who—who are you?" I stuttered.

"I am Hay Fever," said the voice.

"Where are you?" I asked.

"Over here, in the corner," Hay Fever replied. Slowly, I crept on hands and knees over to the corner. He had pressed himself into the corner and covered his face with his hands.

"You needn't be afraid of me. I've just been captured by the black horsemen and don't mean you any harm," I said.

"Oh, you too?" Hay slowly removed his hands from his face. A narrow streak of light came through a split in the wooden wall. Hay put his face in front of the crack so I could see him. He was a thin man and looked at me with large, frightened eyes.

"Hey!" exclaimed Hay. "Why've they taken you prisoner?"

"I wish I knew that myself. I haven't had a chance to ask. Do you know why they captured you?" I asked him.

"Oh certainly, I do. It's a long story, but I will tell it to you. Once, long ago when I was still young, I was riding through the prairie when suddenly a rock avalanche began in the mountains. That's how the black horsemen always announce their arrival. They had no problem catching neither my pony nor me, and ever since that time, I've been held prisoner here. I've learned a lot about these black horsemen over the years through conversations with my guards. Do you know why they always dress in black?" I shook my head no.

"It's because they're too stupid to produce any color! They keep capturing people in the hope of finding someone who can teach them how. They like to steal colorful objects, and then they are as happy as children with a new toy. They haven't gotten much out of me. I was a miner before, so how would I ever know anything about making colors? Miners always wear black and don't often need any other colors. But these black horsemen are stubborn. They are absolutely convinced that I know how to do it but just don't want to teach them. They've taken away everything I had that was colorful. This is all I have left; it's glass and transparent." He pulled out a triangular object from his trouser pocket and showed it to me.

"What a strange thing. Did you get it?"

"Hmm ... actually, I'm not supposed to tell you, but if you promise to keep it among us two? I got this from a water nymph. I had been fishing once, but no matter how long I sat on the bank of the river, I couldn't catch anything. I decided to go home, and as I was walking back along the bank, I saw a boat lying in the water. I thought, '*Hey, Hay, old boy. Use your old noggin. There are more fish in the middle of the river than at the banks, and how does one get to the middle? Exactly! With a boat!*' It is better to come home late with fish than early and empty-handed. So, I stepped into the boat and paddled to the middle of the river. I threw out the anchor and cast my fishing line. I felt a bite immediately. '*Yippie!*' I thought. '*I've got a bite! I've got a bite!*' So, I reeled in the line, and do you know what I had hooked to my line? This glass prism, entangled in a net. I looked it over, and just as I was about to throw it back, a water nymph came up out of the water. 'You can keep it,' she said. 'It will bring you luck; take it wherever you go.' She had beautiful long hair and such lovely eyes. So, I took the thing. 'Please don't try catching the fish anymore,' she said. I pulled in the anchor, and she gave me a shove back to the shore. I ran home to tell the story to my mother. But she didn't believe me and only thought I had made up a story because I hadn't caught any fish. I've kept the glass ever since, though it has yet to bring me any luck."

"May I see it for a moment?" I asked. He handed it to me, and I held it up in the streak of light to get a better look. To my surprise, a rainbow of colors appeared on the opposite wall, beautiful colors ranging from red to purple.

"Ohhhh!" we cried out together. "What beautiful colors!" Then we looked at each other, both filled with the same thought. "Now, we shall be set free!"

"I have a terrific plan!" Hay exclaimed. "Tomorrow morning, the guards will come to bring our food. We shall then let them see the colors. Of course, they will be overjoyed and will want to have this thing. I give it to them, and then they must set us free." I nodded, full of wonder for Hay's wonderful plan.

"First, we must get some sleep," Hay suggested. I prepared a bed out of hay and covered myself with another heap of dried grass. That night I dreamt about triangles, colors, and horsemen in all black.

We were awakened the next morning by someone knocking hard on the door.

"Come in," Hay called out. The door swung open, and a large, broad-shouldered man appeared in the door opening. He, too, was completely dressed in black.

"Ah ha, here's our undertaker!" giggled Hay. The man gave him an angry look. "We have a surprise for you," Hay sang out, though now in a more serious tone. "We can produce colors."

The expression on the black horseman's face changed as if he had seen a rainbow. "Finally. We've waited so long for this moment. We knew you could do it," he said, beside himself with joy.

"However, we will only show it to you under one condition. After the demonstration, we want to be released," said Hay firmly.

"Of course, of course. That is certainly no problem. Now, let me first have a look," said the horseman, almost pleading. Hay pulled the object out of his trouser pocket and handed it to me with a wink. I held it in the beam of light shining through the wooden planks, and a beautiful pattern of colors appeared on the opposite wall. The rider shouted out in joy, ran to the wall, and pressed himself against it. The colors now fell on his body, giving him a green face, purple hair, a yellow shirt, and red trousers.

"Ha, ha!" shrieked Hay. "You sure are a colorful sight. Okay, that's enough now. Let's go and see your leader."

"Oh, yes!" the horseman cried out happily, and together the three of us left the dark little house. We stopped in the square in the middle of all the houses.

The guard cupped his hands around his mouth and shouted, "Meeting! Everyone, come to the meeting!" Black horsemen stormed out of all the houses and stood in a circle around us.

The leader of the group stepped forward and asked, "Well? What've you two got to tell us?"

Hay pinched me in the arm and whispered, "Go ahead. Let them see."

So, I held the glass triangle high up towards the sun, and a lovely colored pattern appeared on the black-dressed horsemen standing behind us.

First, everyone shouted, "Ohhhh!" in surprise, but they quickly began to cheer, "Yippie! Yippie! We've got colors! Yippie!" They all wanted a chance to stand in the colorful pattern.

When everyone had had a turn, the leader came up to me and laid his hand on my shoulder. "We are overjoyed that we can now produce our own colors. We shall also keep our agreement to release you. In addition, you may each choose a horse to take with you." He pointed to the stable. "May we now have the triangle?"

Hay nodded to me, and I handed it to the leader. He examined the piece of glass carefully. Then he snapped his fingers, and another horseman approached, carrying a cushion in his hands. The cushion was made of black velvet. Very carefully, the leader set the precious piece of glass on the cushion.

"Horsemen! You can return to your houses in peace. The glass shall be well guarded, behind lock and key, for our festivals!"

Then, he led us to the stable. It was a large wooden building with small windows. Horses stood in a neat row. Saddles and cloths lay in the corner of the stable.

"Take your pick of a horse and saddle," said the leader. I immediately headed towards the pile of saddle cloths and began to look for the one they had stolen from Sseus. They probably had hidden it well. After digging deep under the pile, I found the beautifully embroidered cloth. At least I had one of my possessions back. Then I walked along the row of horses; they all stood with their heads towards me.

"Yahoo! I've got my pony back!" Hay shouted out. I turned my back to the horses and watched Hay cuddling and petting his old pony. Suddenly, I was firmly gripped by my collar and set down on the back of a black horse. The horse had grabbed me with his teeth.

"*Oh, well,*" I thought. "*This horse is comfortable enough. I might as well take this one.*" I shoved the cloth under me, on the horse's back. Unlike the others, this horse wasn't tied up, and it just walked out of the stable. Hay was already outside on his pony and was shaking the leader's hand. Then he rode off. I followed Hay's example and then rode on after him, quickly catching up.

"Hey!" said Hay. "I see you chose the best of the lot!"

"Well, no," I said. "Actually, the horse chose me."

"Oh, sure, hah hah, you're a real joker!" laughed Hay. He didn't take me very seriously. We rode next to each other for a long time, but eventually, my horse turned off to the right.

"Where're you heading?" Hay called after me.

"I don't know!" I called back. "My horse is doing the walking, not me!"

Hay waved goodbye and soon disappeared out of sight. The black horse kept on walking. I didn't have the slightest idea where we were going.

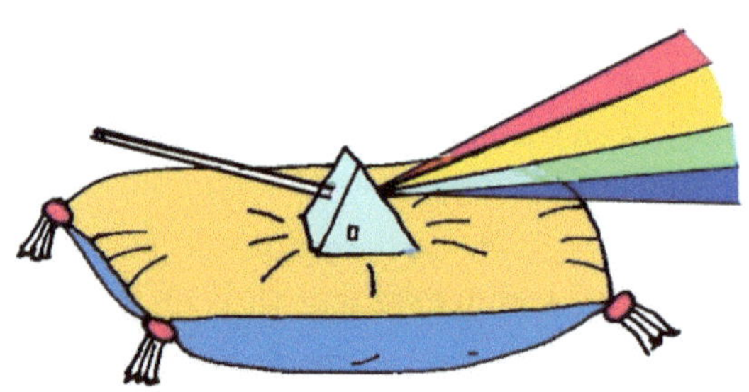

14

We rode through a mountainous region, very hilly and cliffy. Sometimes, the horse turned off to the right and then to the left, and sometimes he just rode straight ahead for hours on end. He apparently knew the way very well. After riding for a long time, I saw a house on the horizon. It was large and well built. The closer we got, the more details I could see, such as a lawn of clover and flowers or the small bronze horse on the roof.

My horse trotted up to the door and said, "You can get off here, Ody. You're expected inside."

I looked at the horse in surprise. This animal could talk. I slid off his back and walked up to the house. Two iron horseshoes were nailed to the door, between which a wooden sign hung. "Horseshoe Villa" was painted on the sign. I opened the door and stepped into a beautifully designed room. Curtains tied up with a bow hung before the windows. The room was reasonably large and probably served as the living room. A few sturdy wooden chairs stood around a wooden table, and thick cushions lay on the chairs. I sat down in one of these very comfortable-looking chairs and waited to see what would happen.

A side door slowly opened, and a brown horse wrapped in a woolen shawl stepped into the room. "Good afternoon, Ody," the horse said. "Did you have a good trip?"

"Ye—yes," I stammered while the horse sat down in a chair next to me.

"You're earlier than I expected."

"Oh!" I said, not understanding quite what he was referring to. There was a silence for a moment. I could hear a whistling noise somewhere in the house. A short while later, the side door opened again, and to my surprise, I saw Sseus walk in. Between his teeth, he carried a small bucket, out of which steam rose.

I ran up to Sseus and hugged him. "Oh, Sseus, am I ever so glad to see you again! But why didn't you come to save me?"

Sseus' eyes looked at me reproachfully as if to say, "But, I did save you." He set the bucket of steaming liquid on the table. I glanced at it; it was hot, brown-colored water. Sseus and I both took a seat.

"I am Flakes," said the brown horse. "Would you like some tea?"

"Oh, is that tea? Yes, please," I said. Sseus took a large soup spoon out of the bucket.

"You can drink out of that," said Flakes. "You know, we really think it's a pity that Sseus can't talk. Normal horses can, but not enchanted ones. Luckily, Sseus and I can understand each other very well, but you can't, of course; you aren't a horse. When you were captured by the black horsemen, Sseus ran to our villa, and together we made up a plan. Corn, the horse which brought you here, would stand guard and watch what happened. If it was necessary, we would attack the prison in order to set you free. But last night, Corn stood outside your prison eavesdropping and overheard you talking with Hay Fever about a glass triangle. This Hay Fever had his own plan of escape, so you didn't need our help. Corn decided to go ahead by himself if things went wrong, but luckily that wasn't necessary. Instead, he waited to pick you up in the stables and bring you here. Do you understand now?"

"No, not everything," I said. "What was that whistling sound that I just heard?"

"Ha, ha," Flakes laughed. "That was the tea kettle!" Then he slurped some tea out of the bucket.

"Oh, Sseus, you are a wonderful horse!" I said, and Sseus smiled. "By the way, I have your cloth back." We chatted for a while longer, and then I suggested to Sseus that we move onwards.

"Oh, no!" Flakes cried out somewhat hesitantly and whispered in my ear, "Tomorrow is Sseus' birthday, and we've organized a party. The invitations have already been sent out."

I looked at Sseus and said, "On the other hand ... um ... why don't we spend the night here." At that, Flakes suggested that we turn in early, so we'd be fit the next day. He headed for the side door, and we followed. We entered a hallway, which led to a bedroom with two beds, one larger than the other. I lay down in the smaller one and Sseus in the larger one. Flakes closed the curtains and left.

It didn't take long before I heard Sseus snoring lightly. However, I couldn't sleep myself. I was bothered by the fact that I didn't have a present for Sseus. What should I give him? I lay a long time thinking until a really bright idea popped into my head; perhaps Flakes had something I could give him. I got out of bed quietly and put on the slippers which I found next to my bed. There was a dressing gown on a coat rack. I put it on, but it was much too big and trailed on the ground. I had to roll up the sleeves. I opened the door very quietly and stepped out into the hallway, closing the door again behind me.

I decided to try all the doors to find Flakes. I hoped he hadn't gone to bed yet. The first door that I tried was locked, but the next one opened easily. I walked into a kitchen, white from floor to ceiling. Two white horses with white aprons were kneading away at dough, and the whole room smelled of biscuits. When the door closed with a click behind me, the two horses looked up.

"Well, Ody," said one of them. "Can't you get to sleep?"

"Who are you two?" I asked.

"Oh, come on now, Ody. Surely your memory isn't that poor. Can't you see? This is Corn, and I am Flakes." I was taken aback and thought for a moment that I had turned color-blind.

"But you two are white horses, and Corn is black, and Flakes is brown," I said.

"Oh," said one white horse. "That is easy to fix." The two horses began to shake themselves. White powder filled the whole kitchen, and I could now clearly see that they were indeed Corn and Flakes. "We were covered in flour! Haha haha!" giggled Flakes. "And now the whole kitchen is covered in flour, including you. Ha ha ha!" Corn and Flakes roared with laughter while I bashfully dusted the flour off my dressing gown.

"Would you like a piece of cake?" Flakes asked, holding out a piece of sweet spice cake under my nose. I could hardly refuse, of course. It was more than delicious, so when he offered me a second piece, I didn't refuse again. Corn and Flakes went on kneading dough while I ate. "We're baking tarts for Sseus! They will be decorated and very fine tarts," said Flakes.

"How old will Sseus be?" I asked curiously.

"Oh, tomorrow, he will see Jacob," Flakes replied.

"Oh yes! I don't have a present for him. Do you?"

"You bet!" said Corn. "We've hidden all the presents in the next room and locked the door."

"Where can I find a present for him?" I asked.

"Sometimes you can find really nice presents in the hills or under the rocks," suggested Flakes.

"Well, then I guess I shall go and look there for one for Sseus," I said and stepped out of the kitchen. I tiptoed down the hallway, past our bedroom, and opened the door at the end, which led to the living room where we had drunk tea earlier in the day. From there, I went to the front door.

It wasn't very dark yet outside, so I could still see well enough. That was lucky since I needed light for my treasure hunt. I lifted up every stone, but the only things I saw were worms and other crawling insects. I had to search further away from the house. There were cliffs ahead of me, and more stones lay to one side and piled up on top of one another. But also here, the lifting up of stones had no good result. Meanwhile, my eyelids were growing heavy. I sat down, exhausted, on a boulder to rest. However, it was growing dark rapidly, and I had little time left.

"Ody," I said to myself, "be reasonable and push on while there's still some light. Soon it will be too dark to find a present at all." I stood up, and just as I bent over to search further, I caught sight of something glittering between two stones. I shoved the stones aside and lifted up the shining object. It was a glass ball hanging on a leather strap. It resembled a collar. The following words were finely inscribed in the glass ball: "No one travels well without good fortune."

"*This is a perfect gift for Sseus*," I thought and put the ball in the pocket of my dressing gown. Luckily, the light from the kitchen was still on, where Flakes and Corn were still baking their tarts. Otherwise, I would have gone in a completely different direction. I returned quickly home, opened and closed the doors behind me quietly, not to wake up Sseus.

Now, as I lay in bed, I was no longer bothered by the thought, "Oh, heaven, I don't have a gift for Sseus," so I fell asleep quickly.

Sseus was still asleep when I awoke the next morning. "*Happy Birthday, Sseus!*" I thought. I dressed and left the room. There was a lot of commotion going on in the living room. I opened the door, full of curiosity.

"Happy birthday to you," lots of horses began to sing out. The room was completely decorated with ribbons and bows. A long, festively decorated table stood in the middle of the floor.

"Happy birthday to you," the horses continued until one said, "Hey! That isn't Sseus. Stop the singing!" Immediately, a silence fell among the horses, who were now all staring at me.

"This is Ody," said Flakes.

"Pleased to meet you," said all the guests simultaneously.

"Take a seat, Ody. Sseus should be here any time now."

I took a seat next to a grey horse with eyeglasses balanced on his nose and glanced around the table. A large bouquet of flowers stood in the center, which Flakes had probably plucked from the garden. All those sitting around the table were well dressed. Some had flowers in their manes, others had a tie around their neck, and Flakes even wore a smoking jacket. Each guest had a package on their lap. The ball which I had found the night before lay between my knees, wrapped up in a handkerchief.

Just as I was about to ask which one was called Jacob, the door swung open, and there stood Sseus. His mane had been neatly combed back.

"Happy birthday to you; happy birthday to you; happy birthday, dear Sseus; happy birthday to you!" the guests sang out together. "Hip hip, hooray! Hip hip, hooray! Hip hip, hooray!" Sseus blinked bashfully. He was shown to the place of honor at the head of the table.

"And now for the presents!" Corn called out. One by one, the guests handed over their gifts. Sseus received a set of horseshoes, a straw hat, a cape, a drinking bowl, a box of chocolates, and many more things that a horse finds useful.

I was the last in line. Modestly, I gave him my gift wrapped up in the handkerchief. Sseus opened it up and saw the glass ball. It gave off a bright light, which reflected in Sseus' eyes. I took it by the collar and hung it around his neck. Sseus looked at me gratefully, and everyone was delighted with the glass ball. It was definitely the nicest of all the gifts that he'd received.

"And now we can eat!" Corn announced. Flakes left the room and soon returned with a large bowl of steaming soup. It had already occurred to me that my place was the only one set with a plate and cutlery. Flake spooned soup into my bowl and then took a seat.

"Bon appétit!" he said.

The horses each took turns drinking out of the soup tureen, and I ate out of my bowl. The soup was delicious, lightly spiced, with the leaves of many types of vegetables floating around in it. Some of the guests asked for the recipe, which Flakes was honored to scribble down on a piece of paper for them. After the soup, a large platter was carried in with a green pig on it. The pig had a red apple in its mouth.

When I looked closer at the main dish, I realized that it wasn't really a pig, but cabbage laid out so that it resembled one. Fried potatoes were scattered around the cabbage with a scrumptious onion sauce. Flakes served me some cabbage leaves decorated with potatoes. Again, the horses each took their turn in eating off the platter. Sseus was given the rosy apple.

Halfway through the meal, Flakes and Corn brought in a number of buckets filled with deliciously cool water. They each carried one bucket between their teeth and three on each arm. The smallest bucket was for me. After everyone had had their share of cabbage, four tarts were brought out and set on the table; the guests "oooooed" loudly.

Each tart was different. The first was decorated with large whirls of whipped cream; "Happy" was written in chocolate flakes in the middle of the tart. The second one was decorated with various fruits: peaches, apples, tangerines, and plums, and had the word "birthday" written in the center. The third was a coffee tart with the word "to" written in the middle. And the last but not least tasty was a chocolate tart covered with candles; "you!" stood in big letters on this one. If you'd have hung from the lamp above the table and looked down, then you'd have seen "Happy... birthday... to... you!"

The tart with candles was closest to Sseus, and he was encouraged enthusiastically to blow them out. Everyone took a quarter of a tart; I chose the kind with whipped cream. Oh, what a pleasure we had eating those tarts. We drew lots for the last pieces, so not a crumb was left over.

After the meal was finished, we all sat around enjoying the taste it had left; but since the meal had lasted six hours and it was already turning dark outside, the guests slowly took their leave. Corn was already busy washing up when the last guest left. Because I was rather sleepy from the large meal, I went to the bedroom to rest a while. I planned to head onwards this evening, so I just wanted to make sure I'd be awake enough to travel.

However, as I entered the bedroom, I saw Flakes sitting on my bed.

"Hello, Flakes," I said. "Are you going to take a nap?"

"No, Ody," Flakes replied. "I wanted to mention something to you. That present which you gave to Sseus reminded me of something. I was sure I had seen it somewhere before, and I suddenly remembered where. The collar belonged to Sseus long ago. He used to come here a lot, and I've seen that glass ball hanging around his neck. He told me that a magician had given it to him. As you saw yourself, there was a saying inscribed inside the ball: 'No one travels well without good fortune.' That magician was a friend of Sseus', and he wanted to give him something which would bring him good fortune.

The magician made the ball so that it could always be found by the bright light it gives off. The closer Sseus came to the ball, the brighter it would shine. One day, Sseus was being chased by fortune hunters who knew about this lucky charm. They wanted it. Sseus managed to escape them, but he lost the ball. He thought that the fortune hunters had picked it up, but now we know that that's not the case. You found it, and we are very grateful for that. You see, Sseus has been rather depressed about it lately."

"Who are these fortune hunters?" I asked.

"Oh, they are old ladies who have encountered so much unhappiness in their lives that they've banded together to hunt for luck. None of them have ever really succeeded in finding any, and I believe that they've all died off by now," Flakes answered.

"Oh," I said. "I see. By the way, Flakes, I am planning on leaving tonight to continue our journey."

"Fine, then I shall pack some food for you to take along."

"Thanks, Flakes, and if you see Sseus, will you let him know that we'll be going?" I asked. "I think he's outside getting a breath of fresh air."

"Okay," said Flakes and disappeared towards the kitchen.

A short while later, Sseus came in completely packed for the trip. He wore his beautiful cloth on his back with two leather saddlebags hanging on each side attached to each other with a strap. A few of his birthday presents had been packed up: the large cape, the straw hat, and the box of chocolates. The food package that Flakes had prepared for us was in the other bag, and the brightly shining charm hung around Sseus' neck. He beckoned me with his big, lovely, golden eyes, and I mounted his back. We walked to the living room, where Corn and Flakes sat, reading the newspaper. When they saw us, they laid the paper down and walked with us outside. They waved for a long time and then reentered their villa.

It wasn't that bad riding in the dark since the light from Sseus' charm illuminated the way for us. We rode for many hours until the cold temperature of the night forced us to stop and build a fire to warm up. While Sseus went to gather wood, I tried to start a fire by rubbing two sticks together. Sseus soon returned with a decent pile and then went to fetch his cape. After a lot of fiddling around, I finally succeeded in starting the fire. We lay down next to it, using the cape as a blanket. We didn't bother eating anything from Flakes' food package since we were still happy with the delicious feast we had had earlier that day. In the pleasant heat from the fire, we quickly fell asleep.

15

I woke up in the middle of the night. Turning over to cover the horse better since we had cooled down quite a bit now that the fire was out, I discovered that Sseus wasn't lying next to me anymore.

"Ss—Ss—Sseus," I whispered anxiously. "Where are you?" There was no reply, so I stood up and looked around. The moon had risen and lit up the whole area. In the distance, I could make out a white figure. I was positive that it was Sseus; I recognized the embroidered cloth.

"*What in the world are you doing?*" I thought. I slowly sneaked closer to see exactly what he was up to. For a while, nothing happened. But then suddenly, Sseus did something remarkable. He took a running start and then sprang high into the air, so high that I saw him shooting across the starry sky. Sseus disappeared behind a large, brightly shining star—the brightest star in the sky.

"Sseus, don't do anything silly," I mumbled and decided to wait until he returned. But it took so long that, in the end, I wandered back to our campsite. With the cape draped around my shoulders, I stared up at the sky. "*Has the horse deserted me again?*" I wondered to myself. "*Oh, Sseus, please come back,*" I kept thinking over and over again.

After several hours had passed, I saw something moving in the sky, coming from the direction of the bright star. What looked like a falling star came shooting downwards, but when the white ball came closer, I saw that it was Sseus. He landed on the ground with a dainty spring and trotted back to the campsite. He wasn't the least bit surprised to find me awake.

"Sseus, where've you been?" I asked, although it would have been smarter not to ask the question since he couldn't give me an answer anyway.

He looked straight at me and seemed to say, "If you really want to know, then you should have come along yourself."

"Well, how could you explain it to me," I said and patted his mane. When I withdrew my hand, it was covered with confetti, small round pieces of paper in red, blue, yellow, and green. I was amazed at this, but I didn't want to worry about this new puzzle right now. The only thing that really concerned me was getting enough sleep before the morning broke. Together, the horse and I began our second sleep that night.

The sun rose earlier than I had hoped. With sleepy eyes, Sseus brought me to a nearby stream to wash. I hadn't noticed the water the night before. While Sseus stood knee-deep in the stream, using his head to throw the cool water onto his back, I dog-paddled—the only way I knew how to swim—back and forth. Two strokes forward, two strokes back. Sseus walked over to the saddlebag, which he had brought along and left on dry land before entering the stream. He pulled out two sandwiches and waited politely until I was ready before he began to eat. They were radish and lettuce sandwiches and very tasty. After breakfast, we prepared ourselves for further travel.

It promised to be a warm day. Therefore, Sseus pulled his

straw hat out of the saddlebag and put it on. I made a sort of hat-like covering with my handkerchief by tying knots in each corner. Then we started on our way, refreshed; the morning swim had done wonders.

After several hours of walking, it occurred to me that Sseus might spring up to the star again this evening. I was terribly curious and really wanted to know what was going on up there. I would really like to go with him once.

"Sseus," I asked sweetly. "Will you be going to that star again tonight?" Sseus nodded his head.

"Say ... um ... Sseus," I asked even more sweetly than before. "Do you think I can come along?" Again, the horse nodded.

I was so excited that I could've yelled out with joy. All sorts of ideas entered my head: the star was a small planet where magicians came together or where fairies bred horses. But then, how could I account for the confetti? No, there must be another explanation. Full of these thoughts in my head, we proceeded on our journey. I was really looking forward to the trip I was on with Sseus. He had appeared so happy last night when he returned; whatever it was, it must be enjoyable.

Sseus took a path that rose up the side of a high mountain. The path was difficult to travel; sometimes, small stones slid out from under his feet and fell down the mountainside. However, Sseus didn't let that bother him. He was very brave and kept on going. Slowly but surely, we made progress until we finally reached the peak. We ate lunch there. I took the package wrapped in paper with the word Lunch written on it out of the saddlebag. There were two lettuce, tomato, and mushroom sandwiches in it, two pancakes with syrup, and two red apples. For Sseus, there was an extra bag, this one filled with clover.

On top of that mountain, our lunch tasted absolutely marvelous. We had a good view from up here; to the left was a barren and rocky area, and to the right was a forest. On the horizon beyond, I saw a blue sea twinkling in the sunlight.

"*Finally, the sea for a change,*" I thought to myself. But how we would ever cross that huge expanse of water was something I didn't dare think about yet. I finished my portion of lunch, but Sseus was still munching away. I was still so hungry that I nearly took some of his clover when he was looking the other way. However, I managed to control myself.

When my horse finished eating, we again set forth on our journey. We now had to come down off the mountain, which was an even more difficult task than the ascent since one false step would send us crashing downwards. So, I dismounted to make the walking easier for Sseus. That proved to be the right move; Sseus almost stumbled, but I steadied him just in time. Together, we came down off the mountainside. It took several hours, by which time the sun had slowly begun to set.

I suggested to Sseus that we make camp at the foot of the mountain before we entered the forest. He nodded in agreement. No sooner said than done. We agreed to get some sleep first; when it was time to go to the star, Sseus would wake me up. We covered ourselves with the cape and fell asleep.

I was awoken by Sseus' nose softly nuzzling my back. "*It's time,*" I thought. "*We're going to go now!*"

The moon shone again just as brightly as the night before. I climbed onto Sseus' back, and we walked to a point directly underneath the brightly burning star. Sseus moved around as if he was looking for a good spot, then bent slightly at the knees and sprang high into the air. I felt cold air race past me. It was almost as if we were shooting upwards along a tight rope. My handkerchief nearly blew off my head; Sseus had been wise enough to leave his straw hat back at the campsite.

The planet seemed to grow larger as we headed directly for it. Afraid of a collision, I closed my eyes until I felt a shock. Had we landed? Carefully, I opened one eye and then the other. Before me was a stone gateway and to the right of it stood a statue of an armless woman, surrounded by all kinds of signs. For example: “Welcome to Venus,” “Make Venus your vacation spot,” “Get away from it all; jump to Venus,” and “If you’re looking for good fortune and want to be happy, try Venus, of course!”

An old doorman doddered towards us. He squinted at the glass ball hanging from Sseus’ neck with his small eyes.

“All right,” he said. “Come inside.” And he opened the gate for us.

Sseus stepped through the gate and walked along the path. It was the middle of the day on Venus; flowers blossomed everywhere alongside the path, large and beautiful flowers. Sseus walked in the direction of a castle on the bank of a river. From the towers of the castle, flags fluttered; on each one, the word “Inn” was written. As we crossed over a wooden bridge, I could make out two people rowing in a boat. Sseus walked through the park as if he was lord of the castle and everything belonged to him.

Then we turned a corner and walked right into a playground. A gigantic slide stood in the middle; someone was sliding down it right at that moment. There was loud laughter and shrieking, and handfuls of confetti were being thrown into the air. The person on the slide landed right before our feet, and I stared in amazement when I saw it was an old woman. She got up quickly and ran to the ladder for another turn. Meanwhile, the next one in line was already on the slide, and again he landed right in front of us. This time I nearly fell off my horse when I saw the face of an elderly man.

“Grandfather!” I cried out joyously.

The man looked up at me and cried back, “Ody, my boy!”

“Joe!” I exclaimed, jumping off my horse. “Grandfather, what are you doing here?”

“I’m on holiday,” he said in his trembling voice.

"Oh," I said. "Let me introduce you two. This is Sseus, and this, Sseus, is my grandfather Joe."

Sseus nodded politely, and Joe replied, "Nice to meet you. Well, come along, let's go and sit over there." He pointed to a bench by a pond. We followed Joe past the slide where the old woman was again swooshing downwards, scattering confetti over us as we went by. Joe sat down between Sseus and me.

"So, you're on vacation," I said.

Joe replied, "Yes, Professor Kugelschreiber is treating me to this one. It wasn't easy to leave the Seventh Heaven."

There was a loud shriek. To our right, an old woman with a wooden horse between her legs was running over the paths and grass, back and forth.

"Yahoo!" she cried. "Yahoo!"

It was a different woman from the one on the slide; I could still see her soaring down the slide. This one wore a red skirt and cape while the other was dressed in blue.

"What's going on?" I asked Joe.

"Why, this is Venus," he explained. "All kinds of people from every walk of life come here to rest or to do whatever they feel like. Some people come here in search of good fortune because this is a lucky planet. Searchers after good fortune can come and visit on the night of a full moon or on the night that follows. On those nights, Venus sends down an imaginary line. Your Sseus probably came that way, too. I see that your horse already has luck." My grandfather indicated the shiny ball. "Don't I know you from somewhere?" he asked Sseus. "Surely, you've been here before. I could have sworn I saw you just yesterday."

Sseus nodded, then stood up and walked in the direction of the castle. I wanted to go with him, but Joe held me back with his hand.

"Let him go. I think he's just going to entertain himself at the castle. In a few minutes, a troop will be passing by here.

Look, here comes one of the troop members now." And indeed, in the distance, a hobbling figure was heading our way. When she was nearer, I saw it was an old woman wearing a green skirt and cape; she was skipping with a rope as she approached us.

"Hello, Joe," she called out cheerfully in a high voice. "Who've you got there?"

"This is my grandson from Earth. His name is Ody, and he's here with his horse, Sseus, who's gone to the cas—"

He didn't get to finish his sentence because the old woman shouted, "Whaat! Is Sseus here? And I thought ..."

"What do you mean, madame?" I asked curiously. "Do you know Sseus?"

"Do I know him?" she said derisively. "Phewy! Why, we used to chase after him, but now we've found our luck anyway."

"Oh, no," I exclaimed in fright. "You're one of those fortune hunters, aren't you?"

"No, no," said the woman. "I used to be one, but I have found my share of happiness here on Venus. It is so fantastic here; I can try anything I please without worrying about accidents happening. If that's not happiness, what is! There used to be four of us, and one day we ran into a man who'd just returned from here. He told us all about it, but Isabella didn't want to come along. She decided to go to an island in the south that her canary preferred."

We slowly began to make our way over to the castle while the little old woman proudly told us about the bandits, which she and her troop had chased after so heroically. Joe, who knew the way, led us to a beautifully designed room wallpapered in red linen. An orchestra sat on a podium in the corner of the room. Each musician—a brown bear, the old woman from the slide, and a wolf—held an ornately carved instrument, none of which I had ever seen before. Along the walls of the room stood rows of tables and chairs where people and animals were in deep conversation or drinking.

Joe led us to a table and ordered water of life from the waiter, a penguin. Three glasses were brought almost immediately. Despite its fluorescent green color, the water of life was refreshing and tasted delicious.

"Oh, isn't it just marvelous here!" the old woman cried out, beaming with happiness. "Look over there; that's Cinder." She pointed to the woman playing in the orchestra. "She's had such an incredibly unhappy youth, poor Cinder. But she found happiness here too. I might add she was a first-class fortune hunter. Always took the lead."

A trumpet sounded, and hoofbeats followed. I turned my chair around to get a better look at what was happening. The orchestra began playing lovely ballet music, and Sseus appeared from behind a curtain, trotting on his hind legs to the middle of the room. My mouth fell open in astonishment as I watched Sseus dance to the music. He danced so gracefully; the cloth on his back fitted in beautifully with the red wallpaper. He made pirouettes and sprang with all four legs, like a cat, always landing neatly on his feet.

"*Oh, Sseus, you dance fantastically,*" I thought, and I was certainly not the only one who thought so, judging by the tremendous applause which followed his performance. Then he disappeared behind the curtain. Joe, the old woman, and I sauntered outside.

Sseus was already standing there, completely packed up for travel and apparently waiting for me.

"Sseus, we aren't leaving already, are we?" I asked. Sseus nodded, yes. "But Sseus, can't I stay just a while longer?" Sseus shook his head.

"That's right, my boy, the old woman said. "We'll be going to bed soon ourselves. And you must return before the sun rises on Earth; otherwise, the imaginary line will be broken, and then you won't be able to get back. Down below, it's already four o'clock in the morning."

So, I reluctantly shook hands with Joe and the ex-fortune hunter who was now just an old lady. Then I mounted Sseus, and we walked towards the gate.

As the doorman opened the gate, he called after us, "Goodbye 'til the next time!"

Sseus shook his head.

"Oh, there won't be a next time? Well, then just goodbye!"

Again, Sseus bent slightly at the knees and jumped downwards. We fell down faster than we had flown up, but nonetheless, we landed gently on the ground. Sseus walked directly to our campsite, and we crawled under the cape again.

16

We slept late the next morning, rising when the sun stood high in the sky. I left the breakfast package in the saddlebag, and I pulled the lunch sack out straight away. This time, there were two covered wooden mugs filled with delicious orange juice, two peanut butter sandwiches, and two wooden cups of yogurt. All in all, it was a scrumptious lunch.

However, we were both still rather hungry, so Sseus opened up his box of chocolates. My mouth watered at the sight of them. Some were wrapped in paper and tied with a ribbon; others were in the shape of a fish. Sseus chose a fish first, and I chose one wrapped in paper. Half was filled with marzipan and nuts, and the other half was filled with chocolate truffle. After we had just about emptied the box, we started riding in the direction of the forest.

It was a rather depressing forest; the trees only grew leaves at their very tops, and many branches were broken off as if they had been placed under too great a strain. I looked around anxiously, realizing that there was no sign of life anywhere; no birds singing, no rabbits hopping about. There wasn't even one blade of grass growing between the trees. I didn't feel very much at ease, and from the manner in which Sseus was walking, I could tell that he didn't either. I hoped we'd soon reach the edge of the forest and come to the sea.

All at once, I heard something creeping up on us. However, each time I turned around, I didn't see anything except the dying trees. When I turned my head back, I'd hear the rustling again. The noise kept getting nearer until I felt a warm breath on my neck.

"Sseus!" I screamed. "Get us out of here!"

The horse didn't obey me at first. Instead, he calmly turned his head around. But then he took off at a run, as fast as he could. His mane and tail waved in the wind as he galloped through the woods, giving the appearance of a very gallant horse. I dared to look back once and let out a scream of fright.

Behind us, a large hairy beast almost as large as Sseus was pursuing us. It had four glistening tusks and enormous claws with sharp nails. Its face was hairless, but the pointed ears were very hairy. Furthermore, it had a large flat nose and small sharp eyes. It drooled out of the corners of its mouth and continuously wiped the drool off with the back of its hairy arm. The monster was very thin; its ribs were easily visible under the loose hanging skin.

It kept repeating: "Yum, yum, tasty dish!" There was no doubt about it—this beast was completely starved. Since there was no food here in this forest, it was certainly counting on us to serve as its next meal.

Sseus galloped on, but the beast, which I had meanwhile nicknamed Broad Beak, kept on right behind us. I could see the light breaking through the trees up ahead; we were almost out of the forest.

Trying to think of something to get this creature off our tail, an idea suddenly struck me. I could throw it the breakfast package from this morning. While it ate that up, we could search for a hiding place. I pulled the sack out of the saddlebag and threw it to Broad Beak. It caught the package in its mouth and swallowed it all in one gulp, not faltering a single step.

When that plan failed, I opened up the box of chocolates and took out the remaining two pieces. Each one was wrapped in paper. I had difficulty with parting from these chocolates, but nevertheless, I threw them on the ground in front of Broad Beak. The monster sniffed at them hastily and gobbled them up, paper and all. Then it continued its chase, having fallen back just a few paces.

Sseus flew out of the forest. We could see the sea glittering in front of us. As we stormed up a cliff that overhung the water, where the rock dropped vertically down into the sea, Sseus didn't slow down at all. I was afraid he didn't see the approaching danger. Nor had Broad Beak given us up. Sseus was now close to the edge of the rocks; we could clearly hear the water murmuring below.

Just behind us, I heard Broad Beak: "Yum, yum, tasty dish!"

By now, Sseus was at the very edge of the cliff, and then ... he jumped.

What happened after that is almost impossible to explain. Sseus simply remained floating in the air! He didn't lose height; on the contrary, he was actually making headway in the air. He had grown wings on the sides of his shoulders, large white wings flapping up and down. And so, we flew over the water, leaving the astonished Broad Beak behind us.

"Is he now ..." the monster called out behind us, but it soon turned back to the woods.

"Oh, Sseus!" I exclaimed. "You saved our lives!" Sseus turned his head around and smiled. I had to hold on tightly to his mane because he was flying quite fast.

The sea passed underneath us. Sometimes, I could see fish swimming in the water or shark fins poking through the surface. We flew for many hours; Sseus didn't seem to tire out at all. As it slowly turned to dusk, I decided to take a nap on Sseus' back. I pulled the cape out of the saddlebag and spread it over me.

However, I only dozed for a short while before my stomach began to grumble. I could also hear Sseus' stomach. There was one last food package marked dinner. We were so hungry that we didn't attempt to save any of this last meal for later. It was a complete dinner, consisting of two potato salads, smoked oats, and pudding. I fed Sseus since he couldn't feed himself while flying. At the bottom of the bag were two wooden mugs

filled with carrot juice. Sseus and I both thoroughly enjoyed the meal, and we wouldn't have minded second helpings of the pudding!

Meanwhile, it had grown dark. Luckily, Sseus' glass charm gave off enough light. I could still make out the black water under us.

"*Will there ever be an end to this sea?*" I wondered. However, I didn't want to think about it too much. I crept under the cape again while Sseus flew the whole time, on and on and on.

Sunbeams in my face woke me up. Sseus had flown the whole night through, and now his eyes were red from fatigue. I wished I could've taken over the flying to give him a rest, but unfortunately, that was impossible. Nor did we have any food left; all we could hope was that we would reach land soon.

All at once, I heard shouts coming from below us. I looked down and saw a few small islands. People wearing flower garlands around their necks were fleeing under palm trees, uttering cries of fear.

"Sseus, let's land over there," I suggested, but Sseus shook his head. The people seemed scared to death of us, and perhaps they would have done us harm instead of just giving us something to eat. So, we flew onwards, leaving the screeching people behind us.

I felt Sseus growing tired. He began to lose altitude and sometimes even touched the water with his hooves.

When that happened, I'd call out, "Sseus, please, you've got to fly higher. If your wings get wet, you won't be able to fly anymore." Exhausted, he used all his strength to rise higher in the air, but he would lose height again a little later on.

Something was drifting in the air up ahead. It was large and round, and a box-shaped object was suspended underneath.

"Sseus! Take a look over there!" I said.

Sseus struggled a bit higher and flew straight towards the object. As we approached, I could see loose ropes hanging down the sides. It was a silk cloth blown up into a ball, with a kind of very large fruit basket hanging underneath. Sseus flew into the basket, collapsed on the floor, dead tired, and fell asleep immediately. I walked over to the edge and looked down. Turning back to Sseus, I realized that his wings had disappeared, and he was his old self once again.

Ropes were drawn over and around the large balloon and gathered together in the basket. Some of them were broken, perhaps due to a storm, and flapped in the wind. Reserve ropes lay in a corner of the basket, and I repaired the broken lines with a few uncertain knots. I just hoped they'd hold until the end of our voyage. Then I covered Sseus with the cape and investigated the contents of the basket.

I wondered why the flying vessel had been abandoned but soon figured out what had happened when I found two different-sized left shoes. The crew had probably run into very bad weather and been thrown overboard. There was a box in a corner of the basket filled with delicious things: smoked ham, dried fruit, biscuits, cheese, and a can of water.

"Sseus, look at this!" I cried out happily. Sseus slowly opened his eyes a crack. He smiled when he saw the food and fell back asleep. I, too, was tired and yawned but decided to take watch.

The floating vessel was blown by the wind, so I didn't have much to do. I sat with my back leaning against Sseus. However, I soon began to feel raindrops. Sseus slept on, undisturbed. Dark clouds hung above us, and it was obvious that the rain would get harder.

I took immediate action. I grabbed the waterproof cloth and laid it over the top of the basket, tying the sides down with leftover rope. It made a cozy tent illuminated by Sseus' glass. I could no longer stand upright, so I crawled back to my spot.

Though we couldn't look outside, I could still hear the spattering of rain on the cloth and the rumbling of thunder. Luckily for us, there were no holes in the canvas. Nor was it blowing too hard, so the basket remained level.

Squatting in a corner, munching on a piece of ham, I listened to the thunderstorm. Every once in a while, Sseus, who slept through the storm, let out a snore. Halfway through the rainstorm, Sseus opened his eyes. They were no longer red and shone in the bright light. He stretched out and then looked in surprise at the canvas covering.

"For the rain," I explained. He crept towards me and eyed the piece of ham with great interest, which I just popped into my mouth. Then he rummaged through the food box himself and pulled out some cheese and dried fruit.

He drank water out of my hands, wiping his mouth with his foreleg. I, too, took a drink; the water was deliciously cool.

The water can was almost empty, so I poked a hole in the cloth exactly above the can, letting the rainwater replenish our supply. It dribbled slowly in, under the watchful eye of Sseus, who made sure no drop fell outside of the can.

We had nothing to do in our basket, so I took a slab of ham and scratched out a tic-tac-toe board with my nail, giving us a game to play. However, I quickly tired of it when Sseus kept winning. Besides, the ham was completely full of scratches.

All at once, the basket shook. It wasn't moving anymore. I quickly loosened the canvas covering to look outside. The rain had stopped, and we had landed!

"Sseus!" I cried out. "We've landed!" We were in a rocky region, with patches of greenery here and there.

Sseus packed up the food in the saddlebags and filled with water the wooden mugs that Flakes had given us. I sprang over the side onto the ground. What a fine, safe feeling it was to have my feet on solid land again. Sseus paced about to stretch his cramped muscles, and I deflated the balloon to decrease our chances of being detected by possible enemies.

When Sseus had loosened his muscles, I jumped onto his back, and we clambered down off the rocks.

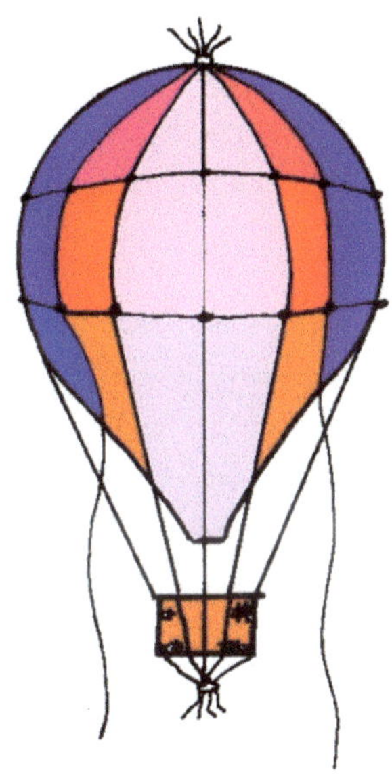

17

The country turned hilly; we'd left the cliffs behind us. The slopes were a lovely green, and I sometimes saw a piece of flooded land with only the tops of the plants sticking out of the water.

"*What a shame,*" I thought. "*Now their whole harvest is ruined.*"

The path we were following was stony. Sseus set each foot down very carefully to avoid twisting an ankle. Up ahead, I saw what looked like a large, wide mountain ridge. Sseus was heading straight for it. It was very peaceful all around us, although I sometimes thought I saw a bush move or heard a tree branch crack as if someone had stepped on it. However, there wasn't a soul in sight, so I must have imagined it. I rode on, my mind at ease.

The mountain ridge turned out to be a high stone wall. Lovely images had been carved in it, and ornamental scrolls were bent like branches around the human figures. Sseus rode right along this wall, so I was able to admire the beautiful artwork. There were scenes of people working in large fields of flowers. The plants had sturdy stems and sometimes were twice as tall as the people. Further along, the flowers had all been plucked, and the seeds lay in the sun to dry. And still further along, a family was shown pouring drops out of bottles onto their food. It was as if a story had been carved into the wall; perhaps it was the history of this area. The wall itself seemed to stretch out forever.

"What shall we do now, Sseus?" I asked. Sseus took a running start and jumped up onto the top of the wall. Just about the same view could be seen to our left and right, except that to the left, there were small houses. There was a reasonably wide path, laid with stones, on top of the wall. Low stone walls ran along each side.

We hadn't walked along this road for long before a large crowd suddenly appeared below us to our right, carrying long reed canes in their hands. They also all carried a leather bag. On an order from their leader, they reached for something inside their bag.

"Hits!" he called. The man had a long grey beard and wore a hat like an umbrella, from under which a grey braid hung down his back.

"Hits!" he called again and raised his hand. At that command, the people shoved something into the canes and raised them to their mouths.

"Blow!" the leader called, whereupon they blew up their cheeks. A large number of objects flew over the wall and over our heads. They hadn't aimed directly at us but at something on the other side of the wall. However, several aimed poorly, and the objects hit us. I managed to catch one; it was a black seed-stone, probably from some kind of fruit. The longer this went on, the better they became at it and the harder the seeds flew.

They were now shooting right at us. The leader waved with his arms indicating for us to move away. As if we felt like sticking around! They were shooting well now; one of the seeds even landed in my ear, and I extracted it only with difficulty. I was hoping there weren't too many of these sharp-shooters. Sseus ran quickly on to bring us out of range.

Because of the shower of seeds, we hardly even noticed the bent figure sitting in the middle of the path.

"Stop, Sseus!" I cried out.

As we came closer, we saw it was a woman; she was crouching down as low as possible against the ground. She had probably been caught in the hail of seeds while walking innocently along the road. I dismounted and walked toward her.

"Come with us!" I said. "You aren't safe here!" She looked at me with distrust. She was a small woman dressed in an embroidered red silk dress.

"To my house?" she offered.

I nodded and brought her over to Sseus. I was about to help her mount, but she nimbly sprang up by herself; in fact, she gave me a hand to mount. Soon we were past the seed shooters.

The woman gave directions: "Jump off here, then turn left and when you can no longer go straight on, turn right ... that's right ... now just go straight 'til you come to that house up ahead." The woman petted Sseus' mane, which Sseus didn't appreciate. It only tickled him.

We rode up to a small house painted white. She sprang off of Sseus' back, grinned, and said, "We're safe here." I tried to imitate the way she had dismounted, but I would have fallen flat on my face if she hadn't caught me. She led us into the house. The door was made of paper, supported by slats of wood. A low table stood in the middle of the room, with satin cushions scattered around it.

"Sit down," she invited us. "I will make some tea." I followed Sseus' example and sat down on a cushion, sliding my legs under the table. A lovely, finely woven cloth lay on the table; it was probably made from silk. The woman reappeared within a few minutes, carrying a tray with a teapot, two cups, and a bucket for Sseus. She set the tray on the table and poured tea for all of us.

"It was very kind of you to come help me, although I can assure you, I can take very good care of myself. My name is Wat Beng. I was on my way to the city when I ran into the seed gang."

"What was actually going on there?" I asked.

"Oh," said Wat. "Nothing out of the ordinary. We had promised Kong, our neighboring country, sunflower seeds because they had used up all of their seeds to make oil. Quite stupid of them, of course. How can one grow sunflowers if one doesn't have any seeds to plant? We, too, specialize in producing oil, but we were smart enough not to use all the seeds up. Then our country, Hong, signed a treaty with Kong to share our seed stock. However, what we actually delivered were watermelon seeds. After all, Kong has always been our competitor, haven't they? So why should we share our fine quality sunflower seeds? While we were planting our seeds, someone from Kong named Chin realized that we had fooled them. So, together with the whole population of Kong, he started an attack. That was what was going on back there."

"Oh," I said. "Is that all? I thought it was perhaps a new planting method. "*Mmm* ... this tea is very good."

Wat folded her hands in her lap. She looked very proud of herself with her grey braid.

"I can do everything," she said out of the clear blue, raising her voice. "Really, everything."

Then she stared at the bright glass ball hanging from Sseus' neck. Sseus returned her look with some distrust, but he continued to sip his bucket of tea calmly until it was empty.

"Would you like to sleep here tonight?" Wat asked while she cleared the table.

"That's very kind of you," I replied. She led us to a side room.

"The beds are already made," she said, pointing to two reed mats lying on the ground in the corner. I lay down on one of the mats and stretched out.

"Sleep well," she said and closed the paper door behind her. It was very warm in the room, so we didn't need to cover ourselves. Sseus borrowed my handkerchief to lay over his glass ball. It shone in his eyes too much and made it difficult for him to sleep. It occurred to me that the ball was shining brighter now than ever before. Neither of us could fall asleep easily on the hard floor without a pillow, so we each used one saddlebag as a pillow, and then we fell asleep.

I awoke the next morning from the singing of a morninggale outside our window. Sseus, too, blinked his eyes and got up. We remained in the room until Wat called for us, which is the polite thing to do. Soon we heard the shuffling of slippers, and Wat entered the room. She wore the same dress as the day before, except now it was blue.

"Good morning," she called out cheerfully. "Did you sleep well?" We didn't have a chance to answer her before she chatted on. "I have breakfast all ready. We're having fish. I hope you both like fish." Sseus looked rather worried but didn't dare say no and appear impolite.

"Um," I replied. "Oh yes, we're crazy about fish, aren't we, Sseus?" Sseus nodded.

"Well, what do you know. That's lucky," said Wat. "Because I've made a lot, you can help yourself to as much as you want; I won't stop you."

Once again, we were in the room with the low table and sat down, putting our feet underneath it. Two porcelain plates, each with a large yellow fish, lay ready for us, and two sticks lay next to each plate. Wat showed us how to grasp the sticks between our fingers. Sseus had a lot of difficulty and finally gave up the struggle. He slowly ate up his fish and was obviously relieved when he saw only the bones left on his plate. Wat cleared the table and returned again quickly. She looked at us both closely with a very serious expression on her face.

"Listen," she said. "I want to ask you something. I have a proposal. As I've already told you, I am capable of doing anything. I can make everything that I want, but no one travels well without good fortune. If you like, I will change your horse into a person."

"Ooooh, but that's fantastic!" I exclaimed, beside myself with joy.

"However, I want something in return," she continued. "I want to have that charm!" She pointed to Sseus' glass ball with trembling fingers.

"But," I said, dismayed, "Sseus will never give that away."

"Think about it, my friend. Sseus will be a person, a real live person!" Her face was very tense.

I looked at Sseus. He was staring at the bright ball. He certainly was not about to make a bad exchange. Then he looked at the woman who had also been staring at the glass ball all this time. She was prepared to do anything to possess it; she'd even turn Sseus into a person.

Sseus sighed deeply. I don't know what made him make his decision, but he took the collar off of his neck and gave it to Wat. She was completely ecstatic.

"I knew you'd see it my way," she said happily. I hugged Sseus, overjoyed by the prospect of his becoming a person. He lay a hoof on my shoulder, and I could see in his eyes that he didn't regret it at all.

"Fine," the woman announced. "Let's get to work."

Wat took us outside and led us under the shade of a tree. She pulled a lovely golden box out of her pocket and opened it up. It contained white powder. Pushing me back a bit, she approached Sseus. She threw the powder over him, and it fell like snowflakes around his body. Sseus closed his eyes.

Wat called out, sprinkling him with powder: "Hocomang ... Bam ... Wam!" When all the powder was finished, she stepped back, and together we waited to see what would happen. A white cloud formed around Sseus. It spun around and around, rising slowly while more clouds formed underneath. In the end, there was nothing more to see of the horse, just a large mass of clouds. For a few minutes, nothing happened, then there was a loud bang.

"He's exploded!" I cried out, shocked. I started towards the cloud, but Wat held me back.

"It isn't finished yet," she assured me calmly. The clouds now rose more slowly and were no longer being formed from underneath. Everything had become rather misty, but I could vaguely make out two feet. The clouds rose higher and higher until a complete figure appeared out of the mist.

"Sseus?" I asked.

The figure nodded. Somewhat nervous, I walked up to him.

"Oh, Sseus! You look terrific!"

A man larger than myself stood before me. He was completely white, just like the horse had been. He had beautiful white hair and lovely golden eyes, and he wore the red cloth wrapped around his middle.

"Sseus, be welcome to being a human," I said joyfully. Sseus smiled. Wat looked very proudly at Sseus, so proudly that he almost grew shy.

"You see!" she said. "Wasn't that worthwhile, now?" Sseus nodded and shook her hand.

"Shall we move on?" I suggested.

But Wat said, "No, you can't go like that. Sseus needs to have some clothes. Come inside with me."

She disappeared into the house, followed by Sseus at her heels, walking in a sort of gallop. She gave Sseus a green silk shirt, woolen trousers, and a pair of boots. With the help of some magic formulas and spells, she turned the red cloth into a jacket. Then she took the saddlebags and handed one to each of us. We thanked her gratefully for her hospitality.

"The honor was completely mine!" she called after us.

All at once, Sseus grabbed me and set me on his back.

"But, Sseus," I laughed. "You aren't a horse anymore. I must walk now, too." He put me down on the ground again and laughed with me. Then we started walking side by side.

"I am really glad that you are a person now as well," I said. Sseus nodded and stared ahead mysteriously.

We climbed a mountain slope using both hands and feet to grab onto the large rocks. When we reached the top, many more mountain peaks came into view. For hours on end, we climbed and climbed. Up and up, and then down and down. It grew colder, and the air grew thinner. Exhausted from all the mountain climbing, we sat down on a stone to rest. Breathing hard, I pulled out some smoked ham, biscuits, and water and gave Sseus half of everything. The food didn't taste as good as it had when we were in the basket, but it hadn't turned moldy either. The biscuits weren't even stale.

We had traveled a long way, and I didn't want anything more than to sit in front of a fire instead of shivering on a stone on top of a mountain. Sseus suffered the most of all, being used to his warm coat of hair. So, I gave him the cape and warmed myself by waving my arms about.

In the far distance lay a 1arge lake, but it would take several days before we reached it since walking on foot went so much slower. After a short rest, we climbed further. Sseus took the lead, placing his feet carefully. I was very tired, and all this climbing was getting very difficult for me. We finally reached the last mountain and descended onto a plateau. Sseus helped me with the descent so I wouldn't stumble at the last moment. Sseus wasn't tired at all; he seemed to possess an inexhaustible amount of energy.

Upon reaching the plateau, I sat down on the ground, shivering all over. Sseus gathered some dry branches and made a fire.

"Ah," I said. "That feels good, Sseus. Thanks a lot."

Sseus pulled the cape off his shoulders and draped it around me. Since it was now too cold to continue hiking, we lay down by the fire using the cape as a blanket. I fell asleep in the pleasant warmth of the fire, but my dreams were less pleasant. I dreamt that an ice-cold spirit slowly settled over me and that it grew colder and colder until I was nearly turned into stone. I awoke with a shock; my feet had suddenly been immersed in something hot.

18

I opened my eyes and saw a friendly face with a thick grey beard close to mine.

"Awake?" asked the strange man.

I was somewhat dazed; I had lost touch with reality a bit and wasn't quite sure where I was. My feet had been immersed in a bucket of steaming water, and I was completely wrapped in blankets in a rocking chair by a fireplace. A rather fat woman was stirring a pan hanging over the fire. She sprinkled in some spices. I was in a wooden house whose walls and floor were covered in woolen rugs.

"Where's Sseus?" I asked the man, but he didn't seem to understand me.

"Sseus?" he asked.

"Yes, Sseus," I repeated anxiously. "My hor—my friend." The man nodded and pointed to a pile of wool. Sseus' face peered out at me through a small opening; he looked relieved. At first, I hadn't noticed him; I'd only seen the pile of wool.

"Ah, Sseus," I called out happily. "What are you doing under there?" Sseus chattered his teeth and pointed to the wool. It was obvious that he'd been cold and had crept under the warm wool.

"What happened, sir?" I asked.

"I was just about to tell you," the man said and pulled up a chair next to mine.

"I'd gone out to gather wood. On the way back, my dog started barking. I stepped off my sleigh to see what was wrong and saw a white head sticking out of the snow. I hadn't seen your friend at first, since he doesn't show up in the snow, if you see what I mean. Anyway, I shoveled him out and laid him on the sleigh; but the dog kept on barking. Then I found you. You two had been snowed under while you slept. Yes, you know. I'd said it to my wife. 'Mjarkova,' I said, 'I feel snow in the air. There's going to be a snowstorm.' And sure enough ... You're certainly lucky that Barksk found you; otherwise, you'd probably have frozen to death. I brought you to my house, and that's where you are now. Here, take this cup of warm sheep's milk."

I took a cup, and Sseus, who'd shuffled closer to us in the meantime, was handed a cup too. The milk was nice and warm, and it did me good because I could feel I was coming down with a severe cold.

"Your friend has recovered unbelievably quickly." the man continued. But I don't think you'll be so fortunate. I think you've caught a terrible cold by the look of your red nose. But tell me, who are you?"

"Ody, sir," I replied. "And this is Sseus." Sseus nodded politely.

"This is Mjarkova, my wife. I am Bjenjif, and this," he said, gesturing at a handsome dog, which came immediately to him from out of a corner, "this is Barksk."

"Glad to meet you," I said and petted the dog. I'd finished my milk and handed the empty mug to Mjarkova.

"Well," said Bjenjif. "We're going to bed now, so it is a good idea that you two go to sleep before we do." He covered us up, poked up the fire, and then quietly left the room with Mjarkova and Barksk.

Sseus fell asleep immediately, but I stared into the fire, my mind blank. Suddenly a gigantic pig began to grunt, on and on and on. The noise came from the next room, where Bjenjif, Mjarkova, and Barksk had headed. After a while, I realized that it wasn't a pig making all that noise but a person. Now I understood what Bjenjif meant when he said, "you two go to sleep before we do." If you're already asleep, then you won't easily be awoken by snoring, but trying to fall asleep with all that noise going on is almost impossible. Nevertheless, after several hours, I succeeded in dropping off.

I was awoken the next morning when Barksk jumped onto my lap and licked my face. I held him off gently at arm's length and pointed to the sleeping Sseus with one finger at my lips. The dog misunderstood me, jumped onto Sseus, and licked his face too. Sseus blinked his eyes open and petted Barksk on the head. Barksk then left the room but soon returned with Bjenjif, who was carrying two bowls.

"Good morning," he said, putting a bowl into my hands. It was deliciously warm oatmeal which we ate up with wooden spoons.

"Bat is bery good," I sniffed, surprised to hear my own strange voice. "Now bhat?" I asked Bjenjif.

He grinned at me. "You've got a severe cold, my friend, and it'll take a while before you get over it."

"Oh no," I said. "I hadn't counted on bat." Sseus snorted and looked at me compassionately.

"I'll get you some warm clothing. Especially if you're planning on traveling in snow that's thirty feet deep, then you should be properly dressed," said Bjenjif. He brought a pile of clothes.

"Here, Ody, this is for you." He handed me a warm fur coat. "An old friend gave it to me long ago," he said. "What was his name again? Job, or Joe, I'm not sure anymore."

I thought immediately of grandfather, who had many friends, although it would be a coincidence if my Joe had given this coat to Bjenjif. I put on the nice warm coat and the red boots which Bjenjif also handed me. Sseus was given a woolen jacket, knitted three layers thick, and also a pair of red boots.

"So," said Bjenjif. "That's that. Oh, wait a moment. You still need a hat." He found a blue woolen hat for me and a brown one for Sseus.

"Come follow me," said Bjenjif after helping us put on the hats. "There's a sleigh outside which you can borrow from me. When you no longer need it, just say to the dogs: 'Gjo hjome njow.' They will find their way back by themselves. I have tied a chest with tents and food to the back of the sleigh, and I shoveled the snow away from the door, so you needn't worry about snow falling inside the house when you open the door. Well, goodbye then."

He shook our hands and opened the door. I thanked Bjenjif profusely for all his efforts. After all, he had saved our lives.

Outside, everything was white except for the sky, which was dark grey. A two-person sleigh with six harnessed dogs stood in front of the door. We sank only to our ankles in the snow since the lower layers were frozen solid. Before stepping into the open sleigh, I slapped the snow off my boots. Sseus followed my example. We laid a blanket over our legs and got ready to go. Sseus took the reins and was quite good at urging the dogs to get moving. Bjenjif, Mjarkova, and Barksk stood at the window and waved.

The sleigh glided swiftly over the snow, leaving a parallel track behind. It was very cold, and the wind blew straight into my stuffed-up nose.

"You do bat bery well," I said to Sseus. "Dis is nice, don't you bink? *A ... a ... choo!*" I sneezed. "By poor dose." I pulled up the collar of my coat to protect my face. I found a pair of gloves and a handkerchief in my pockets so at least I could blow my nose.

We were sleighing through a flat region, which was completely white as if a thick white blanket had been laid over the ground. The snow was beautiful, but after a while, my eyes hurt from the brightness, and I only opened them a crack. Sseus didn't seem to have any trouble with the cold or blinding snow because he kept looking ahead with wide-open eyes. I didn't feel very well and had to continually wipe my nose.

19

I had little to do other than look around, so I decided to investigate the contents of the chest which Bjenjif had fastened to the back of the sleigh. Besides bread, there were also pieces of meat and cheese. I felt around in the box and came up with a decoratively painted bottle. There was a ribbon around the neck, and a card hung from it with the words: "For Ody." I pulled out the bottle. The label read: "Take a large gulp whenever you feel like it."

"Perhaps bis is for by cold," I said to myself, "from Bjenjif." I pulled out the cork and sniffed at it but couldn't smell anything with my stuffed-up nose. So, I hadn't the faintest idea whether the drink would taste good or not. I peered through the opening and saw a rose-colored liquid.

I took a large gulp and swallowed it all at once. The drink tasted bitter and nasty, and it went down like hot steam into my stomach. It only made me feel worse. My stomach burned, and my head began to spin. Pink fireballs appeared before my eyes, and I began sweating heavily.

"Sseus," I said hoarsely, bringing my hand weakly to my head. Sseus glanced at me, took the bottle from my hand, and smelled it, but he didn't give any indication whether or not it smelled as awful as it tasted. He just shook his head and laid me back against the railing, tucking the blanket in tightly. Then he turned his attention back to driving the sleigh.

My eyes slowly closed; I was quickly falling into a trance-like sleep. I lay dead still while everything spun around me; large blue, green, and pink bundles of light shot past me.

"The court is opened," I heard a voice say. "Let him enter." Everything was quiet for a moment. The flames disappeared, and a large hall appeared before my eyes. People sat along the walls and in the middle was a huge desk, behind which a man dressed in black sat. The hall kept getting closer to me until I could see everything quite clearly. It felt as if I was standing on a balcony and looking down upon the hall. Everyone was very quiet. A man stood up and left the hall. He soon returned with a small person walking in front of him. The little fellow wore peculiar clothing: a wide white shirt, grey trousers, and red boots. He walked into the center of the room and stopped in front of the desk. The man behind the desk wore a white wig and small eyeglasses pinched onto his large hawk-like nose. The fellow turned around and looked at me shyly. A shock went through me. That little fellow was none other than myself! Although he wore strange clothing, which I didn't recognize, his face, hair color, and posture were exactly the same as mine. He turned his face away, or rather I turned my face away and looked at the man behind the desk.

"Well, Ody," the man roared. "We shall now judge you!" He pointed to the hall full of people. They all wore masks on their faces and were therefore unrecognizable.

"You are probably wondering why."

I shook my head.

"Well," the man continued. "I shall tell you that later, at the end of the hearing. But now the questions: Is it true that you came here all by yourself? Watch your words; you must tell the truth and nothing but the truth. All the witnesses have already handed in their statements."

My mouth opened to answer, but I couldn't understand what I said; I was talking too softly.

"Ah ha," the man roared. "So, it's true! Is it also true that you have traveled around?"

Once again, my mouth moved, but I didn't understand anything I said.

"Fine! Now don't try any funny business with us because we'll learn the truth in the long run." The man began to speak more softly, so I could no longer hear what was being said. The image grew blurry, and the hall disappeared before me. Slowly but surely, the blue, green, and pink bundles of light reappeared before my eyes. The last words which I heard were: "Very well. Hand me the sword ..." Everything spun around me.

Suddenly, it was over. I carefully opened my eyes and saw the white landscape before me. Sseus, sitting next to me, looked at me strangely. His eyes appeared to bore right through me.

"Sseus!" I called out. "You should hear what I just dreamed about!" I told him what I had seen: the bundles of light, myself, the courtroom, and then the flashing lights again. Sseus stared at me; he seemed to be thinking deeply about something.

The bottle out of which I had drunk stood by my feet. I picked it up and looked at it closely. Had I got that strange dream from this drink? I peered inside and saw, to my surprise, that it was empty.

"Sseus!" I said. "What happened to the rest of the drink? Did it spill?" Sseus shook his head and pointed to our track behind us. I saw a pink trail in the distance.

"Why did you throw it away?" Sseus looked straight at me for a moment and then turned his attention back to the reins. I sighed. Sometimes it was really too bad that Sseus couldn't talk. I reached automatically in my pocket for my handkerchief but then realized that I didn't even need to blow my nose. Both nostrils were clear, and my voice did not sound hoarse anymore.

"Gosh," I said happily. "That drink of Bjenjif's really helped after all." Contented with the fact that my cold was cured, I decided to treat us to something good to eat. I pulled out some meat and cut it with a knife, which Bjenjif had included. Then I did the same with some bread and cheese and gave Sseus the largest part of each. It all tasted very good. To quench my thirst, I hung a hand outside the sleigh, caught a handful of snow, and ate that up. Sseus did the same. The snow melted to water on the tongue and tasted deliciously refreshing.

Sseus pulled back on the reins, and the sleigh stopped. He stepped off and pulled out a package with raw pieces of meat for the dogs. Then he unharnessed them and threw each one a piece of meat. They ate it up immediately. They were definitely accustomed to traveling like this; just like us, they ate the snow for water. I patted each dog on his back.

Sseus and I hauled out a tent made from strong waterproof canvas and supported by poles. Together we set up the tent and laid the blankets which were in the chest inside. The tent was exactly large enough for the two of us. When I went to look for pillows, I found another tent in the chest, larger than ours. I pulled it out, and the dogs immediately came and stood around me with interest. They began to pull at it and succeeded in opening it up. Then they set it up neatly using teeth and paws. There were also six small blankets and pillows, each with a name on it.

I picked them up one at a time and called out the name: "Bestis, Chientis, Dogsk, Comradsk, Yapsk, and Reindisk." As I read each name, one of the dogs approached me, wagging his tail. One by one, they disappeared into the tent, carrying the pillow between their teeth. Sseus and I peered into the dogs' tent. They lay there, six in a row, their head on a pillow and covered by a blanket. The dogs were already sleeping, so what were we waiting for? We kept our jackets and hats on to reduce the chance of freezing and then crawled under the blankets. We soon fell into a deep sleep.

When I awoke, Sseus was already busy folding up his blanket. He had a concerned look in his eyes. I didn't pay any attention to it and started on the breakfast that he offered me. Toasted bread and sheep's milk.

"Have the dogs already eaten?" I asked. Sseus nodded. It was very cold in the tent, and if it had been a degree or so lower, the milk would have been frozen. I stretched and thought, what a life to get up in the morning like this. Then I folded up the tent. The dogs' tent was already folded and tied up. We fastened everything to the back of the sleigh and harnessed the dogs.

"Sseus," I asked. "May I take the reins today?" Sseus laughed, shrugged his shoulders, and finally nodded. That made me happy, sitting behind the reins and holding them tightly. Sseus covered our legs with the traveling rug.

Just as Sseus had done the day before, I raised the reins high above my head and let them fall gently. The dogs shot forward. I pulled the reins to the left and to the right, but the dogs didn't react; they walked precisely where they wanted to and nowhere else. Now I understood why Sseus steered so well; he didn't need to do anything! The dogs had the reins in their own paws.

Glad to know that I, too, was capable of steering so well, I looked around me. The surroundings were the same as the day before, completely white. White piles of snow hung on the green branches of the fir and spruce trees. Sometimes, the wind blew snow off the branches, and once when we rode under a few trees, snow fell right into my face. Sseus wiped it off because I wasn't about to let go of the reins for anything in the world.

"*Finally, I'm the one carrying the responsibility,*" I thought proudly. We rode along, each sunk deep in our own thoughts. I was thinking how wonderful it was not to be sick anymore and what a strange dream I had yesterday. Sseus didn't show what he was thinking about. He just looked silently around.

The sky was dark grey above us. A snowstorm could come any moment now. I thought about setting up a tent over the sleigh and then riding further. But then again, that wasn't very fair to the dogs. It would be better to set up the tent and stop the dogs so that they too could take cover.

Around a half-hour later, Sseus grabbed my hand and looked up at the sky, startled.

"Yes, Sseus," I reassured him. "I already saw it approaching. Surely you aren't afraid of a snowfall?"

Sseus shook his head. He took the reins from me and stopped the dogs. Then he looked at me seriously. In the distance, I heard a whining "*Awoohoohoo,*" which was coming closer. My heart started beating rapidly; I was really scared. Here we sat completely unprotected, not a house nor a cave in which to take cover. Six black spots approached us over the snow. They came closer and closer. It was a pack of wolves!

Anxiously, I made preparations to run away, but Sseus held me back. He stepped calmly out of the sleigh as if nothing were wrong and waited until the wolves came close. First, they sniffed the dogs, who weren't the least bit afraid of them, and then they glared at us with sparkling eyes. They showed their gleaming teeth, ready to bite into a nice, tender piece of meat.

Just when I was about to say that I wasn't very tasty since I was just recovering from a cold, Sseus stepped forward and stared into the leader's eyes. This was the largest and probably the most dangerous animal of the pack. Sseus and the wolf stared at each other for a few minutes, but nothing happened. Meanwhile, the other five animals looked me longingly over.

Suddenly, something remarkable happened. The leader of the pack, whom Sseus had glared at, walked away with his tail between his legs and tears in his eyes. The other wolves looked at him in surprise. One of them became very angry with Sseus, who had intimidated his leader so much that he ran away. He glared at Sseus with angry eyes, but it didn't take long before he too turned away, weeping softly. In turn, each wolf approached Sseus and was stared down. The last wolf didn't bother to wait his turn and just walked away, grumbling and threatening.

When the wolves had all left, I said, "Sseus, how did you ever manage that? You saved our lives! Now we can get out of here."

Sseus shook his head and pointed to the sky.

"Oh, I understand," I said. "You want to sit out the storm, don't you? Well, it shouldn't take long before it starts snowing."

I had barely finished saying this when a few flakes drifted onto my cheeks. The flakes looked like downy feathers on the snow that had already fallen. It was a spectacular sight. A thin white layer formed on my hat and shoulders. Sseus, who kept staring into the sky, was also covered in white. I wanted to set up the tent over the sleigh, but Sseus motioned with his hands that it wouldn't be necessary.

"But Sseus," I protested. "It's snowing rather heavily." However, Sseus shook his head firmly. I gave in and remained sitting on the sleigh. Sseus stared motionlessly towards the sky. He appeared somewhat impatient.

"*Perhaps Sseus has never seen snow fall before*," I thought. I also thought about how wonderful it was that Sseus was now a person. How would he have reacted to the wolves' appearance if he had been a horse? Aren't horses very frightened of wolves? As a person, Sseus was luckily braver than me. As a horse, he'd probably have disappeared into the stomachs of the wolves by now. The thought sent shivers down my spine.

I was startled out of my thoughts by a noise, like a musical saw, which resounded through the dark clouds. A male figure fluttered downwards between the falling snowflakes. He looked angry. He wore a long white robe speckled with black gemstones and a kind of crown on his head which was decorated with wolf images. He landed in his bare feet on the snow but didn't sink into it.

"*This man is dressed for warmer climates*," I thought. He walked up to Sseus and glared at him with savage eyes. Sseus returned his gaze. They remained staring angrily at one another. I didn't have the slightest idea what I should do or why they were so angry.

Finally, the man said, "Thou hast chased away my wolves. Now thou too shalt become a wolf!"

I was stupefied. What did this man mean by that? What did he expect from Sseus?

The two continued to glare at each other. Should I step in? I was desperate! I decided I had to do something and slipped quietly off the sleigh to the back. I quietly pulled out the tent and dragged it towards the dangerous man. As it turned out, my caution wasn't necessary since neither of them broke off from staring at the other.

While I'd been busy, Sseus' face had begun to change. He was still white, but his ears had become pointed, and his nose had grown longer. I was really frightened when I saw how Sseus had begun to resemble a wolf.

"Sseus, stop!" I cried and ran with the tent up to the man. I intended to throw it over him to break his gaze, but he was much larger than I was. I had to make a gigantic leap into the air to get the tent over his head. But I had to do it to save Sseus!

The man collapsed immediately when the tent was flung over him. The canvas cloth lay flat on the ground as if no one lay underneath it. Thanks to my efforts, Sseus' face returned to its normal form, although at first, I thought I saw a horse's head start to take shape. However, it didn't take long before Sseus was once again a person. He sighed deeply and wiped off the sweat from under his hat.

He walked up to me and clapped me gratefully on the shoulder. It was clear that I had saved him, and I was so proud of myself that I could have jumped high into the air. However, I didn't do that because I suddenly thought about the man lying under the tent. I carefully lifted up an edge of the tent, but to my astonishment, I saw absolutely nothing! There was no one underneath the cloth, just melted snow. The man had simply disappeared!

"Sseus," I asked. "How's that possible?" Sseus laughed and gave me another clap on my shoulder. Together, we packed up the tent and fastened it to the sleigh again.

"Sseus," I said. "Why don't you take the reins again. At the moment, I can't concentrate well enough." Sseus laughed again and sat down in his seat. I pulled out some meat for the dogs and flung it towards them. When I saw them eating so greedily, I felt like also having something tasty. So, I pulled out some bread and cheese for us.

Sseus looked tired, but he perked up after having had a bite to eat and became his usual pale self.

It felt almost as if the sleigh moved more swiftly with Sseus holding the reins, but perhaps it was just my imagination. After all, the dogs determined their own speed. While we were riding, it suddenly occurred to me that it wasn't snowing any longer. Actually, it had stopped when I'd thrown the tent over that strange man again.

"What had he expected to get out of Sseus? What'd he come to do?" These questions racked my brains. Since I couldn't ask Sseus, I thought up a satisfying answer. The strange man was the master of the snowy plains and animals which live on them, like the wolves. Because Sseus had scared

them away, the man had grown angry and came to punish Sseus for his deeds. While they stared at each other, he made up a crafty plan to get Sseus out of the way. Sseus, in turn, had tried to undo his plan. All that concentration had made Sseus begin to look like a wolf. That was my answer! And I was contented with it.

Sseus stared ahead, apparently not thinking of anything in particular, though once in a while, a shiver went through his body. "*The cold,*" I thought. It hadn't grown any warmer during our journey, and I wasn't looking forward to sleeping in an ice-cold tent again. Maybe we should light a fire. No, that wasn't very smart. Everything would get wet from the melting snow. Perhaps the best thing to do was to sleep with the dogs, who'd keep us warm and serve as watchdogs at the same time.

When I glanced around, I noticed footsteps in the snow. We were riding precisely in the same direction as the footsteps, which were very strange. A round hollow with four smaller hollows above it, probably the toes.

"It looks like it could be a large cat," I said to Sseus, pointing to the foot tracks. Sseus nodded thoughtfully. The tracks were easy to make out, so they must have been made after the snowstorm. At the rate we were moving, we would soon catch up to whatever was making the tracks.

20

Sseus poked me in my side and pointed to the end of the trail. The footsteps led to a tree, where they stopped.

"He must be hiding somewhere around here," I whispered. I'd hardly finished my statement when I heard a dull thud. A large bear had fallen out of the tree and was now standing up. He brushed the snow off his fur and looked at us in surprise.

"I'm sorry," said the bear, "to suddenly appear like that, but you see, the branch I was sitting on broke." The bear looked at us with small friendly eyes. "*This bear can be fully trusted*," I thought to myself and let out a deep sigh of relief.

"Good morning, Mr. Bear," I said politely and pointed to Sseus. "This is Sseus, and I am Ody."

"Glad to make your acquaintance," the bear answered very properly, shaking hands. Sseus looked the bear up and down. "You know," said the bear while he patted one of the dogs on the back. "I am quite far from home. Do you suppose you could give me a lift? Then you can stay the night or even longer at my place."

I looked at Sseus, and he nodded. "Of course, you may ride with us, Mister Bear. It would be our pleasure," I replied.

The bear nodded, pleased. I stepped out and let him slip in between us. We were rather squashed in together since the sleigh was only meant for two people. But the bear was nice and warm, and his fur was so soft.

"What is your name?" I asked the bear.

"Haven't I told you already? I am Oorsk, Oorsk the Bear," he replied.

"May I ask you something?" I said.

"You just did, didn't you?" said the bear.

"I am just curious as to how you are able to speak. Bears don't normally know how to talk, or do they?" I asked.

The bear laughed and replied, "Well, that's a difficult question to answer. You can better ask him when we get home."

"Who is 'him'?" I asked.

"He is the one who taught me to speak," answered Oorsk.

I didn't ask anything else; I would wait until "he" told me. Sseus grew more and more interested in the bear and sometimes stared at him in a peculiar way. The bear gave Sseus directions to drive to his house.

"I was looking for bread this morning, squirrel bread. In the winter, we have our own special supplier, but when I reached the squirrel's house, no one was there, so I had to go to the next squirrel. That one lives so far from my house that I had to walk for hours to get there. The tree out of which I fell was his house. See, these are his breads; don't they look delicious?" The bear pulled out a handful of acorns from under his fur.

"You know," he chatted on. "In the winter, I don't feel like sleeping at all anymore, unlike my comrades. It's been like this ever since I learned to talk. I have much more fun if I don't hibernate in the winter. Turn right here, Mister Sseus, yes, that's fine, and now straight ahead 'til you see my house."

I saw smoke rising above the trees in the distance. Yet it

still took a long time before we arrived. He had certainly been fortunate running into us. The little house was built from wood and had a stone chimney out of which nice-smelling smoke rose. I was really very curious as to what "he" looked like and what kind of person "he" was. We stepped out of the sleigh, and Oorsk helped us to unharness the dogs. He opened the front door, allowing the dogs in first, and brought up the rear himself, closing the door behind him. It was cozy and warm inside. The bear took our jackets and hats and helped us to pull off our boots.

"Here, put on these slippers," he said, offering us each a pair of soft slippers. The dogs had already gone into the next room, apparently the living room, and lay on the rug before the fireplace.

"Just follow the dogs," said Oorsk. "He is in there, Ody." I entered and looked around the room. A man sat in a comfortable chair.

"Professor Kugelschreiber!" I cried out and ran up to the professor.

"Ody!" he exclaimed. "Vhat are you doing here?" He looked at me in astonishment; he certainly hadn't expected to meet me. Sseus entered the room too and shook hands with Kugelschreiber.

"This is Sseus, a friend of mine. We've been traveling together for a long time now," I said. "But, tell me, Professor; what have you been up to?"

Kugelschreiber laughed in a mysterious manner and began to tell his story immediately.

"As you can see, I have moved here. I have finished my tea research and zherefore no longer need to play the Supreme Chief of zhe crocodiles. I have discovered a very extraordinary type of tea, vhich isn't for drinking purposes but is for producing heat, a burning tea. It is made from a large quantity of dead plants and animals. I have buried all zhat in zhe ground, enough to burn for a hundred years. Vatch!"

He brought out a black syrupy sort of liquid, which burned fiercely when he threw a few drops into the fire.

"Zhen, I left zhe area and have begun on anozher sort of research. I have succeeded in teaching Oorsk to talk by doing speech exercises and drinking a special drink." He held up a bottle containing a yellow liquid.

Sseus watched with great interest. I could easily read his thoughts. Wouldn't it be wonderful if Sseus could talk? I was hoping that Kugelschreiber would be willing to help out.

"Professor Kugelschreiber," I said politely. "Would you like to teach Sseus to talk?"

Kugelschreiber looked at Sseus in surprise. "But he is a person, and people can talk."

"No, you see," I began, "it's different with Sseus. He is actually not a person, at least not originally, but now I guess you'd say he is ..." I told him everything there was to know about Sseus, beginning at my meeting with the magician and continuing up to the present. I also told him about Venus.

"Ach, yah," said Kugelschreiber. "Zhat is true. Joe told me about Sseus. He vas on vacation on Venus, and I might say it did him a lot of good. Vell, I shall try to teach Sseus to talk, but it vill take a lot of time. In zhe meantime, Ody, you mustn't talk to him."

"Well, it's worth it, isn't it, Sseus?" I said. Sseus nodded earnestly.

"Fine, come along zhen vizh me, Sseus. Vizhin a veek, if all goes vell, he vill be chatting avay," said the professor and disappeared with Sseus into a room next door.

"A week," I sighed and lay down on the rug next to the dogs.

Oorsk came and sat next to me. He asked, "Is he going to teach Sseus to talk?" I nodded. "Now, cheer up. Don't let it get you down that it will take so long. We can have a lot of fun while we're waiting. I can show you all kinds of things."

"Thank you," I said.

"Come on," the bear continued, pointing to a bed in the corner of the room. "First, try to get a good night's sleep."

I crept under the covers, and Oorsk tucked me in.

"Sleep well," he said, patting me lightly on my cheek with his soft paw. Then he left the room, leaving the door open a crack.

"Yapsk! Yapsk!" I whispered to the dogs. Yapsk was one of the names on the dogs' pillow, the one which slipped into my mind first. One of the dogs stood up and came to me, wagging his tail. I assumed that that was Yapsk.

"Come lie next to me," I said, petting his head. He lay down close beside me, and we fell asleep immediately.

My stomach was grumbling so loudly the next morning that it woke me up. Oorsk was standing by the fire and pulled out two roasted potatoes with a fork, setting them down on a plate.

"Good morning, Ody," he said. "Here you go, a delicious roasted potato with garlic butter."

I sat up straight in bed to eat the very tasty breakfast. Then I pulled on the clothes Oorsk had set out for me, a thick sweater with a high collar and woolen trousers.

"I'll teach you a game today," said Oorsk, clapping his hands. "I haven't played it with someone else for a long time. Shall we get started?"

"Fine with me," I said, excited to play with the bear in the snow. Oorsk walked outside, wearing a hat and shawl. I wore the warm coat I'd got from Bjenjif.

"It snowed heavily last night," Oorsk remarked. "Are you coming?" I followed him, noticing the same tracks in the snow as the ones we had found the day before. So, they really were Oorsk's.

"It's a fair game," said Oorsk, who'd come to walk next to

me. "You can't cheat at this game, and there are more than enough trees."

After a short walk, we were standing in front of a group of thin trees, planted very close to one another so that there was only a small opening between the trunks.

"These are the rules," said Oorsk. "You walk eight paces away from the trees." He paced off eight steps and turned around. "You may only use the right hand to make a snowball." He bent down low and, using one hand, squeezed a snowball together. He did it very skillfully; the snow was just right, not too cold, so it packed well. "Now, you hold the snowball behind your back with a straight arm." He talked as if he was reading the instructions out loud. "Then you let your arm swing around and release the snowball in the direction of the trees. The goal is to hit one of the tree trunks." He followed his own instructions, and the snowball landed precisely against the closest tree. The tree shook a little, sprinkling snow off of its branches. "Now, you try!"

I measured off eight paces, squeezed together a snowball using one hand, and let it fly. To my surprise, it hit one of the trunks. It wasn't the one I had aimed for, but what does that matter.

"Very good!" Oorsk exclaimed. "You're a fast learner. The object of the game is to see who can make the most hits in ten turns. If you break a rule, you lose a turn." After Oorsk had made several hits, it was my turn. My first snowball flew between two tree trunks.

"Ow!" came a voice from behind the trees. "Great jumping rabbits; who's throwing snowballs?" I looked at Oorsk, perplexed.

"You get a bonus point!" he cried in admiration. "You didn't hit a tree trunk; you hit someone! Such a throw counts for two." I was pleased, but from behind the trees came a soft swearing. A fox stepped out from between the trunks and glared angrily at the bear.

"Well," it said. "It's you again. Are you wasting your time playing that game again?"

"Oh no," I said quickly. "It was me. I'm very sorry. Would you care to join us?"

"Pooh," said the fox, sticking his nose into the air, at which the snow between his ears fell off. "I don't play such silly games."

"This is Crafty the Fox," said Oorsk, with a certain contempt in his voice, "thinks he's wonderful just because he's learned to talk too."

"It's a pleasure to make your acquaintance, Mr. Fox," I said, bowing slightly. "I am Ody."

"Oh, just call me Crafty. We're friends, after all; aren't we?" And indeed, the fox had turned very friendly.

"Are you staying with this Oorsk?"

"Yes," I said. "For a week."

"Oh," said the fox with interest. "Won't you come visit me at my place while you're here? It's very pleasant."

"Thank you for the invitation, Mister ... um ... Crafty." The fox turned back to the woods and disappeared among the trees.

"Should I go?" I asked Oorsk.

"If you want to go, that's your decision," he said and began to form another snowball. We played for a long time and had to keep increasing the number of turns because, in the end, we were equally strong. Finally, we gave up and decided to continue the next day.

The next morning, Oorsk had thought up something new. We built a snow bear. It was quite easy because Oorsk posed as a model. On the third day, Oorsk told me all about his family. His father had been a dancer, his grandfather once was a singer in a local choir, and his sister had married a panda. He also told me about his youth and how he had met Kugelschreiber, who had let it be known that he was looking for a house bear who could make acorn soup.

In the evening, Oorsk prepared the soup, and it tasted delicious. On the fourth day, we had to stay inside because of a heavy snowstorm, and on the fifth day, we dug a tunnel through the snow so that we could get outside. We were completely snowed under the whole day. In fact, the snow almost came in through the chimney.

On the sixth day, Crafty the Fox came to collect me. He insisted that I spend the night. I pulled on my coat and said goodbye to Oorsk. Then I followed Crafty through the snow passage outside.

"I haven't had someone stay for a long time," he said when we emerged from the tunnel. "And they never want to leave once they've arrived, ha, ha, ha!"

I didn't understand why he found that so amusing; I guess l missed the joke. We soon reached his hole. He opened a trapdoor in the ground and let me go first down a steep stairway. Crafty picked up a lantern that stood on the ground. When he had lit it, we walked through the hallway, which led to a living room. It wasn't an unpleasant-looking room, but it was cold and rather dark. There were two chairs and a low table.

"Sit down," said the fox. "I shall prepare a sauce." He licked his lips and walked away giggling. For some reason or another, I didn't feel very at ease. I soon smelled a lovely smell coming from the kitchen. Crafty was busy preparing his sauce. He returned a while later carrying a large silver platter containing only the sauce.

"Here we are," he chuckled. "Now, all I need is the meat." He walked towards me, his eyes glittering.

Then he snatched a large knife from the table and said, "You are nice and tender. Wouldn't you like to lie down on the platter?"

I stiffened with fear. "Nah—nah ..." I stammered in fright,

swallowing hard.

"Oh, come on," the fox tried to coax me.

"Oh, gosh ..." I was almost in tears.

I heard someone pounding hard on the trapdoor. The fox jumped in alarm. He hadn't expected visitors, and he didn't go upstairs to open the door; whoever was knocking would think he wasn't at home.

The fox turned his attention back to me. Meanwhile, the trapdoor was opened very softly; I heard the hinges squeak, but Crafty didn't notice.

He came closer and closer, whispering softly how he would prepare me. "Baked? Boiled?" he mumbled. He was now terribly close. I pushed myself up against the wall.

"Help! Help!" I screamed. Crafty laid his hand over my mouth and put the edge of the knife against my throat. Then, at last, in the nick of time, someone entered the room.

"Crafty, stop this silly joke immediately," said a deep voice.

"Oorsk, you again!"

"Indeed," Oorsk said and walked up to Crafty with his long strides. "Here, take this meat. Fruit meat from dried fruit that will teach you for being so crafty." Crafty took the fruit and laid it on the platter, disappointed.

Relieved and happy, I ran to Oorsk and hugged him. "Thank you so much, Oorsk. You saved my life. If you'd come a minute later, I'd be lying as slices on the platter."

"Yes," said Oorsk. "I saw it coming. Crafty had such a strange expression on his face when he came to get you this morning. I thought, 'He's up to something.' The dried fruit was an excuse to come in, a present for him, you see. And I wasn't a second too late."

Crafty sat in a chair; he didn't seem bothered in the least and ate his sauce with dried fruit. What we had to say apparently didn't concern him. He even stared at us unfriendly, as if to say, "Why don't you leave?"

Shortly later, we were safely on our way back to Oorsk's house, where I had no fear of ending up on the menu.

Once home, I played around with the dogs, one dropping a ball on my lap as if to say, "Come on and play with us."

"Okay," I gave in, and together we rolled the ball around the fireplace and through the room.

Oorsk placed a bowl of beechnut pudding on the table. "Come and try this," he said. "It's much tastier than dried fruit with sauce." Together we ate up the pudding, which melted on our tongues.

"How do you think Sseus is getting on?" I asked. "I certainly do miss him."

"Tomorrow, he will return home, and he'll be talking," said Oorsk. "I don't expect you'll be disappointed."

Oorsk licked the bowl clean with his tongue. I spent the rest of the evening playing with Oorsk and the dogs. We had a lot of fun and went to bed very late. Despite the late hour, I still couldn't get to sleep. I was looking forward to all the things Sseus would be able to tell me. I had so many things to ask him. Finally, after lying awake for several hours, I fell asleep.

21

I woke up the next morning full of expectations; today, I would see Sseus again. I quickly dressed and tossed two potatoes into the fire. Oorsk had set a bucket full of potatoes in the corner so that whenever I felt like it, I could just throw one into the fire and eat it up half an hour later.

Oorsk came in with two mugs of steaming hot chocolate, so hot that I had to be careful to not burn my hands.

"Sseus will be coming back today," I said, taking a sip.

"Yes, I know," said Oorsk. "You have a lot to tell him." Oorsk left again with the empty mugs. A little while later, Kugelschreiber opened the door.

"Professor," I cried. "Did it work? Where's Sseus?"

"Yes, my boy," He replied. "Here he comes." He stepped aside, and there stood Sseus, as white as ever.

"Hello, Ody," he said. I was completely speechless. His voice was so beautiful; the sound was as pure as he was white, so smooth and warm. I had never heard my name pronounced so melodiously.

"I can talk now, Ody," Sseus said, walking toward me.

"That's wonderful, Sseus," I said, and then to the Professor: "Thank you so much, Professor Kugelschreiber."

"Yah," he said. "I have never before performed such a fine job. But now I really must get back to verk." He disappeared immediately.

I handed Sseus a baked potato and said, "You must have a whole lot to tell me, huh, Sseus?"

"Oh, really?" said Sseus, somewhat taken aback. "What, for instance?"

"Well," I mumbled through a mouthful of potato. "For instance, who was the man wearing the wolf crown, the one who descended between the snowflakes? And how did you manage to chase away the wolves?"

"Oh, that," Sseus said. "That was really quite simple. I let the wolves know, through my eyes, that they should be ashamed of themselves for attacking defenseless travelers and that all they had to do to get a piece of meat was to go to Bennie's. He would surely be good enough to give them some if they were hungry. It is an art to be able to impress someone and an art to make someone else think so clearly that he can feel good inside about himself. The man with the crown was the King of the Wolves, their master. They had to give him half of whatever they caught in exchange for information leading to where they could find defenseless travelers. He was naturally angry because I had challenged his authority. Unfortunately, he was familiar with my method and could apply it to me since his level of thinking is slightly higher than mine. So, he tried to make me believe that I was a wolf. One wolf like me would be more than enough for him. Luckily, you saved me in time. Otherwise, I probably would have attacked you, being a wolf and totally under the power of the Wolf King. May I thank you for your help?"

"Oh," I said. "It was nothing. But why did you throw away the medicine I got from Bjenjif?"

Sseus looked at me intently. It took a few minutes before he answered, somewhat hesitantly, "Oh, that was an accident."

However, I knew that Sseus would never do something so stupid. I had a strong suspicion that Sseus was hiding something from me.

"Now it's your turn to tell me about your experience this past week."

I told Sseus all about the snow games and Crafty.

"I had to work hard myself," Sseus said. "That yellow drink from Kugelschreiber was anything but tasty, though it certainly did help to stimulate the speaking organs. The first few days were the most difficult. I had to learn everything right from the very beginning. However, after three days, I had the basics. I might say that I am very pleased with the result," he said finally.

"With good reason," I added.

Kugelschreiber suddenly entered hastily with Oorsk. "Okay, you've chatted enough for now," he said. "Time to make fuzher plans!" He sat down in a chair. "Vhat are you two going to do now?"

"I think we should move on, don't you, Sseus?"

"Definitely," said Sseus emphatically.

"Fine," said Kugelschreiber. "Zhen Oorsk vill prepare some food for you to take along." Oorsk disappeared immediately in the direction of the kitchen.

"Vhere vill you be heading?" asked Kugelschreiber, exchanging a look with Sseus. They appeared to have developed an understanding about one or two things.

"Just on," I replied. Kugelschreiber made polite conversation until Oorsk returned.

"Everything is ready," he announced. "The sleigh is already packed." We all stood up together and walked towards the front door.

"We have a surprise for you," I said to Sseus and pulled on my warm coat, which Oorsk held open for me. "It has snowed a lot the past week; we have to walk through a tunnel to get outside now."

Sseus opened the door but shrunk back when he saw the tunnel.

“Vhy don’t ve say goodbye here,” Kugelschreiber suggested. He shook our hands firmly.

It was really a sad moment for me when I had to say goodbye to Oorsk. I had grown rather fond of him during the week. Would I ever see him again? Oorsk didn’t have any problem saying farewell to me. On the contrary, he was even cheerful.

After we had thanked everyone, we walked through the snow tunnel to the outside world. The dogs were already harnessed to the sleigh, and the chest was fastened to the back. Sseus sat down by the reins and arranged the blanket over our legs.

“Ride on!” Sseus called out cheerfully.

The dogs all turned their heads and stared at Sseus as if they wanted to say, “He can talk?!” However, they recovered quickly and began running over the snowy surface.

Sseus was obviously pleased that he could talk and even tried to recite poems.

We see all around us a beautiful scene,
The dark sky, the white snow,
all under a velvet sheen.
Upon which the stones do glitter,
On his head, the four crowns do flitter.
When we last had this was long ago,
But we are now on the right path, I know.

“Kugelschreiber has certainly taught you a strange poem,” I said, with some admiration for these strange words. Sseus smiled faintly. I, too, felt like making up a poem. Yet when I thought up one, I couldn’t get any further than the first line. “Light comes from the sun ...” I gave up because I couldn’t think of anything to rhyme with "sun."

"You sure have a knack for rhyming," I said to Sseus. I could understand how difficult it was. Sseus just smiled

Traveling was very tiring, mainly due to the very cold air. I didn't have much to occupy myself with, so I started naming everything we passed. As we passed a tree, I'd say, "tree." After a while, it went so automatically that I couldn't stop. However, it was tiring. The surroundings didn't really change much; there were always trees, a grey sky, and snow.

To distract myself, I took a peek inside the chest that Oorsk had filled. I saw the most delicious-looking things piled one on top of the other. On top were a spoon and a small bowl filled with nut pie. I tried a taste of it immediately, and the delicious flavor started me thinking about Oorsk. How pleasant it was to sit with him by the fire, tasting all his various dishes. I missed him a little.

"Anyway," I sighed to myself. "First, Sseus was gone, and Oorsk was around, and now Oorsk is gone, but Sseus is back again." I was so deep in thought that before I knew what was happening, I'd eaten the whole pie up by myself; there wasn't anything left for Sseus. Too late!

"Oh, I'm so sorry, Sseus. I'll see if there's any more in the chest."

"Don't worry about it," said Sseus. "It's all right." Unfortunately, there wasn't another pie; however, I found some bread with herb butter. "*Mmmh.* That tastes very good," said Sseus, chewing on a large piece. I was glad he liked it; otherwise, I'd have felt bad that I'd eaten the best dish all by myself. He finished it quickly and then turned his full attention back to driving the sleigh.

We rode for hours on end, exchanging few words. The sky turned darker and darker. It would soon be night. We wanted to set up the tents under a fir tree. The dogs were tired out earlier than usual since they hadn't had any practice for a week.

We sprang into the snow, landing almost knee-deep. Our boots were just long enough. We waded through the snow with great effort until we reached the chest at the back. The dogs didn't sink as deeply as we did because they were lighter, of course. We dragged the tents under the tree.

"This is much too exhausting," Sseus said, pointing to his legs which appeared to be only half their normal length. "We must balance out our weight. Then walking will be much easier."

He pulled four branches off of the tree and stood on two of them. To my surprise, Sseus hardly sank into the snow at all.

"You see," he said. "This is much better. Come on, you try, too." He strapped the branches to my boots with long pine needles. It really helped. We could make much better progress now. That would certainly come in handy if anyone tried to chase us. We could move a lot quicker now.

The dogs set up their tent as handily as ever, and we set up ours. I pulled out a large piece of meat from the chest, and we and the dogs ate it together. The poor animals were so tired that they went to sleep directly after the meal. We, too, crept into our tent.

We called out "good night" to the dogs and pulled the

covers over ourselves. Sseus fell asleep quickly, but I stayed awake, thinking about him. I was so pleased that he could talk. But where on earth had he come up with such a strange poem as the one he had recited today? Had he learned that before he met me? I lay awake a long time thinking over things like this. There was so much mystery around Sseus. Finally, after I'd counted to three thousand bears—sheep didn't seem appropriate in these surroundings—I managed to fall asleep.

22

The following morning, Sseus was not in the tent. His blankets still lay in their place, but he was gone. I opened the tent flap and peered outside, but I couldn't see him anywhere. I felt rather uneasy; where could Sseus be? Was he taking a walk? I didn't trust the situation, so I crept out of the tent and peeked inside the dogs' tent. To my horror, there wasn't a single dog to be seen. My heart began to beat harder and harder.

"*Where would Sseus have gone with the dogs?*" I wondered. I wanted to go to the sleigh to see if they were there, but it was gone too.

"Sseus," I squeaked. "Where have you gone without me?" I was so sad that if I were a dog, I would have hung my head low with my tail between my legs. I had been completely deserted. Not even the tracks of the sleigh were visible; a new fall of snow had covered them up. I walked forlornly back to my tent.

Brushing the snow off, I crept inside. I pulled off my boots since I didn't know how to remove the branches. I glanced around in the hope of finding a clue, but there wasn't any sort of note left behind. Neither the dogs nor Sseus had left any sign whatsoever. I pulled a blanket around me and waited.

I didn't know whether or not I should be angry with Sseus. The reason for his departure was and remained a riddle. Had he perhaps lost something on the way and gone back to retrieve it? I felt so incredibly lonely; I didn't even have one dog to comfort me. Waiting for Sseus' return seemed endlessly long and not in the least bit enjoyable. There was no one to inform me or calm my nerves.

Suddenly, I sat up in shock. I heard the crackling of snow outside the tent and the puffing of dogs. Shuffling steps hurried towards the tent, the flap was thrown open, and a girl's round face looked in at me with large eyes.

"Are you Ody?" she asked.

"Um ... yes" I replied. I was somewhat disappointed that it wasn't Sseus who stood before me.

"Please, come with me quickly," she said. "Your friend is asking for you."

I hurriedly piled up the blankets and went outside. The girl, who was dressed in a grey jacket and hat and red boots, walked over to the dogs' tent and folded it up deftly. I myself had more difficulty with our smaller tent, but I finally succeeded, although it wasn't nearly so neat.

"Hurry!" she called while she steered the sleigh around using one hand. It was our own sleigh and dogs. Even though the girl didn't look much older than nine years old, she grabbed the reins and masterfully guided the dogs.

"What's happened to Sseus?" I asked anxiously.

"He's been wounded and is lying at our place," the girl answered. Her face was white with two very rosy cheeks. Her news worried me very much. What could have happened?

"Don't worry," said the girl. "He'll recover soon enough." That helped soothe me somewhat.

"What's your name?" I asked politely.

"Yuniska," she answered. "I live together with my sister Kariska in a house not too far from here. I was headed for the village to get some food when I found your friend lying in his sleigh. I brought him home, and Kariska is caring for him. He was covered in claw scratches made by a bear or a wolf, and his clothing was tattered. He hasn't said much yet."

I understood how serious the situation was and nodded. We soon came to a stone cabin with smoke rising out of the chimney. We stepped off the sleigh and ran inside, followed by the dogs which Yuniska had set loose.

I looked around for Sseus. A warm fire was burning inside. There wasn't much in the room; a rug lying on the wooden floor, on which a table and two chairs stood. There was also a bed with a layer of wool and blankets on top. Deep underneath the blankets lay Sseus. A girl stood next to him. She walked over to the fire, where a kettle with water hung.

"Sseus!" I cried out. I kneeled on the floor next to the bed and looked at him with concern.

Sseus slowly opened his eyes. "Ody," he gasped in a weak voice.

The girl was now squatting next to me and laid a bandage on the wound in Sseus' neck. There were scratches everywhere, even on his nose and close to his eyes; they looked like claw marks.

"This bandage has been soaked in an herbal extract. It will help heal the wound more quickly," said the girl. She picked up a glass full of liquid and had Sseus drink up the contents. "This should perk him up a bit," she explained.

And indeed! Within a few moments, Sseus began to talk in a stronger voice.

"You've probably been very worried, Ody. In the middle of the night, I heard a squealing, howling noise, as if one of the dogs had hurt himself. I was afraid something had happened to the dogs, so I went to check. However, everything was quiet in their tent. Suddenly I was grabbed from behind. Someone covered my eyes with a piece of cloth so I couldn't see anything; my hands were bound behind my back, and I was pushed into the sleigh. I heard the dogs being harnessed up, and then we rode away immediately. We traveled for a long time, but even though I was blindfolded, I could still use my ears. Each tree has its own sort of rustle, and I paid good attention to the various sounds so that I would be able to find my way back later on. All at once, we stopped. A person panting softly bent over me and picked me up. I was tossed roughly against a tree. For a while, there wasn't a sound to be heard. The silence was stifling. I didn't waste a moment and began to try to free my hands from the ropes with all my might. It was very difficult, and at first, I didn't succeed at all. Then I heard a low howling sound: '*Ahoo-oo ... Ahoo-oo*!' Everything was suddenly clear to me. That high-pitched howl came from the throat of a wolf, and it was announcing a meeting or gathering. At least now I knew whom I was up against. Wolf number six, as he is known. That was the one I missed when those six wolves came to attack us, do you remember? It was stupid of me not to have dealt with him earlier. I could have known that he'd make this move. He is very sly and probably thought through his plan very carefully whiie spying on us. He'd taken everything into account. He had me blindfolded, so I couldn't deal with him by using my eyes as I had done with his colleagues. Now he planned on taking revenge in order to win back his friends. He was calling—or should I say howling—his pals together to show them that I was absolutely harmless when blindfolded. Meanwhile, I was still trying to free my hands, and finally, the rope snapped. I ripped the rag from my eyes and glared fiercely at my opponent. '*Ahoo-oo*—huh?' he said, astonished. I tried to get him under my power, but he closed his eyes and attacked. As you can see for yourself, he managed to do a good job on me."

"But how did you escape?" I asked.

"Oh, while we were fighting, the other five wolves, which I still had in my power, arrived. I concentrated deeply, letting them know that they had to help me out, which they did. They grabbed wolf number six and calmed him down. I fled immediately. On the way, I was able to find many of the rustling trees, but unfortunately, the wind died down, and the trees didn't make a noise anymore. I didn't know how to get back, nor did the dogs, so we just rode on. However, my wounds hurt very badly, and eventually, I was forced to stop. Then I was found by Yuniska, who brought me here." Sseus closed his tired eyes. Talking had taken a lot out of him.

The girl had heard Sseus' story and looked at him with concern. She said, "We must let him get some rest. He needs it badly." We stood up and walked towards the fire where Yuniska had poured three cups of soup.

"This is fine soup for curing melancholy," she whispered in order not to disturb the sleeping Sseus.

"This is my sister Kariska, who is ten years old," she said, handing her sister a cup. We drank up the soup in silence.

I was thinking about Sseus, who'd experienced such a dangerous adventure. I wished I had been with him, so I could have protected him from the wolf. But I hadn't been awoken by the noise, and so now Sseus was in such a poor state. The girls were very kind and sympathetic.

Sseus slept restlessly that night. He kept calling out in his sleep: "We aren't going to make it! We've got to hurry!" He probably had a fever, which Yuniska later confirmed when she felt his forehead. We decided to take turns nursing Sseus through the night.

My turn was after Yuniska's and Kariska's. I sat down sleepily next to the bed and laid my head on the blanket. I fell asleep in this position.

The next morning, I awoke with a stiff neck due to my

uncomfortable position. Sseus' eyes were already open and were looking at me.

"Good morning, Ody," he said cheerfully. I kept my eyes open with difficulty; I sure could have used a few more hours of sleep. It didn't even occur to me how wonderfully and quickly Sseus had recovered. He looked anything but sick.

"Good morning," I yawned. Sseus smiled, stepped out of bed, and walked around the room to stretch his muscles. I looked longingly at the empty bed but managed to control from the urge to jump in. Instead, l shuffled after Sseus. He had quickly dressed in the new clothing which Kariska had made for him last night.

Kariska entered the room carrying two plates. Her eyes were red from fatigue.

"You all look so tired. What did you do last night? Have a party?" Sseus asked.

"Not in the slightest, Mister Sseus," said Kariska putting the cereal on the table. "This is excellent for curing fatigue."

We cleaned our plates. Sseus was completely better again, and his wounds were almost healed.

"That herbal extract helped a lot," I said happily.

"Yes," said Kariska. "It is an old family recipe."

"I'd like to get going as soon as possible," said Sseus. I nodded.

"Your sleigh is already packed up," the girl said cheerfully, taking the empty plates back to the kitchen. We soon stood by the door in our warm jackets, shaking Yuniska's and Kariska's hands. When we sat again in the sleigh and rode off, they waved goodbye with their handkerchiefs.

23

The weather had turned milder. We were heading south.

"You certainly healed much quicker than I had ever dreamed," I said. Sseus laughed. "I'd almost given up all hope. Do you think we'll run into the wolves again, Sseus?"

"No," answered Sseus. "They will behave themselves now."

The trip progressed peacefully, and the cold no longer irritated my eyes so much. The dark sky which had been with us for so long had disappeared, and the sun even began to shine. The snow melted on the branches, dripping water droplets on the snowy ground. This wasn't so nice for the dogs since the sleigh didn't glide easily on the wet snow. Sometimes, we had to get out and help pull, giving the dogs a chance to sit in the sleigh and rest. But we, too, grew tired and finally gave up the struggle.

"We'd do better to walk," Sseus gasped. "Let's send the dogs back to Bjenjif while there's still enough snow cover."

"Yes," I agreed. "Now, I just need to think of that command, and they'll return home alone without any problem. How did that go again?"

While I tried to come up with the command, trying out various useless attempts on the dogs, Sseus opened the food chest and stuffed some food into his jacket pockets. He left the rest for the dogs to eat on their return trip. Then he taught them to harness themselves up, by which time I had finally remembered the command.

"Gjo hjome njow!" I called out, pleased with myself.

The dogs put their new tricks immediately into practice. They harnessed up each other in front of the sleigh with much barking and bustling and then ran north. They slowly disappeared out of sight.

"I gave Reindisk the responsibility for distributing the food," said Sseus.

We turned away and started walking. I was sorry we no longer had the dogs to accompany us. They had made good companions. As we walked, the snow cover grew thinner, and sometimes we even came across a spot of grass.

"It's melting quickly," I said.

Sseus nodded in agreement. We slowly walked further. It felt as if we were advancing at a crawl; we had grown so used to the sleigh whizzing past the trees. Nevertheless, the exercise was good for a change. After a few hours, we grew hungry, and so we sat down on a stone to eat the sandwiches which Kariska had prepared for us. This emptied Sseus' pockets. The dogs had had most of the food; after all, there were more of them. We went on, having only slightly appeased our growling stomachs. Eventually, we saw a quaint little village laying in the distance.

"We'll find something to eat in the village," we both thought and picked up our pace immediately.

The houses in the village were all decorated with lanterns and streamers.

"Do you think they are celebrating the birthdays of the houses?" I asked Sseus.

He shook his head. "Surely not all of them at the same time."

There was a square in the middle of the village where a fountain spouted water. Many people dressed in gaily embroidered costumes strolled around the square and were telling each other funny stories. I only made out a few words, such as "feast" and "dance." We headed towards the fountain and bent over the side to take a gulp of water.

"It has probably just begun to spout water again," Sseus said, "because if it freezes, then a fountain doesn't work."

"Very true," I said and took another sip.

The fountain was very elegantly built. The water fell out of a large horn, sometimes with so much force that the water sprayed us, and sometimes so slowly that there was hardly even a trickle. Dusk was falling. The lanterns were all lit up in the houses: red, blue, green, and yellow light fell over the streets. The people in the square began to sing joyously while a small band played cheerful music. Lanterns lit up the square with a soft light. Some people started clapping their hands to the beat of the music. Others executed beautiful dances.

Sseus and I walked along with the crowds. The women were dressed in wide skirts with embroidered hems, lace blouses, and high, pointed head coverings. The men wore knee-length trousers, a waistcoat, a shirt, and boots.

I tapped a man on the shoulder and asked, "What are you celebrating? What sort of festival is this?"

The man looked at me with shining eyes and answered, "The thaw has begun. Winter is over, and summer is on its way."

"Oh, how nice," I said happily

"Hey, you!" someone called to me. "Come and try to do what I do and dance your legs out of your body!"

"What a bother," I sighed.

The man who had called me took me by the hand and

dragged me to the center of the square. The people cheered and urged me to imitate the man. First, he made a few simple movements: a kick-kick here, a kick-kick there. But then he squatted down and began to kick his legs one at a time out from under him, his arms crossed in front of his chest. That was too much for me, and I had to give up, just to avoid tying my legs into knots.

"I'm sorry," I said, shrugging in defeat, and drew back into the crowd. The man nodded triumphantly.

The next contestant appeared: Sseus! "Okay, now you must match me," Sseus said to the man.

Sseus sat down cross-legged and leaned forward on his hands. In this position, he danced all around the square to the beat of the music without touching the ground with his legs even once. The poor man was bewildered and didn't know what to do: either imitate Sseus, which he couldn't possibly do, or admit defeat. He chose the latter; walking up to Sseus, he shook his hand. Sseus stood again on his two feet and nodded in a friendly manner at the musicians.

"Long live the man with the flexible legs!" the crowd cheered enthusiastically. Then they all headed for the tables of food, and one at a time, they brought their plates to a place around the bonfire, which had been lit in the meantime.

Sseus wasn't sweating in the least, nor was he out of breath. He acted as if he had done no more than peel an apple.

"I didn't know that you could dance like that, too," I said.

"There's still a lot you don't know, Ody," said Sseus, and he walked over to the fire to sit down.

A girl brought us skewers of meat. We held them in the fire to brown more and then ate the meat. Because we were quite hungry, we helped ourselves to more meat and vegetables from the table.

After this delicious meal, they led us to an inn. The innkeeper was extremely friendly when he saw us and offered us the best beds in the house. We slept well in the nice soft beds, on mattresses filled with feathers. It was a small room, and there was only one candle on the wall, which was giving off light. Everything was quiet outside now. The people had finished their celebration.

The next morning, Sseus shook me awake. “Come on, Ody,” he said, pulling my blankets off me. “It’s late, and we must hurry.”

“But ...” I protested.

Sseus shook his head and said, “No buts about it.” So, I got dressed, and we went downstairs, where the innkeeper had already set up a large breakfast for us. I didn’t dare ask Sseus anything; he was so severe today.

After breakfast, I asked the innkeeper how we could repay him. He shook his head, laughed, and said. “You don’t ever have to pay me.”

Relieved, I thanked him for his wonderful hospitality. When we departed, he gave us a large bag full of nuts to take along.

“That might come in handy,” he said to Sseus.

The streamers and lanterns had all been removed in the village; the houses looked dignified again. We left the village and walked for hours on end; where to, I had no idea.

Sseus often peered over the plains, and then he would shake his head sadly.

“What’s the matter, Sseus?” I asked, but he only shook his head harder. So, we walked further in silence.

When I said, “Perhaps I can help,” he laughed as if what I had said was impossible.

We came to a river from which we drank water. For the rest, we lived off the nuts. We slept on the ground at night since the snow had disappeared by now. We traveled on for days and days. Sseus would have preferred traveling both day and night; he was in such a hurry.

One night, something strange happened. I had just lain down to sleep when I saw Sseus sit up. He kept looking at me, so I pretended that I was asleep since that's what he seemed to be waiting for. And sure enough, when he thought I was asleep, he stood up and walked away.

I lay very still and peered after Sseus through slitted eyes. At a signal from Sseus, a black shadow rode towards him from out of the distance. It was a knight on a horse who slowly approached until he was right next to Sseus.

"Ody," I said to myself. "It's a good thing that you kept your eyes open. You never know if you'll have to protect Sseus from enemies. This knight might try something tricky."

The man got down off his horse, and the two exchanged a few words. The knight pointed in a certain direction, and Sseus nodded. Unfortunately, I couldn't understand a word of what was said. Then they shook hands, and the knight disappeared in the direction from which he had come. Sseus walked back to where I lay and settled down to sleep. He hadn't noticed that I had been watching.

I had the feeling that it was unwise to ask any questions.

24

The following morning, Sseus wasn't nervous anymore; he no longer peered all around but knew exactly which direction to take. He became more talkative and began telling me everything about the area, with which he appeared to be so familiar as if he had been born here.

"Look over there, Ody. In that lake, there lives a silver fish. Years ago, people used to hold contests to see who could catch the silver fish. Whoever did would get a big prize. They could easily promise that because the fish could never be caught. Nevertheless, many people came to try their luck every year. However, one day, the fish turned the roles around. He had laid down a huge net on the bottom of the lake. Then when all the fishermen jumped into the water with their nets, they sprang right into the middle of his net. The fish quickly tied the corners together and pulled the net tightly closed. So, you see, he had caught the whole crowd of fishermen. Everyone, except the fishermen caught in the net, was wildly enthusiastic, and so the fish was given a prize: namely, that he would no longer be disturbed."

"Oh, really?" I said, impressed; the story had captivated me.

Sseus told more stories. About sea mermaids who were washed ashore; about maids who ended up in the sea; and about the birds suffering from pains in their wings, who came to this place in search of a cure. He had never told me these stories before, and hearing them made walking easier and more enjoyable.

I saw an immense forest rising up ahead of us. Sseus was startled at first when he saw it, but then a slight smile spread across his mouth. I really didn't know what to make of Sseus. Lately, he just wasn't himself anymore. We now started walking more quickly and soon approached the edge of the forest. Sseus stopped at the edge and suddenly grew very solemn.

"Listen carefully, Ody," he said. "When you enter the forest, you must walk straight ahead and not look around you. After one hundred paces, turn right and walk fifty paces further. Then take two hundred sidesteps to the left, and then you're there." He stood right in front of me. "Go along now, friend! I must go my own way. Don't look where I am going! Follow the instructions I gave you carefully, and you'll arrive without any problem. Walk well, my friend," he said and turned around.

I was completely baffled! Sseus was leaving me just like that, never having spoken a word about it before. I wasn't even given the opportunity to wave goodbye.

I couldn't get over all this at once. I repeated the words Sseus had spoken to me: "A hundred steps, turn right, fifty steps further, two hundred sidesteps to the left ..." My head spun. I couldn't bring myself to believe that Sseus was really gone, perhaps forever! After I had stood in doubt for ages, I decided to follow Sseus' advice.

I stepped into the forest and carefully counted out my paces. If for any reason I should lose count, I certainly would be in trouble. So, concentrating deeply, I took the exact number of paces that Sseus had instructed. Then, I turned right and took fifty steps further. I had to remember not to glance around me, so I squeezed my eyes mostly shut, leaving them only open a crack to look out of. That was fifty steps and now two hundred sidesteps. I'd never walked sideways before! Despite my inexperience, I managed all right.

At the two hundredth step, I banged into something hard. Startled, I looked up. I had bumped into a huge tree, so huge that one can hardly imagine it. The tree was as wide as a castle with two side wings and so high that it reached the clouds.

"Oh, no," I said, frightened. "I must've gone wrong or lost count somewhere. What must I do now?"

Discouraged, I slumped against the tree trunk and put my head in my hands. Where should I begin? I could never find my way back because I wasn't allowed to observe my surroundings. I'd just have to wait until help came along. Would anyone ever come along this way? It was turning cold, and I wished dearly for a nice warm house. Should I try to retrace my steps?

Suddenly, something strange happened. I heard knocking coming from inside the tree. Someone was knocking against the bark from the inside; a voice said, "May I come out?"

"Um ... yes ... yes, of course," I answered, surprised.

A hidden door in the tree opened, and a clever-looking little man stepped out, wiping his feet on the grass. The man was dressed in red velvet: trousers, shirt, jacket, and a hat tilted on his black head of hair.

"Ah ha!" he cried out cheerfully when he saw me. "You are

just in time. Come along with me."

Glad to have found another living being, I followed him into the tree. He closed the door behind us.

I found myself standing in a long marble hallway with doors on either side. The man walked in front of me and led me through the hallway. Carved gold images hung on the walls, and torches rose out of their mouths, illuminating the hallway. Halfway down the hall, the man turned left, and we walked towards a marble stairway which we ascended. It was very wide with decorative railings, completely carved out of gold. Paintings of kings bearing glimmering crowns on their heads hung along the wall above. I looked around me with amazement. We soon stood before a tall, intricately carved door.

A pile of clothing lay on a chair; my escort handed me them with the words, "Before you may appear, you must be dressed in the proper clothing." I pulled the clothing on silently, a wide white shirt and grey trousers. I shoved the trouser legs into my red boots. It was strange, but somewhere in the back of my mind, I recognized this outfit. This clothing seemed very familiar to me, but I couldn't recall from where. Meanwhile, the little man nodded approvingly and then laid his ear to the door. I could hear soft voices.

"You're next," said the man nervously. "Just follow the man in the black trousers."

The door opened, and a sort of servant took me by the arm, having me walk in front of him. These actions also seemed to have happened to me before. To my great horror, I found myself in a large hall filled with people sitting alongside each wall. All their heads were turned towards me. I couldn't see their faces because they were hidden behind masks. An enormous desk stood in the middle of the hall, behind which sat a man dressed in black. He wore a white curly wig, and a pair of glasses balanced wobblily on his hawkish nose. I felt extremely shy and looked around me in wonder. Everyone was quiet and waited until the man with the wig began to speak.

The man was leafing through his papers and then said in a loud voice, “Well, Ody! We shall now judge you.”

My mouth dropped open in surprise. What had I done wrong? I had only longed for a nice, pleasant house.

All the spectators were nodding in agreement.

“You are probably wondering why,” the man laughed. “I shall tell you that later at the end of the hearing. At the moment, I want to ask some questions,” he continued in a more serious tone of voice. “Is it true that you came here all by yourself? Watch your words; you must tell the truth and nothing but the truth. All the witnesses have already handed in their statements.”

“Well,” I replied, rather baffled. “To tell the truth, I was let in by the gentleman with the red cap. He brought me here if you call that coming all by myself.”

“Ah ha!” the judge boomed. “So, it’s true. Is it also true that you have traveled around?”

“Well,” I answered. “I haven’t been moving in circles. I just kept on traveling straight ahead.”

“Fine,” the man said. “Now, don’t you try any funny business with us because we’ll learn the truth in the long run.”

I jumped back a little. This man was really scaring me. He made me think of Bjenjif and the cold pink-colored medicine that Sseus had later thrown away by accident.

All at once, everything became clear to me. This was the dream I had had in the sleigh.

“Pay attention!” the judge reprimanded me when he noticed I had started daydreaming. “You meet our approval!” At least now, he was addressing me politely.

“I don’t understand yet,” I said.

The judge nodded, took a deep breath, and then began his

explanation. “Ody, it is a long story, so why don’t you take a seat.” The man with the black trousers pushed a chair towards me, and I sat down.

“Once,” the judge continued in a solemn voice, pressing the fingertips of each hand against one another. “Once, we used to have a king. The king was the mightiest of all living beings. He was intelligent and thought through his plans carefully. He was the King of Existence, a ruler over all that existed. He wore four crowns on his head, one each for meekness, loyalty, goodness, and cleverness. He led us through difficult times, and all the people and animals adored him. But one day, he thought too much, and his mind couldn’t handle it anymore. He left, went off to a place unknown to us. No one knows whatever became of him. We all got together and came to the conclusion that we needed to look for another king, someone who possesses the same qualities as he did. We’ve had to work long and hard, and we’ve seen many failures in the process, but now we’ve found that person. And he shall once again rise to be so mighty, and he shall help us.”

“Where is he then?” I interrupted. “I’d like to talk to him about this misunderstanding. As far as I know, I’ve done nothing wrong, so why am I being put on trial?”

The whole room burst out laughing; they laughed harder and harder until they were barely able to control themselves. Even the judge allowed himself a smile.

“No, Ody, you don’t understand. You are this king!” My mouth fell even further open in astonishment. I couldn’t believe my ears; this misunderstanding was only becoming worse.

“I am very sorry, but ... “ I replied, totally confused.

“Don’t worry,” the judge said. “It’s like this. The people you met during your travels are all witnesses. Every one of them is sitting here now.”

The spectators removed their masks and looked at me.

Sure enough, to my great joy, I saw Sseus, Joe, Toodle, Kugelschreiber, Bjenjif, Oorsk, and many more friends.

"Each and every one of them has put you to the test, and they all found you meek, loyal, good, and clever. They were part of a well-thought-out plan. We've often seen our plans fail, but you have come through everything. It has taken us many years to find a new king. Sometimes, some of us were unable to keep completely silent, then Bjenjif let you dream about this, and Sseus recited a poem; these too were part of the test. But you were smart enough not to ask too many questions about it, so we were able to maintain our secret. You often fell into difficult and unpredictable situations because some people"—he glared around the room at these words—"went much too far. But there, too, you succeeded as we would have wished. To put it short, you fulfill all our demands."

I didn't know what to think about his explanation. I had experienced dangerous adventures to become king. They could have made me king from the start. I was terribly confused; everything was happening so quickly.

One of the spectators stood up and asked the judge for the floor. It was my mother! The judge was taken aback; apparently, he didn't know her.

She smiled at me and said, "I owe all of you an explanation too. I am the Wisest Advisor. Years ago, the king came to me, full of despair. His mind could no longer handle all the thinking, and no one could help him. I was his last hope for salvation. The only choice I had was to let him begin his life over again and slowly redevelop his mind. I turned him into a small child and brought him up. But there came a time when I had to let him go. His name is Ody!"

A murmur arose in the room. I didn't know how I looked, but I felt so incredibly bashful. This woman wasn't my mother after all!

I couldn't recall anything from my life as king; the confusion was growing, if anything.

"Long live our king!" the crowd now all cried out together. "Long live Ody!"

I let out a deep sigh. What had I got myself into now?

"Very well," the judge spoke again. "We shall now pronounce you the King of Existence. Hand me the sword."

He approached me with the sword. The servant, too, approached, carrying a velvet cape and four golden crowns. The judge placed them all on my head, one on top of the other. Strangely enough, they fitted exactly. Then he draped the cape around my shoulders.

After that, he touched my nose with the point of his sword and solemnly said, "You shall once more become our king. Please do not lose your power of thinking again." Then he turned to the spectators and called out, "Follow the king to the dining chamber!"

I walked out of the hall, wondering where the dining chamber was, and all the spectators followed behind. Luckily, Sseus quickly caught up to me and could whisper directions into my ear.

"But Sseus," I asked. "Why didn't you tell me any of this earlier?"

"I couldn't do that, Ody. That wasn't part of the plan. As it was, we were afraid that this plan would also fail."

"Oh," I said. "I'm certainly glad that you didn't really go away for good. You gave me the scare of my life, you know."

We quickly came to the dining chamber. Chamber isn't exactly the proper word to describe it; one could better call it a whole building. It was fantastically beautiful, built of marble with silk curtains. Through the windows, one could look over the tops of trees. A long, covered table stood in the room, and at the head was a magnificent chair.

"You must sit in that chair there," Sseus whispered.

I sat down upon the throne, Sseus sat to my left, and the Wisest Advisor who had cared for me for so many years sat to my right.

The festive meal was very extensive and tastier than words can describe. There were eggs in cream sauce for Columbus and cabbage leaves and cakes for Corn and Flakes. Each guest had their favorite dish.

It turned into a large and dignified feast.

I lived in the castle tree and ruled with Sseus' help. Later, I was able to manage alone, and Sseus went to live with Corn and Flakes. He visited me every summer. The people were all very friendly towards me, and all my decisions appeared to be good ones.

Still, I must admit that the whole story isn't yet totally clear to me. Perhaps it's better if I don't try thinking too hard about it all.

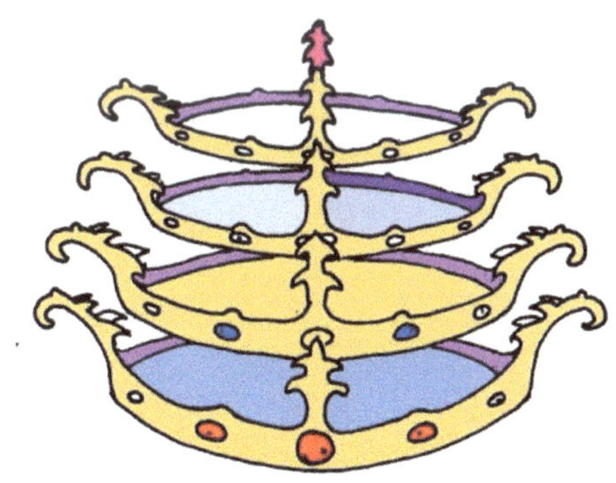

Part 2 of 3

KING ODY

I

I awoke and opened my eyes, hoping to see daylight, but that was not the case this time. I saw no gently tempered sunlight shining through my silk curtains. On the contrary, it made no difference whether or not I had my eyes open or closed. It remained pitch-dark.

I wasn't either in my own bed but somewhere on hard ground, or so it felt. I hadn't really the slightest idea where I was; nothing felt familiar. Rigidly and staggering a little, I got up, stretching out my hands.

I carefully did a couple of steps until I bumped into an earth wall.

"*Strange*," I thought. I could not remember having a room with such a wall. Above me, I felt a low ceiling, which also consisted of earth.

"How could I have ended up here? Did I dream or not?"

I wondered about all this, shuffling along the wall. Somewhere should be an exit or an opening to go outside. It was very quiet around me. I closed my eyes again since it didn't matter in the darkness; I couldn't see anything, anyway. The air around me was slightly chilly and damp. Groping with my hands along the wall, I dared to increase my speed slightly. After some time, I noticed that my surroundings became somewhat warmer, and I felt no longer cold in my pajamas. I stopped for a moment to roll up the sleeves of the jacket.

'"Stop!'" called a voice suddenly, whereas I had stopped already for a long time.

"Don't step further, you hear!" The voice sounded very imperative, which resembled a hold-up by a robber.

I waited already for the next order: "Hands up!" or "Your money or your life!"

But in place of that, the voice said, "Give me only your hand; I'm just behind you."

The man to whom the voice belonged seemed to be very sure of himself, so I obeyed him like a good fellow.

A large, uncovered hand seized mine and drew me backward with a jerk.

"That was only just in time," said the man panting. "You better look out where you put your feet, will you?"

I opened my eyes and noticed that it was no longer very dark, even light enough to observe the man in front of me. He was of small size but strongly built and was dressed in a type of balloon. As a result, he seemed most like a balloon with a head, arms, and legs. The balloon outfit was bright red and had some black dots that seemed to resemble buttons. There were absolutely no fasteners to be seen. I asked myself how he managed to put this outfit on and take it off.

The man nodded kindly at me and pointed to the left of me. Then I got the creeps for a moment because, although it was pretty warm in the tunnel, I was looking into a deep pit. I had almost stepped into it, having my eyes closed. Trembling and with slack knees, I withdrew a step.

"You have saved my life!" I exclaimed.

"Yes," replied the man quietly, looking modestly at his nails. "I am like that. I am always prepared to help somebody.

But come with me; I know a spot where we can chatter enjoyably."

He crawled carefully on hands and feet down the path along the pit. I followed his example. We passed several side passages. I shivered again slightly when I looked to the left at the pit. It was a frightening sight. I had been almost gobbled by that pit. The man turned now to the right into a side passage. This time it was a lot more agreeable; even with my eyes closed, it was possible to see a strange light that radiated from niches that had been dug out of the side walls. We scrambled to our feet and moved further on, upright. We passed again an illuminated niche in which floated some globules of fire.

"What are those light globules?" I asked, pointing to the niche.

"Oh, those are solon-callers; those aren't animals, but simply a substance which one encounters here regularly. You are not familiar here?"

"No, not at all; where I am actually?" I asked.

"Here," answered the man matter-of-factly, "and nowhere else."

I had to admit that my question had sounded somewhat dumb, but nevertheless, I wanted eagerly to know what had happened to me tonight and asked, "How did I come here?"

"On your feet, I suppose," answered the man.

"How long must I remain here?"

"That's up to you. I will not stop you in any case."

My questions appeared to be useless. With his responses, I absolutely did not become wiser. Thus, I stopped asking questions and decided to provisionally accept the situation as it was at the moment.

After a short period, we reached a particularly large but not deep pit in which stood a house. It had been mainly built in the earthen wall so that only the front was visible.

"This is my house," the man said and walked down along the steep slope.

I followed him to the door of his house. There were obvious horizontal tunnels that ended in this pit, as well as vertical ones in the ceiling. On the walls grew large white balls.

I indicated upwards and asked, "How does one get to that tunnel?"

"Very simply, you jump on a Dromble, and you grab the rope that hangs in the tunnel," answered the man.

He opened the door and called something unintelligible to someone in the house. Promptly a second balloon with a head, arms, and legs appeared, but now in a female form, with a balloon child in each hand and still many more balloon children around her.

"My wife," said the man proudly. She sat down on the ground in front of the house with us and her many children.

"This is our guest," said the man to her. "I saved his life in a heroic manner."

She stood up and shook my hand, and I shook the hands of all children.

"My name is Drombless-Large, and these are Drombles-Small," said the woman, pointing to her children.

"Myself, I am Dromble-Very-Large," said the man, "and what do you wear?"

"I am the King of Existence, Ody," I spoke. "I am a Crown-Wearer, but I don't have it at this moment," I added, excusing myself. "But, by the way, what are Drombles?"

"We are Drombles as well as these," he said, tapping at his balloon outfit.

"And those are also drombles," he continued. He gestured to the large white balls that grew on the walls of the pit. "Drombles are useful because they are elastic and smooth. You can jump high up, and you can put them on easily and take them off again."

"Why don't you also put on a dromble," suggested the woman. She picked a balloon from the earth wall and passed it to me. "You must put it on the ground and then lie on it."

I just did what she had advised me. After all, I rather wouldn't like hopping around in my pajamas. So, I lay down on the dromble, which slowly folded itself around me and completely closed itself. The dromble was of a kind of soft rubbery material, a type of jelly rubber.

"Would the Crown-Wearer like to have some food?" asked the woman. She walked immediately into the house without waiting for an answer.

"Thank you very much, Mrs. Drombless-Large."

I turned around to Dromble-Very-Large with a question: "How do you get sufficient oxygen here?"

Dromble-Very-Large scratched himself slowly behind his ear. "I don't know anything about that. I only know that the Large Oxiture takes care of that."

"Who is that, the Large Oxiture?"

"I don't know; there is a big secret about the Large Oxiture. Only he knows who he is."

I looked at the man, curious. Why would the Large Oxiture's identity be wrapped in a secret, and how can he make oxygen? Would he use plants for that? In any case, oxygen was available, and that was, for the moment, most essential. Drombless-Large came out of the house with a couple of clay pots, one of which she passed to me. A remarkable smell, which I could not recognize, filled my nose.

"Zopie," explained the woman. "One does not eat it but just smells it in; you understand, Crown-Wearer?"

I nodded and inhaled the Zopie completely in, just sniffing the last bit. This food does not go beyond the nose.

"What is your profession, Dromble-Very-Large?"

"By Jove! Haven't I said it? I am a hero. My daily occupation is to save lives. A well-paid job because lives are worth gold, aren't they?"

"Oh, but then you are very brave!" I praised him.

"Certainly, I am not afraid for anything and anybody."

"Booooh!" someone suddenly called from behind Dromble-Very-Large, who was scared stiff and jumped backward so high that he landed behind me.

"Ha, ha, ha, ha, ha!" yelled the newly arrived balloon with head and limbs. "I got you, didn't I? Ha, ha!" Dromble-Very-Large restored himself quickly. He tapped firmly on the balloon and said, "Oh, but I knew well it was you, hear. Hmmm ... eh, if I had not pretended to be scared, you would now be very saddened, Boosayer, and as a hero, I can't, of course, be responsible for that. You see, now you are laughing at least!"

Boosayer answered only with a small cough and nodded a bit sneeringly.

I had gotten up to shake hands with Boosayer.

"I am Od—Crown-Wearer."

"Glad to meet you, Crown-Wearer-Sayer," Boosayer answered. And immediately thereafter, he said, "Say, Dromble-Very-Large, you have to save a life, so would you come along?"

Boosayer climbed from the pit, followed by Dromble-Very Large and myself, as I wanted to learn more about this underground world in which I had been dropped so suddenly.

"Brother Boosayer does not feel very well. When I returned from my morning walk, I saw him drunk on Pampus. I think he is unconscious."

The hero nodded understandingly, and silently we ran through a number of tunnels. At last, we reached a large niche which served as an entrance to a house. Boosayer opened the door and showed us to a room lighted by solon-callers. There lay Brother Boosayer in a corner on the ground, just in front of a large jug with the label: "Pampus." Dromble-Very-Large rushed to him and felt his pulse. He nodded.

"Unconscious by sight, as that is called in heroic terms," he concluded.

"What does that mean?" I asked.

"It means that he fainted because he has seen something that he was not allowed to see. It is the habit here to faint if one sees something that is not intended for our eyes. Lately, it happens frequently," explained the hero.

"What is Pampus?" I asked Boosayer.

"Food, sniff, life-keeping," he answered. "Pampus is also the basic principle of heroism because it preserves life."

Dromble-Very-Large was meanwhile very busy with the fainted fellow. He was on his knees beside the patient and was patting him firmly on the cheeks until he slowly opened his eyes.

"Booooh," was his first shout. The hero recoiled slightly.

"Ha, ha, ha; he is as healthy as a worm in the ground again," yelled Boosayer.

Brother Boosayer thanked the hero amply and warmly for his life-saving aid.

"Crown-Wearer-Sayer can stay here if he likes," said Boosayer.

"Naturally," answered Dromble-Very-Large for me. "That's what he wants, isn't it?"

I nodded and waved Dromble-Very-Large goodbye.

Brother Boosayer and Boosayer both now jumped through the room while shouting loudly, "Boo, boo, lalaloo, loolala."

I found them a very strange company. In fact, I could not call these surroundings normal. At least not as normal as it was above the ground. In any case, the two brothers were quite pleasant, and I was allowed to sniff as much Pampus as I wanted.

I was curious about what Brother Boosayer had seen and what made him faint. But when I asked about it, he seemed to have forgotten everything he might have seen after his fall. I considered this seriously.

"Could there be an invisible secret weapon?" When somebody saw something which he was not allowed to see, they fainted and then immediately forgot everything they had seen. I wondered whether this would happen to me eventually, as I was not a native here. But, okay; tomorrow, perhaps I would know more.

I continued to stay at the Boosayers. That went very simple. The food only had to be sniffed, and it could be prepared many days in advance.

To sleep, one just lay on the ground. When the Brothers said it was evening, I stretched and went to sleep. The dromble was deliciously soft and warm. The Boosayers also fell asleep, keeping their outfits on.

2

Immediately after I had gotten up, I sniffed only a little Pampus; more was not necessary. I wanted to ask some questions of the Brothers Boosayers concerning the Large Oxiture.

"The Large Oxiture is very powerful," Brother Boosayer had said so far. With this answer, I was now convinced that I had to find this powerful Oxiture.

"*He could possibly*," I thought, "*help me to escape from this underworld realm where I do not belong*."

But the following remarks of Boosayer discouraged me slightly: "The Large Oxiture wants to govern all alone. He does not tolerate any antagonists or troublesome individuals. He certainly does not like questions, only solutions."

"Where lives the Large Oxiture? I have to talk to him," I said.

The Brothers Boosayers went pale at the idea. Fear radiated from their eyes.

"Eh ... well ... you know, Crown-Wearer-Sayer ... eh ... we have never seen the Large Oxiture. We know very well that you should never come too close to him because then the most terrible things can happen. As a matter of fact, we do not know where he lives. There is a large network of tunnels here; even if you run around for years, you will not find his house."

I was desperately disappointed, but I would not lose heart so easily.

"Well," I answered courageously, "even if I must ramble around here for three years, I nevertheless want to speak with the Large Oxiture."

"Oooohhh," was their only comment.

I smoothed my dromble and got ready to leave the house of the Boosayers.

"Wait," Boosayer called, "take some Pampus with you. We probably don't have enough for three years, but perhaps plenty for three months."

The large pot with Pampus was placed in a dromble. The pot disappeared entirely in it and was surrounded by dromble fabric. Now the Brothers started to mold together my dromble and the dromble with the Pampus. Shortly after, the drombles were stuck together. The Pampus was somewhere on my back.

"Good trip ... and success!" wished the Brothers, and I was ready for a long trip.

The Pampus was fortunately not too heavy to carry; it seemed as if the drombles, not me, carried the Pampus by themselves.

Without having the faintest idea which direction I should go, I simply walked further on. From time to time, I encountered a new Dromble person. To light their way, solon-callers floated around the Drombles' heads all the time as a kind of halo. I examined everyone closely to make sure they were not actually the Large Oxiture, but they had all the typically round and kind faces of Drombles.

One time, I saw a Dromble put his head in a niche in which solon-callers floated. After a short whistle, some of the light balls remained floating around his head. I immediately tried to also do that because, in some corridors, there were few solon-callers niches available, and it could be very dark. I whistled and promptly a number of solon-callers floated around my head. The luminous balls followed my every head movement.

This way, I had become well acquainted with the habits of Drombles.

I nevertheless longed for my castle tree a lot. I feared that the work would pile up at home. Several visits had to be made this week. And next month, a trip to Venus was scheduled. Several Councilors were to come to the castle tree to discuss current affairs with me. Everyone would be worried because of my absence and perhaps would be offended. And I just ran here in my dromble with the Pampus, in search of the Large Oxiture. Fortunately, Sseus was at home in my castle tree, and I hoped that he could meanwhile handle my affairs.

With all these worrisome thoughts, I continued walking on my bare feet until I passed a dromble nursery. It was a large pothole in which drombles of all sizes grew. Some Drombles were very busy with paint in order to give the white balloons a more pleasant look. On the edge of the pothole stood a placard on which was written: "Choose your own dromble. We have them in all sizes and perhaps even yours!"

"*Hmmm*," I thought. "*Would drombles also serve as shoes?*" I assumed they would and descended into the pothole.

"A couple of drombles, please," I said to a painter.

"Have your choice," he answered. "Look for which one suits you best."

After some trial and error, I found the correct size and put on the small drombles. I took some waddling steps when the dromble-painter called, "Hey, wait, I still have to paint those; come here!" The painter took a paint brush and painted my dromble-shoes a shiny red. In brown, he painted a couple of laces. After a look of disapproval at my white dromble, he rapidly painted a couple buttons and a proper tie on it.

"How much are they?" I asked decently.

"That's one pair of small drombles," said the painter.

"Yes, but how expensive are they?"

The man looked at me, slightly cautious as if he wondered whether I was entirely well in my head.

"Oh ... eh ... well, thank you very much!" I said and walked away with the cheerful feeling that one has when he gets new shoes. Apparently, one did not pay here.

I walked very lightly and bounced with every step so that I had a very elegant way of walking. After a while, I got some more experience with the dromble-walk, and I jumped not so high. I walked through the tunnels as if on air cushions. From time to time, I stopped to sniff some Pampus. I did not get thirsty; the Pampus probably ensured I had sufficient water too.

I met fewer and fewer Drombles or Dromblesses and, eventually, none at all. I didn't know whether or not it was already night because I wasn't sure whether the sun had gone down or risen. The Boosayers would've known when it was time to go to sleep.

I don't know how long I had already run around when I had a strange meeting with a Drombless. The tunnel in which I walked was terribly dark and had a sharp turn. I walked carefully because behind the turn could be a gorge or tunnel with a dead end.

I walked around the bend and was scared to death because there stood a small Drombless with a large stick above her head, who shouted, "Waaaaah! ... Gotcha!" But, when she saw my face, her ferocity dissipated, as if she was deeply disappointed to see me!

"Eh ... hello ... do you always hunt this way around corners, scaring the daylights out of people?" I asked.

She was now slightly timid about her previously adopted

attitude and answered, “Well, ha, ha, I had, in fact, expected someone else.”

“Who then was worthy of receiving a blow with your stick?” I asked.

“Not you, in any case; say, it is ... no, I mean, I am doing my daily strength exercises with this stick. That is really terrific for strength development using this stick ... eh ... I mean, eh ... of me ... eh, me ... really very good, say!” she stammered.

But at the same time, she had a very naughty twinkle in her eyes.

“My name is Banelez,” she continued with much more confidence in her voice. This name surprised me. I would rather have expected a name such as “Waaah-shouter” or some other name typical for these underground characters. For this reason, I did not present myself as “Crown-Wearer” or “Crown-Wearer-Sayer” but simply as “Ody.” A slight amazement slid over her face; she had also apparently expected another name.

“Where are you going?” she asked, full of curiosity.

“Oh,” I answered, “perhaps to Fekeluns.”

This name I had invented on the spot because I presumed it unwise to inform her too soon about the Large Oxiture. She seemed very curious to me, and I had no intention of telling her too much about myself. She might like to examine it down to the last detail.

“Really?” she exclaimed, “perhaps I am going there as well!”

I found this very confusing; I had expected that she would say “Oh” and would have moved on, but apparently, I had invented an existing and well-known name. That ended poorly because now I was forced to go to a place called “Fekeluns” without knowing the way.

“I have lost my way and no longer know the way to Fekeluns; therefore, it’s better you don’t join me,” I said in the hope of getting rid of her.

"Oh, but that doesn't matter. I can always find the way, and in any case, we could simply ask someone for directions," she argued.

She grabbed the stick which she had lain on the ground and went in the direction that I had planned to go.

"Come along then!" she exhorted me. "You were the one who wanted to go to Fekeluns or not, by any chance."

I followed her, although I did not want her as a fellow traveler. I was in search of the Large Oxiture, and if I did meet him, I had no use for terrified and fainting Dromblesses. In that case, I would be obliged to save her; I had learned how to do that after all. Meanwhile, the Oxiture would have disappeared, of course.

I could hardly ask her if she knew the way to the Large Oxiture. It remained a strange situation, her standing there with that stick. All Drombles were kind persons. Perhaps was she some kind of warden. I did not belong here; I had no Dromble-face. And wardens do not love strange faces. Fortunately, my outfit was very ordinary for these surroundings. But why did she insist on joining my journey to Fekeluns? No, this little situation did not please me. I decided to shake her off as quickly as possible.

All the while, she talked cheerfully to me and sometimes took, without asking, some Pampus from my dromble. She let me see that there was, with absolute certainty, surprisingly nothing in her dromble.

We walked together through horizontal and inclined tunnels. She chattered in a lively way about the preparation of Pampus and how long one had to whistle to get as many soloncallers as possible around one's head until she suddenly changed the subject to that of the Large Oxiture.

To my stupefaction, she asked, "Say, what you know about the Large Oxiture? I am terribly interested in Large Oxitures."

"Nothing," I said. I did not want to give away that my interest in the subject was possibly larger than hers. "No, I only know some rumors about him. He would be a semi-transparent person."

She nodded and started to chatter again about Dromble households.

After a couple minutes, she suddenly showed an intention to part ways. It seemed she didn't need me anymore. She looked at me with a piercing look and said, "It will be night soon; you better go asleep. I will show you tomorrow the way to Fekeluns, and then you can find your way alone."

Fine, that was good for me. I was indeed a bit tired, and tomorrow I would find out more.

After I slept well, she stood there again, and she pointed at a signpost, on which was written with still-wet paint: "Fekeluns, straight on."

I nodded and saw her hurrying away through a side passage.

Very good, I had got rid of her without too much effort.

"*This way, one could see how an Ody could solve anything*," I thought, satisfied. I was very curious about what Fekeluns would be like and followed the indicated road. Perhaps the Large Oxiture lived in Fekeluns?

I walked on very long until I, after infinitely straight and boring tunnels, ended up in a cul-de-sac. Was this Fekeluns? I walked back a bit and fortunately encountered a cozy Dromble again, whom immediately I asked for the way for Fekeluns.

This one answered laughingly, "I am sorry, young man. I think they have pulled your leg. I have never heard of Fekeluns, and I have already lived here a couple of centuries. Thus, you can take it for granted that it does not exist."

I frowned. Would Banelez have fooled me? And why should she? Well, I didn't tell her the full truth either, but that was still no reason to send me in the wrong direction. I thanked the Dromble for his aid and walked haphazardly into a side passage.

3

Since I had meanwhile drifted through all the corridors, my patience was running out. I had still seen no track of the Oxiture. Nevertheless, I increasingly had the feeling I was close to him. Also, I thought sometimes that something was sneaking behind me. But each time when I turned around, there was no sign of life. I had enough of it, really. I had to invent something better than aimlessly walking around through the tunnels.

I was just in front of an upwards-sloping passage when a Drombless came running at me very hastily. Panting, she called, "My husband has fainted; please, save him!"

I remembered the case with the Boosayers all but too well and therefore considered myself very well able to save the poor man and thus followed the Drombless immediately.

They lived in a small pothole, which looked very cozy. As we descended, she told me how she had seen her husband fainting when she came home with a new dromble, which she had just obtained. He had pointed to something behind the house before he fell, but she had seen nothing. I hurried into the house, where I saw the Dromble lying, stretched out on the ground. I hoped that he could still tell us what or who he had seen.

Would the Oxiture nevertheless be in the neighborhood? I patted the fainted man hard on the cheeks, exactly as I had seen Dromble-Very-Large doing. The fainted man soon opened his eyes, and I immediately asked him what he had seen. He frowned, his forehead crinkling together.

"I don't know for sure, but it was a kind of shadow. I'm very sorry, but I can't say more; my thoughts escape me," he answered. Thus, now at least I knew something more about that mysterious fainting.

The two Drombles were very grateful to me and offered me a meal. While the woman prepared her own type of Zopie, I was sitting with the Dromble man outside the house. I found that living here was dull, everything and everyone seemed the same, and it was the same: the houses, the clothing, the names, and the people.

This Dromble man introduced himself as Nothing-Sayer. He said very little. The woman had made a delicious, hot, and fresh Zopie. Silently, we sniffed the food in.

I asked them straight-forwardly, "Where does the Large Oxiture live?"

Nothing-Sayer just looked coolly at me.

His wife, however, who had the name Everything-Sayer, answered, "It seems that the Oxiture lives in the gold and glittery layers, but nobody has ever been there."

"Then I will be the first!" I exclaimed.

Both looked anxiously at me. They probably wondered whether this was a wise decision.

"How can I get to those layers?" I asked.

Everything-Sayer answered, slightly hesitating, "Take those tunnels that descend, then eventually you should arrive ..."

I warmly thanked them for the meal and the information. I climbed from their living pothole and took the first descending tunnel that I saw.

I was considerably relieved. Now I had at least a fixed aim: the golden and glittery layers. I had many questions to ask the Large Oxiture: how he made oxygen, why Drombles fainted now and then, and especially, how I could leave this place.

The fact that this lord apparently did not love questions would not keep me from asking them anyway. Finally, I was really being brave!

The excursion down was long. It became warmer as I descended. My Pampus reserve was almost empty, and from time to time, I took a short break.

I could still hear the pursuers sneaking behind me, but I was too tired to turn around. As a matter of fact, I could not see anything; I heard and felt them only.

I perspired considerably inside my dromble but granted myself no time to take it off. Then I would have to carry it because I didn't want to throw it away. Who knew how much I might need it again?

After a long descent, my efforts were rewarded! I came to golden tunnels. The walls, the ground, the ceiling, everything was made of gold. Lights of the soloncallers reflected splendidly. This had to be a thick gold layer, such that one could dig corridors. It was so brilliant that it was almost hard to believe.

What a pleasure

it was to walk in these corridors! What a cozy warm light! It did not last long, and then small twinkling diamonds appeared between the gold. The further I went, the more diamonds were to be seen, until at last, there was only some gold between the gems.

The walls and the ceiling shone fantastically in all colors of the rainbow. The floor was entirely slippery, so it seemed to be an extraordinarily beautiful, enormous slide. I sat down and began sliding through the corridors. This way I got much pleasure out of my trip.

At last, I had such a speed that I, like on a toboggan, took corners by sliding up along the walls.

Suddenly there came an end to the fun. I was stopped roughly by a high threshold. This had likely been the last glittery tunnel. I stood up and dusted the fine gold powder off my dromble.

The threshold proved to be my luck because after it was a deep pothole. One could hardly call it a pothole. It was something very miraculous. It was entirely of gold, and a castle was built in it, also of pure gold. The windows had not been made of glass but of diamonds. The castle had four large towers from which hung splendid banners. They moved softly in a small breeze.

I was really gasping for breath when I saw this superb monument, although I was quite used to seeing superb monuments at my castle tree. All this was so much more beautiful and more precious.

I stepped over the threshold of the large pothole and descended by means of a golden staircase, as I assumed this was the home of the Large Oxiture. At the massive gate, I stopped and pulled a golden bell. An elegant tinkling resounded throughout the pothole.

The door opened by itself, and I entered. There was nobody in sight. The door closed softly behind me, just like it had opened. I walked through a golden corridor and went up a golden staircase on which lay a splendidly embroidered carpet. There was only one door on this floor, which I opened.

Now I stood in a hall of gold, and there on a golden throne sat the Large Oxiture! It was a strange character this Oxiture; he seemed somewhat helpless, not at all as I had imagined. He was a lean, small, old man who sat stooped on the throne; the weight of his blue dromble held him to it.

"Come in, Ody," he beckoned and looked at me with tired eyes.

"Can I ask you something?" I asked.

"Don't you get ahead of me as I have to ask you a question. Sit down," was his answer, whereas he drew up a golden chair.

"Ody," he continued, "I have a problem; I can barely make any more oxygen."

"That's terrible!" I said with compassion. "But how I can help you?"

"First, let me explain how I make oxygen."

He rearranged a dromble-cushion at his back and continued. "I make oxygen by sacrificing myself. I look old, don't I'? But in reality, I am only 100 years old; that is very young for a Dromble. Each day of making oxygen costs something of me. Ody, that production is ruining me! But I must make oxygen; otherwise, my people would suffocate. I no longer know what I must do. For that reason, I have brought you here. You, as King of Existence, can help me."

"Of course, I can. But how did you bring me here?" I asked.

"Very simple, by transformalogy. That is a method to divide people into particles as small as possible and transport them by air to where you want them. There you reassemble them again. This is, of course, only possible when one sleeps, such as you did in the castle tree. I transformed myself into your room and then directed us here together. Since I am a bit weak at the moment, you, unfortunately, arrived in the wrong tunnel. But you have found me soon enough, as I had expected."

I nodded understandingly.

"Do you have already a solution for the oxygen problem?" he continued, with a spark of hope in his voice.

"No, but I wonder why the flags on the towers softly flutter in the wind," I said. "I think, to say, that they move due to some draft which comes from outside. Perhaps there is a hole somewhere, the result of which is that air is supplied by my kingdom."

The Oxiture frowned his eyebrows. He did not understand what I meant.

"That would mean, therefore," I explained, "that your oxygen production is superfluous. We must only find the hole to ensure that my conclusion is correct."

The Oxiture nodded happily. "I will stop making oxygen at once since I know of such a hole. In some legends and fairy tales, the existence of this hole is mentioned. Therefore, we will not yet search for it. Should a shortage of oxygen arise after I have stopped making it, we will have to admit that there is no hole, but otherwise, it is there."

The Oxiture recovered visibly now that he had effectively stopped his production.

"And then there is something else, Large Oxiture, that you may not have thought about," I said. "There are still the drombles. They have been entirely filled with millions of air bubbles, air bubbles that produce the substances you use to make air."

The Oxiture smiled, relieved. "I am very grateful to you, Ody."

Now, I intended to ask him my questions. "Tell me, please,

who are you, Oxiture?"

"I am the King of Below-Existence," he answered proudly. Now he was in a good mood.

"The Drombles are, however, rather frightened of you, I found."

"Oh, yes," sighed the Large Oxiture. "That will remain so until they have seen me."

I smiled at him and continued, "Why do the Drombles faint if they see a shadow? And why do they always immediately forget that which scared them?"

The king looked at me with large eyes. "I have never heard of that! This is a new fact for me! I know nothing of that shadow nor of the existence of that sickness."

"Strange," I mumbled. "Anyway, perhaps it is not something serious. I presume that I can return now to my castle tree?"

"No, please, just wait until we know whether the hole really exists."

"Well, but I think your problem has been solved now. You examined the difficulty too long from Below-Existence. It is good to regard a problem also from above, especially when no one is arguing otherwise. Meanwhile, I will use my time to look for a certain Banelez in your tunnels. Before I leave, I want to speak with her."

"Banelez!" exclaimed the king.

"Yes, you know her?"

"Yes ... I mean, oh, gee ... oh, heaven ..." replied the Oxiture hesitatingly. He seemed again very nervous. He needed to recover quietly from his enormous efforts. "Well, well; go ahead, find her."

I got up, shook the trembling hand of the king, bade farewell to him, and left the palace. I wanted to find Banelez and speak my mind concerning Fekeluns and other things.

“If the hole exists, I will have you transformed to your castle tree as soon as possible,” called the Oxiture, who waved to me from a window. I nodded and waved back.

4

I stood again in front of the threshold in the diamond corridor. Just when I had climbed on top of it, I saw two hazies standing behind the high threshold. They had sticks in their almost-transparent hands and rushed toward me. I got a hard knock on my head and knew nothing more.

When I came around again after I don't know how long, I found myself in a large niche, not in a golden corridor but in a simple, earthen dromble niche. In the rear, against the wall, sat a hazy looking attentively at me, probably my guard. This niche was obviously used as a prison because there were heavy bars at the front. The hazy was certainly no Dromble; no, he more resembled a phantom. Nevertheless, he had been robust enough to knock me down.

He looked somewhat pale and had hollow, black, glossy eyes. Around his body, if we could call it that, he wore a kind of thin, flapping fabric. He had the stick with which he had knocked me down still in his hand. He did not speak a word but stayed staring at me with his hollow eyes.

I asked him in a severe tone why I had been brought here, but he absolutely did not react.

I closed my eyes, moaning. I cursed myself that I had not just remained sociably with the Large Oxiture, instead of searching by myself for that Banelez just to ask her a couple questions. That had been terribly stupid!

Hop! The barred door opened with a considerable swing. It was Banelez, accompanied by a second hazy.

"What did you come looking for?" she asked angrily.

I had just opened my eyes and answered, in all honesty, "I paid a visit to the Large Oxiture."

"Ah ha! And what did you have to do with the Large Oxiture?"

"I came to advise him," I said, not without dignity.

She nodded with satisfaction as if she had expected my answer. While I looked at her, astonished, I saw her slowly changing shape. The dromble became invisible, her eyes became black, and her hair, which had been brown before, became deeply black. She simply changed her appearance before my eyes. She now resembled more her hazy companion.

"This is obvious!" she yelled, pointing to me with a thin finger. "I don't have to ask who has sent you; I can guess that easily!" Her voice had not changed in any case.

She ran furiously from the niche, followed by her spooky follower, and slammed the door with a bang.

My guard continued to stand in front of the door to prevent me from escaping.

I was entirely confused. What did she mean, that Banelez? I was the one who wanted to ask questions, not her. This was one large misunderstanding ... or was something wrong with my brain due to that blow? I certainly did not feel myself very clearly at that moment, and I also had a headache.

Meanwhile, there was something happening of which I knew nothing at that moment. Only much later would I hear about it. But it was essential in any case, so I will tell you now.

What was Banelez doing?

After she had slammed the door of my prison, she ran with the hazies straight towards the golden corridors. She did not look for her own golden mirror images, which reflected on all sides nicely, but glided with much speed, yet without pleasure, along the diamond tunnels. She knew exactly where she had to brake for the threshold and soon stood at the golden castle door, which opened for her automatically. She ran immediately to the hall of the Large Oxiture. The hazy remained at the door.

"Grandfather!" she called, then she embraced the king.

"My girl, what brings you here?" the hazies asked.

"I have important news and, moreover, no pleasant news," she said and sat down in front of the king on a golden chair. The king looked at her doubtfully. "Tell, darling child ..."

She swallowed and started her story: "Quost has emerged again!"

Her grandfather jumped from his throne. He was visibly very shocked.

"Oh, gosh! What a calamity! How do you know this for certain? You have seen him?" he exclaimed.

"No, I have not seen him myself, but Tiw has ... And now Quost has caught him."

Her grandfather understood the situation but too well. "He wants us too, for sure?"

Banelez nodded and said, "Grandfather, you must help me; we must disarm Quost. We have caught a spy of his today. He wanted to spy on you and persuade you to work for him!"

"I am glad you were able to catch that spy; he had no word on Quost, I suppose?"

"No, he arrived with a series of thin stories."

The Large Oxiture got up proudly and called, "With united forces then!"

While I lay in my niche, dizzy the whole time, my silent

guard had entered. He could, without effort, go between the bars, in and out.

There was Banelez again; at least, I assumed it was her. This time, she wore an opaque, pure-white tunic and had a type of white mask on her face. She threw another of the same blank tunic over my body and also covered my face with a blank mask. Thus, nobody could recognize me. My guard, who I had baptized as a follower, dragged me by my arm from the niche. The second hazy caught my other arm so that escape would be practically impossible.

In the corridor stood someone else who obviously belonged to Banelez. He was, just like us all, entirely dressed in white, with exactly the same mask. This figure walked slightly bent and gave me a worrisome impression.

Banelez walked with the newly arrived person in front and my guard "appendages" and myself behind. We went somewhere. Except for Banelez, nobody spoke a word. With jokes, she tried to cheer up the person walking next to her.

We moved along steadily and entered all kinds of tunnels that I had not yet seen on my search for the Large Oxiture. I tried to talk, but nobody answered; thus, I talked aloud to myself, hoping that by teasing my companions, they would answer back.

"You're not in a pleasant situation, hey?" I observed out loud to myself.

"No!" was my answer to myself. "I want to leave here as soon as possible. When I get the opportunity, I will escape, good?"

"Excellent friend, keep your eyes and ears well open. These hazies are absolutely not dangerous; you can manage them easily."

Speaking with myself was not really fascinating. I knew already the answer to every question that I could put to myself. One thing was sure; I would not let go of any chance to escape.

We ran into a Dromble sometimes, but not one stopped for a moment to have a chat, and no one even greeted us. They acted as if they just did not see us. Perhaps the reason was the white tunics.

I paid sharp attention to my guards and hoped that their arms would become tired so that I could run away. I wished that the Large Oxiture or one of his men was in the neighborhood, so they could save me from this painful situation. But we passed no golden or diamond corridors. Banelez chose rather steep passages. It became, as a matter of fact, colder, and we kept climbing farther and farther. Our final destination was still a mystery.

After many hours, the company halted when a new hazy emerged. He was completely upset and yelled, "Wit has been kidnapped! Quick, Wit has been kidnapped!"

Banelez and the others were scared stiff, but not me. Because of their consternation, my "companions" slackened their hold for a moment, upon which I reacted instantly. The same moment I had torn my arms loose, I ran into a side passage. I removed my mask; it had impeded me long enough.

"Quick. Bring him back!" I heard Banelez calling to the hazies. Three now came after me. The "Wit is kidnapped" yeller came along too. They were incredibly fast and glided smoothly and agilely over any unevenness on the floor of the tunnel. I stumbled over a stone, and before I had the chance to stand up, they each caught a piece of my tunic.

I had not hurt myself since the dromble cushioned every impact. The three hazies carried me back to the company.

The "white-outfit-wearer" beside Banelez raised an arm and exclaimed, "But, by Jove, that's Ody!"

"Correct," answered Banelez. "He is a spy of Quost."

"Not at all, dear child," replied the man, and I heard from his voice that he was none other than the Large Oxiture. "No doubt, this is Ody. Ody is the King of Existence. He can't, by any possibility, be a spy of Quost!"

Banelez was terror-struck. She slowly became aware that she had made a terrible mistake.

"Release him," she commanded the three hazies.

"Uh huh," I sighed from the deepest of my heart.

The Large Oxiture removed his mask, and Banelez did the same. The three hazies kneeled in front of her on the ground.

She addressed them severely: "Fatheads, I told you repeatedly that he was really the Ody, but you remained carrying on. You insisted he was a spy!"

The aptly named hazies looked at each other, astonished. They opened their mouths as if to protest.

"Ask forgiveness, nitwits; it is your fault!"

Her order was immediately followed, and I forgave them.

Banelez looked a bit timidly at me and said, "I am so sorry, but they aren't the most intelligent beings who don't exist."

I looked at her, asking, "Why 'don't exist?'"

The Large Oxiture took the floor: "She, Banelez is the Queen of Non-Existence. She is also my granddaughter."

We all sat down together on the ground. I wanted a detailed explanation.

Banelez started: "I came to my grandfather, the Large Oxiture, to discuss a problem. The problem of Quost. Quost is, in powerful circles such as ours, a generally feared person. He calls himself the King of Whom-but-Wants. He forces people to work under his authority. Furthermore, he desires to extend his power over everything and everyone, also over us; he wants to play the boss with everything. To get to the point, he can be only made harmless by the joined forces of all monarchs of the Existences working together. You see, it is no trifle."

In something of a less serious tone, she continued, "Now a declaration about me. I can change shape, 'metamorphose' it is called. One moment, I am a Drombless, like at our first meeting, and then I am myself again like I am now. I can change my little self into anything I want. Look, I had taken you for a spy of Quost. I feared you would persuade Grandfather to join Quost. The spies of Quost are very harmful because they can hypnotize someone and thus take power over them. Do you understand now why we caught you? Grandfather knows the situation, and together with you, we can persist. Each of us alone is not strong enough to repel Quost."

It was now the turn of the Large Oxiture to explain to his granddaughter how he had met me and why he had needed me.

"And how you propose to repel that Quost?" I asked.

Banelez looked sad. "I don't know it any longer. I had a plan to use you as bait. I expected that he would send more men to bring back his spy. I wanted to lie in wait and catch them. Just as long as he would come to look for himself, where everyone remained. Then I would have him. But now I know you aren't his spy."

I nodded and said, "You know what? I have, for the moment, a better plan. Let's get some rest!" That we did.

5

After we all woke refreshed, we sniffed each a portion of the Pampus that Banelez and I had with us. The white tunics we had to keep, she said, because nobody could see us while we were wearing them. We were completely invisible. This explained why the Drombles in the corridors acted as if they had not seen us.

Now, the journey could continue. I walked beside Banelez and questioned her once more.

"Why did you hide around the corner with that stick?"

She answered, "I was expecting someone else, Quost's man, not you."

"Is that why you asked about the Large Oxiture?"

"Of course, and I sent you in the wrong direction because I suspected there was something fishy with you. Since we do not, in fact, exist, we could easily sneak behind you; we just made ourselves invisible. And when you found the way to my grandfather by yourself, it seemed to become really dangerous, didn't it?"

I turned now to the Large Oxiture. "Why were you scared when I spoke of Banelez?"

"Oh, Ody, my granddaughter comes only to bring bad news. This time, too, she was the bearer of large worries," answered the king.

Banelez made a point to mention Wit, who had probably been kidnapped by Quost.

"That Quost seems to me a dangerous man," I put forward. "He probably will execute your plan!"

The others asked for a better explanation.

"Look," I explained, "you had the plan of catching his men, one by one, until he turned up. I think he has considered the same. He now already has two of your hazies, Tiw and Wit. Now he waits quietly for whoever comes to save them, and he will catch us."

Everyone was persuaded that the situation could approximately something like that.

"But we have to deliver them!" called Banelez. "We can't let them remain in the hands of Quost, absolutely not!"

It was difficult to find a good strategy here.

"One thing is certain," said the Large Oxiture. "We must first go to the realm of Quost; then we will look at it again in the future."

We kept walking through the tunnels; we were on our way to the domain of Quost.

"Do you know where his realm is?" I asked the Large Oxiture.

"No, not exactly, but in a very old book, I have found these lines and have written them down. The book was called *The Power of the Kings*. Here I have it."

He drew a small piece of paper from his tunic and gave it to me.

I read:

Quost's realm is far from here,
Only on foot one can arrive,

A breach in the wall
will be there at so many hours.
However, the tunnel is long.
Don't fear and never be frightened.
And the end is in sight,
You do your royal duty.
Leaders of every country!
Use then your common sense!

The poem did not say much to me. I wondered how far we could travel with this information. The Oxiture and Banelez thought, however, that it might go well.

The air around us became colder and dryer. The long walk was very tiring for the Oxiture. We had to rest more often for him, and our Pampus reserve was not large anymore. The three hazy figures did not say very much, and if they did speak, it was only with each other in a monotonous singing language, which I could not understand.

Banelez seemed to know the area here quite well, but she always looked cautiously around.

"Because," she told me, "it is not safe in this area. Travelers are frequently assaulted here by Pones."

By the tone by which she spoke about the Pones, I hoped we would not encounter any. At every turn, Banelez snuck ahead with her stick. Generally, there was nobody in view, but sometimes she scared stiff an innocent Dromble. It was a strange experience for them to suddenly hear "Waaah" during their quiet walk around a turn. As Drombles, they could not see anybody since we wore Banelez's white tunics. They must have thought that spirits haunted the tunnels. As a matter of fact, we met noticeably few Drombles. They had probably warned each other.

Banelez started to tell us very scary tales. I really thought that she should not do this in a Pones region. She also told us about another kind of phantom that wandered around here called ground-flappers. They would drift around in the underground tunnels. They came from great depths and could flutter up straight through the ground. These phantoms could sing very beautifully, but listening to them was dangerous. It could bring someone under their power, and they would then fall loosely to the ground.

"The ground-flappers use travelers as an audience. They want to have a grateful public around to listen to their songs. They are phantoms that are dying for appreciation. For everyone else, it is not very interesting. Everyone is summoned to applaud and shout with joy, and one is seldom released."

My heart was beating in my throat, and I would gladly run a bit faster, but that was not possible because of the Large Oxiture.

Below us, I clearly heard applause and shouts of "bravo." Some underground performance was happening and, as a result, they had no time for us, or so I hoped.

The Oxiture took Banelez's stick to support his walking. He had not walked through these tunnels in a long time due to his weakness.

From Banelez's behavior, I could see when we passed a dangerous area and when not. From time to time, she sighed deeply and walked straight and relaxed instead of peering and leering in all directions.

"Ody," said the Large Oxiture, "I think that the hole the poem talks about probably is the hole letting in oxygen."

I did not find this a bad idea. So far, nobody had suffocated; therefore, there really had to be something.

"How do we know whether we walk in the right direction?" I asked him.

"Oh, you can quietly leave that to Banelez. She has a very special nose; she can sense the slightest bit of draft."

"And if there are more holes?"

"The poem speaks of one hole that opens at 'so many hours.'"

Banelez put her nose up and called, "It is almost close!"

She was suddenly scared and stood stiff as a rod. She whispered in our ears, "We must now be completely quiet. We travel the Underworld, and we really shouldn't disturb anything or anybody."

I got a lump in my throat. The Underworld! I had read a lot about it in the books in my library at the castle tree. There were stories about people, living people, who went to that realm to bring back family members. But they did not return alive. And now we needed to go there?

"Isn't it better that we go around?" I asked Banelez.

"Surely not," she answered calmly. "That would be like running around a river which has bridges. That would take much too long."

I sighed, "Let it be then."

Banelez said something to the hazies in their own language. Promptly, they changed shape. The formerly hazy figures now seemed to be people of flesh and blood. Their skin was brown, and around their waists, they wore long, bright blue skirts. On their black hair stood colorful caps, which mostly resembled little self-made, folded hats. I had to laugh for a moment, but I lost all inclination for it when Banelez seized a ball of soil and changed it into handcuffs and masks.

She chained my hands and those of the Large Oxiture and placed masks on our heads. She herself was also chained after a short command to the changed hazies.

"We will play dead. My three men will lead us through the Underworld. Everybody looks like we do now."

We started to walk, accompanied by the sound of our rattling chains. The corridors here were overgrown with strange plants. Some plants had splendid flowers which spread a stunning perfume. Others smelled of incense. It was everywhere very quiet, from time to time, interrupted only by our suffocating coughs.

At the end of a passage, we found a small river. We saw that many more passages stopped there. Those were terribly dark. The river flowed softly, almost without wavelets, in the direction of a large rock. This rock had a deep tunnel cut into it, which the river found its way through.

Right in front of us was a small jetty, against which lay a small boat. It was not attached but remained bobbing in its place. Banelez boarded it as if it was her property and said that we all should sit on the settees.

As soon as everyone had sat down, the small boat started to move by itself, without any aid. It sailed in the direction of the rock.

The splashing water echoed in the rock passage.

"Where are we going?" I asked Banelez softly.

"We will see," she answered.

In this passage, it was dark, but sometimes we saw a lighted rag blowing along. It resembled a thin trail of mist.

We sailed straight through the rock, and when we came to an end, the small boat moored itself smoothly next to a placard: "PRESENT HERE." Left of it were arrows which indicated the way to follow.

The surroundings were the same as on the other side of the rock, only there was no more soil, as everything was of stone: the ground, the walls, and the ceiling.

We had to pass at least three potholes before we saw a man who was dressed like our hazies sitting behind a large table. Banelez had properly estimated how things were here.

When he saw us coming, he beckoned us to come closer. He sat at the end of the passage, which came to an end behind him.

We lined up in front of his table.

"Is this already the new assignment?" he asked, astonished. "But the previous one has just left!"

“There had to be a new assignment,” I heard one of the hazies quietly and assuredly explaining to everyone in audible language. “That was ordered by Operlon.”

The man bowed politely and opened the wall behind him by taking away a stone lump. He preceded us into an ice-cold, almost dark, stone hall. I could only vaguely make out a long file of chained figures. Their masks had all been pointed at a man in the middle of the room. He also wore the tunic that was common here.

We were welcomed by him with the words: “Oh, still more chained people, welcome!” And to the ex-hazies, he spoke, “Let them be examined; attach them to the other prisoners!”

I was frightened, deathly frightened. What was his intention for us? We lived and therefore would be rejected, and then what would happen to us?

We were attached to each other, and the long file got going. The hazies walked beside us.

“We will be judged on being dead,” whispered Banelez. “They do that by seeing if you are frightened. If you are, you are rejected. Therefore, don’t be afraid; otherwise, we can never escape from here.”

We were conducted through a long passage and had to stand with our backs against the wall. I did not feel very safe, although I had been placed between the Large Oxiture and Banelez.

I should not be frightened, that was easily said. How could I do that? In any case, it was an obligation. I decided to think about something very different, on those things for which I was responsible and not my own person.

The guards extinguished the torches which they carried so that it was almost dark.

“Hold tight,” said Banelez. “Here comes a Pon.”

My eyes adapted themselves rapidly to the darkness. There arrived a strangely hopping and jumping character. He hopped along in front of all the prisoners, but not one showed any sign of fear. The Pon removed the masks from their faces, one by one, and again nobody responded.

The Pon took also took the mask off the Large Oxiture, who remained motionless, staring in front of him.

Now it was my turn. With his slimy hands, he rubbed my hair and then seized my mask. I thought of all the people I had to protect and how this adventure with Quost might end so that I would not think about the painful situation I was presently in. Otherwise, I probably would have screamed in fear.

Banelez also endured the test bravely.

When everyone had their turn, there came movement in the file. We were conducted into a space where we had to sit all on the ground. Except for our own hazies, no guards joined us. This was obviously the end of the ride, for the dead at least.

The hazies lighted their torches again so that we could see each other.

"Release us!" commanded Banelez. The order was immediately executed. I felt considerably relieved.

"What now?" asked the Oxiture.

"We must leave from here rapidly," said Banelez. This had everybody's complete approval.

"But we must first find the hole; that must be close by," continued Banelez. "Further on, it is all very simple. We need only to change ourselves into guards. The hole is itself in the Underworld; thus, we must be able to find it soon."

She rapidly adopted the shape of a guard and conjured a couple of guard outfits for us. We each got a burning torch as well and could proceed again. Banelez led us to a stone door. The dead remained quietly seated and looked after us with their staring eyes.

Beside the door was seated a figure which seemed somewhat familiar to me. I approached their face with my torch and was more shocked than by whatever the Pon had done earlier.

"What is the matter with you?" asked Banelez.

"That's—that's—that's—Toodle ..." I stammered, "I—I know her very well!"

Banelez seemed to understand the situation immediately and lifted up the little elf.

"We will just take her along," she said. She gave Toodle immediately to one of her hazies; he had to carry Toodle.

I was so upset that I had to give my torch to the Large Oxiture. After all, Toodle had eternal life. Why was she then here? We walked quietly through the stone door to another passage. It was there very quiet.

"Could Toodle become alive again?" I asked aloud.

"Shhh ..." said Banelez. "We have not yet left the Underworld."

We walked silently along until we reached a cul-de-sac.

"*Now we've gone astray*," I thought.

Banelez whispered, "The breach must be here somewhere." She stuck her nose in the air and explored the walls carefully.

"There we are; we just have to wait for the 'so many hours,'" she said, satisfied.

We all sat down on the ground to relax. A hazy was put on guard to see that nobody had followed us.

Toodle sat slackly beside me, her head turned down.

"As soon as we are out of the Underworld, she will recover," Banelez assured me.

We sniffed the last remaining Pampus and waited without saying a word. Still, nothing happened. Just when I started to doubt whether we were at the right spot, to my large joy, a small beam of light fell on my face.

"Here is the hole!" shouted Banelez with joy and started immediately to dig. We all intently helped until the hole was large enough to crawl through it. We had no more patience to wait and see if it could be made larger. As soon as possible, we crawled through it and dragged Toodle behind us.

With closed eyes, we stood in the sunlight. After all those days under the ground, we were no longer used to so much light. The hazies immediately regained their own shape, and Banelez also became herself again. The Large Oxiture and I saw our guards' tunics disappear, and we got back our white tunics, luckily without the suffocating masks.

We had, however, time enough to adapt to the sun and remained quietly in the green grass to confer. We had no idea where we actually were.

Toodle lay there still very pale and inanimate, and I thought of moving her eyelids, but shortly thereafter, she opened her eyes.

She looked at me, astonished. "Ody?" she asked feebly.

"Yes," I assured her.

She sat upright and examined my companions with an astonished and questioning look.

"We saved you from the Underworld," I said.

"Underworld?" said Toodle. "But I have never been there! I can remember, however, that I had fallen in a hole at my party ... and yes ... after that, I know nothing. In fact, why were you not at my party? Sseus was very worried. He was afraid you could no longer think, just like the previous time. Where you were?"

"I was underground ... you really were not dead?"

'"Here, no," said Banelez. "She was unconscious, probably from smacking into the ground when she fell in the hole. But you did not fall through this hole, so there must be still more of them that connect to the Underworld. Your friends could not save you because those holes can't be seen. However, you are back again."

Toodle looked around. "No, this is not the spot where I left my party."

I told her about my adventures under the ground and of Quost, whose house and territory we were looking for.

"I will help you," promised Toodle. "Since I am immortal, I don't run any risks."

I found it particularly pleasant to see an acquaintance of mine. It gave me still more courage to fight Quost.

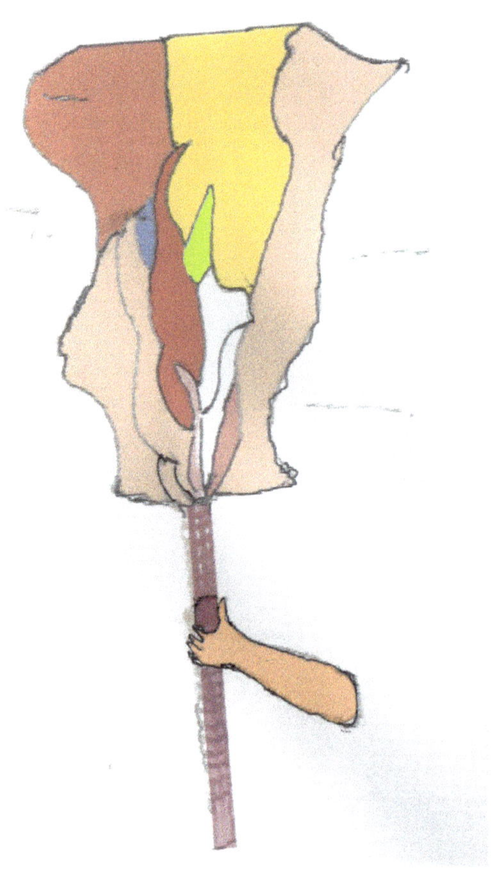

6

We took the time to mostly recover from the events in the Underworld and to get used to the new green environment, but at last, we moved along and continued our travel.

There were many trees, one of which Toodle indicated to us, which had thick juicy leaves. She demonstrated how we could eat them by sucking the clear liquid which flowed in our mouths. It was delicious and very sweet.

There was no path; we walked through high grass and ferns. It was certainly no busy road that we followed. Banelez was leading the way and pushed the plants aside for the Large Oxiture.

Nobody knew the way; we hoped to soon encounter a spy of Quost because it would be nice proof that we were on the right track. But we had to take our chances and not reason too much. We let Banelez decide.

There was a large diversity of plant varieties. Sometimes, there were complete fields full of the most splendid flowers.

Toodle would not be Toodle if she had not picked a couple nice flowers and put them in her black hair. Thus, she looked entirely normal again.

The Large Oxiture felt very happy since he knew that he was relieved from making any more oxygen from himself. He knew now there existed enough holes and could, with an easy mind, leave the Drombles. He already looked younger for his age, and he found more joy in living. The three hazies were, like always, quiet and not sociable talkers.

It was nice to be outdoors again; I just wanted to get rid of the white tunic and the dromble underneath it.

We walked until it became dark. It was again Toodle who taught us, this time, which leaves were suitable as blankets. I did not need them as long as I had still the dromble.

I slept little, however. My worries were too large. Staring at the stars, I thought, "*How could I reach Sseus? How could we fight Quost? Weren't we too few to resist his complete army?*"

The next day, when we were very busy picking berries for lunch, we encountered between the shrubs what appeared to be the first living being of our journey.

It was a fairly small man with a blue cap, red trousers, and a yellow shirt. On his arm hung a basket full of berries.

"Good afternoon," he said politely and tipped his hat to us.

He definitely did not look like a spy of Quost, which was more the pity. Now, we still did not know whether we were on the right track.

He examined the hazies with interest. "Are they feeling all right? They are transparent."

"They are in a good state," I said. "They are like that, but could you perhaps help with some suitable clothing?"

The man looked slightly hesitant but said nevertheless, "All right, come along."

We walked behind the good man to his nice maisonette, which was made entirely of leaves. We were allowed to sit at a round wooden table. He offered us a meal of berries, mush-rooms, and delicious nuts. Afterward, he took some clothes from the cupboard and distributed them to the Large Oxiture, Toodle, and me. The hazies and Banelez needed nothing.

I received short red trousers and a shirt whose sleeves reached to my elbows, but that was nothing. I was glad to be relieved of the dromble and the tunic. I gave my clothes to the little man in exchange, which he appreciated rather a lot. Toodle got a cotton nightdress, which she put over her party dress. Thus, she was less noticeable, she said. The Large Oxiture had to satisfy himself with a morning coat. He put that on over his white garment.

One of the hazies made a sound that resembled laughing. We were not looking very royal this way, but that was not very essential at this time. We were sufficiently satisfied. The dromble-shoes were also exchanged; they were not for running in the outside world, not as nice as in the Underworld. I had now a couple of homemade leather shoes.

There was still another surprise waiting. Behind the maisonette of our host was a small lake, where we could splash and happily wash, one after the other. Banelez and the hazies abandoned their turn. They were apparently not interested.

We thanked the man warmly for his services, all without revealing us to Quost.

"Banelez," I said, "could you and your hazies make yourselves more solid? Otherwise, Quost may soon guess who is in search of him."

She immediately put on a dress, and all three hazies put on pullovers and trousers, all properly in dark blue.

"What are their names, those three?" asked Toodle of Banelez.

"Lim, Mil, and Deb," she answered.

We looked innocent and rural, but we were constantly busy with planning how to disarm Quost. We did agree that, since we were so few and not strong, we had to be clever. We shouldn't let anyone recognize us, under no circumstances be recognized by a spy, and pay a lot of attention so that none of us would be hypnotized.

Everyone made plans to disarm Quost in his or her own manner.

Toodle wanted to give him an elf drink, which makes people listen. Then I must persuade him to abandon his stupid plans and be reasonable.

"I require but a few ingredients," said Toodle. "Ekos plant juice, two grapes, eighteen silent fibers of a noppen tree, and thirty drops of rampart oil. The combination must be completely mixed, very well, and sit for one night in the full moon, and then, ready it is."

The Large Oxiture preferred to transform himself, and then he could easily creep up next to a sleeping Quost. But so far, we didn't even know his place of residence.

Banelez considered all of what she could do in an invisible form.

I found all these plans too weak. We had but to wait to see what our possibilities would be. I asked Banelez to send a hazy ahead to warn us if someone was coming. How good of an idea this was was quickly proven.

The hazy returned in hardly an hour and communicated that there was an armored man approaching.

Banelez, just like Lim and Mil, changed in less than a second into an elegant tree. We dove behind the shrubs and held our breath.

The armored man came barreling down with a lot of noise. He had a bow and arrows with him, ready to shoot. I could clearly hear him panting behind his iron mask. That mask of his would not suit me well. He repeatedly walked a small distance and then turned completely around so that he could continuously observe the entire surroundings. We only emerged when there was no sign of him anywhere.

"What luck!" Banelez exclaimed. "We really can assume

that this was a spy; look what a splendid track he has left behind! Ahead; we are going in the correct direction."

She immediately strode forwards, walking on her tree roots. Now we were really on our way to the house of Quost.

"You know Quost, in fact?" I asked.

"That is to say," replied the Large Oxiture. "I had him over once to visit when he was still small. Banelez was there too. He was an arrogant squirt."

"Oh, yes, I still remember," said Banelez. "Quost could not abide losing. In a game, he did everything to win, even if need be at the cost of his opponent. He wanted to be always the boss, and he yelled, 'The whole world will be miiine!'"

"Yes," resumed the Oxiture. "When eating, he was also very difficult; what he did not know, he did not like. By the way, there sits a small bird in your branches, Banelez. Are you comfortably walking this way, child?"

"Oh, yes, just wait; what shall I become this time?" All of a sudden, there before us stood an iron spy of Quost. I was terribly scared.

"Banelez, don't do that," said the Oxiture quietly. "That's very confusing."

"You are right, Grandfather," said a neat country girl in a beautiful, flowery dress.

We again spent the night outdoors. I now missed my dromble, but the leaves were comfortable enough. Toodle woke me with a bunch of grapes.

"These have been picked by a hazy," she said. The others were also served by her before we continued our journey.

Gradually, our surroundings started to look strange. It soon resembled a prehistoric landscape, with animals that I had never seen before. The most peculiar creatures were hopping around us. Sometimes we saw a crossbreed between a bird and a lizard, snakes with wings. They made no sound.

We knew we were going in the right direction because the

tracks of the iron spy were clearly visible. We walked over a kind of gravel road, so we could see exactly where he had turned around. The crunching gravel under our feet was the only sound that disturbed the silence.

The trees became darker green until they seemed to be almost black. We walked without talking, everyone with their own worrisome thoughts.

Suddenly a small person shot forward from the left-hand side of the path.

"Peekaboo!" he yelled. We were, in fact, too dizzy to be scared, which seemed to disappoint the fellow deeply, as he burst into tears immediately.

That astonished me very much, and I walked to the little fellow. He had a close-fitting outfit that was painted in all colors of the rainbow. It seemed more like he had gotten a couple pots of paint in several colors all over himself.

"Don't worry, hear," I comforted him. "We were very scared, really. Even so terribly frightened that we were nailed to the ground."

There, a smile glided over his face, and he said, "Nool found that nice! You were nice to Nool; therefore, Nool you invited for in house."

His language was poor, but the message was clear. We did not see any harm in following Nool.

Just like a grasshopper, he hopped from the straight path, followed by our entire company. Nool jumped towards a maisonette, which was just as colorful as himself. It was entirely covered with flower petals, which were laid like roof tiles.

"You caming in," he said, whereas he kept the door open invitingly. We stepped into a colorful room, which had been totally covered with flowers. It looked festive and smelled delicious.

"Nool wering preparing something for you!" the fellow informed us. Apparently, he was not familiar with the present tense.

Nool jumped to a corner of the room, from where he retrieved a large calyx surrounded by a couple of smaller ones.

"You would obtaining nectar," he explained. He gave each of us a small calyx, which he filled from a large one. He took one himself too. It tasted very particular, and we indeed recovered. All our lethargy had disappeared.

I wondered, meanwhile, whether we could tell Nool anything concerning Quost; after all, Nool lived in Quost's territory. On the other hand, he could be a confidant of Quost and betray our presence.

It seemed judicious to question him on this matter. "What kind of things you are doing, Nool?"

"Nool wering sweet and were picking flowers today. But Nool not stupid were, because Nool had done also invention. You saw?"

"Yes, let's see your invention," I said, very interested, and the others also pricked their ears.

Nool jumped a couple rounds through the room and then stood quietly with a cylinder in his hand.

"Quiverpipe!" he said proudly and held the tube up high to show it to us. "Here, Nool twins could made were possible! Looked?"

He took Toodle by her hand and placed one end of the tube against her forehead and the other end of the tube against his own.

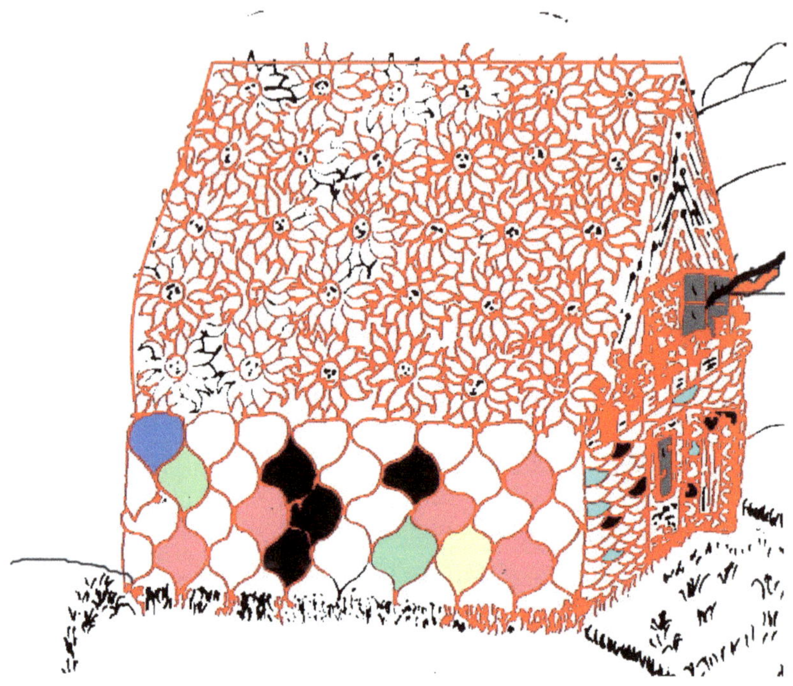

"You now closed eyes!" he ordered Toodle, and she closed them. Upon this, Nool immediately changed his appearance; he became, namely, Toodle!

Therefore, we now had two Toodles, each identical to the other.

"Nicely he?" sang Nool in the same melodious way as Toodle always talked.

We all stood looking with open mouths. The real Toodle just sat down to look at herself.

"I think now exactly the same as Toodle does, and I know what she is thinking at this moment." He spoke neatly now, without errors.

"But this is a terrific invention ... Too... Nool!" called Banelez admiringly.

"Yes," Nool said. "You need only to link two faces to each other with this tube, then one must close his eyes, and the other must them keep open so that he is the one who changes, you understand? He can then think in the same way, ha, ha! Thus, you can change once more, right?"

The same idea probably came to us, namely, to use this tube against Quost!

Nool continued with his explanation. "If I look in this mirror, I only see my own colorful me. In this way, I can become myself again."

He placed himself in front of the mirror which hung between flowers on the wall. Indeed, there was the image of the real Nool in the glass, whereas Toodle stood in front of it.

He put the tube between himself and the image in the mirror, which he ordered, "Close your eyes!"

It had to be a very special mirror, however, because the mirror image obeyed immediately, and the Nool-Toodle became simply Nool again.

"Funnily were, he?" he said in his usual language.

"Yes," said the Oxiture enthusiastically, "but, could we ... eh, I mean ... can we borrow your Quiverpipe for a while?"

Nool became somewhat aloof and asked suspiciously, "For which purpose you wanted using the tube?"

"Because you are so wonderful," explained Banelez rapidly. "You are so clever, and you are also so sweet that you want to lend it to us for a while, right? Just for a couple days ..."

"Well, Nool found it good, but Nool wanted something in return, and Nool there, however, long were thinking over," he said, then he gave the Quiverpipe to Banelez. "When you returned, Nool should let you knew what Nool had wanted."

I let out a sigh of relief; this was at least one more power against Quost.

We still chattered somewhat with Nool, and then he jumped to the path for us. Toodle could not refrain from removing her white dress and dancing in her beautiful blue dancing dress with Nool in the flowers, which pleased the little fellow terribly.

After a short farewell and a last warning from Nool—"Were careful with Nool's tube!"—we left Nool.

7

It had been a refreshing meeting with Nool and certainly not useless. With renewed courage, we dared to encounter Quost. We would keep our eyes open wide, and if he would blink for even a second, we could know exactly what he thought after we used the Quiverpipe. In our reckless mood, we did not doubt that he would lend a willing front to us.

Everyone was delighted and felt careless, and because of this, nobody paid attention anymore as to whether we were followed or watched. The nectar of Nool must have been very nutritious since we felt full of energy and like we could walk a great distance. The day had already started to dawn, and shortly we would witness a sunset in Quost's realm. We had all become extremely lively by our good luck; even the hazies, who usually had such a sad expression in their eyes, looked happy.

I got the responsible task of carrying the Quiverpipe. We intended to even travel all night; nobody wanted to rest, even not the Oxiture.

The sun had only just set when Toodle got a fit of laughter, which could not be cooled off even by an ugly face. She laughed in her melodious manner about everything, even about me.

"Ha, ha, ha, ha ..." she sang loudly. "There we have you, Ody ... ha ha, ha!"

I tried to calm her down because her giggling could possibly be heard everywhere around us, perhaps by Quost.

"It certainly comes from that Quiverpipe," I said to the others. "It must be quite ridiculous to see yourself in living form."

The Large Oxiture smiled too; all the same, he rather preferred that Toodle stopped laughing. But the laughing fits became more and more terrible, and when someone put a hand on her mouth, she spluttered still harder.

"Now, at least everyone knows we are coming," I said to Toodle, who looked at me with tears of laughter in her eyes.

"It can be caused by nerves," said Banelez through the clear, loud, very musical laughter of Toodle.

In the bushes beside us, I heard something rustle. This sound could not have been made by us. I urged everyone to keep quiet. Now I could hear it clearly. There, a branch cracked. With a gesture with my arm, I did send the company ahead, and I dove into the shrub.

I landed on armor. Inside was a spy of Quost! He was at least two heads taller than me. He took me by the arms and lifted me up high, so he could look me straight in the eyes. And this he did.

I saw his glowing black eyes but still could shout to the others. "Go away," I yelled before I was hypnotized. I could not resist. It was a strange feeling; it was as if my body had grown rigid. But I could still hear everything.

I felt myself obey the orders of the spy, such as, "Step in that cart and don't remember anything of what has happened just now."

In normal circumstances, I wouldn't have obeyed such orders, but now I did it without any opposition. Of the following trip, I was unaware.

When I could think clearly again, I was alone in a room that was very familiar to me. It was my own bedroom in the castle tree! The same bed, walls, curtains ... Yes, this had to be my room. For a moment, I thought that I had dreamed everything. But it had all seemed so real. Was I nevertheless in search of Quost? I couldn't figure out this situation until I looked at my clothing. Here, something was not correct! But I decided just to wait.

There was no need for it because, without knocking, an armored man soon entered. His face was familiar, but for the rest, my memory failed me.

"You must appear for Quost," he said bluntly, without waiting to see whether I wanted this.

I was no longer under hypnosis and had no plan to obey his order. What was Quost doing in my castle? And where was my Quiverpipe? I wanted to have it in hand first before meeting Quost. Did I transfer it to somebody or lose it? I did not know, really, but without it, I would be too weak to stand against him.

The spy simply lifted me up; this act I remember, and thereupon he carried me out of my room. If I expected to be in my own corridors, I was deceived. It was a white passage with rough walls.

"Where am I?" I asked aloud.

"In Quost's home."

Uh, oh, that was not very good.

The iron figure carried me up a staircase and along a passage. There, he opened an enormous, thick stone door by pulling on a ring. The stone colossus opened slowly. Not very gently, he pushed me inside and closed the door behind me.

I sighed. I would probably be in a cell and could not count on someone being able to hear me through that thick door.

But I was not alone. Although it was pitch dark, I nevertheless noticed that someone was in the same room. I clearly heard someone breathing. That I found, however, pleasant; at least I was not alone against Quost.

"Is someone here except me?" I called. My voice echoed through the space. It, therefore, had to be a large room.

"Yes," I heard.

There lights flashed from the slits in the rock wall. The entire room was white; in the middle stood a white desk in the form of a Q, and behind it ... sat a pale white man. "I am Quost," he said.

"Sseus...." I said softly, deeply disappointed.

Sseus nodded and offered me one of the white chairs, which stood in front of his desk.

"Astonished, Ody?" asked Sseus quietly.

Rigid as a rake, I stared at Sseus. I was so scared that I couldn't speak a word. This was really a blow, which I had to process.

Quost saw that, for the moment, I had nothing to say. He pulled a string above his desk, upon which an Iron Joe entered with a golden plate full of delicious cookies. He offered them to me, and without thinking, I took one of them automatically.

To my stupefaction, it tasted excellent. How could I admire a cookie under these disconcerting circumstances?

Sseus started to speak during my nibbling. "Ody, I made your own room from the castle tree in this building for you. You will continue to live with me, and for this reason, I want it to make as cozy as possible for you."

"Oh, thank you, Sseus" I could barely strangle the words from my throat.

My brain recovered slowly, but I could ask Sseus some questions.

"How is it that you are Quost, Sseus?"

"That is a long tale, Ody, but I will tell you. I have always strived for power. Unfortunately, I have never been able to reach that, at least never alone. I always needed others for this, such as your aid. You became the King of Existence, not me. What was easier than to take away that power from you? Now I will also get the power of the other, smaller kingdoms. Thus, one becomes King of Whom-but-Wants. There is no further discussion about it. I will keep you here, so, you-want-well, understood?"

Honestly, I did not understand it very well but didn't want to show that. On the contrary, I did see exactly what Quost was up to and already had a counterplan.

"Correct," I said coldly. "There is no other alternative than to submit myself to the situation."

My response must have been smart because Sseus snapped with his fingers at the Iron Joe who still stood behind Sseus' chair with the cookies and ordered him to accompany me to my rooms.

I wanted nothing better because, if I was alone in my room, I could reflect deeply on everything. I was really in a difficult position. No matter how I looked at it, Sseus was and remained my friend. Could he unexpectedly have developed a different character? Would the alleged power make him crazy in his head? Certainly, power is difficult for a human being to carry, but nevertheless ...

It was best to ensure that no rushed and careless decisions were made. I had to protect both Sseus and Banelez, the Large Oxiture, Toodle, and the hazies. Provisionally, I had to ensure that nobody would be trapped. And all that from a bolted room. Quost had no desire to let me escape.

One thing was certain for me. I could not stay here! To start with, I opened my wardrobe. There hung new tunics, so Sseus must not have taken mine. I selected a good and firm travel outfit and put on a pair of well-fitting shoes.

That was one thing. The doors were closed, but the windows could be opened!

When I opened a curtain, I saw it was pitch dark. No moon

to see. Thus, I did not know what height my room was at and if guards possibly stood under the window. The fabrics present in the room were of excellent quality. Thus, I couldn't tear them with my hands to tie them in knots in order to make a climbing rope. I did not find scissors either, so malignantly thorough Quost had been.

Very quietly, I switched off all lights and circumspectly opened a window. Thus, nobody could see me from outside. I listened attentively to see whether I could hear any guards. When, after approximately a quarter of an hour, it still remained quiet, I decided to act.

I took the thick mattress which lay on my bed and threw it out of the window in the hope that it would arrive exactly under my window to break my fall. It was certainly risky because the lowest waft of wind could shift it from its course. However, anything was better than staying in Quost's home.

I took this chance and jumped out of the window.

Splash! I did not arrive on the mattress, but in the water! A moat had apparently been dug around Quost's house. The mattress was nowhere. The water was very cold but not deep. I felt the slippery earthen bottom.

My eyes became somewhat accustomed to the darkness, which meant I could see the bank at a few yards' distance. So, I swam in that direction as soon as possible and climbed soaking wet from the water.

Now it was urgent to find the others. I did not have the slightest idea where they could be. Firstly, I had to leave as soon as possible from this garden. I started to run and fortunately saw in the distance something that looked like an exit gate. I ran through the gate with all kinds of stone "Q"s on it and followed the path further on. I could already see the road more clearly.

My splash in the water might not have passed unnoticed, so for this reason, I made sure to run a reasonable distance from the house. The night was not cold, but he who walks around in wet clothes gets goose flesh, really. I shivered and gasped for want of dry clothes and some sleep. Indeed, I could have had that if I had remained in Quost's house. I ran until I knew that I could no longer. Then I crawled away from the road and under a sheet of leaves. Entirely rolled up and with my arms crossed to protect me against the cold, I fell immediately asleep.

It was a cold hand on my arm which awakened me. Two large green eyes looked at me. The cold hand had not been a hand, in fact, but a gentle paw. The owner of it looked at me with his transparent eyes. I could see in them the rays of the rising sun. There was an enormous, blue, long-haired cat, almost as large as me. He looked deliciously dry and snugglable.

The cat said, "Meow, you must have dry clothes and soon!"

A strange animal. Yesterday we also saw strange creatures here in Quost's realm. The cat helped me up.

"You are very kind, *prrrr*," I said in my nicest tone because I knew that one must always be kind to cats, and it was a very good idea to purr at them.

He gave me a firm pat and went ahead of me, probably to his maisonette.

At daybreak, the landscape looked peaceful, in spite of the almost-black greenness of the trees and the high plants. The flowers were bright enough. Nothing seemed to indicate that Quost made the neighborhood unsafe.

But still, a little shock went through me. Quost was Sseus. Friend and enemy at the same time. Didn't I, as a result, also become my own enemy?

I shook off that idea and remembered that I had been in search of my travel companions. Or had Quost caught them too?

"Meow, this is a spot out of the cold," informed the cat

when we arrived in front of a stone maisonette. We stepped inside, where a huge red mouse was eating cheese. He was exactly as large as his housemate, the cat.

The house had just one room, the floor of which was covered with a thick layer of fuzz.

"Do we have still some dry clothes for this young man, Moos?" the cat asked.

"Yes, sure," said the mouse with a heavy voice. He opened a cabinet, the inside of which was certainly three times larger than it looked from the outside.

"Enter and choose something nice for yourself," said the mouse and pushed me gently into the cabinet. I exchanged my clothes for a deliciously soft sweater in the color of the cat and warm trousers. Now my own togs could dry. The cat took them from me and took them somewhere else, certainly to hang them up.

The mouse had meanwhile put down a considerable piece of cheese for me, which I consumed eagerly.

"I am O—I am Ydo, I meant." I considered at the same moment that neither the cat nor the mouse should be able to repeat my real name to Quost. I did not wish to be caught again.

"We are Moos and Meow; you know it now?" the cat said kindly. He lay, delightfully purring, stretched out on the downy floor.

I wondered whether they had perhaps seen one of the others.

As innocently as possible, I asked, "Do you sometimes see travelers passing by?" I then paid focused attention to the expressions on their faces. But they remained the same.

"Not in ten days," Moos said.

"*Oops*," I thought. "*Then I am badly off track.*" What a pity I could not remember anything of the road which I had taken in the iron spy's cart. I knew, however, that Toodle had been, just like we all were, as a matter of fact, in a cheerful mood, the last time I saw them. If only we could not pass by each other! Who knew how many roads were directed towards Quost?

In any case, I could not wait for them here. I had to go on my way again.

The cat insisted, however, that I stay a while, and to amuse me, he slid a panel aside and showed me his covered garden. The garden had been built entirely under glass.

It seemed many times larger than the maisonette. My clothes hung there, but they resembled an outfit for a giant. Tropical birds and plants clearly felt at ease. There was even a purple parrot with a loud voice who came flying towards me and landed on my shoulder.

"Hello, you!" he shrieked. "Hello. Meow!"

"This is Papa-parrot," said Meow. "There in that palm tree sits Mamma-parrot, and flying there is Child-parrot; you see, Ydo?"

"Hello, Ydo!" called Papa-parrot, visibly glad that he knew my name, and he jumped on my shoulder.

"This is a hobby of mine," explained Meow. "I am fond of birds."

I looked at him suspiciously, hoping that he meant it kindly.

Meow continued with pride, "We had much too little space here until I turned the perspective around; that was very practical."

Now I understood why my clothes seemed so large.

Meow was extraordinarily proud of the catnip that he cultivated.

"The smell fills the complete house," he said. But I smelled nothing. Moos had planted cheesenip.

"Cheesenipshes!" called the bird from my shoulder. "Catnipshes!"

The parrot really was an inquisitive animal. He was happy with each new word he heard.

After I had exuberantly praised their garden, I put on my own clothes, which once back in the room regained the correct size, and gave my farewell to the two kind animals.

They still crammed my pockets with cheesenip and catnip, and Papa-parrot said, "Bye, Ydoolshe!" I went to the path. I wanted to follow it in the hope of meeting the others.

Bravely I said to myself, "Where there is a will, there is a way."

8

I decided on a route, which I followed firmly in my head; it would be in my best interest to either quickly find the way to Quost's house or just remain far away from it.

The situation seemed rather hopeless. I did not want Sseus to be defeated, but neither did I want to be vanquished by him. It was my task to find a solution. I could not expect that the Large Oxiture and Banelez would understand my point of view; in the end, their royalty and the destiny of their nations were at stake. It was therefore essential to divert the attention of the monarchs as far as possible from Sseus, at least temporally.

I could still suggest to Quost that he consent to have my kingdom and my captivity on the condition that he did not besiege the others.

But so far, we were not there yet. I had, as King of Existence, to find a solution. That was now my task in life.

All this did not mean that I felt rather lonely at the moment. It was sultry, wet weather, and there was, except for the sound of my own footsteps, nothing to hear. I saw still no track of the others. What were they doing right now?

Sighing, I continued on my way. I paid sharp attention because it was my intention not to be surprised again. Thus, it came, in time, that I saw in the distance two suspicious spots coming up behind me. I took no risk and dove into the brush instead. I had more than sufficient opportunity to hide.

My patience was rewarded. Two iron figures walked past my shelter, chattering.

"Now we have really searched the complete surroundings without finding something, Kralis. In these few hours, he can't have reached so far. What a calamity would it be if we don't find him? He must be able to do the most terrible things!"

'"I bet he is still somewhere hidden in the castle, ready to seize our leader," answered Kralis. "If that's so, I do not feel safe anymore. We had better return home."

That was fortunate for me. My luck did not let me down. I watched them going away for long enough to be sure that Quost's helpers walked back in the same direction from where they had come. Relieved, I stepped from the shrubs and then immediately dove back in there. On the other side of the road, as it happens, someone had stood up!

"Ody!" called a voice which resembled very much Toodle's. "Is that you?"

I emerged, carefully crawling, and saw her standing. She was alone.

"Toodle!" I called, delighted, glad to have found her again. "Where are the others?"

"I have a hazy with me; the Oxiture and Banelez have returned with the others to look for reinforcements. The Oxiture will try to mobilize a strong army of Drombles. We have in mind to besiege the house of Quost."

"*Oh, help!*" I thought.

"I stayed here with Deb in the hope of finding you, and now I have you. Tell me what happened."

Without too much exaggeration, I told my complete

adventure to Toodle, except, of course, who Quost actually was. It was now essential to mislead her.

"... and thus, I had been locked up in that heavily guarded room, but heroic as I am, I jumped down from at least three stories high. Despite the wild pursuit by the guards, I nevertheless escaped from their hands—" I was fully taken in by my half-fibbed tale.

Toodle interrupted my story by asking dryly, "Ody, what does Quost actually look like?"

"Uh ... who? Oh ... Quost ... hmm, Quost looked, well ... but those Iron Joes were behind me; he ... and then ... well, yes, you have heard how frightened they were of me; you heard it yourself just now how I am capable of the most terrible things."

"Okay, well, you have escaped in any case; that is the most essential thing," said Toodle, making an end to my tale.

"What happened with you afterward?" I asked.

Toodle told me that she stopped laughing after my kidnapping and had taken over the guardianship of the Quiverpipe, which I fortunately had dropped. The Oxiture had then taken the decision to call up his Dromble army. After a general consultation, it was decided to leave Toodle behind with the hazy Deb to look for me, whereas Banelez and the Large Oxiture would return to the dangerous tunnels in the company of Tim and Mil. They blamed themselves for their thoughtlessness, as they had not thought earlier of bringing the army along.

"We now have a splendid plan. We will catch one of Quost's Iron Joes, and by using the Quiverpipe, we will convert all Drombles into armored Joes, and thus the complete army can pass unnoticed through Quost's empire."

"But then the Drombles will think exactly the same as the Joes!" I objected in the hope of finding a weak spot in this terrible plan against Sseus.

"You don't have to worry because Quost is the King of Who-Wants-Best, therefore his people will not be very faithful. We must hide as well as possible until the Oxiture and Banelez return with the army," said Toodle.

"Then I will take the Quiverpipe under my care," I decided and took the tube away from her. It seemed to me to be safest that I had the responsibility. I could, in one way or another, "lose" it and thus remove a weapon against Sseus.

My first care was to ensure that the army stayed away as long as possible. I needed time to prepare a good plan which would bring Sseus to reason. I should first lead Toodle as far as possible from Quost's house. As soon as I knew how to handle Sseus, I would return alone.

I was startled when Toodle said, "I wished that Sseus was here; I miss him. Do you not?"

"Sseus? ... oh, Sseus! Yes, I haven't seen him for a long time ..." I lied. "But, about hiding ourselves, shouldn't we better go part of the way to meet the incoming army? With the tube, I mean."

"Yes, perhaps that's not a bad idea," Toodle answered. "All the sooner we will be in safety. I only don't know exactly how we will get there."

Reassuring Toodle that she only had to follow me, we distanced ourselves more and more from Quost's house.

We walked for hours, granting ourselves but small breaks. The surroundings changed slowly. The strange black-greenness of the trees and the brush changed gradually into soft-brown trunks. The path led us over the soft-springy leaves of a forest. The trees there had no everyday appearance either. I saw a specimen that, in fact, only existed as a trunk. Others had enormous roofs of dense foliage, supported by three trunks at the same time. Toodle noticed a tree that had lively roots waving above the ground. It all looked so very fairy-like that we did not dare to drink from the splashing creeks which frequently crossed our path.

"Ody," said Toodle, worried. "I can't remember having passed this road before. Are you sure we are walking in the right direction?"

"It is perhaps not your right one, but I find it correct," I answered her.

She only frowned for an answer. All of a sudden, she seized me by my arm, and she was all attention.

"Listen," she whispered. "I hear people laughing."

I just wanted to say that this is no unusual phenomenon with people, but I quickly realized that one would not expect such a sound in this forest.

Circumspectly, we walked in the direction of the sound; our hazy went first. Close by, Toodle and I hid behind a shrub through which we could watch.

We saw a remarkable, lively spectacle. It largely resembled one of my most beautiful paintings in the library of the castle. I had frequently looked at it with pleasure. At the colorful dresses, the white-powdered wigs, the picnic baskets full of all kinds of delicious things. And to the little fellow on the left, with his red jacket and a horn at his mouth.

There at a creek, on the grass, sat figures of the same type.

"Emilie, do me the honor of accepting a grape from me," said a gentleman in blue velvet. He sat with his back to us and spoke to a lady in red.

"Your honor increases with each grape," she laughed, whereas she accepted the fruit.

The picnic hosts were visibly amused. There was even an orchestra that provided pleasing music.

Toodle leaped with impatience to join the company. She threw her nightdress into the shrubs and pulled me behind her.

The music stopped immediately when we appeared.

Emilie approached us with the words: "Oh, charming!" All persons applauded.

“Congratulations, you have won!” called the enthusiastic Emilie, expressing it in an elegant way.

“Now we are complete, and you were only two years behind, ha, ha, ha!”

We chuckled politely, although we didn’t understand at all what there was to laugh about.

Toodle miraculously adapted herself quickly and asked,

"And what again was the prize?"

"Much honor, of course!"

Emilie caught us each by the hand and seated us next to a fruit dish on the grass.

With all the worries we had so far, we had forgotten to eat. This lack could now be remedied.

Grooms brought us so many more dishes. Roasted apples, a so-called "honor dish," a mixture of very soft peaches, a most delicious cake, the crispest cookies, and the largest bonbons.

I was nevertheless curious why and how we had won. Thus, I asked a lady dressed in yellow silk, who sat next to me, "Why did we win?"

"The first invitees already arrived two years ago. You know that, don't you?" she answered kindly.

"Oh, yes, I recall it now!" I said as it seemed to be a very bad idea to reveal our identity to this strange company.

"How do you know whether other guests might arrive ?"

"Twenty-five guests have been invited, and we were lacking only two."

With this answer, I was for the moment satisfied with our safety and also with the prize. Everyone tried to bow to us as deeply as possible. I wondered who the real guests were and who we were thought to be. It was my hope that they stayed away as long as possible. I did not want to be considered an intruder.

The long-term festival continued undisturbed. The orchestra played a lively waltz. Everyone stood up to dance. We made a large circle together and danced around and around and around until our heads spun. Exhausted, some fell laughing into the grass.

The festival lasted until very late in the evening. When darkness came, one guest lighted lanterns, and a large campfire was set up, as they had done every evening.

It was nice to stay with these people. I forgot my worries for a moment.

After consuming a couple of warm sausages, we went to sleep around the campfire in order to start the next morning refreshed for the following festival or rather with the continuation of this one.

When everyone was asleep and satisfied, I thought of Sseus, and I did miss him but not Quost. I wondered whether I would tell Toodle what I knew, but it seemed simpler and safer to keep her in the dark. Ultimately, she had nothing to do with my struggle with Sseus.

But I still had to stop a marching army!

Exhausted, I fell finally asleep.

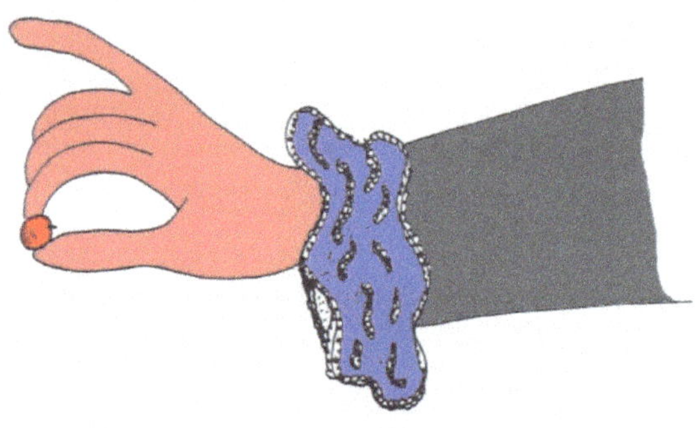

9

In the morning, I was shaken awake roughly by an enthusiastic Toodle. “Come quickly, Ody; everyone has gone already. We must go quickly to the lake.”

Drowsy, I let myself be dragged along to a small lake, where all the guests already paddled quite busily.

“Oh, look here, Ody, it’s terribly delicious, such a morning swim!” Toodle said and went wading into the water with naked feet.

Still not entirely awake, I plopped down on the grass.

“Why are you celebrating a festival each day?” I asked the nearest paddler.

“Each day is a holiday!” he called gladly.

In the lake, elegant white-painted wooden jetties had been built, to which elegant rowing boats were moored. Some of the guests rowed peacefully over the glassy water. I saw Emilie passing, held by a gentleman in green, pulling with all her strength on a fishing rod above water.

“Oof, that must be a big fish!” resounded over the water.

It was an enchanting scene, and the gentle music of the orchestra seemed to blow like a breeze over the lake.

"How poetic," I sighed. "While a Dromble army marches against my friend, am I here looking idly at a water festival."

"Ha, ha, ha!" sounded suddenly over the water. It was Emilie, who had hooked an anchor. "Look here, I have caught our own anchor, ha, ha!"

She roared with laughter. Her fishing rod had been entirely bent over, and she had to be held firmly in place by two people so that she would not fall from the small, unstable boat.

After everyone had waded and paddled enough, grapes, peaches, and cherries were eaten. It was clear that the festival had not paused for long since Emilie came forward with a silk rag, which she tied over Toodle's eyes to loud cheering. "We will play blind man's bluff," Emilie announced.

"The winner from yesterday can be the first blind woman today," proclaimed Emilie, enthusiastically applauding. Upon saying this, she took Toodle by the shoulders and dizzyingly twisted her around.

"Up you go; clear off!" Emilie jumped elegantly away from Toodle.

Everyone tried to avoid the searching hands of the "blind woman." Some even took refuge in the small boats. Toodle was not terribly successful. It was also difficult for her to recognize anyone since she did not recall the names of all guests.

She ran along with a considerable speed behind me. I jumped onto the jetty in the hope that Toodle would not dare to follow me there for fear of falling into the water. But she did not doubt, and with a broad victory smile, she rushed to the extreme point of the jetty, where I stood with bated breath. She could touch me at any moment. But instead of doing that, she twisted herself around with a jerk.

Branches had cracked between the trees. Perhaps she thought she would find there a new victim. She immediately ran in the direction of the sound.

"Oof!" I sighed, but quickly I felt my breath was blocked in my throat, and there was a wave of agitation in me. Near Toodle, two people I had not seen before stepped from the forest. It was a young woman and a man, both with extraordinary and remarkable looks. This was not due to their clothing, because that was of the same type as everyone wore here, but their faces were very particular. The young woman most resembled a white angel. Her face was as white and smooth as the finest porcelain. Her deep dark-blue eyes shone like diamonds. On her head, she wore a high white wig, and she had been dressed in a white silk ball gown covered in gold embroidery, with a wide skirt and a very slender waist.

The man was likewise eye-catching, with a nose that was as straight as a ruler and eyes which changed color all of the time. On his elegant head sat a white wig, with horizontally rolled up curls above the ears and a low horse tail on his neck, tied with satin bows.

Toodle had meanwhile "caught" the man and tried to recognize him. The young man smiled.

"Oh, but this is impossible!" Toodle said, disappointed. "I don't really know this person!"

"Let me present then myself," said the young man with a perfectly mastered and elegant voice as he removed the cloth from Toodle's eyes and gave her a kiss on the hand. "I am called Aristo; at your service, beautiful elf."

Toodle looked astonished. This man had recognized her as an elf! That meant that he was acquainted with the elves and, therefore, must have traveled from far away.

"And this is my ... eh ... sister, Egance," continued Aristo, presenting the young woman to Toodle.

"I am Toodle," answered Toodle to complete her part of the introduction.

The other guests had crowded together to welcome the newcomers.

"I had not expected more guests!" called Emilie. "The last two arrived yesterday.... then you are probably the firsts of the following festival, right?"

The new pair nodded in the affirmative. They did not seem to want to claim the title of "last-arrived guests." There was, therefore, no danger that we might be treated as festival intruders.

"Very good, then we will now start with the following festival." Emilie was engulfed with joy; she enjoyed every festival.

The new pair amused themselves, extremely happy. They chatted with everyone.

"How did you know that I am an elf?" asked Toodle when Aristo came nearby again.

"I have traveled a lot in my life and have encountered many people, including elves, and for this reason, I quickly recognize who I meet," he answered. He looked from Toodle to me, and then his eyes turned dark green.

He told us tales about his travels and adventures. And about regions we had never heard of.

"I was once caught in an impregnable citadel," I heard him saying, "the possession of the 'Angry Brothers.' That was because I wanted to disarm their leader, the 'Most Charming Sister.' She believed, as it happened, that everyone had to become her subordinate because they would be then in safer hands than with her 'Cumbersome Cousins' and 'Awkward Cousins.' But to make a long tale short, I astonishingly succeeded in escaping from the hands of the 'Angry Brothers' in an ingenious manner and placed all property in the hands of the 'Cousins and Nieces.' Not for long, I fear. Recently I learned that the roles had reversed, and the 'Angry Brothers' had once again regained power with their 'Cumbersome Sister.'"

It was a strange tale, seemingly without beginning or end. However, Aristo became, all the same, more sympathetic. He seemed to me a brave and courageous man who would not recoil from any danger. His attitude was proud and lofty, as a result of which soon Toodle and I had an additional friend.

His sister, Egance, remained at a distance but always kept Aristo in view, her eyes with a doubtful expression.

The festival went on and on. I became slightly nervous about it because, in my opinion, I was badly wasting my time when I had something better to do. The Quost problem, by all means, had not yet been solved, and the army of the Drombles could arrive any moment.

Aristo had gained my faith; he was certainly no spy of Quost, and because he was a man who fought for justice, I decided to tell him some details concerning Quost.

"Aristo, do you know Quost?" I asked him in a straightforward manner.

"No, who is that?" he answered in a cold and disinterested tone.

"You are at this moment on his territory. You know that I am the King of Existence—"

"Yes, I already presumed that," he interrupted me and his eyes shone pale blue.

"This Quost is after my power and that of some of my friends." I told Aristo about the Large Oxiture, Banelez, and the hazies, about the Quiverpipe, and that together we would take up arms against Quost. Aristo listened attentively. A thing I did not tell him, however, was the role played by Sseus in this history.

I wished that Aristo would help me in the fight against Quost and stopping the army. If it proved to be necessary, I could always provide him with more information.

"Darn!" Aristo said. "We must firmly tackle that Quost!"

He said "we;" therefore, he was prepared to help!

"Dear Ody, you couldn't have met a better fellow to leave that to! Accept my services. I am ready for you!"

He shook hands with me solemnly. I was glad to have an ally. Later Aristo would understand, however, why I didn't want to have Sseus defeated by an army.

We toasted to our friendship with wine. From the corner of my eye, I saw Egance smiling with satisfaction at her brother.

"We will immediately leave tomorrow; now, we must use our scarce time wisely. It is my plan to kidnap Quost and bring him to other ideas by using the Quiverpipe," I said to Aristo.

I concealed that I wanted to kidnap Sseus in order to bring him to a safe spot. I intended to have him guarded and protected there by Aristo. Afterward, I would have to dupe the army.

It was all very complicated. I had to pay attention so I did not fail. When I had discussed my departure plans with Aristo, I decided to inform Toodle. She was a fierce combatant against Quost; I had but to tell her that I fought not only against but also for Quost.

I explained to her my way of thinking, still half-doubting whether I should do this.

"Toodle," I said. "I have seen Quost."

"Yes, that you have told me already," she answered, disinterested.

"Sseus is Quost!" I said in a more persuasive tone.

Toodle looked at me with large, frightened eyes. She hardly could get a word out except a very soft "Oh, no!"

I continued my story since she would not interrupt anyway.

"Toodle, you must understand that I will not fight against Sseus; he is my very best friend, whether or not he is Quost. I will not allow someone to harm him. I must protect him."

"But Ody, if Sseus is really Quost, would he actually take away your power?" Toodle objected.

"Yes, Quost will do it. But that is not the most terrible thing."

With these words, I probably left Toodle in complete confusion.

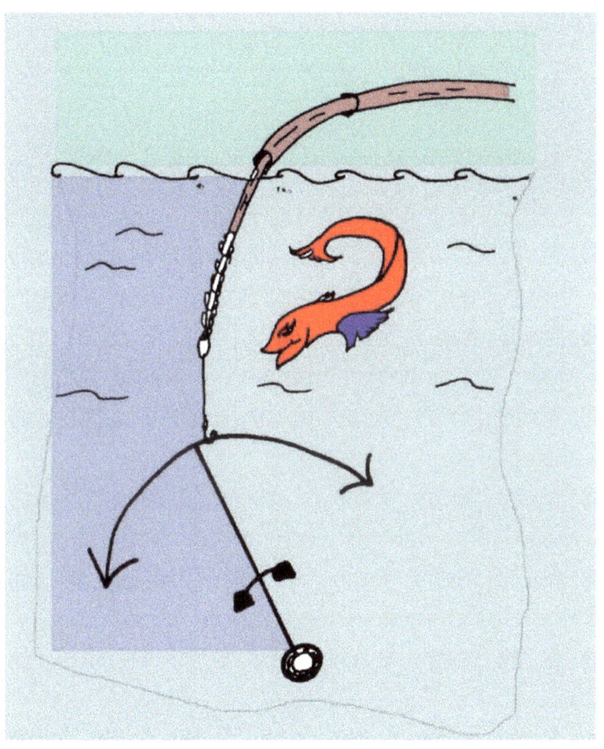

10

The next morning, I was up early. I awoke Toodle and Aristo, who preferred not to bring his sister along. I took the Quiverpipe, and Toodle looked after a basket with something nice that remained from the festival. Aristo left behind a farewell note for the still-sleeping Egance, with probably a couple well-turned phrases, and the three of us left the festival field.

"Follow me; I know the way out of the forest," said Aristo.

We walked through the wet forest with the strangely formed trees. Some rays of sunshine shone through the trunks. We heard many birds singing happily. Some fluffy animals jumped from one tree to another with a loud cracking of branches.

For this reason, we were not scared when, with much racket, something fell from a high tree on our path.

"Ah, that's a hazy," said Toodle, "I almost had forgotten him. He is always so inconspicuous. It is true that I had not yet this morning thought about Deb."

Aristo examined Deb with astonished, pale-blue eyes and said nothing further. Deb said nothing either but floated faithfully behind me.

Now we were four on the way to Quost. I ran as fast as I could. I wanted Quost to be kidnapped before the army could reach him.

Toodle's face looked dull and absent. It must have been a complete shock to her to listen to my tale about Sseus. She clearly doubted my tale; she liked Sseus so much, and her faith in him was high.

The ideas which occupied the hazy were just as unclear for me as he was blurry.

"Do you know for certain this is the right way out of the forest?" I asked Aristo when we had walked for hours between the trees. "Coming to the festival through the forest was much shorter."

"There are many ways," said Aristo. "But first, we must be far away from the remaining guests. It is fairly impolite to leave the festival after only a few days."

I smiled.

"We must arrive, in any case, at rocks," I said. "I have been in Quost's home. It seemed to be a castle that was cut into a rock. It was, however, dark when I liberated myself, but I can certainly remember the way. There was also a kind of canal or river that twisted around the rocks."

Aristo nodded. "I am well acquainted with the surroundings, and if I am not mistaken, we walk in the right direction. You have met Quost?"

Toodle and I looked at each other.

"Yes," I said. "I would recognize him."

Aristo's eyes glowed cobalt blue.

Toodle understood that I had not yet informed Aristo concerning Sseus.

When we had just started resting under a tree, she asked me, "In fact, how do you think we might kidnap Quost? His castle must be an impregnable fortress."

"That's my specialty!" called Aristo enthusiastically. "And I think that the Quiverpipe can help us in good service."

He had already prepared his plan and proposed that we should transform ourselves into hazies by using the tube.

That was a brilliant idea. This way, we could enter the rock castle almost unnoticed.

"In fact, we don't need to kidnap Quost, not at all," said Aristo. "Rather we can treat him on the spot with our secret weapon. Why take the effort to first transport him to another spot?"

I knew that he was right, that it would be more practical, but it was not my intention to make Sseus someone else; I only wanted to isolate him.

"It is safer to take him away from his palace," Toodle, who understood me, said helpfully. "Then we can first try to dissuade him of his intentions, and if that does not succeed ..." She sighed.

It was a difficult problem for her too.

Aristo shrugged his shoulders. "Well, if you both say so."

By then, the picnic basket was half empty, and so we walked further. We decided, as soon as the rocks came in sight, to change ourselves into hazies. We first should have a place to hold the kidnapped Quost, a cave in the rocks or an abandoned house.

We walked the whole day and were already quite tired when Toodle said, "Look, we are there!"

It was true; we arrived at last at the edge of the forest, and in front of us was an unhappy rocky mass as broad as the horizon in the orange glow of the setting sun. Between the forest and the rock lay an open plain. It was too dangerous to cross it without precaution because Quost's spies would see us too easily. I recognized in the distance the stone gate with the Qs, and there behind it were two armored guards. The rock castle was indeed cut into a rock. From the front, it was impossible to see how large it was. The rocky frontage betrayed nothing of the number of corridors and rooms which were possibly hidden inside it.

"We must already be hazies when we cross the plain," said Toodle, "so we travel unnoticed. But we haven't even visited the hazies' cottage."

We sat down to watch the orange sun, which was now disappearing behind the rock peaks. We decided to attack that evening. Aristo declared his willingness, as soon as it was dark, to look for a shelter where Quost could be accommodated.

One by one, we changed ourselves into hazies with the indispensable Quiverpipe of Nool.

When it was dark, Aristo disappeared like a phantom in the night. We three remained behind and, an hour after his departure, would walk in the direction of the gate, where we would meet up with each other once again.

It was a strange sensation to be a hazy because I became Deb not only physically but also mentally. I did not worry for Sseus and had only one aim, to kidnap Quost. The army of Drombles I now waited for with interest, but I was not the least bit concerned for the consequences. I felt in me the impulse for absolute obedience.

After waiting for about an hour, we stood up as one, all at the same time. Three people strong, we descended the forest hill and crossed the plain. As fluff in the wind, we floated over the ground.

It was as if I dreamed. Without tension and without any emotion, we flew towards the large Q-gate. There Deb waited for us already; that had to be Aristo. We could barely discern him when the iron guard looked straight through us in the almost-dark as if we were air. We all easily crawled through the bars of the gate and floated over the path that led to the enormous stone door. There walked an armored guard with a very white man. The man was entirely white, his hair, skin, tunic, everything except the eyes. He had splendid golden eyes. We slid past him without much interest.

Until I turned around. I furrowed my eyebrows because on the back of his white tunic was a golden Q. With my hazy brain, I concluded that this had to be Quost. I signaled the others to follow me, though they had already approached the stone door and had succeeded in opening it to a slit. At that moment, Quost walked out the gate with ease, without even one of his men following him.

"Quick!" said the first of the hazies. "We must take him by his arms and float him to the shelter which I have found." We did what he said, and with Quost hanging between me and another hazy, we flew high in the air, behind the hazy who was most likely Aristo.

The two guards at the gate looked confused by the flying Quost, but they did not sound the alarm.

Aristo led us to the backside of the palace, where the rocks were. There had been an enormous space chopped into the rocks, where we flew inside. We landed quietly on a rough stone floor.

Quost had not said one word the entire time.

"Am I not a genius?" asked Aristo, not very modestly, with a gesture indicating the large space. We nodded in agreement.

Aristo took a mirror from his hazy clothing. Now we knew for certain that it was him; who else would have a mirror with him!

"Now, to be myself again," he explained. He used the Quiverpipe and changed himself into the trusted figure of Aristo, with his wig and silk outfit. Exactly as Nool had demonstrated.

Toodle and I followed his example, and only then did I realize that we had kidnapped Sseus.

"Ody!" was the first thing Sseus exclaimed when he saw

me changing from hazy into my real self. “Toodle,” he said with as much enthusiasm.

Aristo examined us with strange, cat-like green eyes.

“Sseus, we have kidnapped you,” I started with a masterful voice.

“Sseus?” asked Aristo in utmost stupefaction. “Why do you call this Quost ‘Sseus?’”

“Because Sseus is Quost,” I explained to him.

I heard Sseus gasp for breath.

“I only learned a short time ago that my very best friend is also my largest enemy,” I told Aristo with regret.

Then a strange and painful silence fell. Beneath me, I heard water slosh against the rocks.

“Hey, are we close to the sea?” I asked myself, dazed, as it was not entirely dawning on me in these circumstances. I was only called back to reality by the beautiful pure voice of Sseus, who said perfectly quietly, “Ody, I am not Quost.”

Everyone stared at him, bewildered. I was entirely baffled. On the one hand, I was incredibly happy with this declaration, but on the other hand, I was also suspicious. Wasn’t this a clever thing to say if he was Quost?

“You must believe me on my word of honor, Ody,” continued Sseus. “What I am about to tell you is no fairy tale.”

We were curious enough to listen to his plea. We all sat down around him and listened attentively.

“Not so very long ago, I learned from a distant friend that there was someone, who wanted to take your power, Ody. You know that you are my best friend and I know you well. It is inconceivable that whoever could take your place. I decided to not yet inform you of the imminent danger and first to conduct an investigation for myself. After the Toodle’s party, I immediately set out on a journey. Thus, I learned that a certain Quost, King of Whom-but-Wants, had made cunning plans to relieve you of your royalty. I went to his territory, with all dangers that involved, and reached his domain. I wanted to get even with Quost. For you, that would be too dangerous, in my opinion. The King of Existence should not perish. I'd rather myself than you. Don't ask me how, but I astonishingly succeeded in entering his palace, where I found an excellent shelter. There I heard a spy enter, panting heavily and calling to a guard, 'Inform our king that the King of Existence has been spotted on his grounds!'

'Our powerful king is unfortunately not present,' said the guard, 'but I will tell him as soon as he returns.'

'Then do it as soon as possible because I know for certain that my report will interest him.'

I was startled to hear about your presence. It would seriously upset my plans and be very dangerous for you if you were to interfere with the battle. Thus, I had to immediately undertake some plan of action. I knew Quost was not present, and I could nicely make use of that knowledge. I stole to his room and sat down in the twilight behind his white desk. I rang a guard and ordered him, with a disguised voice, which worked out excellently, to catch you. I commissioned a room to be made for you, one identical to yours. I made a precise sketch of your room in the castle tree for them.

Thus, you were kidnapped and conducted before me. It seemed to me safest to provisionally pose as Quost because I knew you would never undertake something against me. You would no longer fight Quost. I wanted to keep you in your comfortable room as long as possible until I had defeated Quost. Who would have expected that you would flee and counterattack? As a result, my plans failed, and I had to fetch you back, with the risk that you wouldn't allow me to continue to fight Quost on my own.

I was just too late. Shortly before my departure, Quost returned home unexpectedly, and I was overpowered. The guard understood that there could not be two Quosts at the same time in the castle. Afterward, I blamed myself for not being alert enough. I have not seen Quost himself. He probably did not know who I was and what I had done because, just before I was kidnapped by you, I was released and expelled through his gate."

I had listened with glowing cheeks to Sseus' story. No, nothing of this had been invented; Sseus was himself again and had spoken the truth. I was glad that Sseus had explained the situation. It was a relief that my brain was no longer under such heavy pressure from the alleged treason of Sseus.

It was now my turn to explain one thing and another. "You have no idea how much I was taken by surprise by the discovery that you were Quost," I said. "You were right that I wouldn't do you any harm, but there is one thing you don't know yet, and that is that Banelez, the Queen of Non-Existence, and the Large Oxiture, King of Below-Existence, are also threatened with a complete takeover by Quost."

I told Sseus what they had told me and how we were going to battle together.

"For this reason, I escaped from your hands. You, as Quost, should have been, as it happens, attacked by Banelez

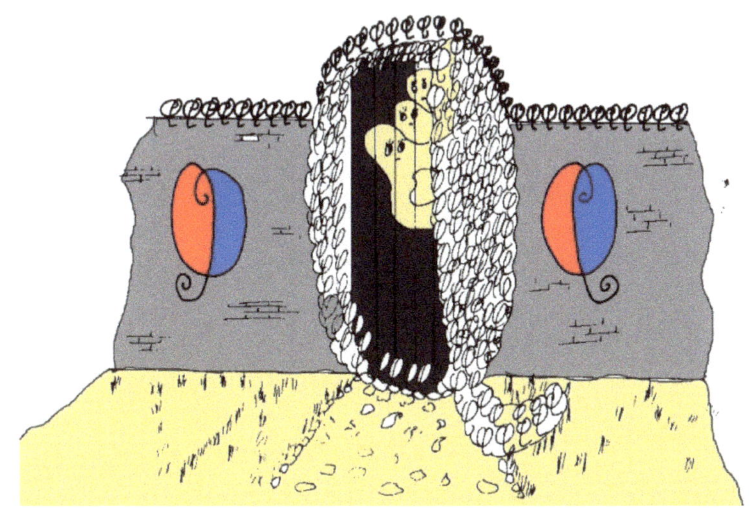

and the Oxiture. Therefore, I had to defend you against that. It is noble of you to protect me, but you cannot stand alone against Quost. Quost can be only defeated by monarchs."

Then I cited the poem recited for me by the Oxiture, which I knew already by heart.

Toodle told Sseus how she had been taken away from the Underworld, and Aristo told once more his tale about the 'Most Charming Sister' and the 'Angry Brothers.'

When we all had poured out our hearts, we fell asleep, dreaming of the drastic changes.

II

"Ody, wake up," Aristo said the next day with much concern in his voice while he gently shook me awake. "Ody, I must wake you with a poorly comforting message that we are now trapped in the cave. There is no exit, I'm afraid."

"Ah ha," I said, nevertheless keeping my self-control. "Then we must look for a possible way to leave here."

It was not as dark in the cave as it was the previous evening, but there was not much light. Where yesterday there had been an entry to our accommodation, it appeared now to be blocked by a large boulder. The barrier did not cover the complete opening, so some thin sun rays could still pass through.

Nobody panicked over this unexpected detention. I sat down calmly on the stone floor and thought about a solution to our new problem. Toodle felt the entire wall in search of an emergency exit.

Sseus, just like Aristo, was deep in thought. I thought how yesterday I had heard the sea sloshing under our shelter.

It was possible that the rocks bordered the sea. This cave had nevertheless been dug by something or someone. Also, the sea might, after so many years, have been able to carve it with her eternal waves.

"Look here!" said Toodle. "This cave is hexagonal. The ceiling and the floor are flat and exactly right, but the sidewalls seem to be dented from the inside. This cave has no natural form."

That was strange because a cave eroded by the sea would have a beautiful, round, and smooth form.

I did not consider this for long. I proposed to my friends that we push together with all our forces against the boulder that barred our exit. With a bit of luck, we could slightly move it out of its place so that we could slip by. Afterward, we could transform ourselves into hazies, slip beyond Quost's house, and meet the army.

It was nice that I no longer had to stop the Drombles. They were even extraordinarily welcomed by me; we could use them in the fight against Quost.

Toodle was already pushing with outstretched arms against the boulder, and Sseus, Aristo, the hazy, and I followed her example.

'"Oooone ... twoooo ... *hup*!"

I had, in fact, thought that the sea had thrown the boulder against the cave and that a lot of strength would be required to move the thing, but when we started together, the boulder shot like a bullet into the air and us behind it as well.

We flew into the air and the sunlight. Under us was the swirling sea, and I prepared myself for a morning dive.

From above, I saw an enormous, steep rock wall full of hexagonal caves. Some were, just like ours had been, closed with a boulder. It seemed that the whole rocky wall was a huge honeycomb. "*Splash*, *splash*, *splash*," I soon heard, and into the water I went, sneezing because it was so cold. Toodle, panting and shaking her hair, came swimming beside me and looked with astonished eyes at the spectacle.

"Look there!" she called, and she pointed with her wet hand to a couple of enormous bees which flew to and from the caves. They were so large that their bodies could just enter the holes, where we had had enough space for five persons. They were very busy with dragging boulders to block the caves and seemed in their hurry to not at all notice even one of us. One bee was just cleaning up our former cave and swept all rubbish from the cave to the sea. I saw how our Quiverpipe, which we had left behind, was just thrown out and disappeared promptly in the waves.

"Oh, help!" I yelled and swam as fast I could to the spot where our secret weapon had fallen in the blue sea. I dove, with open eyes, down as deep as I dared, but I was too late. The tube had already disappeared. The others, who had seen the drama, splashed after me. Sseus had a desperate expression in his eyes.

There went our plan. The complete anti-Quost plan had fallen in the water. Without the Quiverpipe, we could not become hazies. The Dromble army could not be converted into Iron Joes. How could we transport the complete army through the hostile region now?

These thoughts flashed through me until one of the bees allowed herself to notice us. She flew above us, level, and with six legs attached to her hairy belly, she laughed at us.

"*Bzie, bzie, bzie, bzie*!" she said, and continuously giggling, she came down to fish all five of us out of the water at the same time.

"Everybody must hold on to one of my legs, *bzz ... bzz ...*"

"*Leg?*" I wondered, confused as to why I needed to hold onto a leg.

It seemed safer on a large hairy hind leg, which I grasped.

"All well installed?" she asked and looked attentively with her large black eyes at her legs. She did not wait for an answer but immediately shot high up into the air.

I must say that I did not find these bees too nice at first sight after they threw our Quiverpipe away. But this bee seemed to have nothing malicious in her attitude; regardless, we had been saved from the water and flew nicely through the air.

Above me, I heard the fast-moving wings, and I smelled the flowery fragrance of the bee legs.

Our pilot flew into a comb which was still much larger than our place for the previous night and landed carefully on the ground. We each stepped down from our bee legs and waited to see what would happen.

"Say, strange rascals," said the bee, "you don't have to tell me that you have been born recently, do you?"

"No, we are 'shelters-for-the-night,'" said Toodle, slightly annoyed, "and you have thrown away our Quiverpipe!"

The bee came closer to and touched Toodle with the two antennae on her head, and Toodle had to laugh from the tickling.

"You talk gibberish!" the bee finally said definitely.

Aristo, who had so far kept himself aloof, stepped forward and tried in clear words to explain the situation.

"Look," he said.

"I do nothing else," answered the bee with rolling eyes.

"You have thrown something in sea that is for us of vital importance ... was ... now yes, we don't have it any longer."

We explained to the bee how we arrived in the sea.

"*Bzzi, bzzi*," she laughed. "If you sleep in our education combs for young bees, then those combs will be closed, of course," she explained.

"That should be done with wax," I suggested because I had not spent a lot of hours in my library for nothing.

The bee looked at me, astonished.

"We are no slack wax bees!" she spoke proudly. "We are the Stone Bees! Our combs are made of a sound stone!"

"Strange," said Aristo with red-brown eyes. "I've never heard of these bees."

"Oh, but you drip on the stones!" exclaimed the bee and wiped away the splashes from the cave with her legs.

"From that, you get stalagmites," she continued while she put us in the sun's rays to dry.

"Stay here," she ordered, with four of her legs pointing at the ground.

We had a beautiful view over the sea, where the sun was reflected. A lot of bees flew back and forwards in front of us with mouths full of honey. I made use of our rest to explain to Sseus how we would have used the Quiverpipe.

"It will be difficult to move a complete army unnoticed through Quost's realm," said Sseus, "but perhaps these bees can be helpful by diving for the Quiverpipe. That is the least they could do for us."

Everybody was in complete agreement with that.

Our bee had returned with a much larger one; this one had a longer body and broader wings. In her front-most legs, she had two bees just out of the cradle, which she rocked softly to and fro.

"I have brought our queen for you," proclaimed our rescuer, who then pointed at the larger bee. "She will listen to your tale."

She took the two small bees from the royal arms, whereupon she flew away.

The queen bee put herself on the ground and crossed her legs over each other.

"Tell!"

"We first want to thank you for all your hospitality, as we have spent a pleasant night in one of your education combs," Sseus started, "but during the morning cleaning, a bee has been somewhat imprudent in sweeping a very valuable object to us into the sea. We will like it retrieved."

"Nonsense, he who spends the night somewhere must pay the price!" was the answer of the queen. Her antennas moved back and forth in the wind.

Sseus sighed deeply. "You do know Quost?" he asked.

We looked at him carefully, wondering whether he was smart to bring up Quost.

However, the bee gave absolutely no sign of anxiety and said calmly, "I have heard of him, but he does not know of our existence."

"Right," said Sseus. "Then we are safe here for the time being. He tries, as a matter of fact, to gain control over all powers. That we cannot permit. With the use of the now-sunken Quiverpipe, we could have secretly moved a complete army. Now it's your turn. You should and must help us!"

This last said he in such a decisive tone, which ensured the queen that no doubt existed of the seriousness of our situation.

"Well, I'm sorry about the loss of this ... eh ... Quiverpipe? But we bees rather like to remain in the air; we don't belong under the sea's surface. We cannot retrieve that Quiverpipe for you. However, I can be of service in a different way," she said and hung her head toward us as if she wanted to tell a big secret.

Almost whispering, she said, "I am a little bit informed of Quost's intentions, although he never troubles us. He is, as I did say already, out of touch with our existence."

With a somewhat louder voice, she continued, "You said that an army is marching against Quost? Well, I can assure you that you make only him laugh. He will take the complete army under his charge in no time."

"It is already approaching," I said, worried, "with the Queen of Non-Existence and the King of Below-Existence. How can we prevent them from falling into Quost's hands?"

"I can propose for this a modest solution," the queen answered with a nodding head. "We can hardly spare one bee;

it is a busy time now, with the honey supply and the education of the young bees. But for the moment, one is enough. She can fly you to the army so that you can lead them here. I'm sorry that I cannot send the complete colony to fly over the army in one turn, but we can offer safe lodging in the soon-to-be-empty education combs. By the time that you arrive here, the young bees will already be grown-up."

"The way to here is dangerous, and most likely, Quost will catch us already underway. Then he will have all powers in one blow!" I put forward, not very enthusiastic about this plan.

"Admittedly, it is risky, but if you do nothing, the army is lost in any case. You cannot let down the Queen of Non-Existence and the King of Below-Existence. They will be hidden away here safely, somewhere where Quost cannot come."

"Yes, but then we cannot attack Quost either," I objected.

"Everything on its own time," soothed the queen. "You are not yet strong enough to oppose Quost. You, Ody, you are the King of Existence."

She pointed with four legs at the same time to me. I was surprised by her wisdom. She had recognized me!

"That makes that you are the third power, besides the Queen of Non-Existence and the King of Below-Existence. But where is the fourth power?" Here she was silent for a moment, leaving her words to settle with us.

"Powers must equilibrate each other," she continued. "Two opposed powers are each other's anti-poles and therefore neutralize each other. The powers of Existence and Non-Existence together are zero. But who is the anti-pole of Below-Existence? This power you have so far neglected. And now, here lies Quost's strongest point exactly. He can act as the anti-pole of the power of Below-Existence. Since he is not the real anti-pole, he can upset your equilibrium and conquer the power by himself. But he is only an artificial fourth power."

We were stunned by this intelligent statement. Toodle trembled all over, and Aristo's eyes glowed with a grey-green light.

Sseus remained calm and reflective as always, and I wanted to have such brilliant ideas as this clever bee had.

"Find the fourth power, and you are saved!" spoke the bee with a satisfied expression in her eyes. "Powers have to compensate each other, and it is dangerous to leave a power to itself because then the complete equilibrium process becomes out of balance, with all its fatal consequences. That is Quost's objective."

"Who is the fourth power?" asked Aristo, who had followed the whole exchange with growing interest.

"The Queen of Above-Existence is the fourth power which equalizes with the powers of Below-Existence. Very simple," she ensured us.

"How can we find her?" asked Aristo hastily.

"It is for the second power, this means of the power of Below-Existence, to find the fourth power. Usually, opposed powers find each other."

I nodded; this was true. I reminded myself that Banelez had found me in the tunnels of the Oxiture. My anti-pole was Banelez, and I for her. Therefore, we had to now have both the Large Oxiture and his anti-pole.

It was certainly very essential to hide the army until we had found the Queen of Above-Existence.

"We would love to accept your aid," I declared, knowing that my companions thought the same way.

"Smart," said the queen, satisfied, and rubbed her forelegs over each other.

She shuffled to the entrance and produced a lengthy "*Bzzzzzz*," upon which a thick bee entered with flower calyxes full of honey and dew. We were invited to eat the nectar and drink to one's heart's content.

When we were satisfied, the bee queen announced our departure. She became hasty. Due to the waste of time caused by our arrival, she was now behind her schedule.

She shook all of our hands at the same time hands, wished us a hasty "much luck," and flew away.

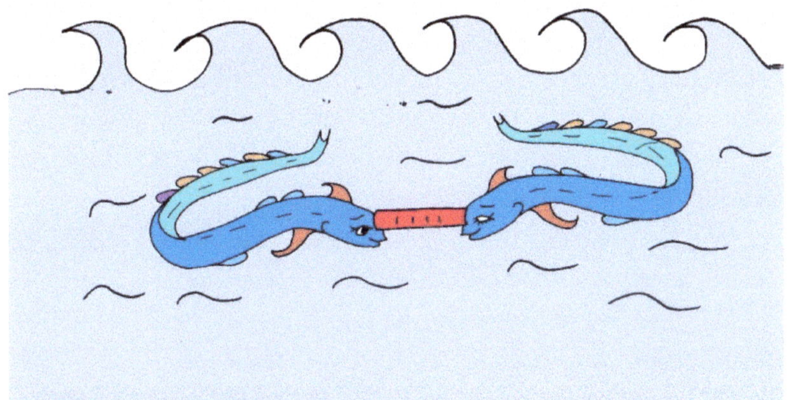

12

The thick bee, which had brought us honey, had been designated by the queen to assist us.

"I am called Nickname," she proclaimed. "I will bring you to your destination."

We did not need many instructions; we could already call ourselves experienced bee-riders.

We grasped her legs firmly, and the thick Nickname took off. She flew very high up so that we could see Quost's rock palace far below us. I had to laugh a moment when I considered that Quost did not even know how there lived, just behind him, giant bees which helped us against him. There was the canal that passed before the palace and on to the sea and into which I had fallen some time ago during my escape.

I shivered at the idea that Quost was far below us, inventing his evil plans. Would we still be on time, or he had already cut the Dromble army to pieces a long time ago? In the gardens of the palace, it was quiet, except for some iron guards who patrolled at the gate.

Nickname hummed further without being noticed. The guards looked very small; therefore, we also looked small to them. Our bee did not make much haste. With a small breeze through my hair, we flew over the bare plain in the direction of the forests. In any case, this was much faster than walking. Nickname did not fly over the forest but followed a path that was to the left of it.

"Because," she noticed very judiciously, "this is a road that is simply practical for an army."

Soon the path bent off to the left, and we no longer saw the forest, which we left behind to the right.

Our Nickname was eagerly looking forward to all the flowers that could be seen; she looked very happy. First, we had passed a bare country, with here and there a tussock of grass, but now we flew for more than one hour over extended flower fields.

The bee flew up and down, which made us seasick. She apparently leaped with desire and impatience to land for a moment on those beautiful flowers. Eventually, she seemed to have made a decision since, without warning, she descended with great speed. The selected flower became larger and larger in our eyes until ... *thud* ... we tumbled into the middle of some pollen.

The flower was very large, and we could easily lie inside without detrimental consequences for the plant.

Nickname put her muzzle deep in the flower and nibbled the flower nectar. She seemed to take a lot of pleasure in it, and her brown belly was completely covered with yellow pollen, just like we were, as a matter of fact.

The flower was pink, lined with white, and had a yellow-gold heart. Toodle danced over the petals, and a hazy hung thrashing on a leaf; he probably wanted to imitate her. Aristo pulled him inside by one of the hazy's vaporous hands. Sseus stood between the stamens that reached to his knees and peered into the distance, looking for the army.

After Nickname had eaten enough to be rounder than she

already had been, she gave a sigh of pleasure and fell asleep.

"Hm," said Toodle. "That one can no longer take off today." And she was right; Nickname still slept when the sun was already almost set.

The flower, which resembled a considerable tree from the ground, closed itself slowly. We sat for the night under a shelter of pink and white petals.

We did not sleep very much. Aristo was impatient and wanted nothing more than to awaken the bee, but Toodle discouraged him strongly since bees require much rest. The hazy continued to sneeze all night from the pollen in his hazy nose.

I thought about the fourth power; the story had sounded very persuasive, but could it also be true? Admittedly, the bee queen seemed very smart, and since she wasn't inclined to be evil towards us, I was inclined to believe the story she had told us. With the loss of the Quiverpipe, we were, as a matter of fact, powerless. Her advice had to be good. We would find the army and hide it until we had found the fourth power. For that, we needed the Oxiture.

"What will happen with Quost when we have brought together the four powers?" I asked Aristo.

He growled impatiently and said, "I want to find that army as soon as possible ... and what happens thereupon with Quost remains to be seen." He sighed deeply and turned around.

It was very cozy in the flower when the sun shone the next morning on the petals. As soon as the flower opened, we prepared to fly away.

There we went, hanging to the sticky and dusty legs of Nickname.

High in the air, we discussed loudly, because it was difficult talking in the wind, which tactic we should follow to bring the Drombles as soon as possible to the shelter.

Aristo had a good idea. "We might have the Quiverpipe no

more, but what prevents us from going to the armory forge of those Quost spies? We can easily burgle it at night or something like that."

"What a good and simple plan," said Toodle. "Is there such a forge? And if so, then where?"

"That forge really exists," said Sseus with a pensive wrinkle on his face, "I know where it is; I had also thought for myself, as it happens, of such a disguise when I went to Quost's. It seems a feasible plan to me."

"How is it possible! I did not even know for certain that this forge exists; nevertheless, how smart of me, eh?" Aristo spoke proudly of himself.

Sseus gave instructions to Nickname on which direction to travel to reach the Iron Joe forge.

We flew over fragrant flower fields, with a tree appearing from time to time. Quost's domain was, in fact, quite large. Which country would it border?

In the afternoon hours, Nickname rustled down at Sseus' request. We were at our destination. At the base of a hillock, a tunnel had been dug. According to Sseus, the forge should be there.

The bee put us behind a row of trees with many thickets underneath. Hence, we had a good view of the tunnel.

There, two people came out of the tunnel, two puffing Iron Joes, who closed the entrance with a wooden door and disappeared in the direction of the hillocks.

We were terror-struck, but this was also proof that Sseus had found the right place.

We waited at least one hour before Aristo decided, "Now is our chance; let's enter."

In front of the closed door, Nickname remained behind; due to her size, she could not go inside and could better use her time to search for honey.

Aristo jerked at the iron ring on the door.

"Gosh!" he said because he had opened the heavy door with one hand. "This door is not even locked! They must do something about it!" He smiled broadly and walked in front of us into the tunnel.

We had been astonished and delighted by this quick break-in. At the end of the dark corridor was a workshop. There still smoldered a small fire, which the room was slightly illuminated by. It was stuffy and warm. On the side walls stood a number of long shelves. On one of them laid some newly forged Joe suits with their corresponding masks. Not enough for a complete army. But quite enough for us.

We each selected one which fit as well as possible and took one in reserve that the hazy easily carried in his arms. He himself didn't require armor; he could change himself into an Iron Joe without the slightest effort.

The suits of armor were not very comfortable to carry, and the masks were stuffy. We were glad to return to the open air again. Aristo, at last, came rushing from the hillock when we were already holding on to the legs of Nickname and closed the door of the forge carefully.

The bee had much more difficulty with our heavy armor and had to pause frequently, but she courageously started again each time.

Aristo, who had been terribly nervous, became now very calm, very self-confident due to his Joe outfit. He had also been particularly outstanding in his ball outfit. I, too, was assured to know we were less eye-catching.

For the army, I had thought of a nice plan. We would just pretend that we had caught the army and lead it to Quost as Iron Joe guards. We would then go in the right direction and would only be encouraged by any possible spies.

With the sunset behind her, Toodle all of a sudden yelled, "Yeeeessss!" Nickname startled a bit and dove down a couple of yards.

Toodle pointed below. There ran, between a large dust cloud, approximately a hundred lively Drombles, all hopping around each other. In front walked Banelez and the Large Oxiture with something that indicated the presence of two hazies.

"Yoohoo!" Toodle called loudly, waving with one free arm.

Nickname made a fast landing, glad to be relieved of her heavy charge.

As soon as we were noticed by the Dromble army, it rushed as one under the brush along the side of the road. Only Banelez and the Oxiture continued to bravely stand upright.

We descended quickly from the legs and ran, as fast as the armor allowed, to our friends.

"Not one step further!" ordered the Large Oxiture. "We have a complete army behind us; thus, you Joes are in the minority. Right; men ..."

Then, he turned around and had to acknowledge that his army had disappeared.

"Oxiture, I am Ody!!" I yelled, and then I took away the stuffy mask and walked to him with open arms.

"Ody, I had recognized you not at all behind that mask; what an excellent disguise!"

We were glad to see each other again, and after this slightly hostile welcome, the army reappeared bit by bit.

The others held back their masks for safety, and I put mine up again on my face.

Banelez magically changed herself rapidly into an Iron Joe, and the Large Oxiture got the extra suit that Deb had brought along for him.

We bade a grateful and cordial farewell to Nickname. She would, I thought, quickly select a delicious flower to once more eat and rest after her heavy task.

With the army behind us, we started on the course to the beecombs. Once underway, I informed Banelez and the

Oxiture about everything. My discovery that Sseus was Quost and then later not Quost, the meeting with Aristo, who had been very helpful, and especially the story of the bee queen. After going from one surprise to the next, this tale of the bee queen was nevertheless a true climax.

Banelez and the Oxiture listened with the greatest attention to my arguments.

"It is absolutely necessary that the Dromble army is safely put away," said Aristo. His voice sounded strange and hollow through his mask.

Banelez and the Oxiture agreed with all our plans.

We would gladly take off our masks, but that really was too dangerous. We had seen only recently, at the forge, some spies.

The Dromble army was again cheerful and sang loud songs about Pampus and Zopie instead of more appropriate warrior songs. All Drombles had a large stock of Pampus on their back, kneaded into a dromble in the same way as Boosayer had done for me during my search for the Large Oxiture.

With alarm in his voice, the Oxiture told us that Quost must have been in the underground tunnels. He had to investigate why Drombles regularly fainted when seeing one shadow or another.

It reminded me of the case of the Brothers Boosayer.

The Oxiture was meanwhile convinced that this had to be the work of Quost.

"What has Quost to search for there?" asked Aristo.

"I think that he watched the activities of Banelez, Ody, and myself" was his answer.

"Perhaps he pays attention to us now as well," said Aristo.

"I hope not," Banelez said and shivered.

"I wonder who my anti-pole is, the Queen of Above-Existence," said the Oxiture. "How can we find her?"

"The bee queen told us," Toodle assured him.

We covered only a short distance before dark. We camped in the open field with the army and marched further the next day, well recovered.

The Drombles were noisy enough the whole day, but we encountered absolutely no spies. Nevertheless, we had to wear our armor in spite of the discomfort. The Dromble singing kept up our spirits there, as a matter of fact.

At night, we camped, all one hundred and nine, on the bank of a river. Everyone sniffed a considerable portion of Pampus and went to sleep.

In the morning, I noticed something.

“All rivers lead to the sea!” I yelled as loudly as possible. The water flowed rapidly enough and ran exactly in the direction we wished to go. The river was not broad, but the transport would nevertheless go much faster than on foot, I reasoned.

I told my brilliant plan to the others. We could let it carry us along easily by floating to the sea, where the bee colony was.

Most of the Drombles had already enthusiastically jumped in the river. They floated quite well on the water. Lying on their drombles, with splashing arms and legs, they swam against the current.

They found this to be a good plan, but for us, we required a raft because the armor made for unpleasant swimsuits.

The Drombles had just climbed, loudly chattering, onto the bank to be able to dry in the sun, when suddenly the complete army ended up again in the water, frightened by the sound of cracking branches behind us.

There, three original Iron Joes stormed from the shrubs.

They had no eyes for the floating army but ran straight to Banelez, who was washing her face further away a bit. For that, she had just taken off her mask. Banelez defended herself violently, and we hastened to help.

Aristo, who was closest to her, threw his mask off and was the first to reach her. The three Joes recoiled a moment but recovered quickly.

"Aristo! You –" called Banelez with a loud and choked voice.

But Aristo already could no longer escape from the arms of the third spy, who had overpowered him rapidly.

The three hooligans ran away astonishingly quickly with their prisoners, without deigning to glance at us.

We followed them as fast as we could, but they seemed to have disappeared without leaving a trace. We searched our surroundings closely. The army searched each tree and shrub, but we did not find the smallest trace of our kidnapped friends.

Depressed and tired, we collapsed along the river. Aristo had thrown himself heroically on the Joes, but he could not help Banelez. Now he was trapped.

I realized that I had lost my anti-pole and a friend.

13

I'll go and deliver Banelez and Aristo!" I called firmly.

"Can I help?" asked a kind voice behind me.

Pleased, I turned around. Yes, there was Nickname; I had recognized her voice.

"Oh, Nickname!" I shouted with joy. "You're just the person we need. What a lucky thing you are still here."

"Well, I did not find it justified, going home already. For this reason, I stayed a bit in the neighborhood. I was just eating delicious nectar when I was disturbed by cries at the turn of the river. I feared that something was not all right with you, and therefore I passed by to see whether you needed some help."

"Particularly attentive of you," Toodle said and caressed the bee on her hairy leg.

"Well," interrupted the Large Oxiture. "Ody, if you go with Toodle and a hazy to Quost's house, because there he most likely holds Banelez and Aristo as prisoners, Sseus and I will go with the others over the river to the beecombs. With Nickname, you shall be there faster than us since the river twists, but you can fly straight to the target."

We found it an excellent plan. In particular, excellent because Quost couldn't catch us all at the same time this way. However, we might run that risk now. If he could catch all three monarchs, he could at his ease go searching for the fourth power. That we definitely could not risk.

Sseus had a good idea for his and the Oxiture's transport over the water. There was no time to lose on building a raft, he decided. He asked to empty two Pampus bottles into some others. The bottles were no longer full, and this way, he had two free drombles. Sseus and the Oxiture stripped off their armor and lain down on the drombles. Thus, they could at their ease swim together with the Dromble army.

We also threw, with a feeling of large relief, our heavy disguises in the river, where they, as far as we were concerned, could rust away. Now, being disguised made no sense anymore. The spies had already spotted us this morning.

Speed was required because we could not assume that Quost would be satisfied with his current hostages. All Drombles jumped in the water and floated on the fast-flowing river to the sea.

We wished them a safe trip and flew with our Nickname in the direction of the enemy. From our high altitude, we saw the river strewn with black spots.

During our travel, I discussed the tactics to follow with Toodle. We agreed that a hazy should do the dangerous work.

The hazy had to change himself into an Iron Joe and liberate the prisoners from their cell, supposedly to bring them before Quost.

It would be our task to diverse the gate guards so that the hazy could escape with Banelez and Aristo.

Our air trip went peacefully; we saw neither spies nor traces of them, but also nothing of the kidnapped. We hung silently on the bee legs, thinking of the coming danger. Nickname did not have to endure much, with only three passengers. She had still breath enough to inform us of something in the history of the stone bees.

"'A very, very long time ago, when our beehive had not yet moved to the rocks at the sea, we lived in rocks which were in the middle of the large pasture with flowers. We had the entire realm just for ourselves. We worked hard, from flower opening to flower closing, without wasting any nectar.

Until, on an unfortunate day, a fey made her entry into our beehive. She was an extremely difficult fey who made our life quite unpleasant. She had, as it happened, qualified herself in the magical art and apparently found this such a pleasant occupation that she couldn't stop anymore.

With her magic wand, she changed every bee into a grasshopper, a rose, or even a bundle of onions. Then she shrieked with laughter as if that was very funny.

On one morning, we were surprised by the fact that she had changed all the flowers into peppermint sticks and lollipops. What was most annoying was that she had vertigo. That was really awkward because she could only bring back anyone to his original shape from a high altitude, flying above her victims with a wand.

She could not be brought to reason and obstinately continued to fly low above the ground with a lollipop in her mouth.

Compelled by the need we have, the last bees, which escaped from her lively excesses, simply took away her wand when she lay asleep. We dared, of course, to fly very high, and we maneuvered the wand above the grasshoppers, peppermint sticks, and onions. We knew, unfortunately, less about magic than the fey, and as a result, the peppermint sticks changed into trees, some only in trunks because there she had eaten off the sweets. The lollipops also got the strangest forms.

You have, for example, already seen during the outward journey such a giant flower. Most of the bees reappeared, however, although some still smell of onions and have tearful eyes.

The fey had also changed a lot. To her stupefaction, she woke up as a bee queen.

You understand that these are essential events in our history. Young bees must learn this history by heart.

Fortunately, the fey was not angry at all. She even was entirely happy because, as a bee queen, she had less vertigo, though she can't work magic as a bee queen, but the magic was already annoying. This is the queen you have met and who protects us."

"And the wand?" asked Toodle.

"Oh, we threw it in the sea to avoid further trouble," answered Nickname.

"*Yes,*" I thought. "*You rather have a knack of throwing things into the sea.*"

The time passed quickly this way, and soon we saw the bare plain and the stone Q-gate, which led to Quost's house. Nickname descended slightly.

We saw absolutely no guard at the gates! Nobody was on duty.

"That's strange," I thought aloud.

"Strange, but handy for us," Toodle replied.

We circled a moment over the gardens, but nobody was there either; we decided to descend.

We had just landed and were busy removing the pollen and the sticky honey, which had been attached to the legs of Nickname, when we heard some noise from the rock house. The stone door, which served as the main entrance, swung open. The sound became louder yet. It sounded as if heavy objects were being pushed around. We heard hastily running footsteps and clanging metal. To our stupefaction and great joy, Aristo stormed from the corridor with Banelez at his hand, who looked very frightened.

"Come here!" we shouted, violently swinging our arms.

Aristo had already seen us, and he descended with great

speed right towards us. Hastily, we caught Nickname by the legs, anxiously looking around for guards, who came running not very far behind Banelez.

Nickname started happily in time with her five passengers, whereas the Joes watched us fly off and, a little while later, returned quietly to the house. Probably to submit a report to the disgruntled Quost.

"How fine to see you again in freedom," I laughed with Aristo and Banelez, who hung on the legs opposite to me.

"What a coincidence," said Aristo, "that you hopped along just now, as we were just escaping."

"When we were kidnapped this morning by those tin gentlemen, they brought us with fast horses to Quost's house. There we were both put, in a mildly charming manner, behind bars with a guard."

"Aristo asked for a glass of water," continued Banelez. "The guard brought it in by himself, which was naturally very stupid of him because we immediately tied him up, and we ran off as fast as possible. We have searched at random for the exit, and there you were."

Our hazy seemed to be glad to see his queen again; at least, he made strange peeping sounds, which Banelez answered with a severe expression.

This was already the third time that we fooled Quost. First my escape, then the kidnapping of Sseus, and now this! All three times had gone rather easily. Perhaps this Quost was not that dangerous. In any case, he could be overpowered, so it seemed at least.

Hopefully, we will also succeed the fourth time with the yet-to-be-found fourth power.

We had passed Quost's house and arrived on the other side of the rocks, at the sea, where the stone bees had their household.

Nickname flew inside the large cave, where we had chatted

with the queen the previous time.

The bee queen was already there. She entertained us kindly with much honey, among other things: lavender honey, blossom honey, blind nettle honey, etc. There were also all kinds of drinks, such as morning dew and evening haze. This was all ready for us in flower goblets.

We satisfied our hunger and rested somewhat from the tension experienced so far. But all too soon, we had to get started again.

Fortunately, I again had my anti-pole with me; otherwise, we would not be complete, although we had not yet found the fourth power.

We did not have to wait long for the army. We heard splashing and sneezing in the sea below us. From the entrance to the cave, we saw the Dromble army splattering awkwardly far beneath us in the water, floating on their drombles.

A number of bees already came flying towards them to grab the dripping soldiers from the cold water and deliver them to the different combs.

Nickname came with the Oxiture and Sseus to our cave. They were extremely glad and surprised to see Aristo and Banelez again. Delighted to see them unhurt, they embraced each other, and afterward, we sat down in the last rays of the setting sun, which cozily invaded our cave.

We told Oxiture and Sseus in short but detailed sentences how we had found Banelez and Aristo and how easily we got them.

"Hum," said the Oxiture, thoughtful, with a deep frown on his face. "A little too easy. I don't trust that Quost, not when he let his recently caught victims go without even exchanging a word with them. What is behind all this?"

"Ah, Grandfather," said Banelez, smiling at the Oxiture. "Quost probably trusted his Joes too much and did not expect we could mislead them. I think luck was with us. Quost nevertheless had absolutely no reason to free us so fast in this way."

Sseus looked cautiously at the hazies but could not put forward anything better.

Meanwhile, the bee queen had provided her new guests with some reinforcing snacks, such as honey.

"It is already late," the bee noticed, peering at the red setting sun, which had now half disappeared into the sea. "You must leave tomorrow morning, at dawn. Our bees have all your soldiers nested in the caves. It will be rough, but we will watch them well until you return."

She hesitated a moment and asked Sseus, "I suppose the excursion over the river was spotless?"

"Yes, it was miraculously quiet on the banks. Absolutely no spy demanded our attention," answered Sseus.

"This gives me so many more reasons you have to start as soon as possible on the way to the Queen of Above-Existence," said the bee queen, while the antennas on her head moved nervously back and forth.

"What are you afraid of?" I asked her.

"I have a suspicion," she explained, "that Quost is up to something and something very sly, I'm afraid. The fact that the army could easily pass is like the lull before a heavy storm."

We sat down around her in the twilight and listened attentively.

"Tomorrow morning," she spoke in a mysterious tone, "I will have a magic potion ready for you. Possibly, you have learned that I am an enchanted fey. I've lost much of my magic power, but I am still able to make magic potions without even using my antennas. If you take this drink, which only some privileged persons know the composition of, one can reach the realm of Above-Existence without succumbing immediately. It will fly you to the stars. But you must be very careful. The star drink works only until the full moon, and today the moon is not shining."

We listened with glowing ears not to miss a word of this enlarging tale of knowledge.

"That is, therefore, the time during which you are allowed to bring the Queen of Above-Existence here. To the place where Quost plots his power-grabbing plans. For the moment, you'd better get some sleep," she decided and flew out of the cave with a sleepy "sleep well."

We remained behind, reflecting on her words. And about her last word, because shortly afterward, we fell into a refreshing sleep.

14

The next morning, we were awoken by the tickling of antennas. We stretched, since our limbs had become rigid from sleeping on the hard stone floor, and looked with interest at the still-unknown bee.

"Our bee queen had to take care of the last newborn bees herself. She has ordered me to give you the morning drink," said the unknown bee, slightly surly.

She distributed flower calyxes filled with a heavenly blue liquid.

"You three hazies stay here," said Banelez to her transparent followers, who just wanted to accept a drink. "We are already enough. You can amuse the army with form-change tricks or make yourself useful by helping the bees as a reward for their services."

The three hazies looked glum but did not dare to ignore the command of their queen.

"This is the star drink, eh?" Toodle asked the bee.

"Don't know anything," the bee muttered as an answer, and after having provided us each with a calyx, she flew silently away.

'"Well, can some bees be lovable," giggled Toodle.

"Let us give each other a hand so that we form a chain," I proposed. "As soon as we have taken this drink, will we fly to the stars, won't we? Thus, we will at least know for certain that we will stay together and not end up on different stars."

This idea had everybody's approval, and so we all drank the heavenly blue liquid, which felt light in the mouth, at the same time. We continued to stand hand in hand in the middle of the cave.

For some seconds, nothing happened. Until all started to turn as if we were on a twisting scale, when I unexpectedly, as first of the row with Toodle and the rest attached by hands, was pulled from the cave with enormous speed by a kind of invisible strength.

Along a tunnel of yellow light, I was flying upwards with my companions. My clothes and hair fluttered in the gust of wind, and I had to regularly blink my eyes to keep them from drying out. Around us, everything was yellow, with a bluish sheen slanting above us, probably the exit of this light tunnel. We rustled there at a breathtaking speed so that the blue light approached very quickly.

After a very short time, we were blown out of the tunnel and fell down with a gentle poof.

Slightly taken by surprise by this high-speed manner of travel, I discovered that I, together with my companions, sat on a blanket of clouds. Toodle also stared bewildered; she plucked somewhat at the cloud, which resembled a non-sticking candy floss. Here and there were some holes in the cloud through which we could look down. I carefully ventured to the edge of such a hole and was bending cautiously over the edge. I saw the dark blue sea far below me. There were more clouds floating above and beside us, which passed with changing speed. They all had several forms. Beside us floated along a dog, a boot, a castle, and many more animals and things.

"What now?" asked Aristo.

"Look, there is a man walking," said Banelez. "Look, there, right in front of us."

Since he could perhaps help us, we hastened in his direction. We walked with bouncing steps to the man, who was very busy with a rake which he tried to close the holes in the clouds with. He was a young man, wrapped in pale-blue semi-transparent fabric, which lightly fluttered with each movement he made. His shoulder-length hair had a strange greenish color.

The young man looked with an impassive face when he saw us standing there.

"Well. Good morning," said Aristo and made an elegant bow for the raker.

"Aha," wearily answered the young man and continued with raking.

"Is this the country of Above-Existence?" Toodle asked the young man outright. This clear language had more impact on the green-hairy young fellow. He seemed prepared to give us some attention.

"Oh yeeessss!" he said, and after some reflection, he continued. "But there is still more. I am only a skyscraper and close cloud breaches with my rake. Someone could fall through them, you understand? There are nowadays so many people who jump a hole through the clouds, which makes it almost too difficult to catch up with our cloud-raking."

"We are looking for the Queen of Above-Existence," I said. "Are you able to help us?"

"Aaah!" said the man, with something of respect in his voice. "Our Queen Aeola has her head in higher clouds, but you cannot find her like that," he continued, with a desperate gesture, pointing to our clothing.

"Come with me," he gestured and walked immediately to the edge of the large cloud, where he stopped a small, rapidly passing cloud with his rake.

"Jump on this one," he recommended. With a bouncing jump, we reached the other cloud. At last, our native jumped and pushed the small cloud apart from the large cloud with his rake. Sitting on this new means of transport, we floated ahead.

"My house is on that mountain top, to the right," said the skyscraper, indicating right in front of him. Indeed, there, in the middle between the mass of clouds, rose a sharp mountain top. Once arrived, the young man grasped the mountain with his rake to hold us still.

"Now change to the other cloud which floats to the right," said the skyscraper. Obediently we jumped on the other smaller cloud, followed by our guide. This new cloud led us straight to a softly swaying cloud in the form of a house. Large breaches on the side walls presented the windows.

"Oh, no!" groaned the young man when we approached his house with great speed.

Thus the two clouds collided hard with each other, which shook us terribly. The clash caused an enormous racket and a lot of lightning.

"Yes, when two clouds clash against each other, you get always rumbling," explained our expert.

When the thunder stopped, the skyscraper helped Banelez and Toodle into his house. With his rake, he first started to repair a couple of windows, which were damaged from the collision. The house was rather empty inside. All the walls, floors, and ceiling were made of white clouds. In a corner stood a couple of rakes, and there lay a bunch of clothes. Otherwise, no sign of furniture or victuals.

After his repair activities, the skyscraper ran to the corner of clothing, where he took six blue tunics from the bunch and distributed them to us.

"These outfits are more appropriate for searching for our Queen," he said approvingly when he saw us standing in the blue tunics. We handed our own clothes to him.

"Can you keep them until our return?" asked Sseus.

"Nonsense," said the man and threw all clothing out of the window, including trousers and even Aristo's white wig. "You won't see me again."

Aristo brushed his hand over his gleaming pale brown hair, which had always been hidden under the wig, and asked with raised eyebrows, "We will not return then?"

"I did not say that; it is, in fact, the other way around. I will not see you again. You see, we skyscrapers are always appearing and disappearing, just like the clouds we maintain. I will, just like the clouds, sometimes dissolve and reappear somewhere else. I can only appear there, where clouds are, and disappear together with them. Very practical because I depend on clouds, not on food. Fat chance that I will be here if you return."

This explained why the skyscraper had not offered us any food, something I had, in fact, hoped on. A star drink is not very nutritious.

"What's your name?" asked the Oxiture.

"It makes no sense to give me a name. Sometimes I exist, and sometimes not," answered the young man.

"Well, skyscraper, can you tell us then how much further we must go to find your queen?" I asked.

"You must go star shooting," was the answer. "That is to fly or to shoot to the stars. The stars are still very far from here; first, you must pass the planets."

"How can we star shoot?" asked Sseus.

"Just like you have come; that's logical, isn't it!" said the skyscraper. He looked around himself, worried. The roof of his house started slowly moving away and dissolving, just like the floor and the walls.

"Hurry away from here! I must go," said the raker. "Transmit my greatest thanks to Queen Aeola for her splendid rain showers. They are of particularly high quality."

"And nicely without holes!" he called after us, and then he jumped through the opening door and dissolved.

"Quick, let's give each other a hand," said the Oxiture because the entire house started to disappear just like our nameless friend had predicted.

We didn't take off, however, which caused sweat to appear on our foreheads. We stood on the last strip of cloud in the middle of the blue sky. Just when the very last bit of white disappeared, everything started to spin, and I was, as an experienced leader, pulled up much like the first time.

This time we did not go through a tunnel. It seemed we went up on our own strength. We could, therefore, clearly see what happened around us. For a short time, we flew through clear blue air, which slowly became white. After a smooth change from grey to dark grey, we arrived in a pitch-black sky. With an open mouth and full of admiration, I examined the superb stars and the sparkling tails of the falling stars. It was a world full of peace and quiet, without any sound. I could almost forget the imminent danger of Quost.

The stars made me think of Queen Aeola. It was a good thing that we were protected by the star drink; otherwise, we could not have traveled freely between the stars.

One of the celestial bodies came rapidly towards us. It became an incredibly large ball, approaching inescapably fast. We already couldn't see the star sky anymore. This frightened us because we could no longer avoid the splendid emerald-green ball.

I swallowed and closed my eyes, waiting for a crushing result. Any moment, we could land ...

Before I realized it, we had landed with six dull thuds on the planet. At least, that was what I thought. I had fallen in a large marble bowl full of yellow jelly.

When I had rubbed the splashed jelly from my eyes, I saw

a most remarkable scene around me.

“Ha, ha, ha, ho, ho!” shrieked a small fellow beside me. He gave me a lively pat on my leg that dangled outside the jelly bowl.

It was a strange creature. Entirely transparently yellow, almost like the color of the jelly in which I was seated. His round head had been decorated only with dark orange eyes and a split as a mouth, which now stood wide open.

The fellow had at last finished laughing at me, and while brushing away some tears of laughter, he helped me from the marble bowl.

“Welle-come” he greeted with a broad gesture, waving around himself.

Now I had to laugh too. Looking around, I saw Toodle’s head sticking out from a whipped cream cake, and Aristo, with an astonished face, sat in a fountain, sprayed by a marble figurine above his head. Sseus, Banelez, and the Oxiture were helped out of a crater in the ground by fellows who showed much resemblance to my helper.

It seemed that we had ended up at a large festival. Many yellow creatures ran lively back and forth. There arrived now black figures as well, which mixed themselves into the party bustle. Long marble tables had been covered with large cakes, with Toodle among them, which were taken off to her regret. She just had started to eat them.

Next appeared plates with colored delicious things that resembled fruit and also green drinks. From somewhere, a certain kind of music played; strange consonances I had never heard before.

“What is going on here?” I asked the creature that stood still beside me.

The yellow fellow, who reached approximately to my shoulders, looked up and answered, “We celebratete the foure daye festivalle. Our planete isse sooo large, that itte isse but seldome day. One complete rotation laste veryy longe. This arere our first sun rays since longe; just now itte wasse still night."

Still talking, he took me by my hand and brought me to a marble table, where my five friends were already installed between other yellow creatures.

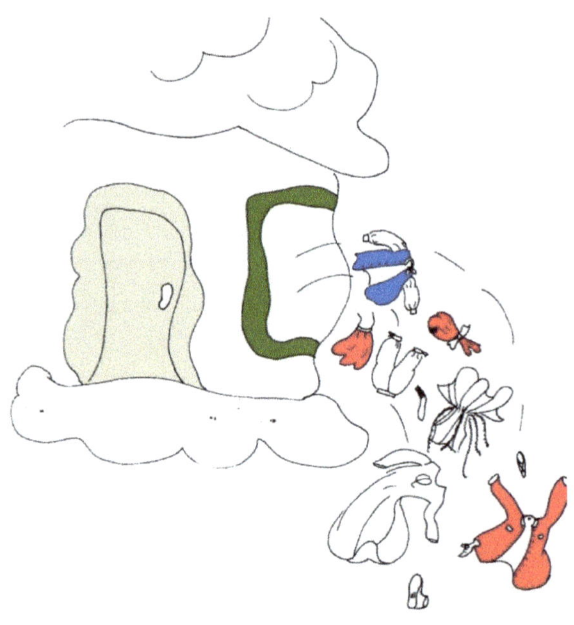

15

A square meal was very welcome for us, and we greeted with joy the pieces of cake and the orange, yellow, green, and purple cookies that were kindly served to us.

"Why are some guests yellow and the others black?" asked Banelez, shoving a mouthful of foam jelly into her mouth.

"We Transpasses changete color with light. The blacke isse juste from the night. I arere here already longer, as a result of which the black has changete for a yellow color. See-e you? Those there becomete already grey."

I looked at the creature which he pointed to and indeed saw a gradual discoloring from grey to semi-transparent yellow. It was funny, too; one could very well see what the Transpasses had eaten, and the pieces of cake, which they swallowed in one gulp, were visible in their abdomens.

The entire festival took place on a fresh-green lawn. That lay between a number of small, square, marble maisonettes with small windows. Fountains jetted their water up high. All the tables sounded of a sociable hullabaloo, which was again reinforced when some man pushed a mobile marble podium with red curtains to the center.

Everyone turned his marble chair in the direction of the stage in order to see what the play would be.

A great acclaim and snapping of fingers resounded when a yellow fellow with a red sash tied around his waist appeared between the curtains.

It seemed here to be the habit to snap with fingers, if one appreciated something, instead of applauding.

After having received his ovation gratefully, the Transpa at the podium cleared his throat and started to read from a sheet of marble. “Dear Transpasses here presente, Ie wellecome you all on the daye festivalle, as well as our burste-inne guests.”

He lifted his head to nod just to us; as such, we attracted the attention of all the other guests.

“For thisse special daye, we havene some players for you designed, who wille playene a piece. Tataritaaaaa ... !” he concluded with his arms broadly spread out.

He moved to the right of the stage, upon which the red curtains were pulled open with some jerks and bumps.

Against the black-painted background decorated with white stars lay some Transpasses on the floor. They were covered with black sheets and apparently slept. There were at least some gentle snoring sounds coming from the sheets.

“Itte wasse night,” started the sashed Transpa on a mysterious tone, “and as itte should be, everybody wasse asleepe. The night man watched over hisse sleeping people.”

A Transpa wrapped in black with white stars made his entry by the podium. He passed hard, stomping in between his sleeping wards.

The public started to laugh loudly.

“The night man isse always brave and scarste offe angry beaste ...”

Now two new Transpasses appeared on the stage, dressed up as hairy brown monsters with large sharp teeth. The night man was so scared that he fled screaming from the stage.

This departure found large approval from the audience, who violently snapped with their fingers.

“The angry beasts grabbede the inocente sleepers and played naughty trickse,” explained the reader, when the dressed-up Transpasses seized their sleeping fellow players by the arms or legs to swing them ruthlessly around.

Large cheering rose from the public, which exhorted the hairy beasts to throw their sleepers into the wings.

I hoped that the Transpasses were built sufficiently firm and elastic to be able to endure these acts. That, fortunately, proved the case because after each sleeper had been swung off the stage, they returned smiling widely and, with the hairy beasts, together thanked the audience for the applause.

“The nights paste sometimes also ...” The reading Transpa kept silent for a moment to listen to something another Transpa whispered in his ear.

After this bulletin, his head became deeply orange, and he called angrily to the public, “Sunne-man hasse disappeared! ... Who muste now be Sunne-man?”

“Leja ... ieieieja! Yes!” shrieked the small yellow Transpa, which sat beside me, “here isse your Sunne-man! Yes, yes, ha, ha!”

He pushed me from my chair, and then I was pushed by the public into the wings, and even Toodle seemed to enjoy the spectacle.

Before I could protest and note that it was a bad idea to let me play Sunne-man because I did not know the text, a yellow sheet was already drawn over my head. On my face, they put a mask in the form of a radiating sun.

The designer of the mask had not thought about any comfort; it was a suffocating thing. I could only be glad that it had some holes to see through, which meant I could examine the stage.

"Once itte wille be day … one wille awake … ." the narrator again took up his tale.

The background of the stage had now become a pale blue, onto which a radiating sun had been painted. On the floor lay the same sleepers. They had exchanged their black sheets for yellow ones.

"Thanne com-me our radiating Sunne-man and greetste his awakene people."

With a poke in my back, I was pushed onto the stage, which almost made me stumbled over my "awakene people." With my hand, I made the promised greeting and wanted to disappear again from the stage. But the "awakene people" held me back by my heels.

"Then camene day and night togethere to dance jointely."

The night man came up again, and all players formed a ring. Then music played, and we danced around until the curtain fell.

The public seemed wildly enthusiastic. Everyone snapped with all the fingers they had. The curtains bounced open and closed. Bowing, we accepted the applause.

I saw that even the Oxiture snapped with his fingers, and Toodle called loudly, "Bravo!"

After the emotions had calmed down somewhat, I threw off the Sunne-man costume and complimented the other actors for their play. The podium was taken away, and everyone returned to their friends.

The strange consonant music, which I had noticed at our arrival, now became louder. Some Transpasses started to dance. They did that by turning around in a big circle, hand in hand, as fast as possible. The dense circle of Transpasses sometimes went so fast that a couple of them flew off the circle, who returned to their comrades, shrieking with laughter.

After we had imitated the trick, we made a circle with our

six and turned, holding each other by the hands, hopping around. After some time, we built up such speed that everything started to turn around us. I released the hand of Sseus but firmly kept a hold of Toodle.

Before we were aware of what was happening, we ascended into the sky. Again, we flew with a tremendous speed to the stars. We had not even enough time to thank the Transpasses for their reception. We saw only the small dots of them on the green planet.

Already, we were surrounded by the stars and silence. A big difference from the fuss below us. This was a pleasant manner to travel to Aeola; still, I was slightly worried about the long time that we had stayed with the Transpasses. How long would the star drink work?

Like a flash of light, we shot through the starry sky. From time to time, we saw falling stars with long tails of fire. A splendid sight. What a pity I could not always remain here. So wonderfully far from Quost. I wondered whether the Transpasses would miss us, or perhaps they were angry about our sudden departure. Chances were, however, that they had not even noticed our retreat in the upheaval and joy.

This third time, star shooting lasted considerably longer than the previous ones. Our speed was possibly quite a bit faster. We passed some planets. Some were entirely in the shade, and others were splendidly colored, red with yellow lines and golden rings around them. One was entirely transparent, as if it was made of glass or crystal. I also saw a flat planet. Not convex this time, but a flat, luminous disk. I noticed that we were approaching this planet.

We prepared again for a hard landing. Close by, I saw trees standing, roots growing straight through the underside of the planet. Dangerously near the edge of it was a maisonette.

With full speed, we shot towards the light planet. With our feet out front to slow down our speed somewhat, we landed on the luminous ground.

"We are on a star!" called the Oxiture, "because a star can radiate light. That means that, at last, we come to the neighborhood of Aeola's star realm!"

"Ah, there are still so many stars," noted a slow voice behind us. We turned around with a jolt and saw a man standing there with a long white beard, dressed in the same blue we wore. Just like the star on which he lived, he weakly radiated light.

"We are Banelez, Toodle, Ody, Oxiture, Sseus, and Aristo," presented Aristo in his charming manner.

"I am the star guard of Queen Aeola," the man notified us in exchange for our names. "Everyone who shoots to the stars must present himself here. Follow me!"

Slowly passing, he preceded us to the luminous star's watch house, which had been built so dangerously close to the edge of the planet. He offered each of us a wooden chair and placed himself behind an enormous wooden desk piled up with papers and books. The room was chock full; there was really no space anymore. The star guard produced a quill, which he dipped with care into an inkpot, careful not to spill.

"These quills are very precious," he told us. "They all have to come from downstairs. Therefore, I hope that there is little to write; otherwise, they wear out too fast."

After taking a piece of paper, he resumed: "How was it again? Your names were?"

Aristo obediently repeated all the names and spelled them out when the guard asked for it.

"Request to stay how long?"

"Until we have found Queen Aeola," Sseus answered.

"Until ... find ... Queen Aeola ..." wrote the man down. "Reasons for staying? Why do you want to see our respectable queen?"

"That is impossible for us to tell you," said Aristo. "It

concerns an extremely delicate and important matter, the reasons for which, on account of security considerations at this moment, should not be revealed for the time being."

The star guard looked at him doubtfully and wrote, "No ... opinion ... doesn't ... know."

"So, enough written! If you all will just sign here."

He handed us the quill and paper, onto which we all scratched our names.

"Before you visit our queen, you must first rest. You look as if you have celebrated for days," said the man in his slow manner.

"It is difficult to know if a day has passed," said Banelez, half to herself. "In space, there exists neither day nor night. Perhaps we already have been underway for many days."

That meant that we did not know when the star drink would wear off. Hopefully, we still had enough time to find Aeola.

I was interrupted in my musing by the star guard.

"Would you please follow me? The beds for short naps at night are here."

He opened a door, and we came into a larger room. There were six wooden beds with simple mattresses ready for us. Exhausted, we fell on them and immediately slept.

The Oxiture and I were the first to wake. Since the others still slept, he whispered, "I don't feel entirely at rest. I have known Quost since he was still small. A child's face can change so much in the course of years, but ..."

Banelez had awoken, and now the others also stretched themselves.

Just the person we needed, the star guard, entered.

"All slept well?" he asked. He did not wait for the answer but immediately went to his desk. Obviously, we had to follow him.

Small, crispy bread rolls and drinks had been put on his desk.

“Please, serve yourself,” he said with an inviting hand gesture. Just like the previous time, he went behind the desk. When we were seated, we each took a roll and a wooden goblet full of luminous liquid.

“That’s star rain,” said the man, as an answer to our inquisitive glances. “It’s very nice and good for the spirit.”

The drink indeed tasted celestially nice. When my goblet was empty, however, the man made no move to pour more star rain.

“Well,” he said. “Your request to stay has been granted. Queen Aeola expects you soon.”

This message made us particularly happy.

“How can we get to her?” asked the Oxiture.

"By star shooting, you will come to the Lion, a constellation. You land there on the right-most star and will find your way by walking through the tunnel. You can't miss it."

I solidly memorized this route description. We should really make haste now; for how long could we still count on the protection of the drink?

I stood up and warmly thanked the star guard for his aid.

"It is my task; therefore, no thanks," he said.

We went outside and gave each other a hand, as we were used to star shooting now. The flat star disappeared rapidly from our field of view. We again shot through a perfect silence.

During our flights, we could not speak with each other. Each sound struck dumb in these void surroundings. I realized that Banelez had been quite silent during the travel. From time to time, her thoughts seemed to stray far away. She seemed lost in thought the last flight.

Sseus had remarked on it too, and from time to time, he looked at her, focused and inquiring. We should not worry too much; perhaps she was only tired from this exhausting travel through strange atmospheres.

16

We had left the star guard planet far behind us already when in front of us, a number of magnificent stars came in view that together formed the image of a standing lion. The legs were raised in pride, and the tongue was out of the lion's mouth in a threatening manner.

This had to be the constellation the guard had spoken about. Besides the lion, there were other star forms, such as a crayfish and a scorpion. It was dangerous to live here.

We rushed in the direction of the tongue of the lion, where the extreme-right stars were. Due to our fast speed, we were in the nick of time at the point of the tongue, where the last star radiated warmly at us.

We could see that the star was attached to a tunnel or tube, which had some branches connected to other stars.

We landed smoothly, without bumping or falling, on the round-as-a-ball star. We clearly had more experience by now.

This star also radiated some light, just like the previous one. Everything looked bare and uninhabited. It was very warm, so sweat appeared on our faces after the small walk it took to arrive at the entrance of a tunnel. Puffing, we walked into the well-illuminated tunnel, where it, fortunately, was somewhat cooler.

"I feel that we come closer to our goal," said the Oxiture, full of expectation. "My anti-pole can't be very far away."

I hoped that the Quost threat would be over soon once we found Aeola. Hopefully, Quost had not already taken her away. But that would have been very difficult for him because the stone bees would certainly not have given him the star drink. Unless Quost had more talents than we dared to fear.

The Oxiture walked in a hurry in front of us and turned himself around now and then in order to exhort us to move somewhat faster. It was not that simple. Our legs were, by then, more accustomed to flying than to running. We did our very best, however, to advance as quickly as possible.

Close to a turn, we heard voices in the tunnel. We naturally had nowhere to hide, but we also had nothing to fear, I thought; Quost was not here regardless.

Two women, also in sky blue, came towards us. They were so busy talking with each other that they walked right past us.

"Twenty-two quills to write and a hundred sheets of paper, she said," claimed the first one.

"No," contradicted the other one, "she said a hundred quills to write and twenty-two sheets of paper."

This tunnel was obviously used by the inhabitants of the star.

After an interminable walk, we would have liked to rest, but the Oxiture would not hear of it.

"We are so close to my anti-pole, so please hang on. I don't know how long the star drink remains effective."

After some time, we arrived at a junction of tunnels. Which of the two should we take? The star guard had not informed us. They looked exactly the same.

"The left!" said the Oxiture categorically, "I am the only one who can find my anti-pole; therefore, you have to trust me."

He was right; we could only follow him quietly. Anti-poles always find each other.

Tired of trudging along, I saw, to my astonishment, a large mob standing in the corridor. All kinds of star inhabitants in sky-blue tunics blocked the way through.

Some, gesturing heavily, were arguing with each other, while others leaned good-natured against the tunnel wall.

"Why would a jam be here?" asked Sseus.

A voice loud enough to hear from the front ranks of the traffic jam drowned over the mob.

"Mister and Misses Standstill," roared the voice, "would you come forward, please?"

Two persons who had been near us cleared themselves a path through the mob.

"Hey, this is not fair, you!" someone called to them. "We were already standing here at the beginning, and you only arrived just now!"

"Silence!" roared the voice. "Orders are orders!"

It was immediately quiet. Here, one clearly didn't question orders.

I tapped the man before me on the shoulder and asked, "Why you are standing here?"

"We wait to be admitted to Queen Aeola. She is very selective, you see? Not one angry word about our queen, hear, but she never admits the first arrivals. She allows the ones she wants to see to come when she wants to see them. Orders are orders, aren't they?"

"Why do you want to see her?" asked Toodle.

"Say, Miss, I must deliver these bread rolls." He showed us a basket full of bread rolls like the ones we had eaten with the star guard. "If she waits too long, I must fetch fresh ones, just like the other time."

I frowned, furrowing my eyebrows. What a strange system of visiting hours Aeola kept. If we had to wait too long, the drink would be used up, and we would never find her.

We decided just to wait for a little, to give Aeola a chance to call us, but nothing had happened so far. The announcer kept quiet, whereas the waiting mob became visibly restless.

At last, we were startled by the sound of the roarer. "Come forward, please, Ody, Banelez, Oxiture, Toodle, Sseus, and Ary Stoo!"

"Next time, I eat my bread rolls myself," growled the man who had explained the line to me.

I ran in front, followed by the others, and pushed a number of waiting people aside with many apologies. We passed ten food suppliers who desperately wanted to deliver their star rain, fruit, and bread rolls.

In the front, we found the broad-shouldered announcer in his blue tunic with a roll of paper in his hand.

"You, listen carefully," spoke Aristo. "We wish to immediately speak with Queen Aeola." His eyes shone angrily green. "And remember, it is Aristo and not Ary Stoo!"

The man looked at him, nonplussed by these severe words, and opened a door at the end of the corridor.

"Excuse me," said the man, while he let us pass. "But orders remain orders!" The door was then closed behind us.

I was overwhelmed by the sweet beauty we now saw. We stood on an even green lawn, looking towards a number of gently murmuring creeks in which splendid birds were swimming.

Over the waters ran elegantly round bridges of carved white wood; from here, it seemed like white lace. There were trees forming a low roof of dense foliage. Particularly beautiful roses grew on lacy summer houses.

In the distance stood a slender castle with fine plasterwork and pretty, carved arcs above the windows and doors. All of this was crowned by slim spires.

The gardens, full of flower beds, contained sculptures so

lifelike that it was as if they could step from their bases at any moment.

One "sculpture" stood on the ground, and it looked like it could step onto a base at any time.

"Aeola!" called the Oxiture, delighted and relieved. We hurried behind the Oxiture, who moved quickly between the shrubs.

The "sculpture" had taken notice of us and moved with smooth steps and open arms towards us.

"Welcome, kind citizens," she said. "Your queen will do everything for you. Come, sit down here on these benches."

She offered us seats on the white benches, which had been arranged in a circle. She was really very beautiful, with waves of red hair that reached her waist. She wore a long, smoothly fitting green dress.

"Listen first to my poem," she spoke, with a gesture to a man and a woman who sat on a bank behind her.

"The couple Staystill, music please!"

I recognized people who had been with us in the line as they started to play two strange musical instruments.

Oh star, in infinity lost,
which secret lies hidden in your heart?
Although the day takes away your sparkling light,
although I seduce you to a poem,
the secret remains shackled in yourself,
as gently whispered in a deaf ear.

Thus, Aeola's recitation sounded.

Admiringly, we applauded.

Aeola bent lightly and said, "I am fond of writing poems; it is for me as food and spirits. I live on them."

"Concerning food," the Oxiture interrupted her, "do you really know that so many food deliverymen are waiting for you?"

Aeola was surprisingly shocked. "Do 'Thou' know many

food deliverymen are waiting for 'Thee'!" she corrected. "And as I said already: Food means nothing for me."

"Aeola, I am afraid you don't know who we are," said the Oxiture, persevering in saying you, "we are not people from your realm. I am the Large Oxiture, the King of Below-Existence, therefore your anti-pole. This is Banelez, the Queen of Non-Existence, with her anti-pole, Ody, King of Existence. Furthermore, I present to you Toodle, Sseus, and Aristo, three faithful friends of ours."

Aeola smiled and said, "How lovely, kings and queens among each other! I have never met you before. Why I am honored with this high visit?"

The Oxiture took the floor and started to tell her the complete story, interrupted by one of us now and then when we thought that he had not explained something well enough.

Aeola listened with the utmost attention and with rising anxiety.

"This is very terrible," she said when the tale had finally finished. "We four must indeed cooperate against this Quost who is so keen on power!"

"Don't let us thereby lose time," interrupted Aristo.

"We have all four powers together now," I said. "Quost can no longer replace one of us with a fake strength and thus upset the balance of power."

"We must go to Quost and there unite our powers," announced Sseus. "Then Quost can be utterly eliminated."

"Follow me, will you? I can send you back to him quite quickly," said Aeola.

We walked along with her to an open spot where trees were absent. There she waved upwards with her hand as if she greeted a flying bird.

It was no bird that came down; it was a wagon. A very beautiful carriage harnessed with four horses. Everything shone with gold, in which the sun reflected. Even the horses

were of the same noble material.

The open carriage descended to the lawn in front of our feet, with much snorting by the horses.

A young man stepped down from the coach box; he was of gold and an exceptional beauty. He bent low and kept the door open for us. Aeola mounted first, and the Oxiture sat down beside her on the golden cushion. We situated ourselves beside and opposite Aeola.

"You mustn't hold it against my poor coachman, but he cannot speak," she said, indicating on the golden the young man who took the reins.

Immediately we took off with the horses loudly whinnying.

"This is a very pleasant way of traveling," explained Aeola. She bent forwards, whispering to the driver in of his golden ears, telling him where she wanted to go.

At this, I sunk agreeably into the cushions, and the gardens and the small castle disappeared out of sight. We came back between the superb stars, where Aeola looked at them delightedly; she probably considered a poem.

Aristo sat in front of me with closed eyes, and Sseus looked worriedly off into space. Banelez was, such as was her habit the last time, vaporous and expressionless. She was no longer the Banelez, who had threatened me with a stick in the underground tunnels and was dead keen on hunting spies. This space flight obviously did her no good.

I was glad that the battle against Quost was coming to an end. We had the four powers together; therefore, Quost could no longer stand up against us. The coachman of our float was an experienced driver; he skillfully maneuvered with a staggering speed between all stars and planets. We shot along past the star guard and the Transpa-planet. The view of all those stars and the obliged quietude of my companions made me sleepy.

It seemed only a short time later that I awoke with a shock. We were in a dense white fog. It was clear that we were already in the clouds.

We looked at each other, pleased; in the coach, the end of travel was in sight. We were back before the star drink had worn off!

17

We shouted with joy when the blue sea lay shining beneath us. There was the rock of stone bees, and as we grew nearer, we saw a large number of Drombles, who waved at us exuberantly from the upland plain on the rock. The bees obviously had already taken the Drombles there from their cells.

The coachman decided that this plain was a good landing place, and soon we stood in the middle of the army. As soon as the carriage came to a standstill, we jumped down in a lively manner and embraced our Dromble friends.

The three hazies, whom Banelez had not allowed to join us, were also glad at seeing their queen again. I doubted whether this joy was reciprocal; Banelez had hardly reacted.

The bee queen was there too. She stepped forward and greeted us with open arms.

"We expected you already," she said. "I am glad that the travel went well."

She greeted Aeola and gave some legs to her.

"It has been very quiet during your absence. Quost hasn't shown himself. Actually, he has never shown himself to us, lucky for us. It is good to see the four powers together. Now that you have found Queen Aeola, Quost's strength can no longer upset the balance of the powers.

But be on your guard! I warn you that he is an extremely bright fellow who will do everything he can to break you apart from each other. As long as he cannot replace a power, we are safe!"

"We will be careful," I assured her.

The bee nodded and said, "Now, you must follow this path that will lead you to the large plain in front of Quost's house. That is the best place to exert your united strengths against Quost. If he is in his palace, he will perceive the powers. However, you must remain together, the anti-poles in front of each other. Thus, Ody in front of Banelez and Aeola in front of the Oxiture.

"Then you must lay hands on each other. Aeola has to put her hands on those of the Large Oxiture, those on the hands of Ody, and at last on those of Banelez. This operation will unite the four powers and make them invincible. Now go and have much success!"

The entire army drombled in front of us on the stone path, which twisted down. The bee queen and the golden coachman stayed behind with the coach.

The three hazies came along too, to protect their queen, in case that would be necessary.

The army advanced somewhat tottering and had great difficulty not falling and rolling down the mountain with their round drombles. It was no pleasant walk. The sun was shining brightly on our heads and there hung an imminent ambiance in the air that gave me an unpleasant foreboding.

Soon the distressing outlines of Quost's white rock house loomed ahead. The path ran to the right and skirted around it. There were no guards in view; the complete complex seemed abandoned. The silence was disturbed only by our stamping feet. Nobody spoke a word. The tension and anxiety increased.

The path headed to the large green plain between the forest and the palace. We walked silently through the large gate with a Q. Still, no Iron Joe appeared. We hoped Quost hadn't moved to another place.

The army seated itself in the grass, trusting fully in our operations.

Banelez, the Oxiture, Aeola, and I went to stand in front of each other, forming a kind of square. I stood opposite of Banelez, who looked nervously in the distance over my shoulder as if she was looking for someone.

We started to lay hands on each other. First Aeola and the Oxiture, then it was my turn and at last Banelez, whose hands had started to tremble violently.

We stood now in the required position, but nothing happened.

Was this now a combination of powers? Why did Quost not appear? Why did everything remain so ordinary? Had we acted correctly?

We looked at each other with anxiously questioning looks.

There went a vibration through me when I heard someone laugh beside me.

"Ha, ha, ha!" sounded in my ears, with a meanness I had never heard before.

I saw Aristo wearing a malicious sneer and running to Banelez.

"Leave immediately!" he ordered her.

Banelez took her hands from mine and obediently stepped aside. She seemed stunned, with a glassy expression in her eyes.

Aristo took her place and was ready to lay his hands on those of mine.

Everything went so super-fast that we hardly realized what Aristo's plan was. Why did he want to stand in for Banelez?

At the Q-gate, behind the back of Aristo, I saw, however, something very peculiarly happening. Banelez came running forward with a hazy. I thought I was seeing ghosts because Banelez was sitting, deathly pale, beside me on the ground, just chased off by Aristo. Therefore, there were two Banelezs in my sight.

Then Banelez, who descended towards us, blew right to Aristo, who did not see her arrive.

Just before Aristo could have laid his seemingly worthy narrow hands on ours, the running Banelez pushed him rudely aside and laid her hands as the fourth of the monarchs.

This was now already the third person who had joined us. I looked at this new Banelez, who in every way resembled the other, except for these lively eyes which lit up.

Now, something did happen.

I heard Aristo calling with despair in his voice, “Oh, no!”

Long flashes of lightning shot from our hands to the sky, where dark clouds merged at an enormous speed, whereas a strong hurricane started to blow, making my hair stand on end. We were lifted by the enormous suction force of the wind. The forest below us was on fire, and the house of Quost became blackened. The Drombles in the army were rolling around each other, frightened.

What I was scared of the most was the fire we could see far behind us in the forest. A volcano erupted, rocketing large scraps of red-hot stones high up as a glowing mass found its way over the rim to spill down to the bottom. The air was hot and almost choked us.

Aristo was sitting between these devastating strengths, crouched down on the ground.

He raised his head to us and called, “Stooop!”

The loud yell echoed in my head. I found all this had lasted quite long enough. I broke the magic by pulling my hands away from between those of the new Banelez and the Oxiture.

It was clear that the four powers had come together, and they had proven their strength.

The eruption reached an end. The wind was falling, and we landed, gently bouncing on the ground. It started to rain considerably hard, which made an end to the forest fire. Afterward, those clouds rapidly pulled away, and the rest returned. Some trees still smoldered somewhat, and from the spot where the volcano had erupted, a white cloud steamed high up.

Quost's house looked still black but was not really damaged.

The monarchs breathed relief, and the Dromble army recovered miraculously fast.

Aristo sat on the ground and wept softly. This all had really made a deep impression on him. No wonder, since Aristo was Quost!

I had understood everything. Aristo, also called Quost, had chased Banelez away to take her place and thus disrupt the equilibriums. In this manner, our strengths would stagger, and he could lay hands on all of the powers. This so-obtained new power could not be abolished by an anti-pole because it became universal, which he could use without limits. Then there would be no more anti-strengths, and without that one, gets only excesses.

Only I did not understand how there could be two Banelezes.

Sseus and Toodle approached us laughing. "It has succeeded! Quost has been defeated!"

We moved into a circle around the now-powerless Quost.

'"*Is he our enemy now?*" I thought.

The lively-looking Banelez took her copy with the tired look by her hand and went with her to the defeated enemy in the circle.

Quost gasped, "You have messed everything up. I had

arranged everything so well. I could assume all power by putting myself in the position of Banelez."

"Which Banelez?" I asked.

"This one," called the radiating Banelez, "and I am glad to see you again at last. I am the real Banelez, and this"—she tapped on the shoulder of the other—"this is only a hazy; transformed into my image."

"I will explain everything. As you know, the first signs of uneasiness were the kidnappings of Tiw and Wit. That happened in the realm of the Oxiture. Quost had then very malignantly hypnotized Wit. That is easy with hazies. They quickly and readily obey.

"This way, he ordered Tiw to change himself into a beautiful lady called Egance. She was to spy on the corridors of the Oxiture. Quost thought that, by her beauty, she could very easily interrogate the Drombles about the Large Oxiture. Wit was used later to represent me during the star travel.

"Quost had already incorporated himself into our company in a refined manner and could follow our movements undisturbed. He arranged to have me and him kidnapped by leaving behind a written task for his men at the forge. I did recognize him then and was solidly locked up with Tiw, who he had sent to the palace, also by means of a letter that he left behind with Egance before traveling along with you.

"Aristo reappeared with fake-Banelez, who was Wit in reality. Allegedly, Aristo 'fled' due to his own cleverness.

Unfortunately for Quost and fortunately for us, Tiw again became obedient to me. He told me the entire story, and I let him very simply transform himself into an Iron Joe. I was rapidly liberated with his aid. I was seriously worried about you. To consider that Quost had hoped to find the fourth power by himself!"

"I am glad I came on time to unify our forces."

"One thing I still don't understand," said the Oxiture.

"Why did my Drombles recently faint so frequently, and why were they unable to remember what they had seen?"

"That's simple," answered his granddaughter. "That was caused by Egance. Shouldn't one faint from seeing such a beautiful lady? Look, but ..."

She said something in the unintelligible language of Non-Existence to the fake Banelez, whereupon the fake Banelez immediately changed into Egance.

Promptly the entire Dromble army fainted, which was, of course, very polite of them, but coming around caused a lot of confusion and required much time.

Egance reformed herself again as Tiw. He looked around, relieved, and searched for the other hazies.

Banelez nodded approvingly. "I do have to teach them not to listen to strange men," she said.

Quost wiped away his tears and waited for his condemnation; he thought his time was up.

But I had other plans. He was a king who existed, and for this reason, he fell under my jurisdiction.

I stood up and spoke, "I will give the fifth power to Quost. Quost, King of Between-Existence. A power formed by the other four powers, each giving a part of their forces to him. The balance is formed by us all four, Banelez, Oxiture, Aeola, and me. As anti-pole, Quost will never be able to take away our powers. Anti-poles cannot levy each other's power. Aristo ... eh ... Quost can no longer be anything more than a fellow king."

This idea found much approval from the other leaders. They agreed completely.

Quost looked pleased. "Better this than nothing!" he thought out loud.

"Quost," I spoke to him, "from now on, you are our friend. You will come to our aid if required, and in reverse, you can count on us. You are no longer the King of Whom-but-Wants, whom nobody wanted. You will take care of the inhabitants who now want to live in your realm."

Quost looked serious. His eyes no longer changed colors every minute but radiated a gentle brown. He promised to be a good King of Between-Existence.

We moved, this time, all five of us towards each other. Quost, in the middle, was surrounded by the powers.

We four laid our hands on the head of Quost. A bright flash of light dazzled our eyes. When this disappeared, a new power arose: Quost, King of Between-Existence.

We greeted the new king, who announced, "We will celebrate this with a party!"

Quost slapped his hands together, and from his palace came a lot of Iron Joes with large platters full of exquisite dishes. It seemed as if they had been waiting until the ceremonies were over.

Aeola sighed poetically at the sight of the feast. "Who thinks of eating?" she smiled, "I must prepare myself to write a heroic poem about this bit of history."

"Then I offer you this document," said the Oxiture and handed her the poem from the old book, which he had carried with him the whole time and that had assisted us in our battle.

The iron men spread out cushions and carpets for us on the ground, and the Drombles also became abundantly served.

The bee queen and many of her stone bees become friends with the new king too.

"I knew what! I knew what," someone called from the forest. It was Nool who hopped lively towards us, together with the man who had provided us with clothes. Moos, the red mouse, and Meow, the blue cat, with Pappa parrot on his back, came along with him.

It occurred to me that Nool should still tell us what he wanted in exchange for the Quiverpipe. This was certainly a good moment for that.

"I wanted a celebration!" he called as if he had guessed my thoughts. "And for that, I had already invited my friends!"

"This ends well," said Toodle.

And thus, we all enjoyed a delicious festival, without stress and with much recreation, before we all returned peacefully to our own kingdoms.

Part 3 of 3

ODY'S DAUGHTER

I

I was sitting at my golden writing table in my castle tree's library. A late afternoon sunshine fell on the paper lying before me. However, I couldn't get a single word on paper because the usually quiet library was now filled with all kinds of noises, which seemed to come from all sides. Above me, I heard the scraping of a saw. The squeaks were only interrupted momentarily by what seemed to be the sound of falling blocks of wood on the floor. The adjacent rooms resounded with a mixture of sounds like "*stamp, stamp, stamp,*" "*tinkle-jingle-clink,*" and "Oops, sorry!" People were hastily walking up and down the corridor. The walkers were in a hurry, almost bumping into each other and passing the oncoming persons with a "*toot, toot.*" In the room just underneath, they were beating against the walls so ferociously that I could feel the vibrations all the way up in the library. The books piled up to the ceiling were shaking on their shelves.

Life in the castle tree had been disorganized for several days now, but today would be the last one. Tomorrow there would be a tremendous feast such as no one had ever seen before. This feast was given in honor of me, as I had ruled for enough years to deserve such a celebration. The banquet was therefore called the Big Thank You Feast. Many preparations had to be made: additional dining tables had to be put together, extra glassware and crockery were needed, rooms had to be decorated, and, most of all, the invitations had to be written and sent out. The latter had been my duty. Fortunately, Toodle and Seuss, who often spent their days in my company, had helped me with this. We had worn out many a goose quill. The whole country had been invited to join the festivities. Everyone had been kindly requested to come to the castle tree, yet many had organized their own more intimate parties, where certainly no more than five hundred people would attend.

At the time, I tried to concentrate on the speech of thanks I had to give at the banquet tomorrow. However, the noise blocked every brilliant thought. I couldn't think of anything better than "Thank you very much for this beautiful feast. I am very happy with it," which the audience already knew very well.

I gave up the brainwork and decided to spend my time reading a pleasant little book that did not demand much of my mental capacity. I walked to the bookshelves in the left corner of the library and climbed up the small wooden ladder that quivered from the diligent activities below. Standing on the last rung, I scrabbled among the gardening and cooking books. I took a small inconspicuous-looking cookbook where an elaborate description was given of how to prepare bookworms.

I was soon sufficiently informed about this and was putting the small book back when I discovered a second interesting book at the back of the shelf. It was a big, yellow, dusty book lying out of sight behind a row of even larger books. Slowly and carefully, I drew the book from behind the row and pushed the small cookbook back. I dusted off the leather cover, after which I descended the ladder sneezing and spluttering and lay the book on my desk. Although I had always spent much time in my library, I had never come across this book before. Thinking that whoever had so neatly concealed the book had probably done so intentionally, I was gripped by my discovery and sat down behind the desk, turning the pages. The paper was old and looked as if any clumsy move would tear it. Written on the first page in sumptuous golden letters were the words:

The King's Finding is Written in This Binding

with a further explanation:

About the Art of Ruling Over Everything That Exists

"That's convenient," I mumbled, "just what a King of Existence needs."

In a few chapters, the book covered various aspects of the art of governance. Thus, there was a chapter on how to treat one's citizens. The book recommended that "the King's Judgment be mild, just, and generous." Another chapter elaborated upon the methods available to make the King's Judgment felt everywhere. Ingenious information systems with messengers and so-called "good-news-bringers" were carefully described in the book. I read it all with a smile, observing contentedly that my art of governance had not diverged much from these instructions, until my eye fell on the last chapter. This last chapter was entitled "About the Maintenance of the King's Judgment," with the subtitle "How to Finish With the People." I read this title, heavily blushing, and my eyes nearly popped out of my head. Did one have to slaughter the people in order to preserve the power of the king?

In the meantime, my desk started to wobble due to the tremendous blows being given to the ceiling of the room below. I did not let it distract me any longer and continued reading: "King of Existence, beware!" was followed by "Disregarding the instructions of this last chapter makes every effort to implement the other chapters useless and without lasting effect. In order to preserve the power of the king, the King's Judgment, over the years, one has to face up to the people's problems. This has to be done on the Big Settlement Days. The king, in person, has to settle his debts with the people. He only has a debt towards those who ask for it. It concerns people with all sorts of problems. It is the duty of the king to solve, once and for all, every problem which is put before him. During Big Settlement Days, all problems and their corresponding controversies can be disclosed."

I heaved a sigh of relief. The "Finish" luckily did not mean a massacre. Reassured, I read the last advice: "Beware, King! The problems presented to you at the Big Settlement Days are not comparable to the daily problems you always solve immediately. They demand much of your personal effort, but once solved, always solved. Or else ..." I quickly turned the page, but there was nothing written on it! I could only see blotchy spots on the paper as if someone had been crying over the book. Nothing but a faint pen stroke was visible between the dried teardrops. I tried to find a good opinion concerning the alarming words "or else."

The sun had set, and the booming noise from below had ceased only to be replaced by soft sounds like "*oof, oof*" and "Well, that's solid." With a pounding heart, I lit a candle on the writing table. The mysterious text of this book made one thing very clear—if there were no Big Settlement Days, all the work of the King of Existence for the prosperity of his realm would become useless and be lost for eternity. I did not fancy this idea at all. I didn't have very long to think about a word of thanks for the feast.

The next morning, I was woken by two nervous lackeys with white wigs and embroidered liveries. "Wake up quickly!" they cried out and ran across my bedchamber. One pulled off the sheets while the other splashed water in my face from a jug. They took off my nightshirt and exchanged it for dark-blue velvet trousers and a white lace shirt. "Your very first Big Thank You Feast," one of the lackeys sighed with delight and asked the other to pass him the royal robe. This one was too nervous to be careful, and instead of reaching for the robe, he tore the bedchamber curtains off the rod. The festivities had really become too much for him to bear. "Oops, sorry," he apologized, shrugging his shoulders and correctly grabbing the royal robe from the chair. They threw the robe over my shoulders and piled the four crowns on my head. After having thrown a contented glance in the big mirror with the golden frame in my bedchamber, the lackeys each took me by an arm and pulled me into the corridor.

A great surprise awaited me there. From top to bottom, the corridor was covered with embroidered cloth showing the text: "Well deserved!" On the spaces on the walls not covered by the cloth, one had painted in swift strokes "The Big Thank You Feast! Hooray! Hooray! Ody deserves it! Tralala!" They had probably continued to work last night, this time in a more silent manner, to finish the decorations on time.

Proudly, the lackeys led me to the Greatest Banquet Hall. They frolicked happily next to me and blushed at my every cry of admiration. I gazed at the sight of the beautifully embroidered tapestries with the laudatory words. The corridor ended at the large wooden doors of the Greatest Banquet Hall. I could hear the thumping and the buzzing of voices behind the doors. The guests seemed to be growing impatient. Each lackey took a door and pulled it with all his strength. I stepped into the sun-drenched hall where thousands of guests had gathered.

An orchestra in the left corner started to play a festive tune. The guests rose and broke into a merry song. "Long live Ody, the King of Existence! He well deserves this feast," they sang from swollen chests and in any fashion. "That's why we join in the chorus: cookies, cakes, and jellies, come and fill your bellies!" Everyone favored this refrain, so it was repeated many times without new stanzas. All had done their utmost best for this party. As far as the eye could reach, one could see streamers of the most beautiful colors suspended from the ceiling that would make a rainbow turn pale. On the walls, thousands of small diamonds and other jewels were attached, sparkling and reflecting the sunlight in the party hall.

Next to the orchestra, they had built a stage above which a couple of dancers were floating in light-green costumes. The singing had ceased, and the crowd responded with thunderous applause. A lackey took me to my chair, which was entirely decorated with bows. There were three enormous tables in the banquet hall, each in the form of a letter. There was the O-table, the D-table, and the Y-table, put together to spell the word "ODY." I had a place at the O-table, from where I had a view over all the guests, even those in the farthest corners of the hall.

Many old and new friends were present. Sseus and Toodle were sitting next to me. I bowed and smiled at my guests, and the banquet began. Many dishes were served, all with the most exquisite tastes and strange qualities. The puddings disappeared from the plate without a trace if you did not eat them quickly enough. The cakes were huge and tasty. They became even bigger if you whistled at them. A loud whistling could therefore be heard when the cakes were served. Great hilarity was provoked by the breakdown of the legs of the Y-table under the weight of so many pastries. With the table on their knees, the merrymaking went on cheerfully.

The feast lasted for many hours. There was a lot of beautiful music, and people danced until the sun went down. The chandeliers were lit, and the guests grew anxious to hear my speech of thanks.

I rose and said, "This Big Thank You Feast is overwhelming!"

Loud cheers of "Yes!" came from the crowd.

"It is my duty to make sure that I will always continue to deserve such feasts. My work for everything that exists should not be rendered useless and without any lasting effect. I have therefore decided to organize Big Settlement Days so that Big Thank You Feasts can be given forever."

There was a sudden silence in the hall. All those present turned pale. They became as white as the tablecloths. Toodle almost choked on a magic candy and coughed loudly. I had not expected that my words of thanks would be so well appreciated as to make everyone silent.

"On the Big Settlement Days," I continued, strengthened by my obvious success, "everyone can present his problems to me, and I will consider it my duty to solve them. For this reason, I will go out into my country and look for the people myself. During the whole journey, it will be a Big Settlement Day every day. It is the only way I can preserve all that exists from doom!" They were still pale and silent.

Trembling all over, Consellus, one of my oldest and wisest advisers, stood up. "You can't do this, King," he stammered, confused. "Our old king, who preceded you, you being a reborn form of him, tried to hold a Big Settlement Day. It was on that day that our king disappeared. That's when his brainpower gave up on him. One has to think too much in order to solve the problems on the Big Settlement Days. We can't take the risk of losing you once more!" The audience nodded its approval.

Now it was my turn to become pale. "But I got it from a book!" I opposed.

"That book was written by the old king himself," declared Sseus, who presently also intervened in my interrupted speech of thanks. "We are acquainted with the contents. However, the book was hidden from your sight since we feared what now has happened."

I was somewhat piqued over these self-willed words but understood the friendly thoughts behind them. Yet, I had no intention whatsoever of letting my government's work be destroyed out of friendliness.

"My decision is made," I announced solemnly, screwing up my courage. "The Big Settlement Days shall be held, and my debts shall be settled. Or else, there will be crying." Some guests already took out their handkerchiefs as a matter of precaution. "Sseus will take over my duties in the castle tree, and Toodle will be my company on my Settlement journey."

The guests buzzed. They discussed the incident among themselves and exchanged panicky glances.

I left the Big Thank You Feast.

2

In my bedchamber, I took off my royal robe and the four crowns. Tomorrow, I would start with my first Big Settlement Day. During the journey, I would visit the farthest corners of my kingdom and make settlements for the people. Some of them had been present at the feast.

There was a sudden knock on the door. Sseus and Toodle came in and sat down on the bed.

"That was a shock, wasn't it? You surprised everyone!" said Toodle joyfully.

"I have spoken to all the guests and explained everything to them," told Sseus. "Although there's still some suspicion left, they now support your decision."

I thanked him wholeheartedly for his help.

"The people who were present today didn't want to take advantage of the Big Settlement Day," said Toodle. "They can't think of any problems."

That at least saved me some work. I told Sseus and Toodle about the last page of the book and the daunting words, the "or else." We did not know what terrible things could possibly happen.

"Perhaps the information in the book is incorrect," tried Toodle. "After all, the old king had been thinking just a little too much."

It could be a good argument, but we decided not to take any chance. I discussed the duties that Sseus would fulfill during my absence and the things Toodle and I had to take with us for the journey. After that, there was nothing we could do but go to sleep. In the background, the noises of a banquet being cleared could be heard.

Everything was quiet the next morning. Toodle, Sseus, and I had breakfast together in my room. Toodle and I had put on convenient traveling clothes. Toodle was wearing a pink elf dress that fell to her heels with a matching cape. I was also wearing a comfortable travel cape over my shirt and trousers. We were wearing supple leather shoes, as the whole trip would be made on foot. Our only luggage consisted of leather bags filled with dried fruits, bread, small bottles of dew-water, goose quills, ink, and paper.

I wanted to take Toodle with me so that she could write down all the details of the Big Settlement Days. It was, of course, possible that I would not always be able to solve every problem on the spot. Toodle had taken this into account and had had the brilliant idea of taking elf paper with her in addition to normal paper. An experienced elf like Toodle could write on this paper, fold it like an arrow, and make it fly in the sky all by itself and arrive at its destination.

After having made sure that there was nothing missing from our equipment, the three of us stepped towards the main exit of the castle tree. The hallways were no longer decorated, and the paint had been washed off the walls. Only vague traces of "Ody! Tralala" could be seen in some places. At the door, many partygoers had gathered to see us off. They smiled sadly, wondering whether they would see me again in good health or whether they should make plans for the election of a new king.

I bade farewell to my great friend Sseus, Toodle and I walked to the forest, and my people waved goodbye with thousands of handkerchiefs. The castle tree became gradually smaller behind us until it disappeared from our sight. It was not long before we left the forest and arrived at a closely cropped pasture.

"*Smack*, yum ... I wonder," spluttered Toodle, who was already trying the dried fruit. "Who are you going to settle scores with today?"

A possible candidate could well announce himself very soon since we could see a small village in the distance. On the outskirts of the village, we saw people actively moving about. Something seemed the matter. We walked up to the people there.

"Good morning, people!" I greeted them when we were closer. The group of men in red suits and women with big white aprons and bonnets looked surprised at me. They had gathered around a stone well and looked as if they did not tolerate strangers near their well.

"What brings you here, young chap?" asked the tallest man in a red suit.

"I'm Ody, the King of Existence," I declared, surprised that someone had already forgotten all about me so near the castle tree. "It's a Big Settlement Day. Do you have any problems? I'm here to solve them."

Large smiles appeared on the faces of the villagers. "That suits us just fine," declared the wife of the man who had spoken first. "Our only non-leaking bucket has fallen into the well. So, it'll be up to you to rescue it!"

I walked to the well and looked down into its dark depths. I could well imagine why no one had fetched the bucket until now. I sighed, a sigh that loudly echoed in the well.

"Bonny, get us a long rope for this young chap here, will you?" called the tall man to a small girl. The girl came back with a thick, coarse rope hanging like a bundle over her shoulders. I entrusted my cape to Toodle, who sat down on a flat stone and, not worrying in the least about my assignment, took out a quill and paper. On the normal paper, she started our travel account with the words "Ody is well-off for wells."

Able hands tied the rope around my waist. I carefully hopped over the edge of the well and let myself sink into the depths. The strongest men kept the rope tight and slowly paid it out. I heard the water splashing below me. The walls were slippery, green, and made my newly washed travel clothes quite dirty. Thus, for some time, I swung my legs to and fro in the air, pushing myself off against the walls. The opening of the well above me was now nothing more than a small spot of light. I heard the villagers chattering busily until a loud "Lunch time!" echoed in my well. As if by magic, the rope around my waist loosened up, and I fell down in a free fall. My rope pullers had probably been very hungry.

"What would you like to drink with your meal, Ody?" enquired Toodle's voice high above me.

"Water!" I called up, and with a plunge, I was served hand and foot. I came to the surface again, gasping and spluttering. The water of the well was cold and deep. Small pieces of wood were floating next to me. They even looked like pieces of a wooden bucket!

"Hey, don't make waves, Trampletrip!" a shout resounded next to me.

In the half-dark, I saw two vivid, blue, elongated lights. They were the eyes of a slim, sleekly hairy, blue animal. It was sitting in a wooden bucket with its hind legs dangling over the edge and paddled with its forepaws in the water.

"Ah!" I called delighted, pointing with a wet finger to its bucket. "That's the bucket I am looking for!"

"Do me a favor, Pannepoon! Bring along your own bucket!" answered the blue eyes, and it pushed itself with its flat feet against the wall of the well to quickly shoot itself in a bucket at my nose and clash against the other side of the well. Wood splinters glanced off into the water. Probably it had already destroyed many buckets this way. Among shouts of "Yoo-hoo!" the well animal floated around in its bucket a little further away.

Suddenly the light went out in the well. Looking up, I could no longer see the bright spot above. Could someone have thrown the lid on the well? I was disgruntled about this development. One could not leave me here in the well! Only the eyes of the animal in the bucket gave some blue light.

"I am a Watergruel," the animal said and gave me a wet hand. "And you are a Trouble-bag and better without a bucket."

"Exactly!" I interrupted the Watergruel. "I want to speak to you about that. That bucket belongs to people who live at the well. I came to pick it up; it is their last non-leaking bucket."

"But then I can no longer go on whining!" called the Watergruel indignantly. "All the other buckets I have torn from their lines are in pieces. This is, therefore, my last non-leaking bucket!"

I began to understand why the problems from the Big Settlement Days were different than the daily problems. Such as this Big Settlement Day problem with a Watergruel.

"It is also for you a Big Settlement Day," I explained to it, still treading water. "I will solve your problem. If you give me your bucket and help me from the well, I will give you a firm barge to bob around. One that cannot break into pieces. Then you can leave the wooden buckets alone when they come descending into the well."

The Watergruel nevertheless looked not entirely convinced but splashed in the water and pushed the bucket over to me. "Agreed, Speakeprat, but no jokes! If you don't give me the promised bobberbucket, I will help myself to a new wooden bucket."

I realized my position with this problem. I did not know yet what kind of solid bucket I could give the Watergruel. That was still a heavy bobber to come.

"Hay there, Rookeronzes! Open the lid and help this Meckermouse!" called the Watergruel upwards as loud as it could, which echoed a long time in the well. Shortly afterward, the light point reappeared above our heads. Then, a rope was quickly thrown down, one that had been fixed at the top of the well. I untied the long rope which was still around my waist and rolled it up in the bucket. The Watergruel attached the new rope to the handle with a firm knot.

"Now, Joke-grol, clear off!" ordered the Watergruel and dove skilfully under the water. I felt its hairy legs brushing my legs. With a short kick, it pushed me aside. I gripped the rope and climbed onto the edge of the bucket.

"A pleasure to have met you, Watergruel," I greeted, but the Watergruel had its own ideas about a new water ballet. My overhead rope pullers hoisted me up rather quickly. The well opening became more clearly visible until my nose came over the edge. The now-well-fed people looked at me somewhat suspiciously.

"Do you really have the bucket?" asked the largest man.

I nodded and stepped from the well with the bucket and the ropes. Their faces brightened up. Toodle came rushing with a blanket, which she wrapped around me in my wet clothes. The lively villagers hopped around me and led me to a diner table under a large tree. Shivering, I put myself in the sun to dry my travel outfit. Bread, water, and large chunks of cheese were placed in front of me.

"Why did you let me fall in the well?" I asked the rope pullers when my teeth had stopped chattering.

"During lunchtime, we put all our problems and occupations aside," they answered. "And you were a problem."

When I asked who had covered up the well, everyone remained silent.

Only a small little boy enthusiastically told me that it had happened when everyone was eating. "Nobody has been near the well," he said. "I only saw a huge bird flying over." Nobody considered a huge bird capable of pushing lids on wells. This was a strange incident.

For this reason, Toodle noted it in our travel report with the words "Huge bird seen at well. Who closed the well?"

"Why did you call us Rookeronzes?" asked Toodle. I told the whole community that was gathered around the table about the Watergruel and the cause of their disappearing buckets.

"So that's where all our buckets went each time!" a woman called.

I told them about the bargain which I had made with the Watergruel. The villagers looked glum. They had no intention of giving the bucket-destroyer a solid washtub. They rather wanted to transfer the Watergruel to the well of another village. It cost quite an effort from Toodle to persuade them of this advantage.

"It would solve your problem and that of the Watergruel once and for all!" Toodle pleaded. "This is also the intention of the Big Settlement Day; once solved, always solved!"

Satisfied with this explanation, a woman fetched a zinc-lined washtub from her house and handed it over to me.

Followed by the children of the village, I ran to the well.

"Here comes the solution to your problem!" I called, bending forward over the well and throwing the tub down. Somewhat later, we heard a *thud* followed by, "It was high time, Dropdral!" Hearing the clunking in the well, the Watergruel, apparently satisfied, tried out his new washtub.

Happy about the good result of the solved problem and my

first settled problem of the first Big Settlement Day, I thanked the villagers for their good meal. We waved them farewell and continued our way in the light of the setting sun.

3

"Big-Well-Do-er!" teased Toodle as we walked out of the village. I smiled modestly. The first problems which I had found on my path had not been difficult to solve, really. If it was all this simple, we need not worry about my health. It would not require too much brainwork from me or use too much of my energy. Calm and with a light heart, we walked over the earthen path that led us through a hilly landscape. We had selected, on purpose, the regions of the kingdom which were less known to me. The people from the well-known parts had already come to the Big Thank You Festival. They didn't seem to have any problems which needed settling.

The sky had become orange-red, announcing a beautiful day for tomorrow. We walked until late in the evening without encountering a living being. Each time we climbed over one hill, a new one loomed up in front of us. The hills were overgrown with crops and long grass, and here and there stood a large tree that seemed black in the darkness. After we conquered a lot of hills, we looked for the shelter of a fir tree with broadly spread foliage. We ate some of the dried fruit which we had taken along and drank some dew water. Afterward, we rolled ourselves in our comfortable capes and fell asleep on the soft moss.

I was woken by a gentle voice. At first, I thought I was dreaming, but slowly it dawned on me that someone really was asking for my attention.

"I wish you a good morning," said the voice most kindly.

I turned around and saw a thin, pale, little man with a large smile on his face.

"Did you sleep pleasantly?" asked the little man. He looked poor. His too-wide trousers with short trouser legs were held together with a thin rope around his waist. His yellowish blouse was torn at the sleeves.

"Yes, I thank you," I answered and woke Toodle, who lay behind me, with a push.

"Waoah?" said Toodle, startled, and got up with a jerk.

"I hope to be allowed to learn also from the young lady that she has spent a pleasant night," said the thin man, turning to Toodle and keeping his polite manner. His voice sounded modest, and the sentences seemed well recited, as a child might when repeating insignificant, difficult texts to his mother.

"I hope you will forgive my discourtesy," continued the man, as if this idea must have already arisen in our heads. "But you have spent the night on my ground. In fact, this is, of course, not allowed, but I would not dare to chase you away." The embarrassed man looked smilingly downwards.

"We will leave, of course," I told him.

"Oh, no," protested the man. "I cannot have it on my conscience that I have chased people away. I have to be nice."

"You are nice, sure," Toodle reassured the man.

"This is the elf Toodle," I explained. "And I am Ody, King of Existence."

An infatuated twinkle came in the eyes of the man, who started to giggle timidly.

"I am Altepan Dolderius of the Bally Meadows. You would

do me a big favor if you just called me Alt," explained the man and shook our hands with his cold, bony hands. A large name for such a thin man. "Can I offer you, great Ody and the exceptional Elf, my humble hospitality?" asked Alt respectfully, bowing his head.

Since we couldn't possibly refuse such a kind offer, we followed Alt to his house. We crossed fields full of wildflowers which moved their heads slowly back and forth in the wind. Soon we arrived at Alt's house. The name "house" was perhaps somewhat exaggerated for this residence since it was no more than a wooden mountain of branches.

This time, less timidly, Alt said, "Please enter this simple shelter." The hut had walls of chopped tree trunks placed beside each other on the ground. The roof was a tangle of branches, with their leaves still green. The inside was just as simple. Alt seemed satisfied with the humblest of necessities, a low wooden table, and a pile of straw in the corner. We sat down on the ground at the table and examined the walls, which were amply decorated in contrast to the rest of the house. Everywhere, wooden placards had been nailed with texts: "I must be nice!" "I must honor the King of Existence!" "I should not do wrong!" "I should not be here!" and "I should be rather glad!"

In wooden goblets, Alu poured some water for everyone, but he took nothing.

Since I was looking to promptly solve a new problem, I said, "It is the Big Settlement Day today. You have a problem, dear Alt?

"Oh, no! Not again!" stammered Alt, confused, and clasped his head with both his pale hands. Toodle and I looked at each other, astonished.

"Why not again?" asked Toodle Alt.

"I have already had all my problems solved recently. I am not allowed to complain any longer," was the answer.

"No one else but me, Ody, King of Existence, can hold a Big Settlement Day. No one else can settle those debts!" I exclaimed.

Alt bowed his head to the ground and started softly crying. "The plump bird said I should not be unpleasant," he moaned.

I jumped upright. I had to settle a few things with that plump bird! "What happened exactly?" I asked in a severe manner. Meanwhile, Toodle was patting the man comfortingly on the shoulders.

"I nevertheless believe it was the plump bird ... I am not allowed to fib," spoke Alt, embarrassed. "The plump bird said it was the Great Big Settlement Day, and on behalf of the King of Existence, all problems had to be solved. I tried to explain that I had no problems, but the thick bird would not listen. *sniff, sniff* ... And then I became a bit angry, boohoohoo. *sniff* ... And then the plump bird said that I had a problem with remaining friendly."

Toodle and I looked at each other with large eyes when listening to this tale.

"And then, *sniff, snurp* ... the plump bird solved my problem. I must be very grateful," he said, raising his head, then continued. "Can I abstain from having any problems?"

"Yes, of course," I replied absently. The only one who had a problem was me! And that was with a fake-problem-settler.

Alt became entirely happy again and recovered from his depression. "Ody, King of Existence, I honor and adore you on all days," he said, returning to his old self, and poured a lot of water into our goblets for the second time.

I had been deeply shocked to hear that some unknown person held Big Settlement Days on his own initiative. The book of the old king mentioned explicitly that the Big Settlement Day could only be held by the king in person. The old king himself could certainly not have invented the operations of the plump bird! The action of a second settler could only be detrimental to my Big Settlement Days. To start with, I had to instill some pride in Alt.

"The plump bird has been so kind to give me these placards," said Alt, proudly indicating the decorations on the wall. "The plump bird has taught me good manners. That was necessary, said the plump bird. Who am I, as a humble servant, to dispute the words of a representative of the King of Existence?"

I did not know whether the plump bird was hostile to me or not. Finally, the plump bird had written on one of the placards that one had to honor the King of Existence. I didn't, however, know a plump bird among my friends. Or has someone from my surroundings disguised himself as a plump bird? Everyone knew what kind of danger I ran with the Big Settlement Days. By holding the Big Settlement Day on their own, the bird could possibly guard me against misfortune. Such a second Settlement Day-haver remained, however, cumbersome, especially if he did not solve problems but, on the contrary, invented them. However, Alt's problem was one I intended to rectify immediately.

"You are too modest, Altepan Dolderius of the Bally Meadows!" I informed Alt, placing a hand on his shoulder.

"But I am not allowed to do nasty things!" Alt protested softly.

"You must honor the King of Existence," said Toodle, who saw what I was up to.

"Correct! You must therefore stop immediately with that humility and remove those placards from the wall!" I ordered.

Obediently Alt went to his placards and removed them one by one, sometimes looking nervously at me over his shoulder. I could understand his confusion. He had to be humble and good in front of the king's accomplice and just afterward had to be proud and worthy before the king himself.

"And now a new house!" called Toodle, delightedly clapping her hands.

“With your approval,” said Alt, still entirely unchanged. “I had a house before the thickset bird came. But that cottage had many needless items for a simple man like me.”

“Let us have a look at it!” I proposed as we left the hut. Toodle and Alt followed.

“I hope I’m not interfering with your journey,” excused Alt, and he led us straight through the fields, where the grass and flowers came up to our knees.

“We were only looking for you,” I replied, at which Alt blushed heavily due to the honor he received.

We passed through a field surrounded by bushes until we reached the top of a hill. To my great stupefaction, I saw a beautiful, square house lying below the hill. It stood on the edge of a forest and was painted white. It had moss-green shutters, rose-flower trim, and beautiful gardens all around.

“See, how sad it was for only one humble man to live in so many rooms,” said Alt with a tired movement of his arm.

We did not share this opinion but didn’t contradict the poor man. We descended the hill until we came to the valley where the large house stood. I was astonished to see that the house was not at all deserted. In the rose garden in front of the house were two sturdy men with brown beards fencing with each other. The glancing sound of their swords echoed throughout the garden. Some children who had disguised themselves with large tunics were running in the garden behind each other. Elegant brown horses grazed in the meadows beside the house. Only when we had penetrated deep in the rose garden did the fencing men take any notice of us.

Straightaway, with his sword stuck into the ground, the left fighter called, “Not one step further, villains! I don’t tolerate invaders in my house!”

“Your house?” Toodle exclaimed and jumped forward. I just managed to retain her by the edge of her cape before she could give the fighters a good talking-to.

"Sure!" endorsed the man, making himself even larger. "Recently, this cottage came into my possession."

"Oh, that's solved then," Alt mumbled and began turning on his heels.

"Just a moment!" I intervened. "How did you come into possession of the house?"

"Oh, from some strange bird, wasn't it?" replied the man, looking questioning to his fighting partner, who nodded in agreement. "Yes, a slightly plump bird. Found that we lived in too close quarters. Gave us this house that was deserted by some ungrateful person."

"The house belongs to Altepan Dolderius of the Bally Meadows. So, actually, you are the invaders," Toodle concluded and pushed the thin, timid Alt forward.

The corner of the swordsman's mouth curled sneeringly upwards. "We are the Proud Knights of the Deep Valleys. We fear nothing and nobody. Our fame nobody can defy!" The new occupants of the house were the complete opposite of Alt, who was far from having any pride. It was time that someone intervened.

"I, Ody, King of Existence, am holding a Big Settlement Day. I will solve your problems. Whatever the plump bird may have done, I am the only problem solver.

"We have no problems," maintained the fighter.

"I am glad," said Alt, who became talkative again. "My simple house has fallen into excellent hands. I thank you for that."

The Proud Knights looked astonished at Alt, who had dropped to his knees. This probably melted their hearts because, in the next moment, we were shaken by the shoulders in a friendly way. "You aren't such bad invaders," said the knights at the same time, and they took us into Alt's house. Two proud women in dark-blue garments conducted us to a dining hall. The corridor was high and royally decorated, and in the dining hall hung many swords, knives, arrows, and bows on the wall. The heavy oak table was set by the hearth, and it was here that we sat down to an excellent lunch.

“You have a superb house. It is an honor to be received here,” complimented Alt. The plump bird had taught him a good lesson on courtesy!

During the meal, I inquired why the plump bird had given this house to the Proud Knights.

“We are ten Proud Knights,” answered the fighter who had addressed us first. “We passed with our families through the fields. We defied deep valleys and tall mountains without a fixed residence. That crazy bird chatted about Big Settlement Days and problems or something like that. Insisted that we had residence problems, so it gave us this house.” Whispering with one hand before his mouth, he bent to me and said, “We did not want to offend that bird, of course. You know how birds are. They have hot tempers.”

I nodded and whispered in his ear that Alt required help. Someone had to repair his sense of honor and dignity. I explained that the Proud Knights would be designated for that. That gave the fighters a proud feeling. Alt could move into his house and learn the tricks of a Proud Knight’s profession.

Entirely satisfied with this solution, I ordered, “Altepan Dolderius of the Bally Meadows, you must return to your own house. The Proud Knights from the Deep Valleys will support you.”

Because Alt did not dare to contradict the word of a king, he accepted timidly. “It is a pleasure to oblige you, King Ody,” he said.

Upon which a bottle of wine was produced by one of the fighters, shouting, “Hurray for our new Proud Knight!” A festive spirit was created, where the disguised children danced on the table with the knights singing in deep voices:

Proud are the Knights from the Deep Valleys
Afraid is Altepan of the Bally Meadows,
He comes to find his sense of honor with us,
Up to large actions, we will lead him.
Up you go, there he goes again,
Upsy-daisy, there comes the honor.

Toodle added her high-pitched voice to the deep basses of the knights. It was all very cozy, but I thought it was time to look for new problems.

With difficulty, we bid farewell to the pathetic Alt and the sympathetic knights. We immediately received some smoked meat to keep in our leather bags, whereupon we were waved goodbye.

"Don't be too obedient, Alt!" I called to Alt, on which he obligingly replied, "No, great Ody. I will be sweet."

We left the cozy house and set off toward the large forest.

4

In this case, is this problem well solved?" asked Toodle once we were underway. "Alt is still very timid, and he has not really recovered his house."

"The Proud Knights are good teachers," I answered. "Within a short time, Alt will have lost his modesty and can throw the knights out of his house—if he still wants to, of course."

Meanwhile, we had arrived at the forest that extended itself over several hillocks. It was a nice-looking forest. Sunbeams fell between the trunks on a mossy path. In a good mood, we followed any path that seemed attractive to us. Streams lapped along our way, working down their courses to lower parts of the forest. The last evening birds flew above our heads or sang up in the trees. There were no plump birds among them. Towards nightfall, we arrived in a valley. We had already eaten the smoked meat that the Proud Knights had given us and now looked for a protected spot to spend the night. We arrived near a small lake that lay in the middle of the forest. This seemed to us a suitable place to bathe and sleep. Toodle ran to the bank and scooped up water onto her face. I followed her example. The water was icy cold but very refreshing for tired travelers. Afterward, we spread out our travel capes behind a large tree that stood near the lake. Fortunately, the night was not cold, and our capes offered sufficient warmth. Under the sparkling stars and gentle moonlight, we fell asleep.

In the middle of the night, a loud splash woke us up with a start at the same time. Carefully glancing from behind the tree trunk, I looked at the lake. There I saw a strange scene! A small girl had plunged into the water. She was slim, with hair that shone silvery in the moonlight and floated far behind her on the water as she swam to the middle of the lake. Her face was thin, and her skin was so light that it seemed to be translucent. She was wrapped in a greenish transparent cloth. Her body was also entirely transparent; only the outlines of it were vaguely visible. In the middle of the lake, she continued to float flat on her back in the water and lie motionless with her gently undulating hair and dress. If we hadn't just seen her alive, we would have feared she was dead. With closed eyes, she lifted her face to the moon.

"I know her!" whispered Toodle, who watched the scene from our shelter. "She is a kind of elf. She calls herself Lunaqua, a water elf, a rather inconspicuous type. She is entirely invisible by day, hiding between the water plants at the shore. In the moonlight, she reappears and then does nothing other than swim and sleep. She sleeps soundly now."

I quietly wanted to go asleep again when we heard a terrifying scream high in the air. "Waaah!"

I was very scared when I saw a plump bird landing on the shore of the lake.

"A plump bird!" Toodle remarked superfluously.

The animal resembled a somewhat-strange bird; it was the size of a man with real hands and legs and feet. Its plumage was a bright yellow. The wings were formed of a leathery substance that stretched from the waist until the wrists, like a bat. At the back, she had a yellow bird tail. The plump bird turned in our direction as if she was looking for something.

"It's a woman!" exclaimed Toodle shocked.

The woman with the bird-like plumage had an impudent mouth, a sharp nose, and very attentive eyes. I could not see the color of her hair because it was hidden underneath a smooth, feathery head covering. Upon seeing this bird-woman, I became very dizzy and almost fainted. Sounds coming from very far away raced through my head, and yellow lights flashed before my eyes. I had the strange feeling that the plump bird was not entirely unknown to me. And yet, I could not place her in my memory. However, I realized I shouldn't worry too much about it.

The dizziness stopped quickly. The plump bird had meanwhile stepped into the lake and waded somewhat awkwardly to the sleeping water elf.

"Go for it, Ody!" Toodle said, but I preferred first just to wait and to see what the bird was up to.

The yellow bird had difficulties keeping her wings dry and tried flapping them, half-swimming with her legs and half-flying with her upper part of the body, to advance. On reaching Lunaqua, the bird seized the sleeping elf from the water and threw her dazed catch on her back. "Oof, saved!" sighed the bird, whereupon she returned, flying with difficulty and splashing, to the shore.

Lunaqua woke and looked around, astonished.

"Uh oh," sighed Toodle, "one shouldn't wake a sleeping water elf!"

When Lunaqua saw the culprit who had disturbed her night's rest, she became visibly angry. Her pale face went a shade of green.

"I have saved you from death by drowning," I heard the plump bird saying. "You don't owe me much gratitude because it is a Big Settlement Day. But a small 'thank you' would not be out of place." The yellow bird-woman was ready to receive some modest words of thanks, but Lunaqua had other ideas entirely. She placed herself in front of the bird and violently shook her head back and forth so that her long, wet, silvery hairs splashed on the face of the bird.

The latter jumped up, severely shocked. "Ungrateful water person!" she exclaimed. "I helped you survive!"

As this seemed a good moment for me to intervene, I ran to the couple at the lake. Now I could reasonably question the plump bird and put right the little matters concerning the Big Settlement Days.

Lunaqua saw us arriving, but the plump bird, rather offended, had already turned, violently clapping with her wings, and flew away without seeing us.

"Too late," sighed Toodle, who, in fact, had wanted me to intervene much earlier.

"What's up now?" asked Lunaqua when we reached her. She was still clearly angry. "Can a water elf never have any rest at present? Everyone, it seems, must keep her from the water ... Well, indeed! Here is the elf Toodle!"

Toodle and Lunaqua embraced each other friendlily.

"Who is this?" asked Lunaqua, looking severely at me.

"This is Ody, the King of Existence," announced Toodle.

"Oh, him!! Lunaqua has never seen him. So, this is him." With a critical glance, Lunaqua walked around me. "Ah, however, Lunaqua takes just a little time for him, not too much, because Lunaqua still has to take a moon bath. Tell me, what brings him here?" continued Lunaqua, who apparently did not like to address someone directly.

"Ody, I mean, I ... hold a Big Settlement Day. I solve any problems which people may encounter on his path," I said.

"Ody was too late to solve my sleep problem!" said Lunaqua outraged, not too impressed by my capacity to solve problems. Added to this, Toodle nodded in approval with Lunaqua, so I rapidly changed subjects and asked Lunaqua whether she had seen the thick bird before.

"Lunaqua doesn't interfere with round, flying, wild animals flying around," she answered proudly. "Lunaqua sticks to water life. Nobody swims faster than Lunaqua!"

Toodle burst into laughter. "I can swim at least as fast as you!"

Lunaqua apparently got the joke because water laughter escaped her.

"Yes, that was nice, wasn't it!" both elves giggled, forgetting me entirely. "And nobody had noticed ... hahaha, hoho ho!" Tears of laughter flowed from Lunaqua's watery eyes.

When everyone had finished laughing, Toodle took the trouble to explain the joke. "When I was still a very young elf, swimming games were sometimes organized by our teachers ... hahaha! These games were always held during the daytime in a neighboring lake. And I never won anything!"

"Each year, Lunaqua saw Toodle finishing last," Lunaqua interrupted.

"Lunaqua lived actually in that lake," continued Toodle. "She decided to make a joke and let me win. Lunaqua is entirely invisible by day. On the day of the swimming competition, she laid me on her back so that I could grip her shoulders. Swimming under me, at a furious pace, I was moved on through the water. You should have seen those elf grimaces when I had won, hahaha! I won an enormous flower! Lunaqua changed lakes during the following game. She was afraid of lakes, they say. To give an honest chance to the other elves, I abandoned the game once and for all that year, hahaha!"

I laughed loudly until Lunaqua said, "Toodle and Ody have kept me awake long enough. Lunaqua goes moon bathing again." With this, she disappeared into the cool water, the same as we had already seen before. We wished each other good night and returned to our sleeping places—Lunaqua in the middle of the lake and us behind our great sheltering tree.

The day announced itself brilliantly. The forest birds were already very busy with their daily work in the berry shrubs and sang loudly. We ate somewhat of the dried fruit and bread, which we had taken along from the castle tree for breakfast. Afterward, we left, throwing a last searching glance at the lake. Lunaqua was, of course, nowhere to be seen, but as we walked away, I thought I heard a gentle “byeee” from the lake, but all we saw were only circles becoming larger towards the shore.

My third large Big Settlement Day started. I hoped to be able to exchange a word with the plump bird. If only this time the bird would not fly away. This plump bird was clearly not a suitable person for solving problems. She made problems or saw problems where there were none. All of this thwarted my plans. It was clear that the actions of the yellow bird-woman had to be stopped.

When walking, I thought about the work which Sseus was now performing in my place. I also thought about the less delightful things, such as the “or else” words from the old book that I had consulted. What would happen if I did not succeed with the Big Settlement Days? It was an alarming thought.

The plump yellow bird perhaps intended to make my Big Settlement Days fail. Would the bird thereby have an advantage? Toodle had less morose ideas. Quoting the good memories from her youth with Lunaqua, she was absorbed in the old tales which were told to her in former days. Thus, she told the history of an old tree that could never take root. In contrast to all other trees, he could go everywhere he wanted.

“He would have preferred a fixed place,” told Toodle. “But whichever forest he went to, he could never find solid ground for himself. At a complete loss as to what to do, he contacted the chief of a gang, who knew that he loved carrot roots. He even robbed them from all the kitchen gardens. The chief promised the tree a lot of roots, in exchange for which the tree had to settle down along the road and let the robbers know if someone came along so that they could be plundered. This the tree did obediently, being so happy with his promised roots. It was only a pity that the tree did not like carrot tops ..."

Entirely absorbed in the carrot tale, I failed to see what was happening in front of us.

"Stop!" a savage voice shouted loudly from nearby. Ten men dressed in purple made a circle around us. Others lined themselves furtively up behind the trees. They had flat heads with large ears and white shining teeth.

"Give us your money!!" the largest man yelled at us.

"Speak of the gang chief," I whispered to Toodle. "These won't be satisfied with a carrot."

"What about it?" shouted the robber impatiently.

The rest of his men droned softly, "Yes, yes, what about it?"

In my imprudence, I had forgotten to bring along any money for our travel. We had nothing that would satisfy our robbers.

"I have no money with me," I said, hoping the rovers would show some understanding.

"Well, darn! How annoying!" was their answer. The robbers beat themselves on the knees with irritation. "How can we do a good thing now?" said the largest robber, extending his hands in interrogation.

"Why a good thing?" asked Toodle, who found this a strange robbery.

"That's what I say, lady! Just give me the old method. Simply take away what you need. No drivel with paying." Raw voices endorsed this with, "Yes, yes, that's right."

"But then that yellow duck came flying towards us. Was

she ever a plump bird," continued the robber. With a drawling voice, he said, "She found that we led our life dishonestly. She decided that we should pay for what we took. She said that we should first earn money." He shouted again in his raucous voice, "Bah! All nonsense! How do we get money? You are lucky if anyone passes along! And then they have absolutely no money on them either! Take now that crumby one who came before you; he could only offer us carrots. Bah! Who likes carrots, anyway?"

Toodle just wanted to tell her carrot tale, but the robber didn't let her interrupt.

"That's what I say, lady! Give me goods only!" The robbers approached and grabbed our leather bags. I would rather have shared our remaining food with them because they should definitely not touch the elf paper. We would certainly need it later on.

"This is the Big Settlement Day, and I am Ody, and I can give you everything that you want but not for a moment," I said, speaking very quickly.

"We have already settled up," they said. "But not yet with you! Ha, ha!" With this, they stormed to our bags. Five rovers

pulled on my cape, which tore in their hands, whereupon they grasped my shirt. Two others pulled on my bag, which I held with all my strength. Toodle suffered the same treatment. Soon, we would break down.

"*Klabberdaboom*!" could suddenly be heard in the distance. It was a deafening slap that made the ground tremble. The robbers also trembled and fled left and right into the forest. We were left behind with torn clothes but with our bags intact.

5

"Oof, saved!" we sighed both at the same time. The plump bird had again caused trouble, and the robbers had run away before I could solve their problems on the Big Settlement Day.

"Let us walk away quickly," I proposed. "I have a suspicion that the plump bird has something to do with that detonation which we just heard." At high speed, we ran to the spot in the forest where the bang had come from. New noises were audible in the forest. Slowing down, we listened attentively.

"*Kra*, *kra*, so here I am!" said a high bird-like voice. "*Kra*, *kra*, me too!" another voice called. Between the trees and leaves, we saw two bird-like figures that looked very much like the plump bird, only smaller and wrapped in green bird outfits. They were less chubby than the plump bird and not female. What they were, however, was not clear. It is sometimes difficult to know with birds. The green birds jumped violently up and down, shrieking, "*kra*, *kra*!" The plump bird stood there too, looking satisfied with her new company. They were in an open spot in the forest. The grass had been entirely blackened, as well as the neighboring trees. This had probably been caused by the explosion which we just had heard. To the right, in the shade of burned trees, I noticed a fourth figure. It was a man with a long dress of blue fabric printed with white dolls. White figures seemed to dance up and down on the fabric. He had a large bald head which he moved sadly back and forth.

"Towards that plump bird!" I yelled and rushed to the yellow bird. "Before she can fly away!" The yellow bird and two smaller, green birds noticed us. Panting from hard running, I stopped before the feet of the plump bird.

"I am Ody, King of Existence, and I require an explanation concerning the Big Settlement Days which you hold in my name!" I said severely.

The plump bird raised one astonished eyebrow. She sighed, "Another problem ... Fortunately, I have now Kra and Kroo to help me." With a compassionate voice, she turned to me. "Ah ... come here then, poor devil! Thinks he is the King of Existence, doesn't he?" With a gesture of the hand, she ordered her small accomplices to take me by the arms.

"No!" yelled Toodle. "He really is the King of Existence! You act foolishly!"

"Ah ..." said the bird with still as much compassion in her voice. "She also sees bats flying?"

I had to admit that for someone who didn't know me personally, it was difficult to recognize me as the King of Existence. My clothes were quite torn by the rough exchange with the robbers. Not exactly what one would call a royal outfit.

"You have a serious problem, young man," continued the bird-woman in her usual bird voice. "But it is a Big Settlement Day, and therefore I will help you. I admit that it is not easy, but I will do my very best to dissuade you of your delusions." The bird took a couple of wooden plates and white ink from her feathers. She extracted a feather from the tail of Kra, her

green helper, and wrote on the plate, "I am not allowed to present myself as the King of Existence." She read it aloud and ordered me to repeat this a hundred times.

"Who are you?" said Toodle angrily to the bird. "You even don't know the King of Existence!"

Then the bird raised both eyebrows and replied, "I, miss, am the daughter of the King of Existence, here in person!"

Stars again came before my eyes, and my head started to become dizzy, just like the first time when I had seen the plump bird. I could not remember having a daughter, certainly not one who was older than myself!

"Come, come, come," said the man with the large bald head, interfering in the conversation. "Leave them to my care, Espra!" With a sigh, he added, "Nobody can stop you from traveling along and from holding Big Settlement Days."

"Correct!" said the plump bird. "But pay attention and do this exactly." She gave the bald man the plate and replaced the still blank plates, ink, and the feather where they came from. Afterward, she flew away, followed by Kra and Kroo.

Bewildered, we remained behind, too confused to prevent

their flight. What were these stories of me having a daughter?

"Please excuse Espra's behavior, King Ody," requested the bald man of me. "She doesn't know better."

"You do recognize me, however, as a King of Existence? Why didn't you immediately explain everything to the plump bird? Many of my daughter's fancies could have been prevented," I said.

"Ah," sighed the man, "that's a long story ... You probably don't remember. I will explain it to you once again ..." The man spoke in riddles. These were strange problems that we encountered on our path! "I would have wanted to offer you a carrot, but I have given that to some purple robbers we encountered. Just follow me ... it is rather burned-out here; I know a better place to pick up old memories."

As we really wanted to hear the solution to this riddle, we followed the man through the forest. He ran quickly for a man of his height and clearly knew the way through the forest. He jumped agilely over small creeks, somewhat holding up his long tunic. From time to time, he looked back to see if we were following him. Finally, we arrived at our destination, a marble castle in the middle of the forest with high-spouting fountains to the left and right! The castle stood somewhat unexpectedly in the landscape, where one would rather have expected wooden maisonettes.

"How did this castle come here?" I asked the man.

"Oh, this I invented myself," was his laconic answer. It was strange that the grass around the castle and the fountains were as blackened as the spot where we had found the man.

Would you like some food?" asked the bald man.

I saw in Toodle's eyes that she was already dreaming of a festive meal. I was thinking of something rather simple.

"Yes, yes, that's good," said the man and grabbed a handful of black powder from his pockets and threw it in the air. A loud bang followed, which threw us backward onto the ground. The few spots of green in the grass had become now also black. Before our eyes, two tables appeared, set up against each other. One table had been set for a festive meal; on the other was a simple bread meal. Just the meals which Toodle and I had thought of!

"Please sit down," said the man generously and drew up a couple of chairs. We took a bite of our "ordered" lunches.

"And what about that plump bird, who calls herself the daughter of the King of Existence? And what is your role in this matter?" I asked after I had recovered some strength.

"Before his disappearance, the old King of Existence also held Big Settlement Days, just like you do now," explained the bold man, looking serious. "On one of his problem days, he encountered me, exactly as I am sitting here now. I had developed a new magic formula, the wish herb. It is quite a particular herb, based on an old saying:

"Wishful thinking is the father of a thought.'"

One must throw the wish herb in the air and wish something. What one is thinking at that moment converts itself into a living being, or if it is a thing, then into a visible form. Thus, I wished myself a castle with fountains and for you a delicious meal ... It's such a pity that the herb becomes useless black powder once it's used for a wish," he sighed.

"And the old king?" I asked.

"The old king came to me and admired my brilliant discovery. He thought long about his own wish, which I, of course, would gladly realize for him. Thus, he wanted to invent a human being who could fly by his own strength, a bird-like person. I satisfied his wish and made his thoughts alive. A plump yellow bird was created by the wish herb powder. Because, as the magic spell says, the wish expressed by the old king made him the father of the thought, so he became the father of that flying bird-person. His thought had been focused on that plump bird."

I was shocked. If the old king was the father of the bird-woman, then this yellow bird had to be his daughter.

"The bird is an illusion!" ascertained Toodle, putting a large piece of nut cake on her plate.

"Not entirely," improved the bald man. "The bird originated from the brains of the old king but leads now an entirely separate life, independent of the brains which had invented her—too independent," he whispered tiredly.

"And then?" I encouraged him.

"Then he took his magic daughter along on the Big Settlement Days. I can't tell you more ... The king disappeared; you, Ody, returned ... The plump bird, who was called Espra by the king, continued the work of the old king. She still holds Big Settlement Days. She doesn't know of your existence, Ody. She thinks that the old king still governs over Existence." He kept silent for a moment, seriously deep in thought, then he continued, asking, "You do not remember much of this, I suppose?"

I shook my head negatively. Espra had only made my head spin.

"Meanwhile, I learned that you were ruling over Existence and would hold Big Settlement Days too. I feared that Espra would become awkward for your work. As the developer of the wish herb, I took on the task of making Espra disappear. I followed her trace, which was easy to find. I found her, tired, on an open spot in the forest. She complained about the hard work she had with the Big Settlement Days and hoped to receive some aid. I did not hesitate and seized the wish herb from my pockets, wishing that Espra would disappear. Unfortunately, my ideas were not strong enough. Espra's wish was stronger. Thus it happened that two new bird-like people appeared out of the detonation to help Espra with her work ... She is now a mother of her thoughts, Kra and Kroo!"

There a long silence fell between us. Everyone considered

these unpleasant developments. Forest birds chirped happily further on, not realizing the kind of problems caused by one of their kind.

Toodle was the first to break the silence. "However, there must be a possibility to make Espra disappear?" she said. "Her father invented her; he must therefore think her away again!"

This seemed a logical idea to me, but the bald man's face was glum, and he shook his head back and forth disappointedly. "It is correct that a brainchild such as Espra cannot have better ideas than their inventor. The old king couldn't pass on ideas to Espra if he didn't have them himself," said the man seriously. "In principle, Ody could make her disappear with the wish herb. I myself was not strong enough for that. But unfortunately, Espra is now supported by her own brainchildren, Kroo and Kra. Together they are just as strong as their mother, and they will not allow their mother to be wished away. Therefore, Ody must oppose both the thoughts of Espra and of Kroo and Kra. That's much too risky, you understand; there is a risk that Ody would not be able to wish their disappearance with the wish herb." We nodded understandingly. "The danger also exists," he continued with a sad voice, "that Espra, Kroo, and Kra together are strong enough to wish you away, Ody!"

I swallowed. The plump bird was more dangerous than I thought. Although she was not really hostile towards me, I was a problem for her. I stood in her way for the smooth execution of her Big Settlement Days. She could be persuaded to get rid of me for getting in her way. It was, however, absolutely necessary that I hold my Big Settlement Days in the most peaceful manner. I hadn't yet forgotten the words "or else" from the old king's book.

"We must try to convince Espra that I am the only real King of Existence and that she isn't allowed to hold any more Big Settlement Days," I decided.

The man sniffed. "That will not be easy," he said, "as

difficult as persuading a mountain that he is a sand grain."

"Unless an official paper can prove it!" Toodle jumped up. The man looked at her without understanding. With a happy face, Toodle turned to me and explained her plan, "With elf paper, we can ask Sseus in the castle tree for an official statement that you are Ody, the King of Existence, and there is perhaps someone in the castle tree who knows Espra. That may completely convince her!"

I smiled radiantly. Toodle's idea was brilliant! The bald man continued to look gloomy. The solution probably seemed too simple, but he remained silent. Toodle took a sheet of elf paper from the leather case, along with a feather and ink, whereupon she immediately and diligently started to write:

"Dear Sseus ... found Ody's cumbersome daughter ... Send immediately proof of royalty. He, who knows Espra, send him to us; nice weather here. Thanks, Toodle."

Under our host's interested gaze, Toodle folded the elf paper to a dart, held it up on the palm of her hand, and ordered, "Sseus, castle tree." The paper started to tremble and shot off shortly to search for its destination. Soon we saw it disappear behind the tops of the trees. We hadn't defended the paper from the robbers for nothing.

"Interesting paper," mumbled the bald man, brushing his chin.

"It is elf paper," explained Toodle proudly. "We call them flyers."

"Now then, only one thing remains for us to do," I sighed. "And that is to find Espra."

"Yes, yes," said the man and got up from the table. "But change your clothes." He signaled for us to stand up. "Think of a nice outfit," he said and had already got a handful of wish herb from the pocket of his tunic. He threw the herb into the air, whereupon the now-well-known *bang* and black combustion in the grass followed.

Toodle and I both wished back our own travel outfits, clean and complete, and that succeeded excellently. We decided, now entirely equipped, to immediately follow the plump bird's track. We bade the man farewell like an old friend and thanked him for his great help with the mystery of the plump bird.

"I wish you a good trip!" called the man after us as he threw wish herbs in the air. The usual *bang* threw us flat on the forest path. Dusting down the substance from our capes, we continued our travel. Behind us, we heard a gentle *bang*, which we assumed was from the bald man wishing the tables away.

6

"Our little man didn't tell us his name," noticed Toodle during our walk in the forest.

"No!" I agreed. "But he was a friend of the old king. I should have known his name, of course, but I must honestly admit that I can't remember anything of the wish herb history."

We walked on, hurrying slightly, because we wanted to catch up with Espra, hoping she hadn't flown too far away. By eliminating the plump bird, I could solve my own problems. Therefore, I was having a Big Settlement Day for myself, indeed.

Our trip went well, too well, in fact. We did not encounter robbers or other dangers on our path, but we were not able to find any trace of Espra! We could not hear any bird cries from Kroo or Kra, only the bubbling of brooks. We walked a long way and stopped shortly for supper. We had the last of the fruit that we had brought along. We ate it together with the rest of the bread. Then, in darkness, we continued our way. Between the dark tree trunks looming ahead, some small lights showed up in the distance. Green, yellow, blue, and red lights seemed to hang in the trees. Perhaps Espra was there with her accomplices. We reached the lights. They seemed to be Chinese lanterns of all kinds of colors hanging in the branches of the trees. All the trees around an open spot in the forest were illuminated. It was very beautiful to see.

"Go away, large softy, there! Away, immediately, you stupid fellow, somewhere!" a malicious voice was heard between the trees.

I was taken aback that they would talk this way to me, so I stepped forward to put this right. On the open spot sat a group of people squatting in the grass. They all looked in the same direction smiling widely. A wooden podium had been set up, on which three figures ran back and forth. It was a kind of stage because behind the podium, between two trees, hung a large dark red tablecloth that represented the setting.

"Disappear fast, you cuss, and don't make a fuss!" I heard the malicious voice say. It proved to be the voice of one of the three players on the stage, and it was not aimed at me but at another player. The voice came from an old woman dressed completely in black, who was clearly playing the role of a nasty character in the play.

An audience member noticed us and walked up to us. He was dressed in a warm, moss-colored tunic and had small funny eyes set into a face with chubby pink cheeks. "Good evening, sir and ma'am. Are you together? There is a place just behind, but come on time, please do mind," spoke the man. He spoke just like the actors, in rhyme.

We thanked him and sneaked by softly, without disturbing the spectators, to the open spot that the man had designated. We squatted on the grass mat and looked down at the stage illuminated with lanterns. At first, I did not understand what the plot of the play was. Besides the malicious woman, there was another woman who was also a cast member, with the same pink cheeks as the man who had spoken to us. She proved to be the daughter of the nasty character, although she did not differ much in age. The third player was a thin, tall man whose body seemed to be made of rubber since he wiggled when he crossed the stage.

"Dear young woman, I love you," proclaimed the young man without persuasion to the nasty woman's daughter. "Give your heart-vow. Oh, give it now. Don't let me wait in vain; your hand will moderate my pain. Your love is what I desire, so proud. Oh, dear, why are you quiet and not loud?"

For a moment, nothing happened on stage, whereupon the young man repeated, "Oh, dear, why are you quiet and not loud?"

"Dear" remained quiet, however, and looked around searchingly until someone from the first row called out, "I feel myself in such pain, whereas I want to be glad again."

Relieved, the young woman on stage sighed and said, "I feel in myself such a pain, whereas I must be glad again. I can't go with you; we will never be two. My angry mother holds me back; she puts me in the cupboard brush rack."

The nasty woman pulled the kind, little girl roughly away by her arm and almost threw her from the podium. Mother explained thereupon why she didn't find the young man a suitable wedding candidate. "Don't court my daughter, you know; my praise on you is very low! You don't know how to eat with knife and fork; washing and bathing, you do with pork! Brush your teeth, comb your hair! Before that time, you are not fair!"

The play plodded on in this way for some time further, with the players accusing each other of bad behavior. Sleep slowly overpowered us in our dark corner, and we were wrestling to keep our eyes open, tired as we were after traveling so far that day. After a last "What can one do with such a guy? He is certainly good for nothing under the sky!" my eyes closed.

Warm sunbeams woke me the next morning. The play had finished. I saw that all audience members were still present. Full of pleasure and with much laughter, the people from the previous evening were having breakfast. The large, dark-red tablecloth that had served as a setting yesterday had been put over the podium, which was used now as a table. The delicious smell of ripe berries rose up from the breakfast podium. The man with the pink cheeks, who had assigned us places to sit, noticed that we were awake and gestured us to join the company.

"Taste this delightful breakfast; better you will not see a better repast!" the man poeticized welcomingly.

Toodle and I stood up and sat down on the suitable wooden stools. Opposite me sat the nasty woman of the previous evening, who now apparently had made peace with the thin young man. From time to time, she gave him a hard, laughing slap on the shoulders, which elegantly bent him.

"This is my wife. Fortunately, you know, she is my life," the man with the pink cheeks said and presented us to the kind, little, young woman who had also played on stage.

"It was a pleasure to see you act," I answered. "This is the elf Toodle, and I am Ody, King of Existence."

The smile of the man broadened. "The Juice-Squeezers we are called, but my name is Laundry," the man said and poured us a goblet full of red berry juice, foaming at the rim. "We pick berries each day, everybody who likes this work, if he wants. Each squeezer has his own task, you see, but also gets a fine if he renounces this task for a fee. He that picks is called Pickery; I, who washes, Laundry. Then there are still the squeezers of the berries, how hard their work is; they can do their work only after a lot of lessons. Finally, one can pour the juice into the wooden barrels, cheerio, and enjoy it then in a good mood, well." After this explanation, he gave a good example by swallowing the berry juice with great gulps. I followed

Laundry's example. The juice was really delicious. First, it was cold in the mouth, but afterward, it felt deliciously warm in the stomach. I could imagine that after drinking so much juice, someone would get such pink cheeks like Laundry and his wife had. The breakfast tasted so good that I almost forgot which problems I still had to solve.

"Laundry," I asked seriously, "Have you ever seen a plump yellow bird here, accompanied by two green birds who always shriek? She is known as Espra."

Laundry frowned. "Well, no, of course not; they flee!" he answered, as if I had asked something stupid. "There are no free birds here, as you can see!" He spread out his arms as a sign that no birds could be seen here.

Indeed, I couldn't hear any bird noises as in other parts of the forest.

"Why are there no birds here?" asked Toodle, touched by this strange fact.

"The birds cannot stand this region one bit; they decided by the hundreds to flee it," the man answered in a mysterious tone. "That is because of the people in the neighborhood who have entirely depleted their lives in the wood. When they see a bird fly, one stands surprised and tricked by how much they will lie! So that's why a poor bird is mistaken by such a cunning double-crossing and taken. They seize him in his neck and fill their stomach quick!"

"Oh!" called Toodle, scared. "The birds serve as a meal?" With fright in her eyes, she stammered to me, "Would that apply to plump birds too?"

"Perhaps even sooner than others!" I said anxiously. Espra might be a cumbersome bird for me, but she remained, in some way or other, my daughter. I didn't like the idea of having her eaten by hungry people without respect for flying creatures. I hoped that she would not be trapped by their tricks. It was better to track Espra as soon as possible.

"I thank you, Laundry, for the gorgeous berry juice and the nice play. It was very relaxing," I said to the man with pink cheeks. "Can I help you by exchanging something for this? I keep today a Big Settlement Day. You can leave each problem to me. I take the task to solve it."

"Hmm!" Laundry sighed. "We only have one difficulty around, and that is really not a little thing to which we are bound. We want to give our berry juice to distant friends, but the road to them does us tremble to all ends. The roads have too many dangers to deliver; we do not want to navigate on the river. Thus, we are denied, unfortunately; our friends are excluded from this juice most certainly."

"Oh, Ody always knows a solution!" stated Toodle, although I was not so sure of it.

"There must be a safe way to get the delicious berry juice to your friends," I said, reflecting. "Perhaps I can first see the barns where you manufacture the juice." Laundry nodded gladly and gestured us to follow him, leaving behind the lively breakfast company who had not paid any attention to us. He led us through the high shrubs between the trees. We followed a splashing stream until we came to a wooden house that was built across the small river. It was a type of bridge house with an opening where the creek could flow freely in the lower part.

"Water is handy for the washing up," explained Laundry. "Very convenient and so close up." On the side of the house, people were busy taking baskets full of berries from a wooden cart and bringing these into the house. "Come in," gestured the man, holding the door open for us. "Then you can see for yourself, what we all invent here; you too, nice elf." The house was dark inside but quite cozy with the sound of the flowing water under the floor and the smell of freshly picked berries in the air. Laundry led us through the entire house, indicating the different operations to obtain the best juice. The baskets with the berries were hung through an opening in the floor to the river. Thus, they got a thorough washing. This was also Laundry's task if he hadn't had a free day like today. He told us that he had to work every other day and that every day a play was set up by those who didn't work that day. This evening, it was his turn to help set up a play. Further on, we saw some women squeezing the berries. They honored their name, Juice-Squeezers; with some berries in each hand, they squeezed with all their strength, and large spouts of juice went into a wooden barrel. Others boarded up the barrels, loaded them on carts, and had them delivered to the consumers.

"What kind of danger are you afraid of which prevents you from sending the juice to your distant friends?" asked Toodle.

The road to our friends leads through a quiet plain. I have already told you, the people who live there catch all those birds," Laundry answered sadly.

"But you aren't a bird," continued Toodle down-to-earth. "Then you've nothing to fear, have you?"

"Unfortunately, those people are unpredictable; before you realize it, it is a bite here and a bite there!" sighed our guide.

The flowing river and the wooden barrels had given me an idea of how I could help the Juice-Squeezers. "Does this river flow through this dangerous area to the place where your friends live?" I asked, full of expectation. Laundry confirmed this. "But that's marvelous," I exclaimed. "You only have to throw the wooden barrels full of juice in the river, and the current will ensure that they arrive at your friends' place!"

Laundry's face brightened up visibly; he had never thought about that. Possibly the barrels could float unguarded down the river. The bird-eating people in the surroundings wouldn't be attracted by a simple wooden barrel, the contents of which could not be smelled. "What a big luck this way; how is blessed our day!" Laundry poeticized in a lively manner and rolled a barrel immediately to the opening in the floor. Soon afterward, we heard a dull splash. The first barrel was on its way.

I had again settled a problem and was delighted about the simplicity with which everything had been solved. It was now, however, time to go after Espra. We had spent enough time solving other people's problems. My own difficulty now needed all my attention. I thanked Laundry once again for his hospitality and took farewell of the Juice-Squeezers. Laundry slipped us two goblets with juice, whereupon we left the house. After a "Come once more, today or tomorrow. They are gone now, all our sorrow," we resumed our search for Espra.

7

We walked in the quiet forest. There were still no birds around and certainly not Espra. Toodle had taken her ordinary paper again and did the travel report while walking along. “Have connected Juice-Squeezers with their friends as is sound, but Espra has not yet been found,” Toodle wrote in an appropriate rhyme. After having walked some time, we drank the berry juice we had brought along, which tasted delicious. The forest changed slightly around us. The trees looked somewhat pitiful, with only a few leaves on their branches. Some trees had become white and seemed entirely dried out. A few dead trees stood nicely in a line beside each other among green and healthy vegetation. I wondered what the cause of the bad condition of these trees could be.

Suddenly, as by magic, two small fellows jumped from the hollow of some tree roots. They did not reach any higher than my waist and had a slight stature. They were dressed in autumn-colored tree leaves, which were lying closely against their bodies. On their heads, leaves also seemed to grow instead of hair. They looked at us with large green eyes from under their long eyelashes and ran agilely towards us.

"Come now, fastshes!" lisped the fellows and smiled widely, exposing two large shining teeth in the front of their mouth. Without giving us any explanation, each fellow took care of one of us. They seized us by our hands and dragged us behind them with all their strength. For their size, these fellows had great strength. Because the men had obviously already made a decision for us, we followed them obediently. "Hurryshes, hurryshes, hastshes, hastshes!" the guys mumbled nervously.

Not really understanding, I shrugged my shoulders at Toodle, who ran beside me. One of the fellows in the leaf outfits stopped in front of a series of dried-out trees with broadly spread roots. Under one of the roots, a hole could be seen in the ground.

"Hupshes, inside, fastshes!" the man said. I hesitated; was the hole large enough for me? The fellow found me too hesitant and didn't want to wait for my decision. He gave me a push in the back so that I landed smoothly in the hole. I was in an earthen tunnel, where the roots of the trees were exposed along the walls. The corridor was illuminated by sunbeams that fell through holes in the ceiling.

Ploof! Behind me, Toodle had been pushed inside. Skilfully, two fellows jumped in behind her. They wasted no time and caught us by the hand again. With speed, we were conducted through the straight tunnel, which fortunately was high enough for us to walk upright.

"Is it wise to go underground?" Toodle asked me. "Any moment now, I expect a letter from Sseus with the proof of your royalty. That letter cannot find us if we are underground. And if it comes in the wrong hands, then the finder has proof that he is the real king!!"

I looked worried but couldn't do anything else than follow the person pulling on me. I saw that the light in the tunnel came from hollow trees above us. I could look straight through the trunks to the blue sky. That's why the trees were in such a bad shape. They were hollow!

"Where are you taking us?" I asked to the running fellow finally.

"I give explainsheshes," he lisped hurriedly. "Everyone wants to know about the trees and why they are so pityful-shes."

At the end of the tunnel, I heard a steady loud "*krrr, krrr, krrr*" sound. It was also darker there.

"Here we are thenshes," called the fellow proudly when we had arrived at the end of the tunnel. I saw dozens of fellows with similar large teeth and the same leaf outfit as our guides. They ran nervously and bumped into each other. The ground was strewn with wood sawdust. Some men had climbed inside the spreading roots and gnawed a hole in the tree above with their large front teeth. This was the cause of the grinding sounds.

"So, we excavate ourshes small trees," our guide explained.

"Why do you do that?" asked Toodle. "That's not good for the tree."

"It is excelentshes for us," the fellow answered, smiling broadly. "It's like this, the sawdustshes are for meals, and the rest is for reinforcing the tunnelshes."

One of the tree gnawers fell from the roots on the floor. He was somewhat chubbier than the others and hiccupped continuously: "*Hupshes*! *Hupshes*!"

"No, yetshes!" sighed our guide. "You nibbled again of the sawdustshes? Don't be so greedyshes, Slisher!" To me, he said, "He is called Slisher because he is lisping so tremedouslyshes, ha, ha, ha!"

He did not wait for comment but pulled us into a light side tunnel. "Quickshes, take a lookshes," he proposed.

We saw some fellows kneading a mixture of sawdust and

water, which they took from trays that stood under the hollow trees.

"Sawdustshes combed with caught rain watershes gives mortar. Just glueshes against the wallshes, let dry, and hupshes, the tunnelshes are solidshes," explained the fellow. "Now it's aboutshes time you must knowshes it."

Two fellows took two wooden chairs for us from a corner. "Go, sitshes!" they invited us to sit down and, with their hands, scooped wood shavings from the floor, which they threw in our lap. "Eatshes, enjoy your mealshes!"

Toodle and I looked at each other astonished. "Eh ..." stammered Toodle. "you know, eh ... What is your name, actually?"

"How would you likeshes to call me?" answered one of the lads.

"Slish—" started Toodle, but I just could correct her in time with "Nicolas ... Wooden Nicolas."

"Very good!" called the man. "Then we are Woodshes and Nicolashes!"

"And we are Odyshes and Toodleshes," said Toodle, entirely in the mood.

"Hasteshes, quickshes," Nicolashes encouraged us. "Eatshes now, all! We must give explanationshes to the next peopleshes. Everyone is so curiousshes."

I stopped slowly, a wood shaving in my mouth so as not to offend them. I did my best not to show my aversion on my face. This was, however, something quite different from the berry juice of the Juice-Squeezers.

"We must really go now!" I heard myself saying before I would have to swallow any more wood shavings. "I am waiting to receive a letter above."

"Yes, goodshes!" Woodshes and Nicolashes lisped and ran away, leaving us behind. Since all that running made us nervous, we decided to remain calm and quiet and find the exit. We passed the tree excavators who made a lot of noise with their gnashing. Slisher seemed not too concerned. He had fallen asleep on a bunch of wood shavings. His supper, perhaps.

"I require an immediate explanation!" a distinguished voice said at the entrance.

"Yes, yes, comeshes, we give explanationshes," was the lisped answer.

"I won't move one step before you explain the reasons for your evil actions to me," it said.

Coming closer, I saw a young man standing in the entering sunlight. He stood straight and upright in a tense position, his arms crossed and his head bowed arrogantly backward. He had a jaunty tip-tilted nose and kept his eyes half-closed under his raised eyebrows. His tunic resembled the outfit which my lackeys wore in the castle tree, but this was a shining blue color. His straight, golden hair was tied up on his neck with a black satin bow.

Woodshes and Nicolashes stood beside him and were becoming clearly impatient. They started to pull at the lapels of his coat, but the young man had no intention of moving one step. "You want explanationshes? You get explanationshes!" called the guys, little impressed by his personality.

Being acquainted now with the way these fellows caught their guests, I could imagine how anyone would be put out by that. "They only want to give you a guided tour," I explained to the young man. "You too must have been wondering why the trees here are in such a bad shape?"

"No!" spoke the man looking at me with half-closed eyes. "I don't wish to interfere with these, eh ... beings. Their chatterings don't fill holes."

"They just make those holes," said Toodle, "in the trees. You hear that?"

"And that excites me greatly," continued the arrogant

fellow, ignoring Toodle's question. "I am a very good musician. One can hardly lean against a tree in the hope of creating a brilliant composition if one is provoked to his soul by primitive '*krr, krr, krr*' sounds!

Woodshes and Nicolashes started to find him an ungrateful guest. With full strength, they drew on his arms, intending to pull him from the hole in which they had just thrown him.

"I will file a complaint with the king himself!" said the musician, controlling himself with difficulty.

"I am the king!" I said with dignity.

"Ah!" sighed the young man, still with the same arrogant expression. "A king proves to be there when one needs one," tearing himself loose of the Woodshes and Nicolashes. "These, eh ... ground-creepers venture to make '*krr, krr*' sounds which disturb my thinking. On top of that, they attempted to control my person. I have spoken!"

The problem seemed to me somewhat exaggerated, but each problem had to be settled.

"I, as King of Existence, keep Big Settlement Days," I said. "I take on the responsibility of solving your problems. Let us discuss this quietly."

"Yes, yes, quietshes!" I heard Nicolashes say by way of exception. Both fellows came along carrying wooden chairs. The musician graciously sat down on one .

"Why have you selected this part of the forest to create music?" I asked the young man.

"Nature's sounds form a source of inspiration for my music," he answered.

"But here, there are neither singing birds nor splashing brooks. Those are in the center of the forest!" Toodle noted.

The man pressed his mouth glumly together. "I refuse to run away to less-worthy areas, as you suggest," he said obstinately.

"Then these surroundings offer you, in fact, too few

sounds from nature. The '*krr, krr*' sounds you find too simple," I concluded.

The man grimaced glumly. "Hmmm ... *hum*, yes ... you could put it that way ..."

"If there were more natural sounds and several consonances, would you be more satisfied?" I continued.

"Oh, positively!" proclaimed the young musician. "There is no better inspiration than a rich collection of sounds."

"Well, that can be arranged!" I called triumphantly and bent myself to one of the lisping fellows who stood near me and whispered my plan in his ear. He grinned broadly.

"Yes, excitingshes," he called delighted. "Nice, much noishes!"

The word "noishes" did not please the musician very well. He looked suspiciously at me with his half-closed eyes. Both fellows ran away to carry out my plan. They quickly returned with about forty other fellows. Some had taken along pine tree branches. Expectantly they looked at me, pushing each other in the tunnel to be able to come closer by.

"Excellent!" I said and levied my hands. "Let the concert start!"

All fellows set themselves at work to make the necessary nature sounds. The result was deafening.

The musician, shocked, made a leap in the air. Some lispers gnawed the trees and made "*krr, krr*" sounds; others were beating with full strength with their branches on hollow tree trunks. This caused dimly droning *boom-boom* sounds so that the tunnel trembled and eroded here and there. This mixture of sounds was in an appropriate manner completed by the rest of the men who stamped with their feet on the ground, applauded, and whistled between their two large front teeth.

The musician appeared to have gained enough inspiration after a while because he called above the noise with full strength, "Stop! I pray you!

I made a stop signal with my hand, whereupon the sounds slowly died out except a small *boom-boom* because some fellows had started to enjoy it.

Panting, the young man admitted, "These nature sounds are somewhat too strong for my sensitive ear. These are not those simple primitive sounds, so gentle and tender, caressing the ear."

I made a naughty smile. The arrogant man started to realize that the nature sounds he first disapproved of weren't that bad. "Didn't I already explain," continued the man, "how essential silences are in music? That silence is a symbol of luck or sadness? I consider just creating a piece of music without sounds," the musician closed his eyes dramatically and seemed to ascend to in higher spheres.

"Correct, yes!" I coughed. "Your problem has therefore been solved. I am glad you take satisfaction from simple primitive sounds. The '*krr, krr*' sounds will no longer disturb your work. And I take it for granted that you have nothing more to complain about with those honestly working tree fellows."

"Actually! No!" exclaimed the man and shook the hand of Nicolashes in a friendly manner. Loud hoorays resounded from the tunnel, which caused the musician to put his hands to his ears.

"Now, quickshes," called Nicolashes, just as hurriedly as before. "We must do workshes. Quickshes, awayshes, enough gameshes seen." The little people pushed us to the exit and supported our feet so that we could climb from the hole where we had been dragged earlier. Thus Toodle, the musician, and I were again in the forest. A last "Byshes!" still resounded from the hole, whereupon we walked away.

The musician walked with us but paid us little attention because he imitated the gentle "*krr, krr*" sounds, which were still audible.

"Yes, that is brilliant!" he praised himself and turned to us. "See there. I must go now, good king. Our ways will part here; a master work awaits me." He bent courteously to Toodle and me but came upright with a yell. "Ow!" With his hand, he rubbed the back of his neck, where something had hit him.

"The letter!" exclaimed Toodle, very delighted, and rapidly picked up the folded paper dart from the ground.

"Those tree gnawers! I shall tell—! What brutality to bombard me with arrows. An attack in the back!" called the musician angrily, becoming red. With large steps, he disappeared from our view.

I tried to stop him, explaining that the lispers had nothing to do with the letter, but it was already too late. The musician had gone.

"He will probably always remain offended," Toodle sighed.

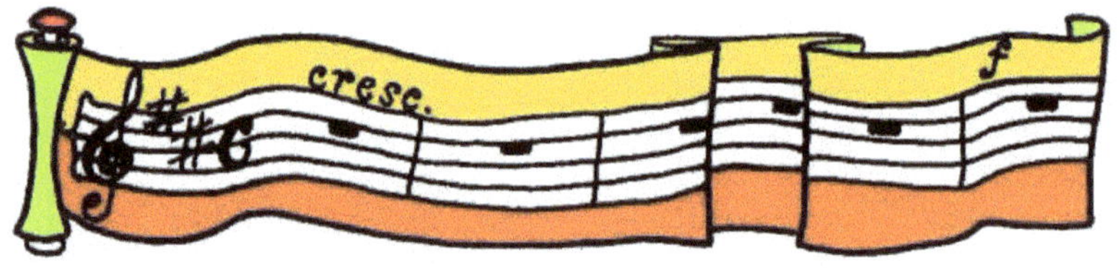

8

Toodle had the folded-up letter still in her hand. "Quick, open it," I encouraged her impatiently. With trembling hands, she unfolded the dart and read out loud:

"Dear Toodle, dear Ody, herewith I send you the proof of royalty.

I declare that Ody, in possession of this letter,

is the only real King of Existence.

Nobody knows here Espra, the cumbersome daughter.

Be careful with her,

don't trust what you don't know.

Your friend, Sseus."

"Hmm," I mumbled, reflecting. "The old king never took Espra along to his castle tree. Why does Sseus insist that we are careful with her?"

"Ah, but we are, aren't we?" Toodle consoled me. "Fortunately, we have the proof of your royalty to persuade her of your high position."

I smiled. "However, let us first find my daughter."

We decided to examine the lower parts of the forest. The number of bare trees decreased greatly, but they were not replaced by green trees. We were still in the bird-free area and would soon leave the forest. We started to descend a slightly overgrown hillock and saw a large blanket of clouds in front of us. It seemed to be a thick mist that lay motionless over a valley. Not one sound could be heard. A threatening and anticipating silence hung there, like just before a large storm.

"Shall we step into that fog?" asked Toodle, whispering and not the least bit enthusiastic.

"Where problems might be; my presence is required anywhere where there are problems, and so is Espra's, or so she thinks," I answered and, full of self-confidence, finished descending the hillock and walked into the white clouds until only my head was above them. After a little hesitation, Toodle followed, and we slowly sank deeper into the fog. We could hardly see a hand before our eyes. We held each other's hands in order not to lose each other. Our shoes made creaking sounds over a gravel-like surface. I stooped and saw that there were large, white rocks lying on the ground. I heard a softly splashing river somewhere, but I could not make out how far away it was. The sound came steadily closer until my feet splashed in the water, and apparently, we had found the river. I felt a light breeze through my hair. The fog patches were slightly blown aside. Thus, I could see the riverbank.

"Look, there you have the berry barrels!" Toodle exclaimed, indicating the wooden barrels which floated gently back and forth, high on the water. Frightened, she concluded, "We are, therefore, in the country of the bird-eaters! The Juice-Squeezers did not dare to pass here, you remember?"

I nodded. I was astonished that, although I stood far into the river, the water did not reach further than my ankles. I waded to deeper parts but did not sink in the water! I scooped a hand of water and took a sip. "*Pfoufft*!" I spluttered. "This is saltier than even saltwater!"

"How interesting," Toodle said and walked with the greatest of ease over the water.

"Those white stones on the ground are probably large salt crystals," I thought out loud.

The fog thickened again. It was difficult traveling in these conditions.

"Let's travel by barrel!" proposed Toodle delightedly. "If we sit together on a barrel, it will certainly not sink in this water."

This seemed an excellent idea to me. The barrel could take us far ahead on the current, and we needn't exhaust ourselves. I waded through the saltwater and searched with my hands, feeling around for a floating barrel. One soon bumped against my knee. I gripped it and helped Toodle to mount, which was not easy since the barrel threatened to tip over. After some spluttering, I took my seat too. Thus, we let ourselves go, sitting comfortably with a leg hanging on each side of the barrel. It was a quiet way to travel. From time to time, I pushed myself off from the shore with my feet to steer the barrel around the bends. We wore our capes to avoid our clothes being soaked by droplets of water and fog.

Toodle remained silent. I noticed she was not at ease in these quiet and foggy surroundings, sailing towards an unknown goal. I was lost in thought about Sseus, my task in the Big Settlement Days, and my daughter until suddenly, I was roughly startled from my thoughts.

"*Kraa*! Waah! *Kraa*!" a deafening shout came from the fog. "*Kroo, krrroo*! Wooh! Keep off your paws off my mother!!"

"Espra!" I exclaimed with my hands to my mouth. I wanted to descend from the barrel, but it started to wobble so that we both splashed into the water, where we remained floating high on the water.

"That was Kra's bird voice!" I said, frightened to Toodle. "We must save Espra!" I stood up and ran to the riverbank. "Come quickly!" I exhorted Toodle, who hesitated to come along. I seized her hand and dragged her to the place where I thought the clamor came from.

"*Kraa, kroo*!! Keep your paws off my children!" now it was Espra's voice.

It was clear that a family drama was taking place somewhere. I ran as fast as possible over the salt grains to solve the problem in time. The fog blankets were less dense here, and with a small puff of wind, I could distinguish a kind of building. It was a blockhouse, a fort made of white salt crystals stuck out high above the fog blanket. A thin sunbeam, which broke through the fog, made the fort shine like one large crystal. On the blockhouse's left, I saw some shadows moving. They seemed to wrestle with something thick and finally threw it into the building with their combined strength.

"How you will regret this!" the bundle yelled in a voice that very much resembled Espra's.

I rushed forward until I had arrived at the wall of the blockhouse. Panting, I crawled carefully along the wall to be able to put my head around the corner. I saw ten very thin beings dressed in wet white rags, which they had bound around their thin bodies. Under their straight hair, two foggy eyes were half-hidden. They all had sharp noses and a mouth that ran from one ear to the other. Furthermore, they all had sharp beaks and itchy hands with long fingers. There was no doubt; we were dealing with the bird-eaters here.

"Ha! Ha!" a voice said. "What shall we do with them? Ha! Ha!"

"Ha! Ha!" was the answer. "Let's discuss this quietly first. Ha! Ha! Let's sit on that fog blanket. Ha! Ha!"

The thin creatures were clearly in a splendid mood. I saw they were light enough to be able to take a seat on the fog blankets.

"We will bake them. Ha! Ha!" someone proposed.

"No, let's stew them. Ha! Ha!" insisted another.

"Let's take them with a grain of salt. Ha! Ha!" said a third one.

"Or cooked or raw or lukewarm or hot. Ha! Ha!" Proposals came from both sides with enthusiasm so great that their mouths drooled. They were all yelling at each other and exchanging the most delicious bird recipes. Finally, after an honest poll, in which those who supported the cook and stove preferences were not allowed to contribute, it was decided to roast the caught birds in a thick layer of salt. This apparently seemed to best improve the taste.

"It must be the best salt in the world. Ha! Ha! Come, let's fetch it. Ha! Ha!" After this appeal, they went in all directions. The fort had been left deserted. The bird-eaters did not know, of course, that bird rescuers were close by. Anyhow, nobody dared to put one step in their area. They assumed they could safely leave their prisoners behind unguarded.

"Now's our chance!" Toodle whispered behind me. I stole around the corner and felt the walls in search of an entrance. "Here is one," whispered Toodle, who had found something. A wooden crossbar had been fastened to a door.

I knocked on the door and asked softly, in order not to be heard by the bird-eaters, "Espra, Kroo, and Kra! Are you there?"

"No!" was Espra's angry answer. "We have escaped!" Espra was clearly in a bad mood.

I slid the bar from its position and pushed open a clammy door made of salt. We stepped inside. There was no fog in the room. In a corner, I saw Espra with a red head, her arms crossed angrily. Left and right of her sat Kra and Kroo, imitating Espra's attitude. Toodle closed the door to keep the fog and any spies outside.

"Espra, we have come to rescue you," I said and approached her.

"Oh, yes?" asked Espra, not very impressed, with one raised eyebrow. "And why so? Because I have cured you so beautifully of thinking yourself the King of Existence?" She had indeed recognized me.

"Yes," I sighed. "That's exactly the subject I want to talk to you about."

"Can't we disappear first?" asked Toodle nervously, looking behind her. "The bird-eaters can return at any moment."

However, I did not think this was a good idea. If Espra escaped, it was quite possible that I would be not so lucky to find her again. And then she would continue with her Big Settlement Days, which was not desirable. I sat down on the ground in front of Espra and told her my story: "Espra, I am Ody, the only real King of Existence; look here!" I took Sseus' letter from the leather case and let her read it.

Espra became even more red with anger. "Why does he say such things about me?! What's this about the 'cumbersome daughter?!'" she exclaimed and fluttered about the room, shocked.

"No! No!" I tried to calm her down. "That's not the point now. It concerns the proof of royalty."

Espra landed on the ground and placed Kra and Kroo behind her. "Well, pale fellow!" she said. "You still have one chance to talk to me, and then I am going to free myself."

I hurried to tell her the whole story. I explained how the king, who no longer could think, had started a new life, how I had been proclaimed the King of Existence, and how the old king and I are the same person, which is why only I had the right to hold Big Settlement Days.

Having heard everything, Espra pressed her narrow mouth together, and tears came to her eyes. "Oh! Daddy!" she exclaimed, sobbing, and threw herself in my arms, embracing me firmly.

"*Ahem, ahem,*" I coughed, half-choked, a bit embarrassed by this plump bird. "Yes, yes ... *ahem* ... you are my daughter."

Also, Toodle blinked a tear away at the sight, a response which I found rather exaggerated. Finally, I delivered myself from Espra's grip, but immediately Kra and Kroo threw themselves on me, sobbing. "Oh! Grandfather!" they croaked.

"Ha! Ha! The best salt I have. Ha! Ha!" said a voice from behind the door.

Everyone grew rigid with fear. The bird-eaters had returned! I jumped back to the door and held my ear to it to listen and discover how many eaters had already returned.

"Ha! Ha! Not at all! I have found the best salt. Ha! Ha!" a different voice said. This back-and-forth discussion arose between the two creeps. I heard no others. There were probably only two of them right now.

I made an escape plan. "Let's run into the thickest fog. Perhaps they will not see us!" It was worth trying. Espra ran to me and even took my hand. Kra and Kroo followed their mother. I opened the door with a crack. Wisps of fog blew in my face. I could hear the eaters argue but couldn't see them.

"Quick!" I ordered, whispering, and pulled the whole fleeing company outside. The fog was now fortunately very thick.

"To the river!" I quietly ordered. I heard splashing in the water and could still remember from which side we had come. "Espra! Fly immediately away with Kroo and Kra! Follow the river. We will follow."

"Will you come back to me?" asked Espra languishing. "Don't leave me alone again, okay, Father?"

I put her at rest and heard myself say, "No, sweet child."

My hands were released. I heard wings flapping, disappearing in the fog.

"Now for us, Toodle."

I again seized a hand in the clouds and started running. "Ha! Ha! How is this for a new game? Ha! Ha!" said the voice belonging to the hand which I had grasped. "Ha! Ha! Are you going to show me where the best salt is? Ha! Ha!"

"Eh," I stammered, frightened, pushing away the cold

hand. "Eh ... do you have problems for me to solve on this Big Settlement Day?"

"Ha! Ha! How strangely you talk, Tom! Ha! Ha!" the voice answered, upon which two bony grasping hands caught me by the shoulders and shook me back and forth. "You have eaten too much salt, certainly. Ha! Ha!"

"Ho! Ho!" someone cried behind us. "The bird has flown away. Ho! Ho!"

"Daughters can never be trusted," I called to the bird-eaters.

"Ho! Ho! Certainly not a plump one. Ho! Ho!" protested the other one. "Ho! Ho! Hold him. Ho! Ho!" Tom's voice advised from behind us.

My one holding my shoulder found this a terrible idea and weakly grabbed me, but then a warm hand pulled me away with a jolt. This hand felt more like Toodle's.

"Ha! Ha! Towards the barrels. Ha! Ha!" she joked.

"Ho! Ho! Ho! Ho!" ordered our would-be captors' voices, but we had already reached the river. We waded through the water, grabbed the first passing barrel, and praised the Juice-Squeezers for their generous consignment of berry juice barrels. After struggling a bit, we were once again sitting on top of a firm barrel and soon disappeared out of the bird-eaters' range.

9

After drifting some time, we sailed out of the fog as if by magic. The banks were no longer of salt but fertile clay on which green shrubs and reeds grew. From time to time, we got bogged down in the reed growths such that we had to jump into the shallow water and pull the barrel afloat. As it slowly became darker outside, I saw a landscape full of plants and trees around us with a heavy smell of wet leaves. There was no houses or cabins to be seen. Toodle and I started to worry because we saw neither Espra nor Kroo and Kra. Had they undertaken something on their own again, we wondered, concerned. This thought was immediately followed by some calling and scraping in the distance.

We heard in front of us "Daddy!" and "Grandpa!"

The current led us nearer to the sounds until we distinguished a dark wooden bridge in the twilight, which railings Espra, Kroo, and Kra jumped up and down on with fluttering wings.

"Yoo-hoo, Daddy!" they said. "Here we are!"

Reaching the bridge, Toodle and I jumped in the water and climbed up the high bank. Espra came to help me and pulled me up by both my arms with such strength that I had no chance to set my feet down and my abdomen was dragged through the wet clay. Toodle received the same aid from Kroo and Kra, who had each caught her by one hand.

"No thanks for the aid," said Espra, loudly laughing without waiting to receive the thanks. "Well, Father, now we must find a spot to spend the night," she continued. "I have selected that tree for the purpose." Espra indicated with a finger a tree with a thick trunk and dense foliage of a kind that I had never seen before. The trunk seemed worked and carved. It contained certain signs and forms. Resolutely Espra stamped to her selected tree, followed by her children, and prepared to fly to one of the branches.

"Wait a bit," I called after her.

"Nonsense; why?" she answered.

"We must check whether there are any people in the neighborhood," I explained. "That bridge may lead to a maisonette where we can find a more comfortable place to sleep."

"Well, this time, I will be tolerant," Espra answered, coming back to me. "But I won't take any responsibility for badly organized sleeping plans."

Wringing out our clothes, Toodle and I passed the bridge, followed by the three birds with "pooh-what-nonsense" grimaces. The bridge was, just like the tree I had seen, decorated with carved forms or symbols. It was not clear whether the planks of the bridge had these forms naturally or if human hands had carved them. We followed a path of flat-stamped ferns which we could easily distinguish in the light of the rising moon.

"What about those Big Settlement Days," said Espra with a hard voice, now walking beside me. "What is my task in that?"

I only wanted to give her a complete explanation of her negligible position in this matter when the yellow bird continued, saying, "You can't snatch my lawful rights. You, yourself, when you were still the old king, took me along on the Big Settlement Day trips. When you ran out on me, I had to do everything by myself. I am willing to forgive you this and to serve you again as an aid."

"I did not run out on you!" I exclaimed. "I was, eh … recovering."

"Your aid has been frequently annoying on these recent Big Settlement Days," Toodle imprudently offered.

Espra roared her indignation but stopped when her head turned green. "'Annoying' says this weedy elf, annoying! And what kind of calamities would have happened if I had not intervened, whereas Mister here was taking it easy, hm?"

Kroo and Kra started to flutter up and down in support of their mother's words. "Dirty elf, boo!" they cried.

Toodle took a deep breath to tell them once and for all the truth about her elf-like characteristics, so I said rapidly, "No, no, there is no problem. Espra and, eh … my grandchildren can simply travel with us. I recognize that Espra's experience, eh … can be useful to us."

The plump yellow bird relaxed her wings slightly and said with a slight suspicion in her eyes, "Correct! That's sensible talk."

The birds started walking again, but Toodle and I looked worriedly at each other. Nobody spoke a word again until we saw a light shining between the trees.

"A place to sleep!" said Toodle, indicating the light.

"*Humpf*, if you say so," Espra mumbled softly behind me.

We accelerated the pace of our walking until we came, to our surprise, to an enormous white temple. Broad, white-marble staircases led to a gallery with pillars, through which a pleasant yellow light shone. Above our heads, the words "Public Rest Area" were written on the edge of the slightly sloping roof.

"Pure chance" was Espra's comment.

We mounted the staircase and found, halfway up, a somewhat plump man, dressed in a white sheet wrapped nonchalantly around himself, came towards us. He had a bald head, walked on bare feet, and said with a sleepy look and a dreamy smile, "Come dissatisfied and leave happy." He bowed as if these were the usual welcoming words and gestured for us to enter the gallery. The main characteristic of the gallery was an enormous peacefulness which dominated the air. The space was bordered by white marble pillars, which were illuminated by a gentle yellow light that came from a round opening in the floor. On the floor around the light source, about thirty people were sleeping, all bald and wrapped in white sheets.

"You can lie down where you like," said our host, handing each of us a white sheet. He gestured for us to be quiet, lay down where he was standing, and fell promptly asleep.

Quietly we each sneaked to a spare spot on the floor. Toodle and I removed our dirty clothes full of river clay, wrapped ourselves in sheets, and followed the example of all the other sleepers. From the corner of my eye, I saw Espra wrestle with a sheet that had been twisted around her legs. She eventually gave up, threw the sheet on the floor, stretched herself, and covered herself with her wings. A heavy smell of roses and unknown flowers sent me into a deep sleep.

Nights later, or so it seemed, I was woken by the bald man with a gentle hand on my shoulder. In my half-asleep and dreamy state, he gave me a bowl of water.

"*A frugal breakfast*," I thought.

"It is good, it is good," spoke the man quietly.

The birds and Toodle still slept, as did all other persons who occupied the floor. I took a mouthful of the breakfast water which miraculously had a lot of taste and was more nourishing than one would have thought.

"This is a public rest area," whispered the man who gave

me water. After a long silence, he continued, "One can rest here."

Since he did not try to revive the discussion, I tried a couple of direct questions. "I am Ody, King of Existence; if you have a problem, I will settle it once and for all. Do you have a problem?

The smile became even dreamier. "A problem? Us?" he asked. And after a silence, he continued, "Everything here is focused on rest, and they who rest have no problems."

"Nightmares, perhaps?" I tried.

"This is impossible if you inhale the flower scent," the man explained. Then he added, somewhat more jovially, "The source in the middle gives rest by light, air, and water. Nobody can resist that rest. Each visitor finds his peace and luck here."

At that moment, some neighboring people woke up, as did my travel companions. Toodle and the birds got their morning bowls of water and gathered around the bald man, who sat down on the ground.

"Don't you ever work?" I asked our host.

"Yes, yes," he sighed. "Ages ago, we built this temple and the bridge over the Sello River, not far from here. From that, we have had to sleep a long time to recover."

"And the carved wood of the bridge?" I asked, interested.

"That was already on the trees ... too much work otherwise," yawned the man. "The temple doesn't have walls. we found the pillars enough ... after not sleeping for so many hours."

"Not sleeping?" asked Toodle.

"He probably means working," I concluded.

"But now something concrete," intervened Espra with a loud voice. Some sleepers sat up, annoyed. "All this sleeping removes all clarity of spirit. You have a serious problem. You must be up early; that's what makes you happy. To work, make those temple walls, and make a neat gravel path to the bridge." Espra had stood up and caught the bald man under his arms, making him stand up.

"No, no, he doesn't have problems that need to be settled," I hurried to say.

"My experienced eye says something else," the yellow bird spoke imperturbably. "You still have a lot to learn from me, I see."

"Stop!" I called, disturbing the rest of the temple. "I am the father, and you are the daughter. Wasn't there a rule that daughters should obey fathers?"

Espra thought, just for a moment, without being convinced. The mood in the temple became more animated. A hullabaloo sounded around us, followed by gentle weeping in the corner.

"What's that?" shrieked Espra turning with a jolt.

"That's nothing at all," said the bald man quickly and opened his eyes a bit more.

In the corner sat a person hidden by a white sheet, huddled together and crying. I wanted to run to him, but Espra hopped rapidly in front of me, seized the person by his collar, and kept him dangling before us in the air.

"This is a bundle of misery," she announced. "Here, we must intervene, Father."

The crying person was roughly rolled out of his sheet by Espra. He was a slim, long young man with dark blond hair. He wore sloppy, white cotton trousers and a white shirt much too big for him. With red, tearful eyes, he looked at us, gasping.

"Why is he crying?" I asked the bald man.

"He came here for rest," the bald man answered. "Rest will heal him. He was brought here by his mother because he always cries so much. Nobody knows why he cries, and it is so sad," he continued shamefully. "Our rest hasn't brought peace to him, and he has been here for a very long time."

"Here sits your problem, baldy," said Espra to the bald man. "Sleep only creates softies. It's much too quiet here for this crying fellow. Adventure is what he needs, wild actions!"

The bald man was greatly shocked. A riot arose between the now widely awake sleepers, who were clustered around the source and scooped water over themselves as in a fixed ritual.

"Papa," spoke Espra, turning to me, "This is child's play. Leave this fellow to me; I will have him alive in no time. I'll take him along with us."

"No!" gasped the young man, for the first time taking part in the conversation. "Do I have to come alo ... along?" His last word led to a heavy fit of weeping, which made the floor wet all over.

"We will do nothing against your will," I put him at rest.

"That's a flagrant error!" Espra exclaimed severely and ran with full speed to the source, where she landed with a large *ploof*. Water splashed up high and soaked the sleepers who had come to drink at the source. A second and third wave was caused by Kroo and Kra, who had faithfully followed the example of their mother, and as a result, almost nobody in the temple remained dry.

"This disturbance is outrageous!" yelled our previously calm host, who made a visibly large effort to remain quiet. "Ody, you are banished from this public rest area. Your company is no longer allowed to enter the temple. Go!"

Never had I heard such words against a king. The bald man stood up and pointed to the exit of the temple. Espra and the green birds stepped happily from the source and shook out their feathers. The yellow bird flew in confusion back and forth, seized a sheet, and hurried to the staircase. Toodle and I hastily picked up our clothes, which we put on rapidly.

"My deepest apologies for my daughter's behavior," I mumbled. The man held his breath and kept his eyes closed.

Toodle and I rapidly ran behind Espra, who had already flown far away. I could see the birds flying high above the trees, like yellow and green spots against the grey, cloudy sky. “We mustn’t lose sight of them,” I said to Toodle. We ran quickly through the forest, from time to time looking up so we could follow Espra’s flight. Sometimes, she disappeared behind the tree branches but reappeared later above our heads. Toodle and I were out of breath. We could hardly keep up with Espra’s flying pace. I was confused and angry. Espra, alone, had disturbed the peace that was so appreciated by those nice bald people; she had created problems where they were none and prevented me from holding a Big Settlement Day. We now approached the edge of the forest, where the trees were smaller and gave way to more bushes. I saw Espra and the green birds landing in high grass. We rushed to the hilly fields, where we found Espra with a very delighted smile. Invisibly in the high grass, we heard Kroo and Kra twitter beside her.

“Great intervention!” said Espra, proud and delighted.

“We have been banished by one of the kindest people I know,” I said, controlling my anger with difficulty. “And I can never take care of their problems. I have missed a Big Settlement Day! You have completely ruined it!”

“Not at all,” replied Espra happily and imperturbably. “Look here, what a surprise.” She pulled a bundled sheet from the grass and threw it in front of my feet.

"Ow!" said the sheet.

"No, look here!" called Toodle, startled and scared. "The crying young man!"

The still-seriously weeping now-kidnapped young man crawled from his sheets.

"You have taken him against his will?!" I stammered aghast.

"For his own good," clarified Espra.

The Big Settlement Days were taking a completely wrong direction. I could not allow people to be forced into a kind of existence which they themselves had not chosen and which would only create problems, not solve them! Stars appeared before my eyes, and my head started to spin.

"Ody!" called Toodle, catching me by the shoulders and putting me down in the grass. The whole world twisted around me, and I had great difficulty clearly focusing on my travel companions. I limply fell down on the grass.

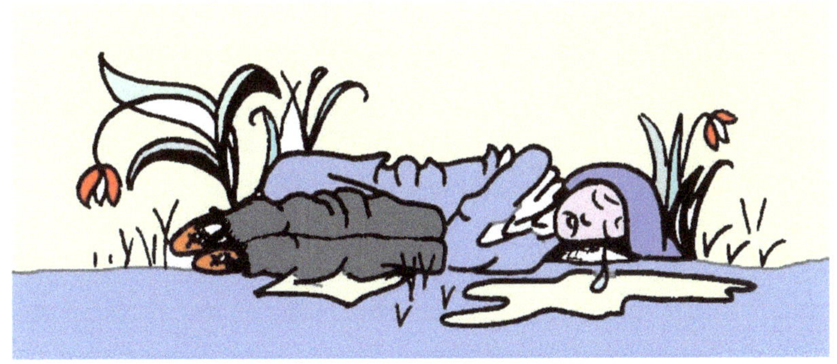

10

I recovered to the sharp sound of a small explosion. Espra and Toodle looked worriedly at me. The crying young man beside me wept softly, with his arms around his bent knees and his head bowed down.

"What was that bang?" I asked.

"A thunderstorm," Toodle reassured me.

Dark grey clouds had packed together; it became dark as night. A strong blast passed by and flattened the long grass flat. Then all of a sudden, it was calm again. I looked at the sky. It was quiet, no sound could be heard, and the atmosphere was strange. Suddenly a flash of light appeared against the dark clouds.

"No, this isn't a thunderstorm," I said pensively.

A belt of light stretched over the sky. The line radiating light came from the left and continued straight on to the right, where it stopped halfway. With bated breath, we watched this unknown natural phenomenon. There, where the luminous line had stopped, we saw a ball of light descending like a falling star. The ball was now above my head and approaching the ground.

"Take care!" I called, pushing aside my travel companions. "It's falling on us!"

We retreated some steps and almost had to close our eyes so as not to be dazzled by the approaching light-ball. A short bump announced that the flare had landed at our feet. A blazing light was shining in my eyes, which I tried to protect with my hand. To my great stupefaction, I made out the contours of a bearded man in a long shirt within the radiating light. He stood before me with long, white hair and a serious face.

"Ody," he spoke with a deep and low voice, which sounded as if it resounded from the deepest of the earth, the voice of a protohuman. "I am the Large Line Artist," continued the lit-up man. "I can only speak once, so listen well. Every King of Existence must, once in his governing period, prolong the Large Line. Once the Large Light Line appears in his sky, he shall let it continue completely to the right, without interruption. A continuing Large Line gives Existence its perpetuity. If the king doesn't let the Large Line continue, the Large Line will stop, and there will be an end to everything that exists and an end to perpetuity itself.

I was greatly startled by these serious and alarming words. "What shall I do?" I asked.

The man did not answer my question but continued, "There is little time before the Large Line comes. Pay much attention to the Large Line."

These were his last words; afterward, he again became a bundle of light and disappeared very quickly into the sky. I followed him with my eyes and saw that the light ball had arrived at the end of the luminous line. After a few seconds, the line faded away and disappeared again to the left from where it had come.

"Look now, that's what's so very annoying with these apparitions," said Espra. "They never answer your question.

Last time, it didn't do so either."

I jumped on Espra's words. "What did you say? What is this previous time you talk about?"

Espra seemed embarrassed. "Now, yes, eh ... the last time," she replied with hesitation.

"Speak the truth," I spoke slowly.

"The last time, when you were still the old king, this light figure came by too," Espra explained.

"And you are only telling me this now!?" I exclaimed.

"You have never asked me whether I had ever seen light balls falling from the sky that announce the end of Existence because they cannot draw large lines by themselves!" Espra said, outraged.

I sniffed.

"What happened with the old king?" asked Toodle.

"Oh, approximately the same as just now," answered the yellow bird laconically. "He didn't say anything about having little time and so on, but yet again, he didn't answer the same question, which the old king had also asked. The 'what shall I do' question."

The sad young man wept even harder, for which he got a correcting punch from Espra, and as a result, the sound became louder. "Stop it once and for all," Espra commented. Toodle tried to comfort the young man by patting him on the back in a friendly way so that he cried for a shorter time.

I continued questioning Espra because I wanted to know everything she knew about me as the old king and about the Large Settlement Days. "What happened afterward with the light figure?"

"Not much," answered Espra. "The old king, my father, sat thinking about what he had done. He mumbled something about problems with stones and stopped holding Big Settlement Days, so I had to take care of everything. One night, he disappeared, leaving me entirely abandoned."

"This is a serious incident," I said, looking earnestly at my travel companions. "If I cannot find out what I must do to let the Large Line continue, if he appears for the last time in the sky, then there will be an end to perpetuity and Existence. Wouldn't holding Big Settlement Days be sufficient?"

We sat down in a circle on the wind-flattened grass, thinking. Apparently, Espra thought very deeply, a frown wrinkling her eyebrows and making her nose look even more like a beak. I seriously wondered if I would ever understand because, when I was the old king, I had apparently not found a solution either and had then lost my capacity for reflection.

After some time of silent consideration, Espra jumped up with a triumphant yell. "I have got it!" she shouted with a sparkling light in her eyes. "I have a great solution! How stupid I was not to have thought of it earlier. There is but one possibility to save Existence, and that is by not holding Big Settlement Days. To safeguard Existence, the King of Existence must himself be ensured and be cured of his inexperience, helplessness, and instability. And for that, there is only one solution: he must get married!"

"Married?" I yelled, frightened.

"Yes, married," endorsed Espra. "Taking a woman as your wife, my mother, and their grandmother." Espra indicated the green birds, who started to hop delightedly around at the idea.

"But Ody doesn't need a wife," Toodle to my aid.

"I don't want to get married at all!" I said, worried about Espra's further reactions.

"That's exactly your great fault," Espra said, approaching me. "Who lost his spirits here? Who is sloppily plodding around with the Big Settlement Days? Who remained motionless in the temple when fast actions were required to save a young man from his misery?" She added, self-assured, "I have more experience with Big Settlement Days and the problems involved than you. You can leave this quietly to my deep insight and be happy that I interfered in this problem."

"No!" I exclaimed. "This problem is too serious to leave to someone else."

"Let your silliness be forgiven," Espra said reassuringly. "But if you don't look for a wife, I will do that for you. And that may be better anyway; otherwise, it would lead to something silly. Come, children; we will go and fetch a grandmother together." When she saw that neither Toodle nor I made any signs of leaving, she said, "Well then, you remain here. I will do it all by myself again."

"Stay here!" I called after her. The young man started to cry harder as Espra and the green birds flew away fast over the fields.

"Oof, we've gotten well rid of them," Toodle sighed.

"But not for long, and who knows what they are all up to," I thought aloud.

Because of the sudden departure of Espra, Kroo, and Kra, I was able to reshuffle my ideas, so I could think quietly about the two remaining problems: the crying young man and the Large Line solution. In the interim, the first problem noisily claimed my attention.

The thin lad gasped heavily. "I don't want to exist any longer ... *sniff* ... I even don't want to want ... *sniff* ..."

Toodle and I looked up, astonished. This young man was really feeling very sorry for himself.

"Why don't you want to exist any longer?" I asked him gently and full of compassion.

"Better stop with that Large Line ... *sniff* ... Existence has no sense anyway. What does it matter ... *sniff* ... when everything no longer exists? New problems are continually being created ... and still more and more ... boohoo ... boohoohoooo ..." sobbed the man.

A sudden idea flashed in my brain. "But of course!" I called delightedly, and the young man raised his tearful eyes and stopped gasping, astonished. "Just like Existence, all problems are also indefinite and infinite. Although all problems can be solved once and for all by the Big Settlement Days, new problems will always remain to be settled. That process will never stop unless Existence comes to an end."

Toodle looked at me expectantly.

"We can travel years and centuries around in search of people and beings whose problems must be solved, but each time we turn around, we face a new problem. How can we permanently remove all difficulties? That is the question."

I turned to the sad young man who looked as if his end was approaching and was not even pleased about that. "Would you still like to exist if your existence had sense?" I asked him.

Hesitating and blinking a tear away, he answered uncertainly, still weeping, "Yes ... Perhaps."

I continued my reasoning. "If we want to solve all problems in perpetuity and infinity of Existence, then everyone must be able to go somewhere to have his difficulties solved. That's my task now with the Big Settlement Days, but not everyone knows that I do this and where I am. Not everyone can come to me with a problem at any time."

"Then what do you propose?" asked Toodle, slightly suspicious because the solution seemed so simple.

"I propose to build a tower which is so high that everybody in the existing kingdom can see it. In the tower, we shall put all people and beings who can help with solving problems. Everyone's problems could thus be solved, and all could exist without difficulties. If one knew that there is always a solution for each problem, without exception, one would have more time for all the other things of Existence, namely happiness."

"And what about people who cannot come to the tower?" asked Toodle, looking for a weak point in the plan. I had not yet considered this. How could a potential problem be solved as soon as possible in the tower if the person was not able to travel rapidly to the tower?

"However, I know of something," said Toodle answering her own question. "We will use elf paper. There are elves all over the kingdom of Existence, and I can call them up. Elves can handle elf paper very well. When I inform all elves of the kingdom about our tower, they can act as our local representatives. There is always an elf in the neighborhood to whom problems can easily be passed on. They will write the difficulties on elf paper and send these to the tower so that the problem can be solved quickly; in short, a Big Settlement Day at a distance."

"That's a brilliant idea," I said delightedly. Toodle's face radiated happiness.

The sad young man followed our conversation in silence, too astonished to think of weeping.

"Well," I announced solemnly, as I stood up, "now there is only one thing left for us to do—find the center of the kingdom and build our tower there. We will call it the Solvetower!"

Toodle clapped her hands but sensibly remarked, "How can you find the center of the kingdom if everything that exists is infinite, and for this reason, the borders of the kingdom are also infinite? Isn't then each point a center?"

"My kingdom indeed has no structures," I answered. "It is not round, and it is not flat, but includes all forms that exist. We must float very high up in the sky, look around as far as we can see, and then put the Solvetower down in the middle."

This got Toodle's approval, and we were greatly surprised to have found the solution to this serious Existence problem so quickly. However, our laughter died down as we considered further arrangements for our plan.

"How can we fly in the sky?" I thought.

"We could have used Espra for this purpose," Toodle sighed. "But she is only there when she is not wanted and disappears when she could be useful."

"Do you want to fly?" asked the sad young man, intervening. "I can fly," he continued hesitatingly and melancholically.

"You can fly for us?" I said, astonished about the hidden capacities of this young man.

"Not now," he answered. "But my flying bird can."

"Flying bird? What do you mean by that?" questioned Toodle.

"I am not allowed by my mother to fly ... *sniff*," He started crying again. "She finds it too dangerous ... *sniff* ... but I built my flying bird secretly ... *sniff*, *sniff* ... you want to see it?"

"Of course!" I exclaimed hopefully.

The young man got up, staggering, and gestured for us to follow him back into the forest.

"Actually, what is your name?" I asked him, now that our conversations had started to take a more serious course and there was less weeping.

"Frint," he said without enthusiasm, clearing himself a way through the high ferns.

The sky had brightened after the Large Line's appearance. The sun's rays shone through the roof of foliage and between the trunks so that we could easily distinguish all the different green colors of the foliage.

"I built the flying bird by myself without my mother knowing about it," said Frint, showing a brave face. "Then I hid it in the forest and didn't look after it anymore; there was no point anyway." His face became sad again. "When it was finished, I didn't find it very nice any longer ... and then came the Public Rest Area ... *sniff*." He wanted again to stop in order to let his tears flow, but Toodle and I took him by the arms and encouraged him to find the flying bird first and cry afterward. After a short walk and some searching left and right, since Frint could not find the hiding place immediately, he dived into the sumptuous plant growth and signaled to us with his hand.

He dug somewhat deeper between the ferns and other ground plants, pulled a couple aside, and said, “Here it is.” Behind the foot of a large tree, which had the same figures in its trunk as those at the rest area, lay a bunch of branches and leaves. Frint had already removed the upper layer of plants and now shoved away the dry leaves and branches. We helped him with his work and soon discovered a medium-large metallic bird. Its tail, wings, fuselage, and head slowly became visible. The bird was made of thin flat metal blades with small holes which were fixed to each other with iron wire. In the head of the flying bird, two balls acted as staring eyes, whereas a sad and painful smile was painted on the flat metal beak, which left no doubt about the builder of this vehicle. Two settees, one behind the other, had been placed between the wings at the back of the flying bird. One for the pilot and a passenger and one for two slim people. The metal blades were a silvery grey color and were rusted here and there on the corners. The dense branches and the layers of leaves had sufficiently protected the bird from the air, and they had not rusted entirely.

“Get in,” gestured Frint. He was seated in the driver's seat. Toodle and I wriggled ourselves on the hindmost wooden settee. We sat up to our waist inside the bird; the rest of our bodies were above so that our view was not obstructed. Frint pulled on some handles. The head of the flying bird moved up and down, the tail wobbled from left to right, and the wings started to move with moaning sounds. Frint was busy and very focused; he grimaced gloomily but did not weep. “Hold tight!” he recommended, which did not prove to be superfluous advice. The bird shook up and down as the wings started to flap faster. With each ongoing movement, we heard “*peep, peep.*” After a sharp crunching sound, the flying bird lifted a bit off the ground and swerved to the left, finally ascending right through an opening in the foliage to above the forest. The flying of the metal bird was very strenuous for Frint, who operated both wings by working with his feet on two pedals. He controlled the direction of the tail and the head with his hands to steer it on its course. We clung to our settee and looked down, surprised, as we saw the forest and the fields disappearing under us.

"Go as high as possible," I shouted in Frint's ear. He nodded and continued diligently with the pedaling. How lucky we had been! This flying bird served us terribly well. Everything was running on as if wheels, and I could hardly imagine why the old king had had such a problem finding a solution for the Large Line, as Espra had explained. I was probably more difficult when I had been the old king. In the depths below, I saw the forests, the foggy field of the bird-eaters, and even very far away, my castle tree. The wind blew through our hair, and it became colder. I drew my travel cape close around myself. It also became more difficult to breathe as we ascended still higher, and we could no longer endure the cold. On the horizon around us, I started to look over the extent of my kingdom. Frint made a final extreme effort, which resulted in us rising several meters higher. There I saw that, very far away, the horizon became black. Apparently, I could not see any further because there the Kingdom of Existence reached that of Non-Existence, where infinity and zero touched each other.

I gestured to Frint to bring the flying bird in such a position that a black edge was visible on all sides at the horizon. This was the center of my realm. With much effort, Frint succeeded in bringing the flying bird to the correct place. Now we had to go straight down to the spot on the ground, where the Solvetower was to be built. Frint stopped pedaling, and the flying bird made a free fall down at an alarmingly high speed. The wings groaned under the weight and folded up-wards. Just when I thought that we would crash on the ground and could forget about the Solvetower, Frint started to pedal again, the wings unfolded, and the bird descended in a spiral. We could already see the earth clearly as the bird decreased speed.

"Look!" Toodle exclaimed. "There is already something standing at the place of the Solvetower!"

11

The flying bird arrived moaning on the ground in a region where trees were not so high and stood far from each other. We jumped from the vehicle and examined the place where we had landed. It was an open spot in a young forest where thorny plants grew everywhere. Looking carefully in order not to be hurt by the thorns, I came close to the object that Toodle had indicated, which stood exactly on the spot where I wanted to build my Solvetower. It was a stony construction, partially in ruins, surrounded by large blocks of stone and rocks. I walked around the structure, which was round and rather large. It consisted of one floor, which had eroded partially at the back. Some rose shrubs had wormed themselves between the mass of stones. At what seemed to be the front, I saw a reinforced entrance without a door. The large stone strut pillars indicated that this building had once been decorated with a majestic door. In the harsh grey stones above the door opening, a text had been carved. One could read "Solve ..." The text seemed to be incomplete because some space had been left for more characters. A strange feeling of fear overpowered me as if some misfortune radiated from this construction. Toodle approached.

"This seems to be the ruin of a Solvetower," she whispered as if she did not want to be recognized. "Look, there stands 'Solve.' They have forgotten to carve 'tower' in order to make 'Solvetower.'" I nodded. This was what I already suspected, and strangely enough, this discovery did not please me. "It seems as if someone has preceded you without success," continued Toodle in a gentle tone.

"The old king?" I suggested. "Hadn't he, according to Espra, had problems with stones or something like that?"

"What should we do now?" sighed Frint, leaning tiredly over his flying bird.

"Pull!" we heard from the ruin. "Pull! Still harder!" a loud voice yelled.

Toodle and I jumped aside as fast as lightning and hid behind the wall of the construction from where we could see the entrance. Frint slipped adroitly under a wing of the flying bird.

The ground groaned. "Forward! March!" the hard voice called. "And oof ... and oof ..." some other voices answered equally loudly.

I glanced carefully at the entrance. We could just as well, of course, have remained there where we were, but the anxious atmosphere which hung around the ruin and the hardness of the voices had scared us. It was better to be careful. A heavily muscular man with a tanned upper body, wearing a broad leather belt around his waist and short brown trousers, came out of the ruin. He levied a fist in the air and shouted, "Stone out!" The "and oof" callers now appeared. They were six similarly muscular men who wore the same outfit as the "stone out" commander. They pulled outside a wooden cart on which lay a stone block hauling on two rope cables, three men at each side. They synchronized their steps with their "and oof" calls, the right leg always at "oof" and the left leg at "and." Without noticing us, the group disappeared to the left. I gestured to Frint that we should follow the men to see where they were going and what they were up to. Frint crawled from under the bird wing and shrugged his shoulders as if he didn't care a fig. Toodle and I kept hidden, carefully walking softly from trunk to trunk and following the men. This was sometimes difficult because the trees were not close to each other. Behind us sneaked Frint, who preferred not to be left behind. The group walked, stamping, out of the forest and arrived after a while on a stony road. The cart's wooden wheels rattled so loudly that we could walk with less caution. The trees had now disappeared so that we had to run directly behind the cart, ducking below the stone block. We had arrived in a rocky and arid area where nothing grew or flourished.

"Stop!" the first walking man ordered suddenly. "You there, behind the cart. Come forward." I was surprised that someone had noticed our presence. Since we had no choice, all three of us stepped forward from behind the cart. "What's all this spying?" asked the man with dark eyes, towering above us. Frint started crying, as was to be expected.

"I require an immediate explanation!" I bluffed. "Who gave you the right to take away stones from the ruin?"

"Those stones are ours," answered the man, somewhat restrained. "They were brought there for nothing and must therefore return."

"I am the King of Existence," I explained. "And I want an explanation as to how that ruin came here in the forest."

"Ha, ha," chuckled the man, contorting his face as if he wasn't used to laughing. "You are not the King of Existence. He looks quite different, ha, ha. A bit more thickset and older, ha, ha." It was really awkward traveling around in my kingdom when so many people persisted in telling me that I wasn't the King of Existence.

"He is the new king," Toodle hastened to add. "The old king has disappeared.

"Was high time," the man commented. "In that case, you better follow me to my house."

"That is exactly what we will do," I said, taking Frint by his arm to soothe his weeping. The "and oof" men took up their heavy work again, throwing me glances of disbelief from time to time. We approached a group of houses enclosed by blocks of rock at the foot of a bare, grey mountain. In front of what seemed to be a large cave excavated in the mountain stood many carts such as ours, with and without stone blocks.

"Discharge!" ordered the forerunner with a loud voice. The men pulled the cart into the cave, and somewhat later, a hard "*klapperdaboom*" could be heard. The cart reappeared from the cave empty.

"Follow me, then we talk," ordered the muscular leader in his usual commanding tone. He went into a stone house, which contained vent openings but no windows, gestured us to sit down on stone stools around a stone table, and fetched some goblets and plates of crude earthenware. The man seized a stone pitcher from a niche and a sack of broad beans, which he put on the table for us. As he poured a dark grey juice into our goblets, he spoke, "So they have appointed a new king. What brings you here, new king?" The man had not been introduced to formal language, obviously.

"I want to know more about the ruin," I answered.

The man sat down in front of me at the table, shoved some dark red broad beans in his mouth, and said with his cheeks full, "That ruin, as you call it, was built by us a long time ago. It was to become a Solvetower, built for the King of Existence for delivery before it was too late. Man, what a lot of gold and gems we got for that!" He chuckled, satisfied with himself, and continued, "An old man came by one day, claimed he was the King of Existence, and wanted a tower to be built on that spot and nowhere else. I warned him that this spot was not strong enough; the ground is too soft to support a very high tower. But, no, no, it had to be there and nowhere else, so we started the work. Man, how long that old man took before he came up with a construction plan. I told him explicitly that it contained errors, but he was as stubborn as ... well, yes, something which has little to do with a king."

"What happened to that tower then?" Toodle asked.

"Nothing but misfortune and misery," he answered. The man shook his head as if he had seen what was going to happen a long time before. "Don't get involved with high towers; that's my advice," he continued. "Sooner or later, they fall on your head."

"The tower then fell on the head of the old king?" asked Toodle, strained.

"No," answered our host; he really wasn't much of a gentleman. "The tower was never completed. It collapsed before then because of some kind of lightning."

"The Large Line!" I called.

The man continued imperturbably. "The reason was never really understood. Technical errors, if you ask me. We had arrived at the hundred-and-second floor when a thunderstorm struck, and at least fifty floors thundered down. What a fright! And what a mess of stones. We had to clear everything by ourselves because the king had disappeared after that short but violent lightning. Vanished! Never to be seen again. Now, we have broken everything down and demolished the rest of the floors so that the stones can be used again. Just imagine all those years of work, and we still have not finished taking away the remains of the tower. What good would it have been to leave that ruin as it was? The stones can now be sold again." He bent to me and whispered, pointing to Frint, who chewed on a broad bean without tasting it. "That thin pale one is not very well. A bit of hard work would do him good. If you want,

I can put him at work."

"No, he belongs to me," I whispered, "at least provisionally." I thought about the accident which had occurred to the old king. The Large Line had thus already appeared to him, and it had destroyed and disapproved of the Solvetower. Did I have to adapt my plans now, and should I consider this as a warning? The muscular man now became interested in Toodle, with whom he spoke with pleasure on the techniques of quarrying. Toodle's presence obviously made him somewhat timid because he blushed from time to time. Still deep in thought, I occasionally heard flashes of their conversation.

"I am called Steno," I heard the man say, offering a large hand to Toodle. "I am of the people called the Stenodiggers. We dig up the stones, in short."

"Do you always live here?" asked Toodle.

"Yes. These are our workplaces, our, eh ... women live further on. Stone-digging is no woman's work, you understand?" Frint remained quiet, still chewing without enthusiasm and hardly aware of what he was eating. Some more stone juice?" said the man, startling me from my reflections.

"Yes, thank you," I answered absentmindedly. I had a serious dilemma. My mind told me that I had better think about a different Large Line solution because, in all probability, the old king had had the same idea for the Solvetower, and he had failed greatly. However, some inner urge told me to continue with the plan of the Solvetower. Maybe I could make a better design; perhaps the plan had indeed only failed because of technical errors, or the storm had indeed been only a storm and not the Large Line. Additionally, I was unable to consider a better plan to solve the Large Line problem. My brain was simply blocked. For this reason, I announced to Steno, "I want the Solvetower to be built again."

"Oh no, oh no, out of the question," said Steno, startling and moving backward. "I don't want any more trouble on my neck. Repetitions are always wrong."

"Not even for gold and gems?" Toodle asked impudently. I lifted my eyebrows. Where could we obtain gold and gems from? I knew that the treasury in my castle tree was not very full. We had only enough for what we needed, but no more. In days long ago, the treasury must have been well filled, but the old king must have used all the funds for the construction of his Solvetower, I considered now. I saw Steno hesitate.

"Agreed," he spoke, biting on his lower lip. "But then I want twice the amount paid the previous time."

"Double?" I was scared.

"Yes, you must understand," he explained to me in a laconic way. "If this plan fails and the tower collapses again, then I have been already paid for the clearance work."

"Excellent, we will do that," Toodle said, offering a hand to Steno without any hesitation.

"This is a reasonable person!" Steno said to me as he shook Toodle's hand firmly.

"Elf," I corrected him.

"This deserves a party!" said Steno in his loudest voice. "Wait here." He ran out of the house, and we soon heard cries of "hooray!" outside.

"Toodle, I don't have gold and gems," I said when we were alone. "I can't borrow either because how can I ever pay them back?"

"I have no treasures either," answered Toodle, untroubled. "But I know where to find them! There is a river called the Goldstream, which is only known to elves. No mortal knows of this, and it has been heavily guarded as a secret. If non-elves hear of the existence of the Goldstream, there would be too many disputes and too much fighting." She bent herself closer to me. "However, I believe that this is an absolute emergency. The elves would commit a crime if they did not exploit the secret of the Goldstream just now. Existence is at stake.

However, there is one problem: only you and I can fetch the gold and gems. Nobody is allowed to know about it. Tomorrow we must leave. We have not much time to lose." I nodded, assenting.

"Come up, fellows! The festival is starting!" Steno called very loudly through the window opening and gestured for us to come outside. Frint let out a deep sigh and dragged himself behind us to where the twilight had fallen. Frint still seemed sad but wept less, although I saw some tear spots on the table where he had been seated. Steno had not been stingy with the festival. A large fire had been lighted, which the Stenodiggers danced around somewhat stiffly. Stone blocks served as seats. On a large flat stone, a really festive meal had been displayed. It was astonishing how fast the Stenodiggers had arranged this banquet. Their stamping and hand slapping accompanied the dancing Stenodiggers. Toodle jumped gladly towards the dancers and followed them with her elegant elf moves.

Although the festival was extraordinarily tempting, I decided to absent myself for the first time in my life. Since Toodle and I were leaving tomorrow to fetch gold and gems, I wanted to have the construction plan of my Solvetower ready before that time so that the construction could start in our absence. Time was precious, and I felt a certain agitation within myself. The Solvetower must be built as soon as possible, before the Large Line arrived. With some regret, I excused myself to Steno, asked for some sheets of paper, a feather, and ink, and locked myself up in Steno's house. Frint lay down beside the campfire and had fallen asleep without participating in the festivities.

"Then we shall but dance with you, charming elf!" called Steno with joy, taking Toodle by the shoulders.

I installed myself behind the stone table and looked for a small piece of stone on the ground which had a flat, straight side that could serve as a ruler. I placed three sheets of paper beside each other. Steno had given me two candles, which were not quite straight, but they gave sufficient light to the paper. I needed three sheets because the tower was to be very high. In total, there would be a thousand floors so that it could stick out above the highest mountain tops. It should be a round tower, broad below and narrowing at the top. The last floor would therefore be very small. Inside, a staircase would be built that continued right up to the last floor above. Only some lower floors would get windows, to avoid weakening the walls. On top would be a hole through which one could look out over the Kingdom of Existence. Everything would be built with the grey stones that could be provided by the Stenodiggers. Because the Solvetower would, due to its height, be very heavy, I considered that the ground underneath it should be reinforced first. A large hole had to be excavated and filled with stone rubble and rocks and covered with a thick layer of flat stones. All this should help avoid it sinking, leaning over, or falling down.

After some hours, I examined my drawings, was satisfied, and decided to inspect the quality of the stock of stones. The bottom floors especially had to be constructed of the strongest stone material to be able to support the other floors, which could be made with lighter stones. I picked up a candle and ran in the direction of the cave where I had seen the Stenodiggers discharging the stone blocks.

The festival was still in full swing when I sneaked along. Toodle sat with her face to the fire with a circle of Stenodiggers around, who listened intensively to her powerful elf tales. "And then that giant elf descended on me with his sharp teeth ..." said Toodle to her listeners, who started chattering their teeth with the tension.

Once in the cave, I saw that there were all kinds of stones of different sizes and types. The cave was gigantic, and it seemed as if it had been excavated by the Stenodiggers with sharp pickaxes. Thus, they had large and small stone blocks. The light of my candle shone on the cave's walls. With my straight stone, which I had used as a ruler, I tapped on some rocks to see how porous they were. In the rear of the cave lay a high pile of stone blocks reaching almost to the ceiling. I looked between the blocks to see what kind of stones lay underneath. It seemed that the underlying stones were of a very firm material. I climbed on the stone pile, and from the top, I levered a smaller rock cube aside with the ruler. It rolled, thundering down, the crash causing an echoing in the cave. The underlying stone was now visible. It was of mixed grey color, just like the others, but with some metallic grey veins. Tapping with my hard stone ruler on this block, the block promptly broke to bits under my fingers. A small tap from the ruler had been sufficient to split it into pieces. This stone the ruler was made of was the stone material that I wanted to use for the foundation and the lower floors of the Solvetower! That type of stone could carry the weight of a thousand floors. Happy with my findings, I wrote on paper which stone type should be used for each floor. I stowed my design away in my travel bag and left the cave, yawning. Meanwhile, the festival had reached an end, and close

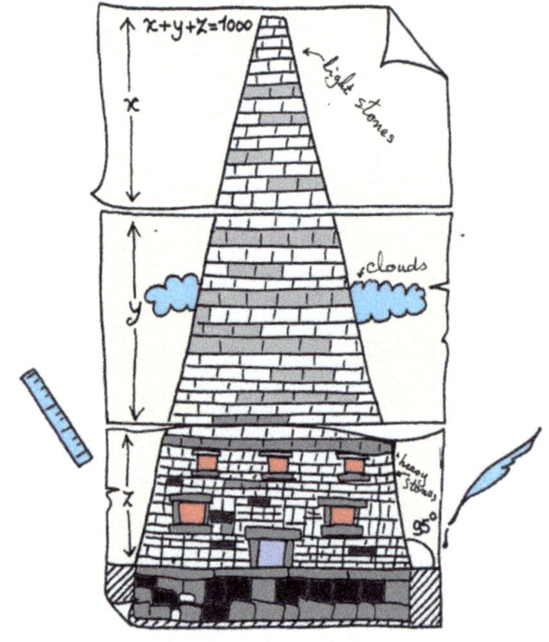

to the smoldering fires, the Stenodiggers had fallen asleep. Some snored almost growlingly. In between them, I saw Toodle rolled up in her travel cape. Overcome by sleep after my nocturnal work, I rolled myself in my cape too and lay down on the hard ground under a radiating starry sky.

12

The next morning, I was woken very early by a hard slap on my back. "*Uche*," I coughed.

"Worked hard, right?" asked Steno with a broad grin and grimacing laboriously. He offered me a couple of beans and a rough cup of stone juice.

"Where does this stone juice come from, in fact?" asked Toodle, who approached us with a similar goblet in her hand.

"That's something very rare," answered Steno, quite ready to explain something about the Stenodiggers' specialties. "You get this when you leave a stone soaking in water for twenty-five hours and then squeeze it by hand. Only our hands have this secret. I wouldn't try it out, agreeable elf."

I took last night's papers and spread them out in a line on the ground for Steno. I looked around for Frint, whom I found squatting by yesterday's festival stone. "Frint, come here, please," I called, waving him over. Frint stood up slowly and shuffled to us.

All four of us leaned over my Solvetower design, and I indicated with my finger from top to bottom the plan for the technical construction of the tower. "Filling a hole with stone gravel," Steno mumbled, reflecting. "That could succeed, perhaps. We didn't do that last time, but the existing ruin must first be taken away. I had not counted on that. You made me understand that we could build on the existing ruin. This changes the deal, of course. With the removal of stone and the digging of a hole, you will need to pay some more gold. The costs for me will be higher."

"Well, then we will pay even more than we had already agreed," said Toodle, undisturbed.

"And then I'm still with you," said Steno, smiling crookedly and moving his head back and forth in agreement.

"The bases and bottom floors must be made of that stone with dark grey veins that I found in the cave," I explained, indicating the spot on the paper.

"Oh no," replied Steno, upset. "No way. Those stones cannot be used, no way. I cannot give those for any amount of gold!"

"But Existence depends on it!" pleaded Toodle.

Frint considered this a suitable moment to start crying again.

Steno said, "Existence? My existence, do you mean? The armed stones are intended for our own houses. And I know how urgently we need them. All our homes, not far from here, have been built with that stuff. Thus, our women, who remain behind, are well protected against hostile people. No arrow or javelin can pierce those stones; for this reason, we call them armed stones. This is a question of strategy, you understand?"

"Who attacks your women's houses?" I asked, shocked by the fact that armed conflicts existed in this part of my kingdom and I was not informed about it.

"Oh ... the Stenoblockers," answered Steno almost timidly. "They do about the same work as we do, only worse," he hurried to add.

"And, of course, you never attack the Stenoblockers' houses and women!" said Toodle smartly.

"Us!" said Steno indignantly with his hand on his heart. "Us? Never! And if we did that, it would fail because the Stenoblockers also live in houses of armed stones. Thus, we keep a good working balance between us. I cannot endanger this balance by selling all my armed stones, even in exchange for much gold and many gems, you understand?"

I saw my Solvetower was in danger. "Well," I spoke, grasping my papers, "then I'm obliged to submit my proposal to the Stenoblockers."

"Ho, ho, not so hasty" was Steno's immediate response. "Perhaps I can still do something ..." There was a solemn silence, and he moved his shoulders slowly back and forth. "We can make the bases and first floor half and half. A mixture of armed stones and ordinary hard construction bricks. Then I can still keep some as a reserve and needn't sell my complete stock. They are difficult to get because they cannot be quarried from the mountain. Much too strong for a chisel. Thus, the tower will be firm enough, but ..."

"But then the costs will become higher," Toodle filled in, sighing.

"That's it," nodded Steno with closed eyes. "Let's say three times as high as what the old king paid for his tower, but then you will get a splendid quality of work."

Toodle nodded approvingly and again shook Steno's hand as she had done yesterday.

We can trust this elf!" called Steno, delighted.

I had explained the last details of my construction plan and then announced, "Toodle and I will leave now for a short trip to obtain your gold and gems." I said this last part vaguely on purpose because I could definitely not disclose the secret of the Goldstream. "I appoint Frint as a construction manager during our absence. He will supervise the construction activities."

Steno raised his eyebrows to show his lack of faith, and Frint raised his eyebrows with even more surprise than Steno and abruptly stopped snivelling. "You have only one thing to do, Frint," I assured him. "Take care that the tower is built according to my plan and postpone crying until after your working day." Frint nodded like a child and accepted my construction papers with care.

Toodle and I stood up. We had already wasted too much time negotiating with Steno. Steno gave each of us a bag of beans for our travel and waved goodbye. "So," I heard Frint say with a gentle, hesitating voice, "let's start with the construction if that suits you."

Toodle stipulated which direction we took. She ran with such quick steps that I could hardly keep up with her. We walked on the left flank of the mountain, where we eventually found a small stone path. The arid, rocky landscape lay far behind us now. It was Toodle's intention to walk around the Stenodiggers' mountain. After some time, the stone path changed to short grass.

"From now on, we will not find any path," announced Toodle, now half running.

"Is the Goldstream still far away?" I gasped breathlessly.

"Not if you don't think about it," she answered.

We had arrived in the green fields which lay behind the mountain. To my right in the distance, I saw a number of houses standing close together, which, as far as I could see, were built of armed stones. These must be the houses of the women of the Stenodiggers or of the Stenoblockers. Toodle resolutely crossed the fields in the direction of another mountain chain, the tops of which were obscured by the clouds.

"Do you think that Frint can handle the supervision of the construction work?" asked Toodle.

"Some responsibility and trust won't be bad for him," I replied in an attempt to reassure myself too. "As long as he believes he can do it."

A bit later, I asked, "Where is the Goldstream situated exactly?"

"On top of that mountain chain, directly above the cloud boundary," replied Toodle.

I swallowed. We faced a rough climb; the trip would last longer than I had expected. We heartily walked on, but not for very long at a time. We frequently stopped to eat some of the beans from Steno, and Toodle used one of these resting places to update our travel report. There was a small delay in her reporting because she hadn't had time to put her experiences on paper. It was a miraculously quiet journey, and in spite of the hefty physical efforts which we had to put forth each day, we felt very relaxed. This was due to the fact that we didn't encounter anything or anybody.

"You didn't think that the Goldstream flowed between highly populated urban areas, did you?" remarked Toodle. "Where it could be discovered too easily? There isn't even a fixed road to it." Toodle seemed, however, to have a fixed pattern to reach her destination. From time to time, we took strange turns around the fields and forests instead of going in a straight line to the foot of the mountain.

"There is no right track to the Goldstream," explained Toodle, "but many wrong tracks."

At night we slept under a thick tree or a shrub. We felt completely tranquil and full of self-confidence. In the end, everything went smoothly. I had removed all the Solvetower's technical errors that had been made by the old king. The foundations and solidity of the bottom floors were ensured. Since we were not disturbed by anything, Toodle and I had time to discuss further arrangements for the Solvetower. I would get my own room in the Solvetower on the hundredth floor. The floors below would be occupied by councilors and solution coordinators. Those who came to the Solvetower with problems could select to which person or being he would explain his problem. These persons or beings would inform me and make proposals for the solution of the problem. They were, therefore, the solution coordinators. They had to specialize in solving certain types of problems, like everyday problems, once-a-year problems, once-a-century problems, which required a particular skill, and constant problems, among which would be emotional problems and some work problems. Finally, the never-again-returning problems, which were easier to settle. Of course, one could also come directly to me and ignore the solution coordinators. This I left to everybody's choice.

During one of our breaks, sitting next to a deliciously smelling flower shrub, I proposed to appoint Frint as a solution coordinator for emotional problems. This would, at least it seemed to me, perhaps give him a purpose in life. Toodle hesitated, however, and looked serious. "He is perhaps sensitive but has not yet experienced all emotional feelings." Therefore we provisionally kept it under consideration. To my large consternation, Toodle did not want to have an official position in the Solvetower. When I asked her why, she answered enigmatically, "No, when the Solvetower has been completed, I must disappear ... I cannot stay with you."

I urged her to clarify her statement and asked if she really had to leave after the completion of the tower, but she refused to say more and gestured kindly not to disturb her anymore. This was the last topic we discussed concerning the Solvetower.

After some days, we arrived at the foot of a mountain. Toodle walked to a crack that resembled a narrow valley, through which only one person could pass at a time. We entered it. Left and right of us were high mountain walls, enclosing narrowly around us. Above our heads, I saw the white clouds which, according to Toodle, always hung around the summit of this mountain. The crack became narrower and eventually came to an end, and we faced a rocky mountain wall.

"Here we must go upwards," announced Toodle, as if this was the simplest job in the world. The mountain wall was quite vertical and stretched hundreds of meters above us. Toodle, however, wasn't at all discouraged. She placed her foot in a small cavity and started to climb up the wall in the same way that lizards do. I took a deep breath and followed her example. To my great stupefaction, the climb was easier than I had thought. At each step and with each hold with my hands, it seemed as if the mountain bent itself backward, becoming less vertical. This made a strange impression, but one should not be astonished where elf business is concerned. The higher we climbed, the more the mountain wall leaned over as we climbed. I saw the layer of clouds approaching. Toodle already had her head in the clouds and pulled up the rest of her body. My head was now flat against the bottom clouds. One last push and I would also disappear into the clouds. But however strongly I pushed, I did not succeed in getting my head in the clouds. Soft though the clouds seemed to be, they felt as hard as steel, so that I hurt my head by pushing and without any result.

Grasping at the now-ever-steeper mountain wall, I called, "Toodle! Help, I can't pass the clouds." I could neither hear nor see anything through the dense cloud masses.

After a while, above my head, I heard a voice saying, "He cannot pass under any condition. This is not a free-visiting resort." It was the voice of a young man who produced the same singing tones as Toodle, which made me conclude that it concerned an elf.

"We do not come here for a tour," I heard Toodle's voice. "It concerns a case of paramount importance!"

"I'm sorry, but non-elf-likes are refused access. We have never, in all those centuries, made one single exception," the other voice persisted. "Only you can go further."

"I refuse to go further without him," said Toodle firmly.

"Fetch Flotasio, the Elf chief; I want to speak to him." It was quiet after this command, which made me conclude that the order had been followed. I carefully moved my aching hands. Small stones fell off the rock from this displacement and rattled down the mountain wall.

After a short period, I heard a voice calling, "Give me a hand, King!" A pale, delicate hand was put down through the cloud, groping for mine. This I quickly gave him, although I wondered if such a delicate hand could carry my weight. With his strength and this time without any effort, I passed through the cloud blanket. With a jump, I ended up above the clouds, where the sun was shining sumptuously and softly warmed me. In contrast to the bare rock walls below the cloud border, everything was green here. It didn't seem as though we stood on the top of a mountain because the ground was flat without much of a slope and covered with short deep-green-colored grass. Here and there stood small trees with fine trunks with sparkling gems of all kinds and colors stuck on their leaves. You could not look at them very long without being dazzled. Beside me stood a kind of elf-like man, the one who had given the pale, delicate hand to me. He was smaller than me but had a large round head with dark-gold, shining tresses and bright, blue, glowing eyes. Around his elegant body, he wore a green tunic of no particular fashion and a dark-green cape studded with gleaming stones.

"Flotasio," Toodle presented him to me, saying, "the local Elf chief."

"King," Flotasio said, bowing his large head slightly to me. An elf youngster stood beside him with a javelin in his hand and wearing a tight, light-yellow outfit without decoration. He looked me up to down suspiciously. This had probably been the other elf, the one whom Toodle had spoken with earlier.

"Follow me, King," said the local Elf chief. Leaving the youngster elf behind, we followed Flotasio over the lawn. I heard a brook splashing in the distance but could not see it. Around the lawn were motionless white clouds which enclosed the landscape like a soft wall. With the light-footed steps so characteristic of elves, Flotasio preceded us. We encountered many elves on our path, who all seemed very busy. Some of them had bandages around their hands and stopped with dumb stupefaction when they saw me. Consternation and a slight resistance could be read on their faces.

"Take a seat under my tree, King," Flotasio said while motioning with his hand. We had stopped at a medium tree with a delicate trunk which, like some other trees, was decorated with sparkling stones; all three of us sat down in its shade. A gentle breeze moved the top of the foliage.

"This is a particular moment, King," spoke Flotasio with his elegant voice. "Never before we have allowed a non-elf-like to the Goldregion. You are informed, I think, of the mysteriousness of these regions." He turned to Toodle, who nodded. "I count on your confidentiality; without that, we cannot let you go from here, King."

"Nothing will force me to give away this secret," I assured him.

"Toodle has explained that you require gold and gems for the construction of a Solvetower."

"Yes," I confirmed this intent.

"However, I must disappoint you," the elf continued, stretching his neck. "Our gold and our gems cannot be delivered to non-elf-likes. That is a law of nature that we cannot go back on. Gold and gems do not simply come apart from their bed when a non-elf-like grips them.

"But Toodle can nevertheless catch them?" I asked, not understanding.

"Toodle doesn't need gold and gems. You are the one who needs them, King. Only those who need gold and gems can take them from the Goldstream—at least when he is, of course, an elf-like."

"Isn't there any other possibility?" I asked, confused by this situation, which would mean the end of my plan.

"Build the tower without payment," suggested Flotasio laconically.

"That won't work," answered Toodle with certainty in her voice. "We have given our word to the Stenodiggers, who have already started with the construction works. We have shaken each other's hands on this agreement.

"In that case, there remains only one solution," the Elf chief said slowly, seemingly unconvinced that I would accept the solution. "But this one is radical and permanent."

"Which solution is that?" I asked, prepared to consider any proposal.

"Becoming an elf-like, King," he answered.

"Me?" I stammered in stupefaction.

"Yes, you, King. The impact will be permanent. Be aware: You don't need to become an elf such as Toodle and myself but nevertheless an elf-like. At least one-quarter elf; otherwise,

you can never tear loose the gold and the gems. However, consider that your life and possibly your royalty over Existence will be changed by it. It is difficult to forecast to what extent. I know it is possible, but I can't remember a human ever becoming elf-like. The unknown risk is yours, King."

This was a difficult decision for me because I had to count on an unknown factor. The change in me could be serious, and I was a bit frightened of giving up a quarter of my human existence to be changed into an elf-like. However, the matter was too serious, so I didn't have much choice. Existence was at stake; I couldn't wait any longer because the Large Line would come soon, and the Solvetower had to be completed in any case. I could not permit myself the same errors as those of the old king.

After this hasty decision, I forced myself to say, "Well, I will become a quarter-elf."

13

The construction of the Solvetower demanded many sacrifices on my part. To become a quarter-elf was one of them. With a slight apprehension for the unknown, I persevered. "I want it to remain secret once I have become a quarter-elf," I announced. "My existence and my royalty could be affected by it. Should this be in the negative sense, then I must do my best to rectify the shortcomings. I want to do this undisturbed and without commentary. The quarter-elfness must therefore remain secret.

"That suits us too," said Flotasio. "If not, people will wonder why you became a quarter-elf. All indications which lead to the Goldstream must be avoided. You can be ensured of our confidentiality. Which does not imply that you will not be obvious as a quarter-elf."

I nodded solemnly. The young elf came along and put a bowl of food in front of everyone.

"Caterpillar porridge!" Toodle called, delighted, clapping her hands. "I haven't eaten that for a long time."

I tasted some of the green porridge politely. The taste was actually rather good, as long as one didn't reflect on the contents.

"Toodle Hidoo!" someone suddenly exclaimed gladly. A handsome, tall elf, much taller than the average elf man, ran with open arms towards Toodle, who leaped up enthusiastically.

"Rover!" Toodle called and jumped into the arms of the newcomer. He had a fine face with a straight, sharp nose and a naughty laugh playing around his mouth. He wore a pink elf shift with dark red lines and a sharp-pointed cap of a bright, light-green color bent backward and ending in a tip.

"What brings you here, little girl?" asked the tall elf, continuously laughing. He held Toodle by the shoulders when the greeting ceremony had finished.

"Ody," she replied, pointing at me.

The long elf went to me and gave me a hand. "And who is this one?" he asked with an arrogant smile in his eyes, shaking my hand.

"That you know very well," said Flotasio, apparently annoyed by the arrival of the tall elf. "Get lost, Rovericus; you disturb us, as always."

"Come, come," spoke Rovericus, undisturbed. "Can't one greet an old study friend when unexpectedly seeing her again after so many years?" He caught Toodle by the hand and drew her towards the fields. “Come, Toodle, let's go and play,” he called enthusiastically.

“He is inoffensive,” excused Flotasio. “But he loves naughty jokes.” I saw the elf laughing in the distance, twisting around a tree, whereas Toodle tried with great pleasure to hide behind another tree or to run fast in front of him.

“We must now start the learning process,” said Flotasio, claiming my attention. I turned away my gaze from Toodle and Rovericus. From under his cloak, Flotasio brought out an old, much-read book and passed it to me. The elegant elf writing on the cover declared the title to be *Elementary Handbook for the Beginner Elf*. “This book contains the basic principles of elfness,” explained Flotasio as he sat in front of me so that he could designate the major points in the text. “You don't need to know more as a quarter-elf, but learn it thoroughly by heart without skipping a word. Each word in this book takes its value from the reader. This means that, depending on the brightness of the reader, the words have more meaning. Let's start at the beginning.”

Flotasio gave me the first chapter, which he allowed me to read entirely, and subsequently asked what was in it. I explained that the chapter concerned the construction of an elf house out of the leaves of a giant four-leaf clover. I knew that Toodle had had such a house too and now discovered how the four-leaf clover could best be prepared to make a comfortable house. Complex fluids had to be poured over the roots of the clover to give the leaves their required firmness.

“That's correct, King,” nodded Flotasio, satisfied, as he showed the next chapter. I learned all technical aspects of the elfness, the preparation of caterpillar porridge, and the making of elf paper, which, as a matter of fact, is very interesting since the paper obtained its flying capacities from the addition of butterfly tears—it's difficult to obtain this fluid since butterflies are always so lively. Also, elfness involved dancing in elf rhythms, speaking with elf-likes in Old Elfish, and making and picking gold and gems in the Goldstream. This last interested me, especially at this moment, and Flotasio took the effort to explain each aspect of the Goldstream seriously. Thus, I learned that elves, using their hands, could press gems from rain drops and gold nuggets from hailstones. This was only possible at the beginning of the Goldstream. The gems and gold nuggets created in this way had to be thrown immediately into the river, whereupon they grew fixed to the riverbed. Once made, the gold and the gems had only a short life unless they were fixed fast in the Goldstream. After only two full moons, it was possible for elf-likes to retrieve the gold and gems from the riverbed, whereupon they could be kept forever. At the end of the Goldstream chapter, the book mentioned that pressing gold and gems could hurt the fingers and palms of the hands but that some bandages soaked in rose juice could relieve the pain considerably. This explained the bandages I had seen on some elves' hands I had met.

"That's very upsetting," I mentioned to the Elf chief. "However, are gold and these gems worth the pain? Can the gold and gems be pressed with hands bandaged for protection?"

"No, that's not possible," he answered without much conviction, staring in the distance. I remained silent about this problem and read that the Goldstream changed into an underground river under the cloud boundary, without any gold or gems on its bed, and it ended up in the sea. Flotasio pressed ahead with the teaching process, as a result of which I had soon understood all of the technical tricks of elfness. However, I still lacked the basic core of elfness; I didn't think, jump, and talk like an elf-like.

When Flotasio realized that I understood every word in the handbook, he got up, stretching his legs. "So, now for the practice," he announced. "Toodle!" he put a hand to his mouth. In the distance, I saw two figures jump from a tree and run to us. Toodle had pink cheeks of joy, and in her hair, she had put red and blue gems. "Give him his practical lessons," ordered Flotasio to Toodle then. "Start with the fire test and the pick test," he said and, turning to me, continued. "You will make it, King; don't worry. I must leave you for a moment to solve some delayed matters." Flotasio bade farewell and walked away.

"So, you finished the book?" asked Rovericus, who could hardly be dragged away from Toodle. "Wasn't easy, wasn't it?" Slight sarcasm could be read on his face.

"I have read many far more theoretical books," I answered coolly.

"On to the practice tests," Toodle said, taking me by the hand and pulling ahead.

"That's what I want to see," Rovericus said and laughed, coming beside us.

Toodle drew me to one of the elegant small trees that were loaded with sparkling green stones. "This is the pick test," said Toodle, pointing to the tree. "The gems in this tree have been collected by elf hands from the Goldstream and stuck in these leaves. You must now try to remove a stone. It is less difficult than catching a stone from the Goldstream because you don't need to be elf-like. But without knowledge of some elf-like principles, you will not manage the removal technique."

"He will never succeed!" Rovericus joked, throwing his head backward with a howl of derision.

"The limits to my powers as King of Existence are unknown and, for this reason, without restrictions," I explained to Rovericus, keeping a kind tone in my voice. Rovericus pressed his lips together and kept silent. Next, I took a leaf of the tree in my hand and tried with the other hand to remove the gem attached to the leaf. I gave a short hard jolt, but the stone didn't move an inch.

"See what I mean!" said Rovericus, giggling softly. Toodle looked at me, worried, taking pains not to give away the secret removal technique. It annoyed me a lot that I couldn't detach the smallest gem from a tree leaf. I should and had to succeed, I decided firmly. I wouldn't allow Rovericus any amusement at my expense. I took a deep breath, closed my eyes, and concentrated deeply. Then I took the stone between two fingers and pulled it softly from the leaf. The stone came loose without any effort!

"Success!" Toodle exclaimed, full of joy.

"But not in the correct way," Rovericus grumbled, astonished.

"Yes, that's strange," Toodle admitted. "This was not the elf way to remove a stone from a leaf. The secret is to pull the leaf from the stone and not the other way around. Strangely enough, you have succeeded in taking the stone without moving the leaf. In fact, that is not possible according to the books. I don't understand it." Toodle looked at me, curious.

"It succeeded because I wanted it to," I proposed as an answer, although I did not know exactly how I had found the solution or if it would work again.

"The fire test is another matter entirely," said Rovericus, rejoicing in advance.

Toodle picked up some leaves of an adjacent shrub which was not covered with gems and piled up them up in front of me on the ground. The leaves were wet and heavy.

"Try to obtain the fire from these leaves," Toodle told me.

"Fire?" I asked with raised eyebrows. "But there is no fire in these leaves. They are completely wet!"

"I can only give you one hint," said Toodle.

"Would you?" asked Rovericus.

"Think of flint," continued Toodle, ignoring Rovericus.

I reflected on how I could set fire to a wet bunch of leaves with flint and then remove the fire again and where could I obtain flint from. Rovericus started to chuckle and sat down on the ground with his arms crossed as if he expected a long wait. I started to consider how I could dry the leaves first before I tried to ignite them with flint, but I soon saw that this reasoning had reached a dead end. Drying leaves would take too much time, which was probably not the point of the fire test. Slowly, the idea came to me that the task was possibly not meant in a literal sense but figuratively, implying a riddle. Considering that idea further, I playfully toyed with the gem I had picked up in my hand. Toodle looked sharply at my hand, ensuring that Rovericus did not see her look. I followed her gaze and opened my hand. The last sunbeams fell on the green stone, which sparkled violently and reflected the light in all directions.

"But of course!" I exclaimed. "This gem shoots fire! It glows like fire!" Toodle couldn't suppress a naughty smile. I placed the fire-shooting stone on the bunch of wet leaves and said, "Now fire sits on the leaves." I took the stone again away and said, "Now I have obtained the fire from the leaves!"

"Yippee!" Toodle said, clapping her hands.

"I succeeded much faster in my earlier youth," Rovericus said, little impressed by my success.

"We can inform Flotasio that everything has succeeded excellently," Toodle said as she returned to the tree where the Elf chief sat once again.

"Can't we put him through another small test?" Rovericus asked with a simulated begging voice.

"That's not according to the rules," Toodle answered, shaking her head.

"What if we only ask how you can get butterfly's tears for the preparation of elf paper?" Rovericus persisted.

Toodle burst out laughing. "You are a master of that by accident! I remember the last time when you did it. We could not recover from laughing." Toodle giggled some more.

"Tell me," Rovericus said high-handedly, with a hand on

my shoulder. “How would you make a butterfly cry?” Toodle gasped with pleasure.

“By telling him a pitiful tale,” I suggested, wishing that these useless elf riddles would stop once and for all.

“No!” Rovericus announced triumphantly. “By telling him such funny riddles that he gets tears of laughter in his eyes. You want to hear a couple from me?”

“Oh no, stop, ha, ha, ha,” laughed Toodle. “I’m beginning to cry with laughter just thinking about it, ho, ho, ho.”

“Well,” Rovericus spoke, gladly forging ahead with his successful advance. “Why do one-day butterflies only live one day?”

“Yes, I know that one!” Toodle called, her shoulders shaking with laughter.

Rovericus threw a mischievous glance at me. “Because they have such a bad name,” he answered his own question. Toodle laughed still harder.

“What do butterfly caterpillars like to play with the most?” Without waiting for our answer, he continued, “With pupas! And why do butterfly caterpillars eat tree leaves? Because the trunk is too hard.” Now Rovericus laughed to his wit's end.

I smiled daintily. These riddles were undoubtedly great fun for butterflies but did not make me roar with laughter.

Still gasping from laughter, Toodle led us to Flotasio.

“I understand that the tests had joyful results,” the Elf chief spoke with some tension in his voice.

“Yes, ha, ha,” Toodle said. “He succeeded in everything.”

“Not really as it should have been and not terribly quickly,” Rovericus hurried to clarify.

Flotasio gave him a disapproving look such that Rovericus visibly writhed and gave no further comment. “Then tomorrow we will make a beautiful quarter-elf of you, King,” Flotasio said, turning to me with a smile.

I was tired after this stressful day and so didn’t want to

ask for any further explanation on how one eventually became a quarter-elf. We ate some caterpillar porridge and drank the dew water that Flotasio offered us. The night had meanwhile fallen. Rovericus returned to his sleep tree, whereas Toodle and Flotasio each climbed up to a branch in the Elf chief's tree. I continued to lie at the foot of this tree, preferring a more human place to sleep.

The next morning, I was awakened by Toodle and Flotasio, who jumped down from their branches. Not long afterward, Rovericus came running over to us, across the field with agile and lithe steps. "The big day has come, King," Flotasio said solemnly, snapping his fingers. I did not find it such a big day because I wouldn't have chosen to become a quarter-elf, not if Existence hadn't depended on it. A young elf had rushed to Flotasio with a glass of clear water. Flotasio drew one of the soft sparkling gems from his mantle and let it fall in the water. The water in the glass started to sparkle and dissolved the gem entirely.

"When you have drunk this, you will become a quarter-elf," Flotasio announced, handing me the glass. I put the glass to my mouth without knowing what would happen to me.

"Goodbye, human!" Rovericus called in a dramatic voice with an arm in the air and his other hand on his heart. The dissolved gem water had absolutely no taste. It was even astonishing how tasteless this could be. Even a mouthful of air seemed spicy compared to this drink.

When I had finished the glass, Flotasio caught my head between his hands and twisted it a quarter of a turn to the right. I praised the fact that I did not need to become a full elf, thinking how painful it would be to twist my head a full turn. Slight nausea rose within me but immediately disappeared again. I started to shiver in all of my limbs, unable to stop. My eyes closed of their own accord, whereas I continued to see clear flashes of light.

Suddenly everything was over. I opened my eyes and saw that Toodle and Flotasio looked at me delightedly. Rovericus grimaced glumly and moved his lower jaw from left to right. "That's better!" observed Toodle with satisfaction. I did not feel changed. A bit lighter, perhaps. I examined my hands, arms, and legs and saw that my bones had become slimmer. Not much, but enough for an attentive observer.

"You gleam more," Toodle explained to me. "Your eyes, your hair ... Walk just a bit." I took some steps and saw to my stupefaction that with each step I took, it seemed as if the grass was pushing me up so that I waltzed with light steps over the lawn. I tried to make this new movement look as human as possible but only partially succeeded.

"Just a grasshopper," sighed Rovericus, his head shaking back and forth.

"Let's go to the Goldstream," I proposed impatiently. I was shocked by my own voice, in which new tones could be heard. It seemed as if some glass-clear bells had been put in my throat for strengthening. Toodle and Flotasio praised my new elf-like characteristics, like every elf except for Rovericus praised me at the recognition of my elf-like signs. Flotasio beckoned with his hand, waving in the direction of the Goldstream, and walked in front of us. I could hear the clear splashing of the brook as we came closer. The stream lay on a higher lawn between rocky stones. We now stood beside the Goldstream, where uncountable gems and nuggets of gold were glowing on the shallow bottom. The reflection of the water made the stones shine more than above water.

There was great activity around the Goldstream. To the right of us was the highest rock, where the stream had its source. Strangely enough, a dark grey cloud from which rain fell hung exactly above this rock, but the rest of the sky was quite clear. I saw some elves catching the raindrops and squeezing them with their hands. I was surprised to notice that these elves had bandages around their hands and yet managed to press gems.

"Bandages!" I exclaimed in a clear voice.

"That was a terrific idea of Flotasio, our Elf chief," explained an elf wading in the water as they quickly fixed the pressed gem to the riverbed. "Now, we don't have any more pain in our hands. Incredible." The wading elf continued, "Nobody had ever tried to press gems with bandages before!"

I turned with a questioning look to Flotasio, who looked timidly at the ground. "That is indeed an excellent idea," I said slowly. I could, of course, have made a loud protest and given away the fact that it was my idea and not Flotasio's, but I considered that the Big Settlement Days were not yet over and the fact that I had thus solved a problem for these elves. More discussion about it would be superfluous.

Flotasio raised his head, relieved, and hurried to help me with my next task. He caught a rough-looking bag of old brown linen that lay on the ground at the riverbank. "You fill this bag, King," he said.

"But it is very small," I protested. "The Stenodiggers will certainly not be satisfied with one bag."

"Fill it; then you will see," consoled Flotasio. I took the bag and walked into the Goldstream until the water came to my waist. A fast and strong current of water flowed around me, but I was able to stay standing in spite of my legs, which had become thinner. I put my hand under water and grabbed haphazardly in the riverbed. Gold nuggets and gems came off without any effort. Thus, I filled my bag and was astonished that it never became entirely full to the brim, no matter how much I put into it. So that was the secret! With this special bag, I could take along an infinite amount of gold and gems. Even better, this elf bag had been so made that the weight of the bag was never too heavy.

"Watch him grab!" Rovericus sneered.

This was too much for Toodle. “Rover!” she yelled in a punishing voice that would have made even the nastiest fellow cringe, which is exactly what Rovericus did.

When I found that I had picked up enough gold and gems, I stepped out of the Goldstream with my elf bag over my shoulder. “I thank you very cordially for your help,” I said to Flotasio, giving him a hand.

“I can say the same, King,” said Flotasio with a gleam in his eyes.

“We must go now,” I announced. I nodded to Rovericus, whose head was bowed slightly, and walked to what I thought was the exit, the edge of the lawn where the clouds formed a border.

Toodle took farewell of Rovericus with less joy than she had greeted him with yesterday. “Take care of yourself, Rover,” she recommended to him with her hands on his shoulders.

“That’s what Rover always does,” Rovericus answered, tapping with one finger on the edge of his cap.

The young elf with the javelin who had received us yesterday still stood there. He gave Toodle and me each a giant cloverleaf that felt thickened and reinforced.

“For the descent,” explained Flotasio.

Toodle knew how to use the cloverleaf. With two hands, she kept it clasped under her bottom and let herself glide into the cloud blanket. After a last farewell, I followed her example, holding the elf bag in one hand and my giant cloverleaf in the other. I was glad to be able to return to the Solvetower.

14

When we had jumped through the blanket of clouds, we ended up once again at the steep rocky wall. Although the slope was less steep, it was still steep enough to allow us to glide at a fast speed. The giant clover leaves really served as sleighs. You had to hold them tightly; otherwise, they slid from under you, leaving you to uncontrollably roll down the mountain. Because I could use only one hand, it was more difficult for me than for Toodle. Although my hands and my arms had become thinner by the transformation into a quarter-elf, they hadn't lost their strength and had perhaps even gained some. Toodle enjoyed the ride. Her hair flew out behind her due to her speed. The advantage of this descent was that very soon we were below. Toodle jumped to the ground, soon followed by me. We had arrived once more at the mountain crack. I looked back to the mountain wall and saw that it was entirely vertical towards the cloud boundary.

It was quiet, and nothing suggested that above the clouds lived a colorful elf people. Toodle preceded me towards the exit of the crack.

"Your hair!" I noticed. "There are still gems in your hair.

You better remove them; otherwise, the robbers will get bad ideas.

"Ah, yes! I stuck those in my hair yesterday," said Toodle. She removed the colorful jewels from her hair and put them in her travel case. "Those are for me," she decided.

When we came out of the crack, we saw the fields and forests in front of us again. The return journey could now start. Toodle followed the same invisible track as on the outward journey. It was a calm trip which relaxed us a bit more each day. Toodle discovered to her joy that someone had secretly put a little pot of caterpillar porridge in her travel case. On an accompanying note were written the words: "These caterpillars will never become butterflies. A pity for them! They will never hear my latest joke!"

"Rover," sighed Toodle with some compassion. Nobody had hidden anything in my travel case, so Toodle shared her caterpillar porridge with me until I had gradually had enough of the taste.

Just as on the outward journey, we encountered nobody. We didn't tire rapidly either because I had become more light-footed than before, so Toodle proposed we walk on, deep into the night. It was very pleasant to walk in the limpid moonlight under the clear, starry sky. Toodle knew the way by heart, so we didn't go astray even in the darkest parts of the forest.

During a long walk one night, I saw to my great stupefaction that luminous eyes were staring and blinking in the thicket and between the branches of the trees. I did not stop because the beings belonging to the eyes were not hostile; they just looked at me, astonished and staring but remaining mostly invisible. Toodle did not even seem to notice them. I went walking closer to Toodle and whispered in her ear, "A number of luminous eyes have been watching us in the darkness between the leaves."

"Naturally!" Toodle laughed loudly. "They are astonished

to see a quarter-elf, and you are astonished to see elfluffs."

"Elfluffs?" I asked louder, trusting she was right.

"Since you have become a quarter-elf, you can see more. A quarter more, especially at night," answered Toodle. "The elfluffs are beings who descended from elves. A subspecies, we say, although they don't like to hear that. We help each other sometimes in periods of great need. The elfluffs cannot be seen by humans, and they sometimes abuse that in a funny way. Haven't you ever lost something which you didn't know you had lost and which you never did get back?" Toodle looked nonchalantly around for a moment. "There are always so many that I don't pay attention to them anymore ... and then you still miss three-quarters of what I can see," she added, giggling. I pressed Toodle to explain to me what the three-quarters implied, but Toodle wouldn't. "That cannot be told; it is elf business. You only see what you can manage, not more."

Full of unanswered questions, I threw a side glance at a couple of passing eyes. They stared at me and then gave me a wink.

To my pleasure, the return journey took less time than the outward journey. On a beautiful sunny morning, the stone houses of either the Stenodigger or the Stenoblocker women came in sight. We walked around the mountain and arrived at the Stenodiggers' rocky workshop.

The Stenodiggers were very busy, to my great satisfaction. Carts, loaded with rocky blocks, were being pulled from the cave. Other Stenodiggers were twisting two round, flat stones against each other with a handle so that smaller stones were crushed to powder between the flat millstones.

"That must be the cement mill," I said to Toodle, indicating the millstones. From the cave and also in the distance between the trees, one heard the crash of chisels and pickaxes mixed with the workers' raw cries. "Hacking! Discharging! Loading!"

were the commands heard in all directions.

"Where is Frint?" I asked, looking around, seeing a passing Stenodigger with a bag of cement on his back.

"At the tower," he answered, indicating the direction with his head. Toodle and I walked down the stone path, sometimes jumping aside for the carts that came rattling along. It had become a very busy path. Appearing from between the trees, I saw the beginnings of my tower. It looked promising, which reassured me. Nearer by, I observed that the foundations had already been laid and that two floors were completed. These floors were round, just like the ruins had been, but much broader and made of crude, rough stones and grey armed stones. My tower occupied a larger surface than that of the old king. Not too-large window casings and a large door opening were visible. The door opening was square and supported by stone posts. Above the door, nothing was yet written. Looking up, I saw that some women were smearing a layer of cement onto the highest stones of the highest floor. Some strong Stenodiggers then pushed the construction stones into the fresh cement.

Steno descended from just behind the tower and ran towards me with open arms. "My large gold and gem donors have returned!" he called loudly. He seized me roughly by my shoulders. However, his welcome enthusiasm was rapidly dulled when he saw the elf bag on my back. "What a small one!" he said, dismayed, shrinking backward. "I am not doing it for that! That was not the agreement!"

"You will not be disappointed," I soothed, throwing my bag at his feet. I pulled the elf bag up by two edges. The glowing gems and shining gold splashed on the ground. An enormous pile formed before us. Steno squirmed with a sort of mad joy, his hands together. His eyes glowed like the gems. A celestial smile spread around his mouth so that his face had a pleasant look to it.

When the bag was empty, a huge pile of gold and gems lay before us, and Steno disappeared entirely behind it. He stepped straight-faced from behind and said, "Well. That's it approximately." I passed him the elf bag, whereupon he put his head in the bag to examine the bottom. Afterward, he scooped the received payment up with his large hands and put the gems and gold back in the bag.

In the meantime, I asked him, "Have you also employed your women in the construction?"

"Yes," he answered. "That was Frint's idea. He has right. Cement smearing is a woman's work, doing something other than weaving and spinning. Of that, I was already certain."

"Would it be possible," I heard Frint's voice suggesting timidly, "to accelerate the activity a bit. I don't know how much time we have left, but it will not be much." He added this last bit rather pessimistically. With an upraised finger, Frint descended to Steno, the design of my tower in his hand.

"That's him 'gain!" said Steno grumpily, and the corner of his mouth turned up. He quietly continued to fill the elf bag.

"Good idea," I said. Frint startled. He had not noticed me yet.

"Ody?" he looked at me, top to toe, with a deep frown. I nodded and greeted him warmly. "I had not recognized you. You are somewhat, eh ... thinner."

"That comes from all that running and carrying of those gems," I hurried to explain. "You have acquitted yourself excellently of your task." Frint looked a moment to look at the shrinking gold and gem pile.

"Ah," he said. "No one else could have fulfilled the task better."

Steno had now finished filling the bag. He patted it, satisfied, and said, "So! Now we will hide this booty," and he waved and walked away.

"How do you want to accelerate the work?" Toodle asked Frint.

"Yes, ah, I don't know," he replied modestly. "By a better allocation of the work perhaps ..." Frint took my plans to an area where there were now some cement stains. "At present, the Stenodiggers insist on building the tower in their own traditional manner. That means that each Stenodigger cuts his own stone from the cave, puts it on the cart, pulls the cart, unloads the stone, and stacks it on the tower. The work has already improved because I have asked to let the women do the cement smearing; otherwise, they had to do that by themselves too. There is now only one separate mill for the cement milling. Perhaps we can—it is, of course, a bad idea—have special Stenodigger teams for each section of the construction, for cutting, transport, unloading, et cetera."

I looked at Frint inquiringly. Some responsibility had done him good. Although his eyes were still wet, I couldn't see any real tears.

"That's what we'll do!" I called happily. "It's a terrific idea!"

"However, it is sure to fail eventually," Frint sighed, falling back into his old habit.

"Not at all! Not at all!" called Toodle hastily so as to prevent a rising fit of weeping, which was thus avoided.

"Well," I said, "then we too will go to work!" Frint had the task of assembling the Stenodiggers during a short break and separating them into workgroups. In spite of the fact that some cried, "*Moah*! That will not succeed! All these innovations will have to be reversed!" Frint persisted, and the Stenodiggers eventually agreed. Toodle decided to take a hammer and a chisel and do some decoration on the stones of the Solvetower. I took over the general supervision and decided which stone was placed where. We worked the whole day, hardly granting ourselves any rest.

At twilight, we returned to the stone workhouses of the Stenodiggers. Since everyone was too tired to prepare a large meal, we ate raw beans, which tasted sweet because of our hunger.

The women of the Stenodiggers were nice but spoke little. They were wearing brown dresses and were all the same, slim and muscular. The Stenodiggers were very lively that evening. I didn't know whether this was due to the presence of their women or to the gold and gems. We slept deeply around a smoldering fire and rose again at sunrise, full of courage. Thus, our days passed in routine with little change. The tower now shot up more rapidly into the sky and was already far beyond the treetops.

I regarded it with satisfaction and was just praising myself for the good design when I heard the hard, heavy stamping of running feet in the forest around, added to by loud shouts and indecent words. All Stenodiggers and Stenodigger women around and in the tower were startled.

"Take cover!" shouted Steno in a panic. I saw a large group of muscular men heading for us with pounding steps and at full speed. They resembled the Stenodiggers but wore black, not brown, short trousers and black leather belts. They surrounded us and roughly pushed the Stenodiggers in their way to the ground. In their hands, they had armed stones tied with string, which made it possible to swing a stone threateningly above their heads. The Stenodiggers ran away, frightened. Some succeeded in hiding between the legs of the attackers, but the rest fled anxiously into the tower.

"Go away from my site! Clear out!" Steno shouted at the wicked people as he barred the entrance of the tower. However, when the crowd came near him, he rushed within, followed by some attackers. Frint had already fled into the tower at the first cries, whereas Toodle and I had quickly run to a tree and jumped on its highest and strongest branches. For the first time, I was happy that being a quarter-elf had worked. Panting, we examined the sad scene which was taking place below us. The attackers bludgeoned the bottom floor of the tower with their stone weapons. Some pieces of the grey stones crumbled off. The armed stones remained unchanged, to the large dissatisfaction of the attackers. Inside the tower, the Stenodiggers' footsteps were audible as they rapidly climbed the staircase, followed by the invaders. I had the impression that the attack was more targeted against the tower than against the Stenodiggers themselves. In the tower, walls were attacked, and some stones fell down. Soon I saw the top above the heads of the Stenodiggers. With a jolt, they pushed their heads away. The attackers did not interfere with them anymore and concentrated on destroying the edge of the upper floor, which soon disappeared. I could see now all the Stenodiggers, keeping together with the stronger men.

"Scum you are! I have always said that!" I heard Steno shouting from above. The muscular attackers were now able to destroy the floors of my tower one by one, and I sat completely powerless in the tree. "My tower!" I sputtered, biting on my lower lip. The attackers were by now slightly tired but continued destroying the upper floors. They were visibly disgruntled and annoyed. Any attempt to calm them by negotiation was deemed to fail. With a heavy heart and sighing deeply, I had to observe how the tower was shrinking to the level of the highest trees. Kept under control, the Stenodiggers were forced each time to go lower down.

Suddenly I became startled by a little stone which fell from the sky onto my arm. "Ow!" I called, clenching the spot on my arm with the other hand to reveal a large blue spot.

"Ow! Ow! I now heard from the tower too. The attackers kept both arms protectively above their heads. A rain of stones fell down from the sky. The Stenodiggers shrank down too.

"Look!" Toodle yelled, pointing to the sky in supreme stupefaction. I saw, high in the sky, a plump yellow bird with two small, green birds that had a number of well-filled bags around their waists. There were probably holes in the bags because a flood of stones fell down from them. The three birds circled around and over the tower, frightening those who were underneath them.

"Espra!" I called, for the first time in my life delighted by her arrival.

"Beat it!" Espra shouted to her victims below.

The angry attackers ran out of the tower, ducking, with their hands on their heads. "That's not a fair game, men!" the most muscular attacker yelled to his comrades. "They've got reinforcements! They collaborate with birds!" Running confusedly into each other, they escaped to the forest, and finally, we heard their steps die out in the distance. Espra, Kroo, and Kra followed some of them with their last stones.

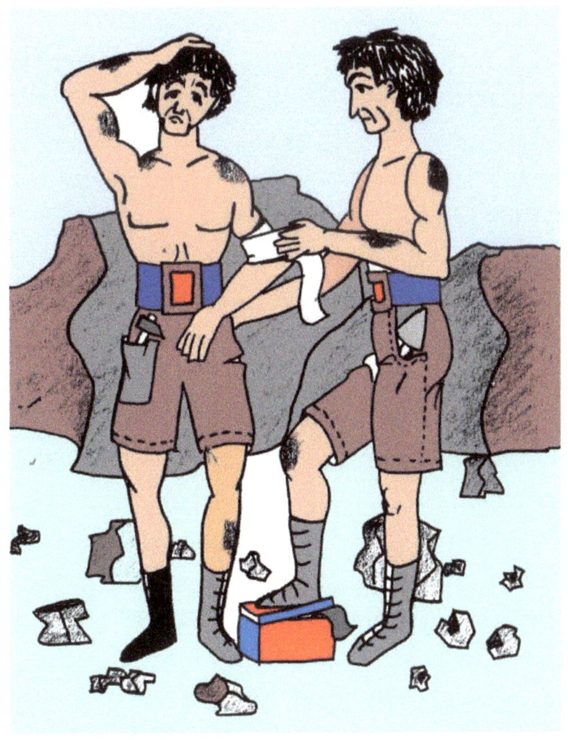

15

Toodle and I agilely jumped down from our hiding tree. We walked up to the tower, where we found the Stenodiggers angry and beaten. They came, one by one, out from the destroyed tower. Some had red spots on their arms and shoulders from the rain of stones.

"Revenge! Punishment!" growled Steno between his teeth. "For that, they have to pay heavily!"

I tried to calm Steno's anger because I didn't want to have the tower as an eternal battlefield of hostile people where they would keep fighting their vendettas. "I will find an appropriate solution. That's my task," I soothed.

"With that scum of Stenoblockers, no solution can be found." Steno gnashed his teeth. "Eradication is the best," he added excitedly.

The situation had become dangerous, I decided. "First, take some rest and a cold bath," I proposed to Steno, pushing him softly in the direction of his workshop. The Stenodiggers were covered in dust, grit, and cement. They followed my advice for the moment and walked slowly to their houses. Mutually, they discussed the revenge they had in mind and vowed that the Stenoblockers would remember it for a long time.

Frint strolled out, the last one free from the devastated tower, completely overcome by the heaviest fit of crying that I had experienced from him so far. Toodle hurried to him. He leaned against the eroded outside wall of the tower and hid his face in an arm. From time to time, he bumped his head against the wall. "Everything is lost!" he gasped violently. "It is all my fault!"

I wanted to walk to him, but Espra and her green birds came flying low above me and landed before my feet. Espra looked very angry and put her hands on her waist. "What misconceptions are these!" she called with great disapproval in her voice, as if she had forgotten that she spoke to her father. "I only go to fetch a mother, and here you are causing the greatest chaos and the most violent wars and then creeping, frightened, into a tree, leaving everyone to his own sad destiny!" Espra was particularly disgruntled. She started to pace worriedly up and down in front of me and grumbled, half about me and half about herself. "They should depose you as King of Existence! This exceeds all limits! I must take steps, and quickly too. If I had not been there, you would have already fallen short and become a good-for-nothing king! And yet he still calls me annoying for the Big Settlement Days!" Espra was terribly good at finding the correct reproachful words if she was angry. Even Kroo and Kra sat listening, slightly shocked by her speech.

"I am glad you have intervened ... this time," I said, mumbling the last two words to myself.

"That you'd better be!" called Espra, leaping and pacing up and down. "I was so clever to fetch a couple of bags of stones nearby, at a type of stone workshop. I found a solution." Espra stressed the "I" strongly with an expressive frown. She discovered the violently weeping Frint and clapped her wings against her body. "Oh, this too!" she sighed, almost despondent from my ignorance. "Now he is at present even deeper in misery than before! What abusive situations you have caused—what mismanagement!" She shook her head back and forth and didn't give me a chance to intervene. I wasn't really planning to defend myself. I found her charges too inept and too exaggerated to make any effort against them.

"Yahooo!" called a woman's voice from one of the treetops, asking for our attention.

Espra tapped herself on the head with her hand. "I almost forgot! Your wife!" Espra flew up and put her legs in the upper branches of a tree close by. "Mommy!" she called. "I'm coming to get you!" Some softness now resounded in her voice. Hold tight," she advised the woman in the tree. Just a bit later, Espra was flying up again, now with difficulty. Clenched to her legs, I saw a small, chubby woman hanging down who looked delightedly left and right at the landscape underneath.

"Oh, heaven! What now?" Toodle said softly. She had pulled Frint away from the tower and looked with anxious foreboding at the sky. Frint did not look at all. He had now somewhat calmed down.

Espra landed before us and put the delighted chubby woman on the grass before me. Kroo and Kra came hurrying happily and put their faces in the woman's skirts, clasping her legs. It was a strange, winking figure that I was looking at, surprised. She was pretty, although her cheeks were somewhat round. She had long blonde tresses that reached to the ground and light blue eyes with long black lashes, looking full of expectation at this new world. She was young and plump. Her clothing struck me as strange. It consisted of thick layers of a transparent, flapping fabric of soft greens and different shades of pink, blue, yellow, and white, which overlaid each other in so many layers that they became non-transparent. A tight belt had been stretched around her thick waist. The dress had a nice vest with wide sleeves. Pink and pale-blue downy feathers had been sown over the entire dress. Under the skirts, which reached just above her ankles, I saw soft shoes covered by a layer of feathers.

"Haven't I made an excellent choice?" asked Espra, looking delightedly at her chosen mother.

Before I could answer that the young woman was attractive and nice, but I still had no plan to marry, the chubby woman looked happily around, found Frint in her sight, and hopped to him in an unwieldy way. "King Ody! I am engaged to you!" She clasped the bewildered Frint in her arms, and standing on her toes, she gave him a cordial kiss on his cheek. "He has tears of joy in his eyes now that he has found his ideal woman," she said with a happy face. "Ah, gosh, gosh, gosh," she continued while sweeping tears from Frint's cheeks with her finger. Frint gasped a bit but stayed stiff as a rod. Overcome with surprise, he stopped crying.

"No, Mommy. That's the wrong one," called Espra, correcting the young woman. "This is him." She caught me by the shoulders and held me in front of the nice, chubby woman.

"That thin, scanty thing?" said the young woman, deeply disappointed.

"That's true," said Espra, examining me sharply. "You have lost much weight during my absence."

"Because of hard work," I explained.

"You should not come to me with that excuse," said Espra, slightly annoyed. "I know what work implies for you. Just admit that you have missed me." I nodded since I had just about enough of this.

The nice, chubby girl approached, dragging Kroo and Kra still clutching at her skirts. They seemingly could not have enough of her presence. "Have I made myself beautiful for this?" she sighed. "Now, yes, go on," she continued without enthusiasm. "I will sacrifice myself. Existence seems to depend on it."

"That's my girl," Espra said. "I have an intelligent mother!"

"Not so fast!" I could intervene at last. "There is absolutely no chance that I will marry anyone. You are free, Mothe–eh ... young lady."

Espra started to stamp one foot on the ground. "I should have known. It is my own dumb fault," she spoke. "He who is too stupid to bring his royalty and Existence to a good end is also too stupid to see and recognize his own rescue." And with her voice predicting misfortune, she said slowly, "You are a lost cause. I know what I have to do!" Without further notice and without asking our opinion, Espra flew up in the sky. "Come, children!" she ordered. Kroo and Kra departed unwillingly from the skirts of their chosen grandmother but did not dare to disobey their mother's demanding voice. Thus, Espra and the green birds flew away, leaving us behind and full of anxious apprehensions as to Espra's next action.

The nice young woman was seated on the grass, and tears started welling slowly in her eyes. This picture was too much for Frint. He shot to her aid and said, weeping a little, "Why do you cry, dear lady?"

"My daughter has just flown away ... *sniff* ... When will I see her again?" Frint kindly patted her on the shoulders. Toodle and I looked at each other, astonished.

"Treason! Treason!" shouted Steno behind us. He looked fresh again and rushed, quite upset, between the trees to us.

"What's the matter?" I asked, worried.

"What's the matter? What's the matter?" he panted with a cracking voice. "My gold and gems have been stolen, disappeared, vanished–that's what's the matter!"

"But didn't you hide the bag with gold and gems extremely well?"

"I know for certain that the Stenoblockers have stolen it while they kept us busy with their destruction party at the tower. Nobody could have found the bag. I am the best hider. Even as a child, I sat in hiding for many nights because nobody could find me during hide-and-seek games." He gasped for breath, which caught in his throat, and continued, "There is a traitor among us. Only by treachery could the Stenoblockers have found my good gold and gems!" He took another deep breath.

"A traitor?" I asked, frightened.

"I know, however, who it is ..." said Steno, closing his eyes for half-second. "He there! That blubberer!" He pointed a trembling finger at Frint, who only now started to pay attention and was startled from his consolation activities.

"Frint?!" Toodle and I yelled together. "Impossible!" I said with great force, defending Frint.

Frint burst into tears again. The chubby young woman looked at Frint, shocked, and started to comfort him, "Ah, gosh, gosh, gosh."

"This disorder must come to an end," I spoke with a resolute voice, upon which everyone became silent and paid attention. "Steno!" I announced. "You and I will visit those Stenoblockers at once and put an end to this brawling situation definitively."

"You'd better do that!" growled Steno without much courtesy. "You are the one who involved this howler into our activities."

"Toodle, would you please take care of the activities and meanwhile see that things run on well-oiled wheels!" I asked Toodle. "Up to the Stenoblockers!" I encouraged Steno. He stamped sulky in front of me to the workshops. Toodle, Frint, and the nice, chubby young woman followed us.

When we arrived at the houses, Steno and I turned to the right. "This is the shortest way," he said. We walked past the mountain without exchanging many words. I had to retrieve the gold and the gems because I did not expect that the

Stenodiggers would repair the tower and complete it without their treasure. At a particular moment, we arrived at a second type of stone workshop, which actually wasn't far from the Stenodiggers but was out of their sight. There were some workhouses, which didn't differ much from those of the Stenodiggers, and also a cave identical to the Stenodiggers' cave. There was nobody in sight.

Without hesitation, Steno walked up to the cave. He stopped before the cave opening with outspread legs and clenched fists.

"Well, at last, there you are. I have been expecting you for a long time," a heavy voice called out from inside the cave.

I went closer to Steno and could make out some dark characters. Steno and I stepped inside. When my eyes got used to the darkness, I saw a group of Stenoblockers sitting around a large oval stone table, whereas some other Stenoblockers leaned against the walls and regarded us with defying looks. Blue spots were visible here and there on their muscular bodies.

"It's going to be tough for you, Block!" Steno roared at the strongest Stenoblocker, who sat at the head of the table in the distance.

The one who was called Block gave a short jeer. "Who is that poor starved dirtbag beside you?" asked Block, pointing a finger at me.

"That's Ody, King of Existence and so much more!" Steno answered with some pride in his voice.

"Oh," said Block dryly. "I didn't know that."

"You had better return my bag of gold and gems very quickly, or bad things will happen to you!" Steno beat on the table with a fist, on our side where nobody was sitting.

Block laughed, not at all impressed. "Oh, how scared I am!" he said teasingly. "If not, you will probably set that weedy fellow on me." Block looked to his men, grinning, who all laughed at their leader's wit.

"You are an impostor!" exclaimed Steno without granting me a word. "You have used a traitor. How could you otherwise have found my bag? Come up with it! Who is your traitor?"

"A traitor?" said Block, drawing his mouth corner up. "Don't put on airs. I need no traitor to find your so-called hidden treasures. Even without searching, blindfolded in the night, I would stumble over your bag with gems. Really ... under your bed? Even my little son, who is not as clever as his father, can think of a better hiding place." The company of Stenoblockers started to giggle again. This was a hard push for Steno, who slowly started to see red. Block accepted a goblet which one of his men passed to him. He started to drink contently and left us still standing before the table.

"Darned badly paid as a matter of fact," he continued. "One small bag of gold and gems for a complete tower. I had expected better of you, Steno."

Steno and I held our breath. It was clear that the Stenoblockers hadn't emptied the elf bag with gold and gems.

"Here is my proposal," said Block, drinking the last rest from his goblet and wiping his mouth with the back of its hand. "I keep the bag with gems, and you, Steno, disappear far from my sight so that I will see you never again, and I will ensure that that tower is rebuilt for a more reasonable price."

Steno sniffed. "And this is my proposal," he resounded loudly in the cave. "You return my legitimate property to me, you pay a strong fine for the damage caused to the tower, and you never put your sordid feet on my ground again!" Both men growled. The negotiations were completely stuck at a standstill.

"Whatever you consider," I intervened, "the tower is mine. It's in my interest that it is completed as soon as possible, and not only I but all of Existence also depends on it. It is now more necessary than ever that you put your disputes aside."

"That may be," said Block. "But we must earn our bread. Without that, we cannot exist either!"

I didn't want to go once more to the Goldstream for more gold and gems only to bring quarreling parties together. This would last too long, and now I wanted to stay with the tower to make sure of its fast completion. So, I came to a decision and gave my proposal. "Block, you must, in any case, return the small bag with gold and gems to Steno. Anyway, it is not much, and I, as King of Existence, must take unpleasant steps to punish you if you unlawfully keep the small bag." Block regarded me doubtfully, not knowing what kind of steps I could take as king. To be honest, I didn't know either since I did not have an army. However, it seemed to me that bluffing was called for.

Block snapped with his fingers. One of his men came along with the bag with gold and gems. Block threw it next onto the long table and quickly pushed it over to us. Steno skillfully caught the bag and clenched it firmly against himself. "Now I'll get you, pal!" he growled threateningly.

"No; silence!" I ordered. The muscular men obeyed, asking themselves slowly what I had to offer. "I want you Steno-blockers, together with the Stenodiggers, to repair my tower and complete it. Then the tower will be finished that much faster," I said. Loud snorts of indignation resounded in the cave from both the Stenoblockers and Steno. "In exchange for that," I yelled above their grumbling. A silence fell in anticipation. "In exchange for that," I continued in an ordinary voice, "I will not punish the Stenoblockers for their destructive actions." Block sneered. My argument was not apparently strong enough. "Moreover," I continued saying, "after the construction of the tower, the Stenodiggers will give up their share in construction and stone market and cede that to the Stenoblockers."

"What?!" called Steno with much fear in his eyes.

Block laughed, satisfied. He stood up in his chair, walked away from the table and to me, and stuck out his hand to me. "Excellent, we will do that," he said.

"Not at all! We do nothing! I'm going home! As for me, the complete matter has been solved!" said Steno, incensed and intending to leave the cave.

"Steno!" I called him back. "Haven't you got, eh ... enough with this small bag of gold and gems to live without further hard work in a pleasant resort somewhere?" Steno looked a moment at his clenched bag.

"If you do so sparingly," teased Block with a large grin.

"Yes," said Steno. "I am reconciled to the idea ... however bad it is of our king." Steno shook the hand of Block as quickly as possible and took his hand back just as quickly. He did not smile but had a calculating look in his eyes, which didn't put me at ease. I hoped that Steno would stick to his word.

"Tomorrow morning, we start the activities up again," I explained to Block. "We will continue until we can't any longer. The tower must really be completed now."

Block nodded understandingly. "Now we, the Stenoblockers, will help; you totally don't need to worry about that. There are no better craftsmen than us—are there, Steno?" Block added, baiting and laughing.

"You are a

block to my leg," mumbled Steno to himself and left the cave hastily.

"See you tomorrow," I said to the Stenoblockers and walked away after Steno.

16

When Steno and I arrived at the Stenodiggers' workshop, everybody was already asleep. Twilight had since settled in. Steno didn't exchange a word with me and fell asleep. I went to the fire, where most of the Stenodiggers had the habit of sleeping when they did not want to lie in their houses. It was a beautiful night, and the stars glowed in the dark-blue sky. Everyone slept except Frint, who sat squatting beside the fire, staring with large eyes into the flames. He hardly blinked and looked very much like a sitting sculpture.

"Frint?" I asked. "Aren't you sleeping?"

"Ah, why should I?" he sighed deeply, but the sigh did not correspond with his usual misery.

I lay down and paid no further attention to him. I was glad that the construction of my tower would be accelerated so quickly. What would happen next? We will see later.

The next morning, we were startled by the rough voices of the Stenodiggers. "Cover!" they called, running off in all directions. I blinked my eyes sleepily and saw in the distance a large group of Stenoblockers arriving with contented sneers on their faces.

"Stay here! It's nothing!" I called around me. "They come to help us!"

Steno appeared from his house, woken by the noise. "Johnny perfectionist," mumbled Steno, drawing his belt more tightly.

"Hey, Steno! Too early for you, isn't it?" Block called to him, waiving with his hand.

"To work, men!" Steno shouted at his astonished Steno-diggers.

"What's this?" asked some of them, coming closer and examining the Stenoblockers suspiciously.

"The person who ordered the tower has considered something new—cooperation. That's what has to be done," Steno explained, heaving his shoulders.

"Pooh!" said some Stenodiggers.

I wanted Frint to inform the new employees of our partitioning work and the plow services. "Frint!" I called, looking around. To my surprise, Frint still sat in the same position as yesterday evening. He seemed to stare in the fire's ashes. "Frint!" I said again because he did not seem to hear me.

"Hm?" was his absentee answer as he continued to look at the ash.

"Will you explain to the Stenoblockers how they should work on the tower?" I asked, looking inquiringly at him. Without answering, he stood up and ran drowsily to the Stenoblockers, staring in front of himself. He didn't even ask why the Stenoblockers were now involved in the construction of the tower.

The Stenoblockers and the Stenodiggers walked to the tower, keeping some distance between them. First, the stones and stone blocks, which lay around the tower, spread out in the grass, had to be cleared in order to repair holes in the walls and restore the floors.

Toodle and the happy, nice, chubby young woman came to

me. "Ody!" Toodle called. "I am glad that all has gone well with the Stenoblockers." The chubby girl looked at the ground, somewhat timidly laughing. "Since Landa cannot leave," continued Toodle, "I have decided that she can help me with decorating the walls."

I nodded. The chubby girl was therefore called Landa, I concluded. All three of us went to the tower. It swarmed with Stenodiggers and Stenoblockers, who were working hard as if they wanted to show each other that they and not the others were the fastest and best workers. Sometimes they stood in the way of each other and regarded each other growingly while Frint, without much result, said, "Tut, tut." However, it never came to an open fight.

I was very busy because I had to keep double the supervision and could not make mistakes in pointing to where this or that stone had to be put. After one day, the tower had been repaired as if there never had been any destruction.

"We build better than we destroy," Block said with satisfaction, at which Steno said, "You do both badly!" Block tried to remain nice since the faster the tower was completed, the earlier he would have exclusive rights over construction and stone works.

After a while, it was decided that the Stenoblocker women would also help with cement smearing and even with the decoration and layout of the tower, to the large dissatisfaction of the Stenodigger women, who found them nothing but weaklings. The Stenodigger women were very competent in weaving curtains; some of them could be called real artists. Some Stenodiggers and Stenoblockers already specialized in the making of furniture. The furnishings would, by force of circumstance, be of stone because the workers had no ability with and knowledge of wooden furniture. After some days, the tower had reached high in the sky, such that it took a long time to go up the stone staircase to the highest completed floor.

Toodle and Landa had done their very best on the inside and outside decoration of the walls. With much attention and joy, Toodle had chiseled above the entrance the words "Solve-tower – welcome." She piled up a number of stones, jumped on top of them, and chiseled other designs and ornamentation on the outside wall. It became all very nice and welcoming. When Toodle and Landa could no longer reach any higher, they chiseled artwork in relief on the inside walls. Landa found it heavy work and hated going up the staircase. Frint then rushed to be helpful to her, and she waved back. Once, I caught him taking over Landa's hammer and chisel and finishing her work, forgetting his own activities. Frint's strange behavior was more and more notable. In the first place, he cried but seldom, not counting some tears at night by the fire. In the second place, he was full of servile attention for Landa, who frequently smiled at him with fluttering eyelashes and timid looks. He followed her the entire day with his eyes but turned away with a jolt if he thought that Landa had noticed his looks. Although Frint watched only Landa, they never spoke to each other for long. Frint's face radiated with joy when Landa picked a flower and put it playfully behind her ear. Frint and Landa were, in fact, the only ones who didn't work with full effort on the tower. Because the system of plow services ran now smoothly, Frint no longer had to supervise the division of labor so much.

Because of this, I decided that Frint, Toodle, and Landa could concentrate on what the Stenodiggers called "the non-stony matter." This implied window frames and the provision of curtains and carpets for the chambers. One of the Steno-blockers was skilled enough to make glass for the windows. This Stenoblocker, a cousin of Block, had learned glassmaking because, as he said, "The future is not in stone, but in glass," an explanation which had so far been sneered at by his uncle. The glassmaker had his own cave and the required ovens.

The fabric for the curtains came from the stocks of the Stenodigger women, and the carpets were made by the Stenoblocker women. During their husbands' long absences, they had weaved an infinite number of carpets and cloth with their looms. From their stock, one could deduce that their men had frequently been absent. Thus, we could cover the stone staircase up to the hundredth floor with carpet, along with all chambers of the solution coordinators, and provide my office with a large carpet. To Frint's delight, Landa was very clever at sewing the curtains, and she had refined taste in selecting the colors of the curtains to match carpets. Thus, she decided on a different color for each floor so that one could always remember which floor one was on. Frint and Landa did this work jointly and joyfully.

I had entrusted the decoration of my office on the hundredth floor to Toodle. I had given her a free hand so that it remained a surprise for me in how she would arrange the office. After some days, she came hopping over to me and invited me to the hundredth floor. It was a long climb, which I managed more easily than I would have done in former days because of my recently obtained light-footedness. On the hundredth floor, the tower was more narrow, so I had but one large room. After our staircase excursion, Toodle drew the door curtain of my office aside. I stepped inside my sun-drenched study furnished with a large stone desk with stone chairs, a large niche in the wall with carved shelves for the books and papers, and a long conference table with stone benches around. Heavy curtains hung from the two windows, and an enormous carpet that almost completely covered the floor was of the same colors: grey, light pink, red, white, and black with square and other straight-edged shapes. It was really nice against the grey stone wall, but I found the relief paintings the most beautiful. Toodle had chiseled into the walls here and there, showing some of the events which had led to the construction of this Solvetower. Above the door, she had drawn the book of the old king about the Big Settlement Days; to the right of my desk, Toodle had chiseled Espra, who looked kind and nice, the Large Line appearance, the ruin of the old king, the attack on our tower, and finally, right behind my desk chair, a picture of the newly finished Solvetower.

"Terrific!" I praised Toodle. I was delighted with all of this but could not oppress a small feeling of fear when I saw the carving of the destroyed Solvetower. Although I had been careless last time and, in fact, had had no time to have extras in case they are needed for a good result, I was shocked for the first time. I did not mention it to Toodle, but I doubted whether we would ever arrive at completing the tower and hoped that this relief would not represent a never-happened event.

At last, we had reached the five-hundredth floor. Since we were halfway through the construction, I decided that we would take a day's rest and have a five-hundredth-floor festival. Everyone was getting ready for the banquet and decorating the trees that stood around the tower with Chinese lanterns and garlands. The festival was to be held on the open spot in front of the Solvetower. When twilight fell, the lanterns were switched on, and a large campfire was lighted as the Stenodiggers did every evening. Everyone was delighted over the rich meal, which did us good after all those days of raw beans. Stone juice flowed abundantly in everybody's goblets, and we took large portions of the cakes, which were sometimes as hard as a stone, but that was the way it should be, said the Stenodigger and Stenoblocker women.

Landa looked a bit lost, looking timidly around. The Stenodiggers and Stenoblockers were not interested in her, and Frint looked into her eyes but was unable to say a word. Landa herself hadn't been terribly talkative so far, and I knew little of her, except that Espra had brought her from very far away. Now that we didn't have to concentrate on the tower, I tried to learn more about Landa. "Where did Espra find you?" I asked her, biting firmly into a stone cake.

"In Marka," she answered delightedly, glad that someone, at last, talked to her.

"Marka?" I said, astonished. I had already heard of this place earlier and had read about it in the books of my castle library. Marka was the area that lay close to infinity; that's where the borders of the Kingdom of Existence were.

"That's infinitely far away!" said Toodle, who seemed to also know the region.

"But then you are Markese!" I exclaimed, astonished. Landa nodded and timidly looked at her lap. It astonished me that Landa was Markese because, according to my books, the Markese people were long, slim, and, to quote one notebook, "of the most noble character." Although Landa was friendly and also a nice person, she was neither tall nor slim. Frint looked at her with even more interest.

"I am a bird keeper," Landa explained to us. "I take in and nourish all kinds of traveling birds, so they can recover their strength before flying to infinity. I have seen many different kinds. We have a large cage, which takes up an entire field and reaches to the sky, to receive birds coming from and going to infinity. And then they are very tired." Landa giggled up her sleeve. "One day, your daughter, Espra, came flying towards us with her sweet young birdies," she continued. "I had never seen such a strange bird ... and how upset she was! She couldn't find a mother that pleased her anywhere. I had to soothe her for hours before she calmed down. They enjoyed the large birdcage and everything that I did for her and the other birds. She gave me many suggestions on how I could improve the cage and the bird reception. She has so much energy and so many good ideas, which I immediately acted upon."

Toodle and I glanced at each other significantly. This was the first time that I heard someone praise Espra's initiatives.

"After some days, when she had entirely recovered, she asked me whether I would like to become her mother and the grandmother of Kroo and Kra. If so, I had to marry a certain King Ody," continued Landa. "How could I refuse such a pleasant request from a nice bird? But, yes ... then everything went wrong." She sighed deeply.

"No, no," said Frint, who gripped her by the shoulder and had found his voice again. "Nothing has gone wrong. Ody does not want to marry you, full stop, and that is not so terrible—is it? Unless?" Frint looked at me with eyes full of fear and perplexity, anxiously wanting to know if, now that I knew who Landa was, I might nevertheless change my mind.

I laughed understandingly. "You must, in any case, not let go any tears," I said, upon which Frint's face brightened up. Landa was more special than I had thought at first sight. She was the only one I knew who had handled Espra peacefully and pleasantly. I found myself feeling the way fathers do when their daughters are appreciated by strangers.

We finished the festival with a bout of dancing around the fire; we were pulled away by the Stenodiggers' and the Stenoblockers' strong arms, and our feet hardly touched the ground and flew around outside the circle. Landa was having a great time. When deep into the night, everyone had tired feet from the dancing, we decided to sleep close to the tower and continue to the following morning. With a lingering pleasant after-festival feeling, we went to work again in the morning.

Then it was time for me to send a letter to Sseus on elf paper to explain that I would shortly have a Solvetower and that he should look for suitable people or beings who could act as permanent solution coordinators. Toodle had more writing to do than me because she had to write all Elf chiefs to inform them of the existence of the Solvetower. She asked them to be the local representatives and, with the use of elf paper, to send the problems of those who could not come to the tower. When we had written all the letters, they flew as darts by air to their destinations.

On a quiet evening, when the construction of the tower had already progressed far, Frint came to me hesitatingly with a small note. "It is a letter for Landa," he explained, stammering. "Would you give your opinion on whether it's well written ... asking if ... if Landa ... she was, eh ... finally to become my wife." I was just about to explain that I would not read the letter, having the fullest faith in his writing style and the kind reception Landa would give it, when I saw for the first time in days a small tear in his eyes again.

"She thinks nothing of me," he started, gasping more and more. "I never know what I should say to her ... probably she does not want me. Oh, forget it!" At these last words, he cried as hard as ever and withdrew his letter.

"No, let me see it," I said to help him. "It is perhaps a very good idea to write down what you cannot say to her." I took the letter that he offered to me with trembling hands.

"My very sweet Landa" was at the top, written beside a dried tear spot. "I was looking from my tearful valley and saw you falling from the sky. You held me in your spell at once, and I never can escape again. Your eyes, your hands, your long tresses will remain chiseled indefinitely in my memory. I put my life in your hands. You can knead it to your will, and if you don't want it, you should throw it in the deepest and darkest sea where it will fall apart, forever, far from you, into a thousand bits and will be food for fishes."

I looked up from the paper, surprised, and saw Frint's anxious look. He dealt quite severely with his life, I thought. I read further. "Forgive me my existence because that does not make much sense. But before I die, I want to know if you have but the smallest feeling for me. However, it will not be this way. Who am I to dare to hope? My last tear will be for you." It was signed "Frint, who adores you."

"Die?" I called, returning the letter. "That's not your intention, I hope. Naturally, Landa thinks of you!"

Frint smiled painfully. His pessimistic nature made him uncertain of it. "I'll give it to her tomorrow," Frint said. I nodded. I restrained myself from saying "with much pleasure" since these words seemed not to fit with Frint's ideas—everything except pleasure—and his life-risking letter.

The next day was almost a historical day. Toodle and Landa had made a flag of bright red so that, once on the top of the tower, it was clearly visible in the distance. With united strength, the Stenodiggers and the Stenoblockers had finished the last floors in one day. This work was the hardest because the workers became very tired from the cold and thin air. Frint had partially helped them by carrying them to the highest floors on his flying bird, but the stones had to be drawn up the staircase with a rope because they couldn't be transported with Frint's machine.

Landa, who must have received Frint's letter by now, looked a bit glum and avoided Frint's anxious look.

At the end of our working day, the tower was completed except for one thing: The flag! Tomorrow, I would place the red flag on the highest floor, leaving it there forever.

"We have managed it!" exclaimed Toodle with joy. Everyone, except Frint and Landa, was full of joy. Full of pride, I examined the enormous tower from the ground. It extended high, very high, above me and seemed to move slowly back and forth against the blue sky. Everything was ready for tomorrow's great day.

Toodle had only received good bulletins from the local Elf chiefs, who were prepared to give their support to the Solvetower. The Solvetower was ready to solve all problems indefinitely. The large opening yawned before us, welcoming.

I had decided not to put a door in so that the Solvetower should be accessible to everyone and always.

"The job has been managed!" Block said proudly to me.

"In spite of you!" added Steno.

I was just about to praise them for their thorough work when I saw a dart of folded elf paper flying towards me. I caught it in the air and started to read it. It was Sseus' answer.

"Dear Ody," it said. "Enough good solution coordinators can be found. I will personally send them to you, so you can select for yourself. Much success with the tower construction, but think about the Large Line. There is a report that Espra is taking particular actions. I don't know what yet, but you take care! The danger is not yet over."

Toodle came closer by. I gave her the letter to read, after which she raised her eyebrows. "We will see," she said carelessly and proudly examined her red flag.

At nightfall, everybody was too tired to celebrate the evening before the flag festival. I went to sleep outside and dreamed about the good results I hoped for the tower. A better success than that of the old king, and the Large Line was still absent from the sky. We had been well on time. Frint did not sleep and started writing a new letter to Landa in Steno's house. Landa's evasive glances had made him suspect the worst.

The night was quiet when I awoke suddenly to the soft sound of a horse's hooves. I was surprised and noticed that I was not the only one who had been startled. Whereas everyone else still slept, I saw Landa standing with her back to me. A horse rider approached her gently. It was a strange black horse with grey spots, which wasn't the body of a horse I was used to. His head was longer and sharper, his neck rounder, with a long grey mane, and he stood very high on his tendril-like legs. The rider was, insofar I could see, a long, slim young man with a dark flapping cape, gleaming boots, and a straight posture. He walked to Landa, bent himself to her, and said, “Hello, Deary.” He seized her by her waist and put her behind him on the back of the horse. Landa said nothing but went with the young man without protest or hesitation. The rider and Landa immediately rode away at a trot and disappeared between the trees on the fast horse. I was shocked and did not have the courage to stop them or ask prying questions. I feared only for Frint.

17

The next morning, everyone could only think of one thing, a grand festival that would last the whole day and night to celebrate the flag-raising, the successful completion of the tower construction, and a free life without work for the Stenodiggers, now that the Stenoblockers would take over their stone and construction company. The Stenodiggers themselves didn't find that this last reason deserved a party but reconciled themselves with the facts. During all the festival commotion, nobody noticed the absence of Landa. Frint was still nowhere to be found. I quickly ran to Toodle, who was explaining a new recipe to the Stenodigger women so that their cakes would be less hard.

"Landa has disappeared," I whispered, taking her aside. Toodle was startled. I told her what I had seen that night.

"You must tell Frint this," she said, nevertheless. "Look! There he comes from Steno's house." She pointed to Frint coming out of the house and blinking from the bright sunlight.

I went to him.

"Hey, Ody!" he said. "Tonight, I wrote a new letter for Landa. This one is somewhat clearer; perhaps she didn't understand yesterday's properly. Do you want to read it?"

"No," I said with a sad voice.

"What's the matter?" asked Frint anxiously.

"Landa has disappeared. I saw her being picked up by a rider tonight on a horse."

"What!" called Frint, almost scared to death. "She's been kidnapped? And you haven't done anything about it? Why didn't you call me?" He panicked completely and, in his nervousness, tore his letter to pieces without paying attention to what he was doing.

"She hasn't been kidnapped," I said calmly, showing my compassion. "She went along with the rider willingly." I spared Frint some details which would have saddened him even more, such as the fact that the rider was a young person and had called Landa "Deary."

"Another man," said Frint with a deep and hollow voice. I expected that he would burst out in a very great fit of weeping, but to my stupefaction, he didn't do that. What happened was more awful than crying because his distress was too great and too unbearable. Frint turned quite white, as white as the paper pieces on the ground. His hollow eyes no longer gleamed. He started to tremble throughout his entire body.

I was deeply concerned by what I saw because his situation seemed beyond consolation; a simple fit of weeping would do no good. "We will search for her," I tried. Frint looked around inanimately, dark circles forming below his eyes, but he remained silent.

"I will bake cakes," he announced suddenly without some enthusiasm and ran sadly away from me.

"The flag! The flag!" called Block, coming to me with the flagstaff in his hand and the fluttering red flag. "Hurry up! Then I can at last take over the little business here!" Without waiting for my reply, he seized me by my waist and put me on his shoulders, with one leg on each side of his head. He gave me the flag and rushed at full speed to the Solvetower. Toodle, the Stenodiggers, and the Stenoblockers walked in a group behind us. We had decided that I would go with the flying bird and fix the flag on the thousandth floor in the special opening made for it in the stones. This would save time and allow us to avoid climbing the long staircase.

"Hurry! Where is the tearful toot?" called Block, getting impatient.

"He's baking cakes," I said from my high place, looking around.

"We haven't seen him baking cakes," said some Stenodigger women.

"Neither have I," endorsed Toodle. I looked but couldn't see Frint anywhere in the company.

"I cannot wait for him," said Block, stamping his foot impatiently.

"Oh, we are not in such a hurry, are we?" asked Steno slowly, who would gladly play for time and so delay the moment when Block would take over his business.

"Then I will fly!" said Block and jumped ponderously into the flying bird which stood beside the tower. "The crybaby has flown me frequently enough to the highest floor. I know now how it works—a piece of cake for a Stenoblocker, isn't it? I jumped from his shoulders and put myself behind him on the seat. I saw Block's large muscular back as he started to pull on all kinds of lines and handles so that the bird started to strangely hop in the grass. Block had not really paid much attention during his flights with Frint. I looked desperately at Toodle and then around, hoping Frint would still show up. However, Frint remained hidden, and some Stenodigger women who had looked for him returned alone, shrugging their shoulders. I didn't have much choice: either I took the long staircase, which would take a lot of time, and the flag would arrive at night, or I must trust in Block's flying skill.

Meanwhile, Block had found the correct handle, and the neck of Frint's flying bird came up, and after some starting failures, the wings started to flap. Block worked the pedals with all his strength, and the bird made fast peeping sounds. I wondered if he would destroy the bird with his strength. At last, the flying bird rose up vertically from the ground.

"Hooray!" the crowd below cried, and Block's men called, "Push him up into the sky!" Block seemed to enjoy this experience. After a while, having gone straight up, he found out he could make the bird circle around the tower, and it went up in a spiral. "This is nice!" he called over his shoulder to me. I didn't find it so nice because circling the tower made me a bit nauseated. The air became colder, and here and there, small clouds floated by. In contrast to Frint, Block didn't easily tire of pedaling, so the flying bird kept a constant and fast speed. Under us, I saw our construction comrades. In the distance, I saw the forests and fields, and away to my right was a dust cloud as if a large group of people was running over the fields.

"You get ready!" Block called. "There we almost are!" The last narrow floor came into view. Block maneuvered the flying bird near the tower top's edge and tried as well as he could to keep the vehicle in a steady position. I stood up carefully, grasping the plane with one hand, and leaned forward. It was a harrowing job because the flying bird didn't stay steady, and I had but little support. I stretched my arm as far as possible, holding the flagstaff firmly. With one short push, I put the flag into its slot. I pushed it down firmly, ensuring that it wouldn't be crooked. Block took care that the machine's wings did not touch the wall as I carried out my operations between the tail and the wings. After I had made sure that the flag could not come off, I gestured that we could descend. I sat down carefully and admired the elegant red flag flapping in the wind.

"Yippee!" Block exclaimed as he let the flying bird go down in a free fall, as Frint used to do. The flying bird began to crack on all sides, and I saw some metal plates coming loose alongside me. "No panic! I have everything in my hand!" said Block, who had also noticed the strange sounds, starting to feel proud now that he had everything, in his opinion, well under control. Some dozen meters above the ground, he started to pedal diligently and brought us down with a hard bang on the ground.

"Hooray! The Solvetower is finished!" shouted everybody with joy. I stepped, still trembling from the exciting trip on the flying bird.

"Ha! Ha! Child's play!" said Block, patting his chest. "You can't imitate that, hey, Steno? There is gold in those flying birds, that's what I say! Handy and adventurous, that's what people want!"

Steno said with a wry mouth, "You aren't such a high-flyer, Block. Keep yourself to stones."

"My stone business and yours, you mean to say," Block laughed with a sinister expression in his eyes. "You'd better count your bit of gold. Your stones are now mine. After the festival, you disappear. That was the agreement!"

Steno growled between his teeth, looking maliciously at me, and then was silent. Everyone rushed down to the banquet. Some danced in a large circle around the Solvetower.

"We really must find Frint now. I am very worried about him," said Toodle, coming over next to me. We went towards the trees and the thicket first. Overwhelmed by his sorrow, possibly Frint had hidden there, far from everyone. I was looking between the branches of the trees when I heard a dull drumming sound of footsteps. It seemed that a whole mob was marching toward us.

"What's that?" asked Toodle, who had noticed the sound too. The memory of the dust clouds, which I had seen on the ground from the flying bird, came back to me. A large group of people was heading in our direction.

"Perhaps they are the first people to come to the Solvetower with their problems," I suggested, but I was not certain of my explanation because the droning footsteps seemed ominous.

"I hope not attackers again?" sighed Toodle.

"No," I said slowly with a gripping feeling around my heart. "It is ... Espra."

The partygoers were surprised at seeing these uninvited guests. Espra came first and led an enormous mob of people, birds, and other beings that I did not know. She was frowning deeply and tapped on the ground with a stick to a rhythm that her followers had to run to. There were hundreds of walkers and stampers, all with imminent looks in their eyes. Some held up wooden signs which stuck out above the dark mob, and the following slogans had been painted: "Away with Ody!" and "No more mismanagement!" and "Espra, Queen of Existence!"

"Give me a stone! Who are those disturbers of peace?" said Steno coming closer with heavy steps. I stood stiff as a nail, fixed to the ground. An insurrection! This mob was entirely in Espra's power. I feared most terribly for what they would do, but I had to save the Solvetower and keep Toodle and the others away from eventual hostilities.

"No, but," Steno said, brightening up, "if that isn't the crazy bird who saved us from the attack of the Stenoblockers!" He descended to Espra, suspecting nothing, to thank her again for her rescue operation.

"People!" said Espra, her hand up and bringing to halt the grumbling mob. "This is one of Ody's victims. Under his control, this poor helpless man was attacked with violence! Aren't you grateful that I saved you?" Espra looked penetratingly at Steno.

"Yes, naturally, but ..." answered Steno, not understanding and sticking out his hand.

"Enough!" ordered Espra, and she turned to me. "Here he is!" She spoke with a very loud voice so that her followers could hear her well. The partygoers looked confused. "The sad picture of a king who only has wrongdoings on his record," she continued. "Fortunately, I am here to take over his tasks, his own daughter! And Existence will be saved!"

I was deeply incensed and mastered myself with difficulty. "You go too far," I said with a stiff jaw and stiffer cheeks.

"We, the people here, can depose the King of Existence; you know that very well," said Espra severely, her eyes semi-closed. "Well, here are these people. Step aside; I am the new Queen of Existence."

I didn't move from my place and tried to give a quick explanation to Espra and her followers so that they would leave us alone.

"Goodbye! Until never!" a hollow voice suddenly rang out from high above us.

"Frint!" startled Toodle, turning around. The whole company was dismayed by what we saw. On approximately the fifteenth floor of the Solvetower, Frint sat with his legs over the edge of an open window. He pushed himself further off with his hands and clearly had the intention to jump from the tower.

"Look here, people!" said Espra, raising a hand accusingly. "He even drives others to life-threatening jumps."

Murmuring mounted from the mob. "Ooh!" came suddenly from all mouths. I saw Frint flying in a free fall beside the tower in the sky. Espra hesitated not one moment and flew with great speed to the falling Frint. With a clever swoop, she flew under Frint and caught him with a slap on her back, where Frint continued to lie with an astonished look. Espra flew back to us and shook off Frint so that he rolled to my feet on the ground. Toodle squatted by Frint and kept his head between her hands, close to herself.

"More proof!" said Espra, speaking again to her followers. "I am a much better Queen of Existence!" She turned to me and said in an almost compassionate tone. "Step aside. It's much better this way. I will take very well care of you; you won't lack anything."

I still did not move. I couldn't possibly endanger my Solvetower because if Espra became Queen of Existence, she would certainly not maintain the tower since it was my slick idea. If that happened, the Large Line solution would be in danger, and I could not allow that, as Sseus had already warned me in his letter.

"It's impossible for me to leave," I said shortly.

"Don't force me to take unpleasant measures," Espra whispered to me as her followers became impatient. "I still grant you an honorable way out."

I crossed my arms over each other and waited to see what the mob would dare undertake against me. Frint burst into tears, which I thought was a good sign. He was still the same and barely consolable. I could hear fast hoofbeats from a horse coming up behind the mob. A white rider rushed at full speed towards us, slowed down when he had arrived at Espra's supporters, and slowly cleared himself a passage through the shifting mob until he stood before me.

Full of joy, I received the white rider on his panting white horse. "Sseus!" I called happily.

Sseus looked serious and descended from the horse. "Espra, you go too far," he said calmly, hardly looking at Espra and removing the bridle of his horse.

"I have heard that tale before!" said Espra.

"Go away, pal!" called Kroo and Kra, flapping about. They had hidden between some followers' legs and now found the courage to support their mother.

"What do you actually want?" asked Sseus, looking straight at Espra.

"Be careful how you speak, stranger. You speak to the Queen of Existence!"

Sseus smiled subtly. "I thought that Ody was the king?"

"Not anymore," was Espra's short explanation. It was clear that she did not know who Sseus was and was becoming slightly uncertain of his peaceful intentions.

"You don't have the right to depose Ody," explained Sseus, his eyes smiling.

"Oh, no?!" exclaimed Espra. "We will see about that!" She motioned with her hand and bade her supporters to walk past us to the tower. They moved their wooden plates back and forth threateningly.

"No, not to my tower!" called Block, startled. "Keep off of my tower!"

"Hear who speaks," called Steno as he rushed with his men to the tower to protect it against the imminent mob.

I looked at Sseus anxiously. What can we do against this mob? And this time the tower would be really damaged.

"Break down the tower!" Espra told her supporters. "Then he will have to admit that there is no one better than myself to be Queen of Existence!"

"No!" I called out in an unfruitful attempt at reconciliation.

"There must be a better solution!"

Espra did not listen. Frint wept loudly. Dark clouds packed together in the sky and announced a big thunderstorm. I looked up as I already heard the first crashes echo off the tower's stone walls. The sky became darker. A sudden solemn placidity fell over me. I forgot everyone around me.

"The Large Line is coming," I mumbled to myself. I was peaceful, ready for what might be my last ordeal.

18

Soon I saw the luminous white line arriving from the left. Slowly the band of light crawled to the right. I swallowed and hoped that the Large Line would continue uninterrupted to the other side. If this happened, it meant that I had found the correct solution to save Existence forever. However, if the Large Line stopped, then Existence would also end and no longer extend to infinity. Anxious, I followed the course of the line.

Espra and her followers looked inquiringly at the sky. "The Large Line!" called Espra. "It will, at last, confirm that I am the only good Queen of Existence!"

Everyone ceased their activities and looked to the sky anxiously. The Large Line was now almost above my head, where it stopped abruptly.

"Oh, help!" said Toodle. Scraps of stones started to fall from the Solvetower. Espra called for her supporters to quickly come away from the tower.

I couldn't believe my eyes. Had the Large Line really been interrupted now? Had I not found the correct solution? Hadn't I been better than the old king? The ground started to tremble under our feet, and I heard thundering sounds around. The partygoers looked searching around as if they wondered what they could best do, run away or stay. Existence was staggering.

A strong feeling arose in me. I didn't want Existence to end, whatever the Large Line indicated and whatever the Large Line Artist had claimed.

"Nooooo!!!!" I called loud in the sky, with my hands to my mouth.

Suddenly something extraordinarily unforeseen happened. Everything around me froze and became stiff as a rod; only I could move freely. In front of me, I saw Sseus, who stared stiffly at the sky. Frint lay on the ground with an open mouth, as if taking a breath, ready to cry, but without actually weeping. Espra hung in the sky, ready to fly away with Kroo and Kra behind her in an attempt to escape from the falling stone blocks. Both the birds and the stone blocks remained motionless, suspended in the sky. It was as if this moment had been frozen in time like a painting.

The Large Line still hung in the sky, interrupted and without movement. I sighed. "What now?" I said to myself.

"Now, you must make the correct choice," answered a voice to my right. The voice sounded familiar, but I could not place it immediately. I turned and saw an old man standing before me. I was surprised because much of this old man reminded me of myself. He wore my king's mantle and had my four crowns on his head. His face resembled mine but was older, much older. The man had a short grey beard, and because I recognized so much of myself in him, I thought, "That beard does not suit me."

The man was somewhat stouter than me but had the same look in his eyes. "I am the old king, as they call me now," spoke the old man.

"But that isn't possible," I sputtered. "I am the old king, at least the one I have always been. How can you stand then here before me if you are myself?"

"I'm not really here," was the quiet answer. "I appear here. You are now in a timeless moment. Everything stands still. We are in another dimension, where time plays no role. Soon you must return but listen first." The old king examined me from top to toe. "What made you so thin," he said.

"Oh, hard work," I explained to him, using my now-old excuse. Strangely enough, I wouldn't give away my secret that I had become a quarter-elf even to myself.

"I once searched for the Large Line solution," continued the old king, walking back and forth slowly. He raised a finger and said, "I made a number of errors then. Oh, yes! The Solvetower was a terrific idea, but to keep it undamaged and permanently up high is another matter, as you have noticed. The Large Line came and stopped flat above me, just as it now is above you." He stopped a moment to commemorate this sad moment in his and my life. "Then I knew that I had made a mistake somewhere, but where? I thought and thought so much that, at last, I could no longer think ... and then I was given a last chance by the Large Line Artist. I got a delay, a second chance. My tower was not yet finished, and as he said, 'You haven't had enough time to collect all elements for the Large Line solution,' the Large Line was withdrawn, and I had to look for a new solution. Therefore, I decided to start anew from the beginning, living as a child and learning everything new so that I got a fresh view of everything. This way, I came to the 'Wisest Advisor' who made me a child—that became you." He looked at me inquiringly, examining to see if he found that he had improved my appearance. "Well," he sighed. "Here we are then. I have appeared as the old king in you and will give you some last wise advice. I know why the Large Line does not go further than your Solvetower. The tower will only continue to stand if you give yourself up to it completely, locking yourself up forever and never to leave again.

Otherwise, how can you solve all problems of the Big Settlement Days? You must give up everything, your castle tree, your friends, your festivals. Make use now of this timeless moment, move quickly into the Solvetower, and close yourself up in your office. Then the tower will continue to stay, and the Large Line will continue. Existence will go on indefinitely; you must make that choice and sacrifice yourself. It's not very much, really. You restrict your own life to one office in a tower, but you ensure happiness for everyone else. Go ahead, make that choice now; it's your only and last chance!" The old king urged me with tension on his face.

I was desperate. The old king was most likely correct. He had faced this problem earlier. I walked slowly to the entrance of the Solvetower. Almost at the door opening, I threw a last look around. I would never again see this forest and could never talk with these people unless they came expressly to me to solve a problem. I looked at Sseus and Frint, and then suddenly, I was incredibly frightened by the image of Toodle. She stared straight at me. In her eyes was despair, very deep sorrow, but also resignation. What shocked me most was the fact that I had difficulties clearly seeing Toodle's body. Her image was blurred and almost transparent. Only light colors indicated her outlines, the fine lines of her face and eyes. She had become a shadow of herself, but the other people around had not been blurred.

"What happens to Toodle?" I asked after I had regained my voice with some difficult difficulty.

"Toodle? Who is Toodle?" asked the old king with some impatience because I still had not entered the tower. I indicated Toodle's image, which was becoming more and more vague. "Interesting," said the old king brushing one finger over his beard. "An elf fading herself away."

"Is she fading herself away?" I asked, dismayed. "But why?"

"Hm ... this must be the finest and noblest elf of Existence," concluded the old king as he went nearer to Toodle's blurring image and examined her thoroughly from top to toe.

"Of course, Toodle is the best elf of Existence," I said with some indignation. "She is ..." I swallowed my last words with fright.

"She is mine; that is what you wanted to say, isn't it?" said the old king turning himself suddenly on me and pointing with his finger. "That's the core," he continued. "This elf has understood and sensed that you will not enter that Solvetower as long as she walks freely around outside when you can no longer visit her. For this reason, she is fading herself away. If you do not enter the Solvetower, Existence is ended. The elf Toodle has taken the bravest decision of her existence—she disappears. You should be grateful to her for that."

I remembered Toodle's refusal to accept a task in the tower, which she had spoken about during our travel to the Goldstream. "I am not at all grateful," I exclaimed desperately. "I cannot give up Toodle. I want her to be with me in the Solvetower."

"That is exactly the problem. You cannot take her along because she is fading away. And even if you take her with you, do you seriously think that you would ever have time to talk with her other than about business? Moreover, her presence would distract you. You can't think of yourself and your own pleasure. You must always make your time available to others. It is much better this way, believe me. Toodle is doing you and Existence a noble service. Elves always make their own decisions; you can't do anything about it."

Blood throbbed through my head. I had the Large Line solution within arm's reach. I only had to catch it, and Existence would be eternally secure. The Large Line solution, of which I was once so proud, now struck me as something as sorrowful as I could imagine. My task as a king was obvious and clear: Walk into the Solvetower and forever solve all problems presented to me with a cheerful smile. I had lost Toodle and had myself to blame. My decision was simplified and decided for me. Could I risk all of Existence and sacrifice my good relations for an elf? No matter how unpleasant the decision was for me, surely the existence of all people and beings was of much greater importance.

"Stop dawdling," said the old king, impatient for me to stop thinking about it. "You really must go into the Solvetower now!"

I considered all the tribulations which I had endured during my life and my royalty that had brought me to this sad but unavoidable moment.

"Go then!" called the old king, his arms extending to me.

I clenched my fists. My hesitations had given way to a previously unknown feeling that I had never heard anyone speak of. I looked at Toodle's shadow, and a tear welled up in my eyes. The old king looked at me desperately. The strange feeling within me became stronger, coming, it seemed, from the depths of the earth. It was as if a thick-link iron chain united Toodle and me together.

A chain so strong that no saw or strength could possibly break it. I had never noticed this feeling between Toodle and me before, but I understood clearly now that this collar had always been there, unnoticed, from the moment when I had first seen her, with her harp, dancing toward me over the flower field. It was not a feeling of love such as I had heard of in poems and songs. It did not resemble Frint's feelings for Landa. It was much more than that. It was an unbreakable chain that made the words "marry" and "love" sound hollow. How unreasonable and fatal my decision would be—my relationship with Toodle could not be denied.

"I'm not going," I announced finally to the old king. It was impossible to give any other answer. Neither the whole of

Existence nor the threat to eternity could change that.

The old king started to fade. He had been struck dumb. I walked to what remained of Toodle and took both her hands.

"Oh, misfortune! Oh, sadness!" lamented the old king, flinging his arms to the sky.

A loud thunderclap followed. All the characters around me came to life again and continued their interrupted movements. Frint cried desperately. Espra flew with Kroo and Kra over my head, and the stone blocks of the Solvetower continued to fall down. Everyone around me ran anxiously together each other. Toodle's image regained its color, and she regained her normal shape.

"You haven't gone!" she said, looking at me, astonished and with questioning eyes.

"No," I said with a certain sadness. "And you are not wiped out. But Existence will end now."

Toodle took her hands from mine and said, "We are too strong. I had hoped that my disappearance would force you to choose the whole of Existence and not us; it is now too late ... we are together, but not for long."

"That's outrageous! The Large Line is cheating!" Espra came down again; she had her arms akimbo and looked stubbornly at the sky.

Toodle and I followed her look and saw to our utter amazement that the Large Line stretched out as a broad band entirely uninterrupted from left to right over the sky.

"The King of Existence is confirmed to be a softie since he hasn't even found the Large Line solution, in spite of my good ideas," continued Espra with indignation. She looked at us inquiringly. "You have become very light," she remarked, "just as light as you are in your head!"

Light from the Large Line illuminated our heads for a short moment, then the Large Line went out and ... never appeared again. The ground under our feet had stopped trembling and droning. The shower of stones from the Solvetower had ended abruptly. Espra's followers and the partygoers looked surprised and glanced around, relieved. The signs of Espra's followers with the negative statements had been broken and hung slack in their hands. They threw the broken signs on the ground and looked at Espra in anticipation.

"What now?" asked one of them.

Espra turned to Toodle and me and bunched up her cheeks. "I am too good for you dimwits," she spoke. "I know when I'm not wanted! The Large Line was awfully mistaken. Existence may still be saved, but don't ask me how! There will be eternal chaos! And that they call indefinite existence!" Espra shook her head at the idea of so many silly things. "I will save what still can be saved; you can't expect more from me as I wasn't made Queen of Existence. There is at least someone who will do something to save your image." She remained silent for a moment and looked at me full of compassion. "Come, children!" she said, drawing Kroo and Kra to herself. "A new task awaits us." Turning to her assembled people, she said, "You will not be disappointed. I will create a spot where you will be protected against this poor dimwit, where chaos and abuse will not dominate. You will hear from me!" With these last words, she rose into the air, followed by Kroo and Kra.

"But daughter!" I called after her. "Stay here for once!" It was the first time that I really had any fatherly feelings for Espra without caring what mischief she would be up to. I wanted to see her happy and content.

Espra's followers watched her going and called, "Hooray for Espra!"

"You have made the correct choice!" Sseus exclaimed, laughing and slightly shocked, when he walked up to us.

I explained briefly to Sseus and Toodle exactly what had

happened between the old king and me. "The old king was wrong," I concluded. "At least under these circumstances—he hadn't counted on the existence of Toodle."

"That was the reason he could not find the Large Line solution in former days," interrupted Sseus looking fascinated. "He had never had the unbreakable chain feeling. If you had gone into the Solvetower and been locked up, you would have lost everything: Toodle and also Existence. That wasn't the solution! Then the Large Line would not have been continued!" Sseus observed us both inquiringly. "What is that the bond between you two which ensures eternal existence?" he asked.

I searched my thoughts for the true answer to his question. I knew it was correct and that the Large Line had accepted my choice, but I didn't really know how or why.

"Because we now form an entity," answered Toodle. "We know what we should have known for a long time. Ody or I alone were incomplete. We were interrupted and not whole, just like the Large Line. Because Ody made himself an entity by choosing me, he became a complete and uninterrupted person, and so the Large Line also got the chance to go on without interruption ... but I didn't know that in the beginning." Toodle looked a bit timid and continued. "I think that the origin lay in the king himself. He had to experience enough freedom to be able to feel and understand everything—the Large Line then just had to follow." Sseus, Toodle, and I looked at each other. Although we didn't know for certain that we were right, things seemed to have worked out well.

"Celebration!" the Stenodiggers and the Stenoblockers around us cheered. They had been put at ease and even drew some of Espra's followers to the tables, those who didn't really know what to do next without their mentor. At seeing the cakes and delicacies, Espra's followers gladly jumped up.

"*Tss*—yes," said Steno looking at the nails of his hand and taking Block by the shoulders. "You certainly saw to it that the Solvetower was broken down again. Obviously, it was the stone blocks cemented by you and your half-measures that caused the tower to fall down. Mine are still there." Block wanted to grumble at hearing these grotesques lies, but Steno quickly continued, "However, the Solvetower is incomplete once again. Therefore, eh ... my stone business is not yet yours, not until we have repaired this thing under my good leadership."

Block growled a moment but had to admit that he couldn't yet take over Steno's business now the Solvetower had again broken down. Both men sat down companionably on the grass and raised a toast with their goblets of stone juice. "To the tower's repair!" said Steno. "On its quick completion," toasted Block with a grin.

We were startled by Frint, who was sobbing on Sseus' shoulder. "I am a good-for-nothing," he sneezed. "I couldn't even jump from a lousy tower."

"Who is this?" asked Sseus, astonished at seeing the crying Frint, who was getting Seuss' shoulder completely wet. Frint was scared at hearing Sseus' voice which he did not know.

"Who is this?" he asked in turn.

I presented both men to each other.

"I am Frint without Landa ... *sniff* ..." Frint wept, running one hand over his eyes and extending the other to Sseus.

"We must quickly retrieve Landa," Toodle suggested, becoming impatient with Frint's constant weeping.

I nodded. "Let's leave immediately for Marka; perhaps they will know more," I said. I briefly explained Frint's history to Sseus and asked him whether he would take on the surveillance of the Solvetower's repair by the Stenodiggers and Stenoblockers during our absence. The mob collected by Espra might find its way here again. Sseus nodded and wished us a successful trip.

"The flying bird!" said Toodle, dragging Frint with her. "We'll go to Marka with the flying bird, which is much faster. Take heart, Frint; think of Landa, and you will soon be near her." Frint let himself be dragged along without protest by the speed with which Toodle arranged our trip.

"She doesn't want to see me ever again," he gasped, seating himself in the flying bird. "We will be chased off by her like bandits ... *sniff* ..."

Toodle and I jumped up behind him. It seemed clever to help Frint with his search for Landa before he gave up completely because I knew approximately where Marka lay. The flying bird ascended. A long trip awaited us.

19

Espra's followers and the other partygoers waved us goodbye. The festival was still in full swing, and they looked astonished by our hasty departure. Frint pedaled hard, lifting his airplane up in the sky. With my arm, I indicated the direction in which he had to fly to reach Marka. According to the books I had read, Marka was "where the sun approaches the ground and goes to sleep."

It was the longest flight that I would ever make with Frint's flying bird because Marka was the settlement that lay the closest to infinity. After Marka, the Kingdom of Existence continued, but nobody knew what beings lived there. The birds that sometimes flew to and from infinity couldn't talk to say anything about it. The sun started setting, and its last golden-red beams shone right in our eyes. The flying bird sometimes made strange sounds; as well as the usual "*peeps*," we also heard "*cling, clang*" and "*cur, ssst*" sounds coming from the wings. Frint looked down questioningly at the beating wings.

"There are missing some metal blades," he called, turning to us. "Someone has treated it roughly."

"Block," I called back in his ear. "He helped me to put the flag on the Solvetower."

"We must land," announced Frint, as he steered the flying bird on a downward slope, with the bird's neck stretched straight ahead. Frint tried to land the machine gently, only half succeeding because the wings had lost their carrying capacity due to the missing blades. We landed on an open lawn. This emergency landing suited us fairly well since twilight had started, and we didn't want to travel by night. Frint got off and inspected both wings carefully. With the weak light of the falling evening, he rapidly and skilfully repaired the wings. He took away some blades of the lower part of the flying bird's abdomen where they were not needed and fixed them carefully onto the broken parts of the wings. In our hasty departure, Toodle had quickly seized a couple of sponge cakes and put them in her travel bag, so now we ate them with great pleasure.

Frint did not cry much during the journey. He looked as if he considered the trip doomed in advance but limited himself to subdued behavior. Each night, we slept on the ground under the outspread wings of the flying bird. Since the trip was to last a long time, Frint proposed to give flying lessons to Toodle and me so that we could relieve each other and wouldn't have to stop for rest pauses on the ground. This delighted us very much and seemed a practical idea. Toodle was the first to get a lesson. One morning she sat in the driver's seat beside Frint. I went behind her. Frint explained all the operations which she had to carry out. Soon Toodle started to pedal, and the flying bird ascended. Strangely enough, it felt different with Toodle flying the bird. The flying bird felt lighter and seemed to dance a bit in the sky. This had been different with Block. The flying bird had made many turbulent movements in the sky when he flew it. Frint was very enthusiastic about the way Toodle was flying and patted her appraisingly on the shoulder. In spite of her delicate construction, Toodle kept pedaling for a long time. One of the most sensitive operations occurred when changing the driver. Because we didn't want to lose time with landing and taking off, we decided to change places in the sky, to switch out pilots. I had to take over from Toodle. To make space in front, Frint crawled over the edge beside me. I stood up carefully with bent knees, holding myself by the edge of the seat. Then I stepped over the first seat and next to Toodle. With one leg after the other, I took over the pedaling, and Toodle went behind me next to Frint. To begin with, the flying bird headed down when we started changing pilots in the air, but soon we became very skilled. Frint gave the necessary instructions to keep the vehicle going. The handles, which I had to pull on from time to time, were very sensitive, and the bird jumped in the air or shook back and forth like a small boat at the slightest movement. Steering the bird in the correct direction was rather simple: straight ahead to where the sun went down.

It frequently occurred that birds flew around us and stared at us with unconcealed stupefaction. Many looked at us from a higher altitude and made it clear that they didn't consider the flying bird very elegant. We could admire many landscapes from our altitude: forests, fields of all colors, lakes, and jagged mountains. Below us in the fields, I sometimes saw people at work or children following us, laughing and pointing at us. The weather remained perfect during our entire trip, with just a few floating clouds. A gentle wind blew through our hair.

Although Frint remained resigned and expectant, Toodle and I constantly had a strange, happy feeling. Since the moment when I had found the Large Line solution, Toodle and I had become aware that we always formed an entity. We realized that, up to now, our personalities had not yet been complete. There had been a vacuum within us which needed to be filled. Toodle and I understood each other very well for this reason, especially when we were tired, hungry, sad—which was rare—and happy.

Since we only landed on the ground at night, we did not encounter many people on our trip. Everyone was usually asleep at that time, and we were near only the elfluffs, who stared at us from the small woods with luminous eyes without coming any closer. I had advised Frint to frankly tell Landa the truth about what he felt for her without considering the men who had taken her away on a horse. However, I couldn't ignore my slight concern that Landa might possibly send Frint away. How could we find comfort for Frint then?

After what seemed to be an endless flight, during which we strengthened our leg muscles by pedaling, Marka came in sight. Marka lay in a wide-open field and consisted of a large group of round houses much like beehives but made of hardened clay. From the sky, I saw light-red clay houses lying densely packed as if to obtain protection from each other. Marka was also recognizable by the large gathering of all kinds of birds, some well-known and others unknown, who flew back and forth in a giant cage. Landa had already described this huge birdcage at the edge of a housing settlement, a cage reaching high in the sky and extending over an entire field. The round maisonettes seemed small beside this birdcage. We flew over the cage, searching for Landa, but couldn't discover her anywhere. The birds in the cage made a lot of noise. They twittered and chirped happily, telling each other the longest tales.

"You see, she isn't there," Frint sighed, peering down. "We'd better return." Frint looked a bit frightened, seeming to harbor intentions of fleeing.

"We haven't made this long trip for nothing! I haven't worn my legs out for that!" I exclaimed, incensed.

"Let's look for the cage's entrance," suggested Toodle. We examined the edges of the large cage in search of a door. Frint flew the flying bird around the cage. Suddenly I noticed a young man with boots, black trousers, and a white shirt staring at us from the cage. He was tall and slim and stood there proud and erect.

"Deary!" he called. "There is a new bird for you. A very strange one with three heads sticking out from its back!" I thought I remembered the voice of this man as the rider who had greeted and kidnapped Landa that evening. The young man walked up to the outside of the cage and opened an almost invisible large, barred door to let us in.

Frint hesitated. "Come on!" I exhorted him. "Fly into the cage!" Frint obeyed my command without joy and landed the flying bird on the grass inside the cage.

"Deary!" called the young man, frightened. looking behind himself when he saw us descending. "The heads of that bird are coming down!"

In the distance stood a round, clay maisonette out of which I saw Landa exiting. Frint saw her coming and fell to the ground, slapping it with his knees. Shame-faced and with an anxious look in her eyes, Landa came closer. She stopped before the kneeling Frint, who regarded her with appeal.

"Will you marry me?" Frint implored, his eyes full of tears.

You cannot ask her that, only me!" called the young rider beside Landa, angry since his authority was being ignored.

"But I don't want to marry you!" exclaimed Frint with even more indignation than the young man. "I want to marry this very sweet Landa!"

"In the absence of her father, who is far away on a trip, you must ask for approval from her oldest brother," persisted the young man. "That is me. I don't want her to be brutally rejected once again by a ... a king, it was." The rider sniffed, still angry at this memory. I looked at him and Landa with big eyes. Landa glanced at me, ashamed.

"I thought that you, eh, were ... a fiancé of Landa or

something like that. I heard you call her deary," I said to the young man, who claimed to be her oldest brother.

"Naturally, I call her deary!" he said proudly. "Isn't she exactly that! Try even once to say she is not!" In his pride, Landa's brother seemed to be easily offended. He looked at me, proudly defying me.

"Well then," Frint admitted, turning on his knees to the rider. "Do you want my dearest Landa to marry me?"

"No!" was the fast and short answer.

"Oh," said Frint softly and looked disappointed at the grass. "Then I will go away again—my life has become too long." Frint started to gasp violently and allowed several large teardrops to fall on the grass before Landa's feet.

This scene was, however, too much for Landa. She squatted and bent to comfort Frint, saying, "Oh, no! My lad, my lad, my lad!"

"Why do you object to Landa marrying this young man?" Toodle asked Landa's brother.

"Because it will only produce misery," he answered. "I have bitter experiences. The previous time, her hand was asked for by a king's daughter and two king's grandchildren. In her foolish kindness, Landa accepted without informing me and without asking for my permission. And what was the result? The poor innocent young woman was roughly treated and was forced to heavy labor in a stone construction company!" Landa got up and started softly scratching her brother's sleeve as if she wanted to explain something.

"I was that king," I said without any fear. I clearly noticed that since the Large Line solution, I no longer felt fear, no fear for anything or of anybody.

"Mister!" exclaimed the rider haughty. "How dare you appear here before us?! Your feet stain our clean grass!"

I remained calm and smiled. "I did not reject Landa ... at least, it ... was all completely different; it was not my idea to marry, and I only refused the obligation to marry made by my, eh … daughter."

"And the forced labor?" opposed the brother.

"It was Landa herself who wanted it," I explained.

"But Lando," soothed Landa, still scratching her brother's sleeve. "I told you …"

"I only need half a word to see into the real unexpressed truth," said the brother, as he carefully calmed down. "My sister is, I know from experience, always too modest and too kind. She would describe a slap in her face as a caress!"

Frint regained some hope and looked at Landa appealingly. "Then now I can marry her?" he asked with dried tear tracks on his cheeks.

"Of course not!" answered the brother as he turned his back on us and made intentions to walk back to the clay maisonette. "What an idea!" he said to himself while Toodle, Landa, and I followed him. "A howler!" he continued to himself, making large dramatic gestures with his arms. "A supplicant, without any pride, kneeling in the grass and unable to retain from crying—that is not worthy of a proud and noble Markese!"

"He is prouder than you think," I pleaded. "When you carried away Landa that night, he no longer wanted to live any longer without Landa; that is proud and noble, isn't it?"

Lando stood quietly, looked just a moment at our waiting faces, and said, "Is that proudness or weakness? In any case, she cannot be spared from here. That's why I fetched her on my quickest horse. Everything here was becoming disorderly here, with all birds that came for protection and care before they continued their long flight that were deeply saddened by Landa's absence. My brothers and I couldn't manage any longer. The birds only wanted to be fed by Landa's hands. They all became very thin." He indicated a passing blue bird with a long, elegant tail. "Can you see his hollow cheeks? He only started eating yesterday, after our return."

Frint dragged himself up, dangling his arms and dragging his feet. "In that case, I will become a bird and remain eternally in Landa's cage," he said when he was nearby.

"And if we find a good substitute for Landa?" suggested Toodle, who seemed to have an idea. I thought immediately of Espra but wondered where and how I could find her immediately. We moved on and reached the door of the maisonette.

"No way," called Lando, keeping the wooden door open for us. "Landa is irreplaceable."

"But she does not need to go," Toodle proposed, standing on the doorstep. "Frint may like to stay here!"

"He is not a Markese," continued Lando obstructively. "Only a Markese who is born in Marka can continue to live here; otherwise, our proud and noble people would be diluted, so Marka would become less proud and noble."

From the maisonette, I heard the sounds of a lively and already well-advanced meal, the clanking of glasses and knives and the clashing of plates. We entered the room and saw four other young men joking gaily and sitting at a long table. The room was sociably arranged with pieces of wood-carved furniture, wide curtains of a flowery fabric, similar cushions, and elegant chairs. As I already knew Landa's talents for room arrangement from her work on the Solvetower, I recognized` her style immediately. At our arrival, the four young men looked at us and gaily raised their glasses.

"Welcome, strangers!" called one, whereupon he, followed by the others, drank from his glass.

"These are my brothers, Landus, Landi, Landen, and small Landosi," Lando presented his brothers to us. It was probably a Markese habit to give children one name and make variations of it for other children, I thought. "Please sit down and enjoy our hospitality before you leave again," said Lando, as he carried in some extra chairs. Landa went to the kitchen and brought new plates of food which she put before us on the table. Landa's brothers looked at us inquiringly. Landa explained their presence by saying, "They came to ask for Landa's hand, but they did not know that we would never permit it." The brothers burst out in laughter.

I put some pudding on my plate and said, "If I understand correctly, our Frint cannot marry your Landa under any condition."

"I see that you have understood," laughed Lando, without any indulgence. I understood then why Landa hadn't asked for her brother's approval when she had gone with Espra.

"I knew it," sighed Frint, sadly chewing on a seed biscuit. He looked very pale and very upset, not even having the strength to consider a plan to shorten his life.

Landa's own opinion and desires did not seem to be important in her brother's eyes.

I looked at Landa searchingly when she brought a fresh plate of honey sweets and asked, "And you, Landa, do you want to marry Frint?"

Frint lifted his head but let it fall again immediately.

"Yes, eh ... I mean no," she answered, frightened by this direct question. The brothers looked at me threateningly. "I have no parents here; right now, my father is making a distant trip to the infinite. My brothers know what is best for me. It seems that one becomes blind by, well ... love." She swallowed the last word almost inaudibly and continued. "In such cases, it's better that others make the decision for you."

I understood that Landa's brothers didn't want to give up the homely kindness and coziness and certainly did not want to let her go with a strange man. Every argument for keeping her with them was good.

"But now I will remain in the cage," sighed Landa, walking slowly back to the kitchen. "The birdcage has also become a Landa-cage. How nice it was to discover all new things with my daughter, eh ... your daughter, Espra." She sighed in a way that produced worried looks from her brothers.

"You are completely right," said Toodle suddenly, looking Lando straight in the eyes. "You have the fullest right to protect Landa against greedy wedding-hungry brutes. Forgive us for coming. You are the best brother I have ever encountered!"

Lando relaxed and looked at Toodle gladly. Frint gasped softly into his plate. The brothers had been put at their ease and started to like us. The subject of marriage was no longer brought up, so they were prepared to talk a lot about Markese lives and their parents' travels.

"They are visiting the unknown people of the infinity," explained small Landosi eagerly. "We don't know exactly what lies beyond Marka."

I found this extraordinarily interesting and said I hoped to receive a travel report from them shortly.

"Our horses are the fastest horses of Existence," blustered Landi with pride. "They are noble souls just like us! They are even faster than your bird."

"We are an important people," explained Landus to me, tapping with a finger on the table. "This is the first border settlement as far as we know. We seize by the collar every invader who passes. We are the five brave brothers, and with our horses, we can pursue anybody!"

The brothers wanted to tell us everything about themselves, but I found it time to return to the Solvetower, which I had left behind in a hurry at an essential moment. Moreover, I had winked knowingly at Toodle. We both had our plans ready.

"We must leave now," I announced as I got up from the table. "I thank you warmly for your welcoming reception. It was an honor to make acquaintance with the Markese."

"A Markese always remains reasonable and fair," said

Lando, who accompanied us to the door, “as long as one does not come with dishonorable offers. Marriage is one of those in our eyes.”

I nodded understandingly and gestured for Landa to come along with us. Lando and Landa took us to the flying bird, which was surrounded by confused-looking and inquisitive birds. One had hopped on the seat of the pilot and tapped his beak against the handles so that the tail of the flying bird started wagging, all to the great pleasure of the other birds.

At our arrival, they flew up, disturbed. Lando shook our hands warmly, whereas Frint, with bowed head and looking as though he was eternally damned, took Landa’s hand and said, “Goodbye, my curse. Destiny is too much for me. No consolation is possible for me. In a while, I shall only be a breeze for you, lost in the game of the hurricanes.”

Landa started to gasp, making a face similar to Frint’s.

“Well, no! It’s not as bad as that!” Toodle said as she tore Frint away from Landa and into the flying bird. Toodle and I went behind Frint. I encouraged him, whispering, “Keep up, Frint! Pedal even more!”

The flying bird started moving. Lando began to wave goodbye to us. We were approximately one yard above the ground when I called to Landa, “Oh yes! I forgot which direction we must take from here; do you know approximately where the Solvetower is?” Landa, wiping away her tears, came closer to give us the answer above the moaning noises of the flying bird.

“Now!!!” I said to my fellow travelers. Frint made the bird swing abruptly so that Landa was just under us. Toodle and I bent to the right-hand side and stuck our arms far down. “Come, Landa! Hurry!” I exclaimed. We each seized an arm and tried to draw her into the machine. Frint pedaled hard, as a result of which the bird shot high into the sky outside

Lando's reach. Frint had some problems keeping his vehicle stable because we keeled over to the right from Landa's weight.

Landa continued to hang from our arms, astonished but delighted. "Yahooo!" she exclaimed brightly, greatly relieved.

"Landa! Deary!" we heard a scared Lando calling below us. "You don't want this!"

"Yes, I do!" called Landa back.

Frint steered the flying bird to the gate, which fortunately hadn't been closed by Lando. The birds around us wondered what this spectacle meant. Lando stood in the cage, upset. I saw him questioning whether he would follow us on his fastest horse, but he gave up eventually. His face tightened. As long as we remained in the sky, nothing could happen to us.

Thus, my relations with the Markese people remained stressed for a long time. It would be quite a while before their offended pride was healed.

"Oof!" sputtered Toodle, who tried to pull Landa up. With our united strength, we succeeded in drawing the chubby Landa onto the seat. She carefully sat down beside Frint, who pedaled higher up with pure joy, having regained his full strength. She gave him a kiss on the cheek and said, “With regard to my answer for your question—it is ‘yes!’” The flying bird shot again much higher and made elegant turns in the sky.

20

The return trip to the Solvetower was long again but went more rapidly than the outward flight because Frint and Landa, who now had also learned the art, pedaled especially fast and for long spells. Perhaps we had done something mischievous, but I didn't have the slightest remorse about that. I appreciated the Markese people very much for their border defense and their "noble soul," as they said of themselves. The trip was pleasant since all travelers were lively and had no thoughts of crying.

One evening before sleeping near a calm lake, Toodle said to Frint, "You have now experienced a lot of feelings from deep sadness to celestial gladness. Your heart was broken and is now repaired." She looked for a moment at me. "I have already discussed the possibility with Ody that you could become a solution coordinator in the Solvetower for emotional problems. Now you have experienced the complete range of emotions; you are extremely eligible for this task."

I interrupted Toodle and endorsed this idea, saying, "Everyone with emotional problems can benefit from your understanding. For this reason, do you want to help me in the Solvetower?"

Frint nodded gladly, and for the first time, he spoke words that he never could have uttered in former days: “Well. That seems a good idea to me!”

The trip approached its end. I was happy to return to the Solvetower where so many problems awaited a solution. Strangely enough, I had no more doubts as to whether I would always find a good and correct solution. During the whole trip, I had always been able to see the red sign of the Solvetower’s flag. The tower was, therefore, high enough to be seen all over the kingdom, as had been exactly my intention.

On a sunny morning, we approached the Solvetower. We flew over the forest and circled just around the highest floors. Below us, everything was quiet. There was nobody to be seen. To my luck, I saw that the tower had been entirely repaired and that no stone was lacking. The Stenodiggers and Stenoblockers had done their work well. I gestured to Frint to fly to the Stenodigger workshops, but nobody was there either.

“Where are they all?” Toodle asked herself.

Frint flew to the Stenoblocker workshops. There I saw a desperate scene. A whole mob, looking like one of Espra’s, ran behind the fleeing Stenoblockers. Leading the menacing mob, I saw Steno standing.

“Chase them off, people! They want to take over my little business!” he called.

Sseus, on a stamping, high-spirited horse, rode back and forth in front of Steno. Sseus wanted to stop the mass but was only pushed aside. Frint let the flying bird descend with great speed so that we landed exactly between the demonstrators and the fleeing Stenoblockers. Sseus was surprised and waved to us.

Steno also caught sight of us. “Back so soon?” he asked, disappointed.

We had landed just beside Sseus and jumped rapidly from the flying bird. Steno held his hand up as a sign that the group should halt. The first row understood this but not the last row, which continued pushing, so some of the forward line fell over themselves and turned around threateningly. The Stenoblockers still ran on, but when they saw that the attackers no longer pursued them, they hesitatingly shuffled back.

"What's the matter here?" I asked Steno with some severity.

"Oh, nothing in particular," he answered, sweeping with a foot over the ground. "This is a little matter between Block and me in which we don't want any nosy parkers. Better go; I've everything under control."

Block furiously came closer. "Be sure, we want nosy parkers and how!" he exclaimed, stamping. "So that those nosy parkers can see once and for all what kind of a shifty-eyed person you are! Mister doesn't like to keep his promises, does he?" Block roared with indignation and continued. "You know very well that the agreement was that I would take over your little business when the tower was finished, but now when it comes to the point, you incite everyone against me!" The two men continued to stare at each other with their rudest looks.

"Where did that mob come from?" I asked.

It's been here since Espra's departure," answered Sseus sighing. "Steno was very hospitable and until today threw them parties with lots of spirits and delicacies while his men and the Stenoblockers repaired the tower. The mob could not be persuaded to go home because the festivities became more important every day. The Stenodigger women took care of that."

"That was the least we could do!" interrupted Steno. "You can't send those people home just like that without a small bite when they have traveled so far to admire my Solvetower's construction!"

"You outsmarted them under my own nose!" exclaimed Block. "And I was a fool to have trusted you, especially as I have known all my life that, in any case, Stenodiggers can never be trusted!"

"I am as honest as gold!" replied Steno for his part, talking over our heads. "This idea of giving over my little business to you was not mine! It was forced on me, you know very well. And it was my 'reward' because you gave me back my own grubby bag of gold and gems!"

Sseus took advantage of the moment when Steno paused for breath to continue his report. "When the tower was finished," he said to me, "the Stenoblockers came, as agreed, to install themselves at the Stenodigger worksites and in their workshops. Then Steno informed the merry-making mob that the Stenoblockers had unlawfully invaded their houses. On hearing this, the mob was only too happy to help their do-gooder and host to help chase out the so-called invaders."

"Hey there, what about it!" someone called from the mob. "Should we go on helping now or not?"

"You had better return from where you came," I called with a loud voice. "There is nothing more for you to do here; all festivities are over."

A murmur arose from the mass. Steno looked annoyed but did not dare to contradict my proposals. Slowly the mob, men and beings alike, dispersed in all directions. Some of them still grumbled: "I call that impudent." "We are sent away as good-for-nothings when we helped so nicely!" "Don't be surprised about anything," said another one, whispering in one's ear. "That's that king of those sillies."

When everyone had gone home, I gestured to Steno and Block to follow me. Toodle, Landa, and Frint went to the Stenodigger workshops as Sseus joined our company. I walked to the Stenoblockers' cave and took a seat at their long stone table, followed by Steno, Block, and Sseus. This cave had now almost become our traditional negotiation cave.

"It's all rather simple," I said immediately to break the ice.

"Steno, you must now cede your workshop to Block. That was the agreement, and we cannot come back on that." Block nodded furiously, satisfied.

"But that's nothing in comparison to my small bag of gold and gems which I received for the construction!" Steno sputtered. I looked at him severely for a moment, whereupon he no longer dared to touch the subject.

"That doesn't mean," I continued, "that Steno can't do another job. Wouldn't it be a good idea if you, Steno, concentrated on making flying birds according to Frint's model? Many would like to have such a bird, and it would really facilitate traveling to the Solvetower."

"Oh, yes!" Block jumped up delighted. "Can I have one? I was the first one who saw a gap in the market! As soon as I flew that thing myself."

"You are crazy," said Steno calmly with half-closed eyes. "The king wants it for me, and what the king says, you must hold to."

Block leaned, his fists on the table, in Steno's direction. "You are a terrible harpy," Block accused Steno. "You are never satisfied."

"We could also mutually share the flying bird market," Sseus proposed.

"Share?" Steno startled. "With this impostor? No, that would never work."

"Well," said Sseus and got up. "Then I will make the flying birds myself." I looked at Sseus for a moment inquiringly. Did he mean that, or was it a tactical move?

"Now, you shouldn't be so ready to blame," said Steno uncertainly, swaying back and forth on his stone stool. "Let's examine the things clearly. I wouldn't mind sharing the flying bird market as long as I have a part of the construction market."

"Agreed!" exclaimed Block. "If it is only a small part."

"The quarry on my ground remains mine," added Steno. "I give the rest to you to be exploited." Block sneeringly laughed for a moment, but soon the two men shook each other's hands in the expectancy of some good businesses.

It was now time to solve the last problems concerning the Solvetower. The Stenodiggers and I were invited by the Stenoblockers for a small meal on the square in front of their cave. Steno and Block slapped each other on the back, sometimes really hard, as they continued to argue on the mutual distribution of the flying bird market. "Half and half," Block proposed. "Well, no!" said Steno laughing as if he had heard the most foolish proposal. "I have gold and the gems to buy the metal blades; therefore, you can only get much less than half." Block drew a mad grin but did not protest further.

After the meal, I asked Sseus, Frint, Steno, and Block to come to my office in the Solvetower, where I held my first meeting. We sat around the stone table in the center. There was a pleasant, quiet atmosphere in the room, as a result of which one would think that any problem would always be solved. I threw a glance at the relief carving of the Solvetower and saw to my astonishment that Toodle, at the last moment, had carved the flag on the top.

"Friends," I spoke, turning to my auditors. "There are still three things to do: In the first place, the solution coordinators and their assistants have to be appointed."

Sseus comforted us and said, "I have already summoned several. They may arrive any moment to the Solvetower."

"In the second place, Block and Steno, too, should ensure that houses are built around the Solvetower so that the solution coordinators and the solution seekers have somewhere to stay," I continued.

"Ha, ha!" resounded Block. "Leave that to me. That will be arranged in no time! Especially if this one here doesn't thwart us." He jokingly indicated Steno with his thumb.

"Wait and see," teased Steno.

"Third," I went further. "Frint must explain his flying bird to Steno and Block, so that they can find the necessary material somewhere and copy his design."

Frint looked full of pride and felt slightly honored since his invention was considered so significant. "It's not much," he explained modestly. "But if it pleases you, I will explain how the flying bird should be constructed. I have also thought about some improvements so that there is less jerking about." Satisfied with their collaboration, Frint, Steno, and Block left my office for the long walk down the staircase.

A moment later, Steno put his head between the curtain which fenced in the door opening and said, "There are all kinds of strange guys on the staircase! They say that they want to coordinate solutions."

Sseus, who had remained behind, jumped up to meet the "strange guys." "Ah!" he exclaimed. "Those are the men whom I have summoned for you." With Sseus's letter in their hands, they were admitted one by one to my office. They were all very different men and beings with high qualities. I usually agreed with Sseus's choice, but then better candidates submitted an application, and questioning the candidates for solution coordinators took much time. For each type of problem, they had to have particular skills. There were no Markese among them, although they had been invited; after Landa left with us, they had found my plans suspicious. Some young elves were appointed to receive, send, and prepare the elf paper. The century problems would be treated by a very old man, two centuries old, who had become so old by eating ancient, preserved food and who had already experienced these problems twice in his lifetime. The once-per-year problems were given to a yearling, the everyday problems to day-trippers, the constant work problems to a hard-working little girl who was religiously called "Impatiens," and the never-returning-problems that never lasted long to a very good, short-term thinker.

When all solution coordinators and their assistants were selected, dusk had already fallen. Satisfied, I walked down the long staircase with Sseus.

"You have become considerably more light-footed," panted Sseus, stopping just to regain his breath. "I've noticed for some time that you've got thinner bones."

I turned around on the staircase and looked mischievously at Sseus from a lower step. "Yes, that's because—" I started to explain.

"Because you have worked so hard," Sseus finished my sentence. He started to laugh conspiratorially and said, "Yes, I understand. I understand very well ..."

We continued to descend the staircase until we reached the forest. Large white X-shaped marks were on the ground here and there. Those were the places where Block had planned the construction of the new houses for the visitors and the solution coordinators. Sseus and I walked back to the Stenodigger workshop where we would spend the night. I saw some solution coordinators walking in and out of the Stenodiggers' houses, tapping the walls, and examining the window openings.

Block stood beside them and made wide gestures of explanation. "But there are only two possibilities," he explained. "Either you take a maisonette with a door and no windows, or you take one with a door and three windows, but then the price is higher."

The full moon illuminated the now-peaceful settlement. At the traditional campfire, Frint and Landa sat looking speechlessly at each other with illuminated smiles in their eyes. Toodle sat a bit further away, staring into the fire with her head in her hands.

Sseus and I joined the company. "Everything has been settled," I announced to my friends. I sat down beside Toodle and continued, "Everything but one thing."

I looked at Toodle and said, "We must give the Unbreakable Alliance Festival. That will be our wedding feast." Toodle caught my hand and smiled.

"We return tomorrow to the castle tree," I said to the others. "The great festival will be held there, and you are all expected there at the next full moon."

"Oh, that will be nice!" called Landa, delighted and clapping her hands.

"We will marry sometime later," Frint said. "First, I will present Landa to my mother, who will certainly shed tears of joy at seeing this marvelous young woman. In the meantime, I will explain how Steno and Block can make the flying bird."

The fire died down slowly, and only small remains of the logs remained smoldering. With a peaceful and calm feeling, we fell asleep. Our Unbreakable Alliance Festival had to be held soon because the first men would soon be arriving at the Solvetower to have their problems solved. Provisionally, the solution coordinators and their assistants would have to

handle them. I would soon see my castle tree again, but I was no longer the same Ody as before. With Toodle, it seemed I had become double, although we seemed together only one person.

21

The next morning everyone was already busy and working hard. The solution coordinators examined their offices and tried their stone chairs with curiosity. Block put his men to work on the construction of the maisonettes around the Solvetower, and Steno let Frint explain the flying bird more thoroughly once more.

"I find those metal blades are nothing but weak material," muttered Steno. "Wouldn't it be better to make stone flying birds? I have more faith in that."

Frint ensured Steno that, except for the stone owl, birds cannot be built of stone.

Toodle and I made preparations for our return to the castle tree. Sseus would stay behind, giving explanations to the solution coordinators about their future tasks. Since the flying bird had to stay behind with Steno as a construction model, we were allowed to borrow Sseus' horse. The horse could easily carry both of us because neither of us was very heavy. Everyone bade us a lively farewell, whereupon we sped over forests and fields with the wind flapping in our travel coats.

Since we had already taken the road between the castle

tree and the Solvetower once before, we knew how to avoid the unpleasant regions, such as the bird-eaters' foggy area. Moreover, I remembered the landscape from our trip with the flying bird when we had selected the spot for building the Solvetower. Thus, we could work out a quiet way back. We seldom stopped and took only short pauses for rest because Sseus' white horse had an almost inexhaustible strength, although it wasn't the kingdom's fastest horse. Since we were eagerly looking forwards to the oncoming celebration, we even tried to travel at night. We slept as much as we could on the back of the horse by taking turns in the back, leaning against the other while they sat in front. We encountered people and beings on our path that we greeted pleasantly without, however, taking the time to get acquainted with them or asking about their problems for Big Settlement Days. That would all come later at the Solvetower.

Having traveled some days in this way, the castle tree came into sight. There it stood in full glory with its huge trunk and its spreading branches. We jumped off the horse and let it go in the grass field. We went through the main entrance of the tree trunk and walked along the long corridors. There is a great quietness in the castle tree as if the occupants had already noticed that the Large Line had been prolonged. Arrived in my castle tree's study, I sent, first of all, for the Highest Festival Chief, who had this function because he had a large red nose. I explained that at the full moon, from the afternoon to the night, the Unbreakable Alliance Festival was to be held for Toodle and me and all our friends. Then I called the tailor who was to create Unbreakable Alliance outfits for Toodle and me. Soon, the entire castle tree was in commotion. Invitations were sent, large and expectant gift tables were built, festive recipes were considered, fabrics were cut and sewn to each other, flowers were selected for their smell and color, and jewelry was crafted.

The symbol of the Unbreakable Alliance between Toodle and me would be gold necklaces that we would wear around our necks. A competent goldsmith of an old wizard line would craft the two necklaces. When they were ready, he proudly let us see his work. They were simple necklaces with golden rings melted into each other. They were nevertheless light so that we would not be weighed down by them. The necklaces had a special power; so as long as we were both wearing them, we would know exactly where the other one was. The image of the other one would rise spontaneously inside us. However, this was nothing new for us because this already happened without the necklaces.

It promised to be a gentle warm day for the Unbreakable Alliance Celebration. For this reason, we had decided to hold the festival outside. Since the castle tree was surrounded by trees and a low thicket, it was necessary to clear an open spot at the foot of the castle tree in order to be able to receive all guests. With manpower, some big trees and their roots had been removed and replanted at the edge of the forest. Although this job was difficult and required much technical skill, the result was quite satisfactory. From the window of the library, I could see the clearing lawn downstairs. A lot of elongated tables had been put on the grass, and chairs had been arranged. It was nice to follow the furnishing of the lawn. The tables were covered with white tablecloths, and each chair had a downy white cushion. Additionally, large white lanterns had been hung in the surrounding trees, and arches of white flowers were put between the tree trunks. Everything would be white, and we—the guests, Toodle, and I—would all dress in white.

At last, the moment had come. Tonight, the moon would be full and would regard us with its appropriately white, round face. Now, however, the sun shone, which made the white crockery and crystal glasses sparkle. Toodle and I dressed so that we could go down and receive the guests. Toodle had an enchanting white elf dress of a fabric that one hardly dared to touch, fearing it would fall apart between the fingers. In my eyes, her long black hair had, for the first time, a golden blond sheen; Toodle had put on the gems which she had picked up from our visit to the Goldstream. I wore a white blouse embroidered in white silk with a pattern on the collar. It had a high square collar and a white band around the waist. The long white trousers were made of a soft fabric.

From my window, I saw that some guests had arrived already. They walked over the lawn and examined the cushions on the chairs where their names had been embroidered. More and more guests streamed in, some with large, wrapped presents in their arms, but of Sseus, Frint, Landa, the Stenodiggers, and the Stenoblockers, there was still no sign. As it was getting late, Toodle and I went down. I feared that we were obliged to start the festivities without our construction friends.

Exactly as we entered the garden and when the people with presents greeted us warmly, I heard high above us soft moaning sounds. Everyone looked up at the sky, where the sound came from. To my relief, I saw about twenty flying birds arriving in the distance. They were straining less than Frint's first flying bird, from which I concluded that Frint had improved his invention. We now clearly discerned Sseus, Frint, and Landa, who sat together on one flying bird and waved to us with white handkerchiefs. Steno, Block, and their men and women were divided onto the other flying birds and forcefully pedaled their vehicles ahead. Under the enchanted cheering of the other guests, who had never seen flying birds before, my construction comrades landed on the open space left between the tables. They put their birds between the trees and told of their joy upon their arrival.

When everyone had found his seat and nobody else was

missing, trumpets announced the beginning of the festival. The ceremony of the Unbreakable Alliance was simple. I hung the golden necklace around Toodle's neck, and Toodle did the same to me.

"Now he has been chained up!" someone from the company of guests loudly proclaimed in a voice similar to that of Rovericus and then laughed.

After this short exchange of necklaces, Toodle and I took places beside each other at a table, to the cheerful acclamation of the guests. The most crucial moment of the festival was, however, the banquet, for which so much care had been taken—more so than I had ever experienced. At the dinner, the guests, who were in a lively mood, dominated the festivities. The evening was settling in, and the moon was shining through the trees. An orchestra of flutists and violin players filled the air with light and elegant melodies, whereas the lackeys served successive platefuls of delicious spices. All food was white or transparent. We drank water that tasted as one hoped it would. Thus, many raised their glasses in a toast and exclaimed, gladly surprised, "What a delicious wine!" or "Such a delightful glass of milk I have never tasted before!"

The banquet consisted of ten courses, each of which was so light that at the tenth course, we wouldn't have been disappointed if another ten had followed. There was everything on our plate, including, for example, white rose leaves drenched in crocodile tears, rice castles with small flags of rice paper, white sugar clouds floating in white nut juice and white caterpillar porridge in a sheath of silk web, which was particularly and loudly applauded by the elves present. After our tenth course, a huge Unbreakable Alliance cake was brought in to much cheering and whistling. The cake had been made in the form of an enormous chain of soft fluffy cakes with whipped cream layers, all wrapped in white marzipan and studded with small, superb, edible diamonds. Every guest got at least one ring of the chain cake. Under the candlelight, the cake rings shone enchantingly brightly on the plate. Everyone was very pleased, and lively chatter came from all tables. The lanterns had been switched on and gently swung back and forth between the trees. The moon had risen high and was shining above a canopy of foliage.

When all the cake rings had been consumed, and before the guests got the chance to ask for more chain cakes, the tables were cleared to make space for a big dance floor. Several orchestras alternated between each other. First, it was an ensemble of shell players, then there were players with strange, plucked instruments, such as a kind of harp in the form of an “S” with two turns of “S” strings, and finally, some flutists who accompanied two mermaids from the sea singing splendidly, who had come onto land especially for this occasion. Their voices rang clearly and high throughout the forest, and they had a large repertoire of swan songs, howling wind songs, and of course, sailor songs, which they had frequently heard above their heads and remembered well.

We danced in large circles or in rows and jumped high and low until our feet refused to carry on. That was the agreed-upon signal for the giving of gifts because the large gift tables still remained empty. On arrival, most guests had hidden their gifts between the trees, under the thicket, or in cavities and searched diligently for their surprises. Some could not find their hiding spot, including Steno, who had found such a good spot that he couldn’t find it again.

Block used this as an excuse to jeer, then closed his eyes, and started to walk back and forth between the trees, where he quickly stumbled over Steno’s hidden gift. Triumphantly, he held the parcel up.

“You are a cunning stone-gnawer!” Steno blamed Block with an appropriately indignant face. “You must surely have removed my gift from my hiding spot beforehand and laid it down in front of your feet! You are a deceitful hard-head!" Steno and Block let out friendly laughter and punched each other in the side.

Toodle and I got the most well-thought-out and original gifts: Spring shoelaces that automatically fastened in a bow, plants that answered if one asked them a question, an old Elven poem compilation for Toodle from Rovericus, a mirror from Frint and Landa in which we could only see ourselves when Toodle and I looked at it at the same time. From Steno, we got a number of metal blades and other flying bird parts.

"And from me," said Block, when we had unpacked Steno's parcel, "as a gift, I will put a flying bird together for free for you both, one better put together than any flying bird has ever been before!" We were glad to get our own flying bird so that I could travel faster back and forth between the castle tree and the Solvetower.

When everybody had delivered the presents, and the gift tables almost knuckled under with the weight, Sseus came to us with a small parcel. Strained, I unwrapped the white paper from it. A simple grey stone with small sparkles and with roughly broken sides lay in my hand.

"This is the philosopher's stone," explained Sseus. Toodle examined it with admiring, cheerful eyes. "I have had it in my possession for many years and have saved it for you. It was entrusted to me a very long time ago by the last of the wise men. I was to wait until you should be wise enough to be allowed to have the stone in your possession. This moment has come now. It is yours or rather both of yours because you can't be regarded as separate.

"But Sseus ..." I said almost silently with stupefaction. "You've never told me that you had this stone."

"No," answered Sseus with prudence in his voice. "There was always the danger that you would not find a solution for the Large Line and for this reason didn't deserve the stone."

He looked at me with great friendship and continued. "There is more than the Large Line; there is always more. With this stone, you can go increasingly farther. The philosopher's stone stores all knowledge of its holder in itself. If it is given to a new person, then this person should know at least as much as the previous owner. That becomes a starting point from which the stone will continue to store more knowledge and wisdom. It will always lead you and will absorb everything you learn. The stone is no more than a tool, but you will see how fast you will understand things and can assimilate.

"I'm dumbfounded," I said, thanking Sseus. "You remain a surprising and transcendental person."

Sseus laughed a moment and joked, "But now comes the attractive part! You are obliged after a number of years to find someone who knows at least as much as you so that the philosopher stone can grow indefinitely and can be passed on. Have lots of pleasure with it!"

"It'll work for certain," said Toodle, full of trust. "Everyone can always think farther ... if his nose is long enough."

Hard slaps became audible above our heads. "Yippee!" called the guests looking up. "Flying fire!" Colored fire arrows were shot in the sky, and bouquets of silver-white diamonds exploded and spread out over the sky to fall elegantly down. Flying fire shot in the air from all sides and illuminated our faces at every "*boom*" and each "*bam*."

The Unbreakable Alliance Festival approached its end. After the last loud *bangs*, the eyelids of the guests started to become heavy. It was time to sleep before the sun came up. The guests slowly walked to the castle tree, where a convenient chamber and a soft bed had been prepared for each guest.

Landa and Frint walked up to us with sleepy, half-aware looks. With unconcealed regret in her voice, Landa asked, "Where is Espra, my almost-daughter?" Since Landa had promised to marry Frint, she picked up the habit of calling Espra her almost-daughter.

"We haven't been able to find or reach her," answered Toodle.

"I don't know where she is, and I hope all is well with her," I said for my part. Landa nodded, disappointed.

As the red of dawn became visible in the sky, all people present in the castle tree were deeply asleep now. A new part of our life started. We never heard anything more of Espra, until one day ...

22

Years passed by, and just like the day when I had found the large book of the old king, which stated that each king had to keep Big Settlement Days, I sat in the castle tree's library at my golden desk. For a long time now, I hadn't had enough time to sit at this table since I was, for the largest part of my time, in my office in the Solvetower. The Solvetower had attracted an inconceivable number of problems that needed solving. The Kingdom of Existence was infinitely large, and there had been more problems concealed than I had imagined in the beginning. It hadn't always been easy to solve problems, especially because one problem often hid another one. With the united strengths of my solution coordinators, we had, however, always found a solution because we knew the solution did exist and it was only the search for it that could be difficult. It also happened that Toodle and I, or I alone, sometimes solved the problems ourselves. The representation system of the local Elf Chiefs worked particularly well. If we received a report of a problem and the man in question could not come to the Solvetower, we took the flying bird to solve the problem on the spot.

Moreover, besides the solution coordinators, I had also appointed some problem-forecasters, whose duty it was to consider problems even before they came up so that we could solve them in advance and prohibit them. Although there were an infinite number of problems, a permanent solution to every difficulty was made. The Solvetower would continue to exist up to eternity, and we knew that for this reason, the problems would one day disappear entirely. We thought a lot and learned more and more.

The Solvetower no longer stood in a forest. The Steno-blockers had moved all trees or burned them up with their nocturnal campfires. They had built houses in the cleared area. Every house purchaser was obliged to buy a flying bird, without which they could not get housing from Steno and Block. Their business was run very successfully, and they were busy educating their sons in the stone, construction, and flying-bird businesses. Steno and Block wanted their sons to cooperate seriously with each other, but this only half succeeded because both sons called each other "son of an impostor!" and "child of an experienced dummy!" The Steno-digger women had given up weaving and now specialized in making jewelry with bits of the gold and gems that, after the completion of the Solvetower, their men had given them after many threatening appeals and sour faces. They made beautiful and exclusive jewelry which they sold to the Solvetower visitors at unreasonable prices.

Frint and Landa had been married for quite some time now and lived in one of the most beautiful houses that Block had built around the Solvetower. Frint had presented Landa to his mother, who, as he had expected, burst into tears, not of joy but of sorrow, because she found that her son had thrown his life away and that "such a chubby girl was nothing for him." Frint and Landa had then left the mother's house with everyone weeping and had married the next day without

Frint's mother's approval or the permission of Landa's oldest brother. Their wedding festival at the Solvetower, where Frint and Landa had seen each other for the first time, had been terribly cozy. Frint's flow of tears was of luck and joy, for which nobody needed to comfort him. Toodle and I had also come to the festival and had given them a pile of soft silk handkerchiefs that had an immediate comforting impact when used to wipe off tears. Moreover, if one had a cold, the handkerchiefs immediately healed the inconvenience with one blow of the nose. They had now four chubby children whose weeping could only be stopped with large effort. Frint and Landa were among our very best friends. Frint worked with much zeal and pleasure as a solution coordinator for emotional problems. He always found the correct consoling words for everyone. He never cried again, except for weeping together with the people with emotional problems who came to see him. Landa said that she felt very happy, but I noticed that she sometimes missed Marka and her family. They had never wanted to see her again, although they seemed to have nobly forgiven her errors. However, Landa had much pleasure going on trips. She loaded all four children in the latest model of flying bird, which Frint had again improved so that pedaling was no longer so difficult and tiring, and flew in every direction, visiting much of the world.

I was glad to have the time that day to sit behind my golden desk in the library. In front of me lay a brown notebook which I had just unpacked. On the cover was written, "Report of a Trip to Infinity: The Work of a Noble Markese." I had received the report today from Landa's father, who had returned from his travel to infinity. He had not traveled too far because of a lack of time but had nevertheless written a most interesting report in which he described the strange beings beyond the Markese area. It was the first time since Landa's departure that the Markese had given some news of themselves. The letter that was added to the report warned me that the noble Markese people would not withhold this report from me, in spite of the fact they could never forget my detestable behavior towards them. I took up the notebook and walked to the window so that the sunbeams could fall on it and I could read it more easily. "On the Unknown Beings of the Darkness" was the title of the first chapter.

"If you give me the ball now, you get ten points; otherwise, you only get five," said a clear, high-pitched voice from outside. I looked up from my book and saw through the window my two children playing on the lawn before the castle tree.

"But I rather prefer five points and the ball than ten points and no ball!" replied another young voice. A boy with blond hair and a fine posture hopped over the grass as he threw a red ball high above his head and caught it in his arms. A little girl with dark-red, gleaming hair and a similarly good posture as the boy stood quietly with crossed arms, looking at the game without commenting on it. They were both considered three-quarter elves, Toodle's and my children, as Toodle was a full-elf and I a quarter-elf. Since nobody yet knew that I was a quarter-elf, one assumed that the children were half-elves. The truth would come to light one day because people who are more than half-elf have eternal life, and half-elves or less do not. Simor, my son, and Albana, my daughter, the first real one after Espra, were still young. Their lives were filled with pleasure and free of troubles. With great joy, they learned the elf outlook on life from Toodle and happily invented elf-like tricks that nobody could free himself from. Nobody, except Toodle, Sseus, and naturally myself, although we had more and more difficulties in solving their riddles and reading their plans. Sseus visited us frequently when he was not in what Simor and Albana called "the Sseusen world," the area and house where he lived and where we had never been, because he wanted to have one spot where nobody could come to visit.

"You don't have much more choice now." Albana's voice came from the lawn. "This morning, I filled the ball with solution powder," said Albana, looking at her brother with a satisfied smile. "If you don't give it to me now, within two seconds, it will dissolve."

"Whiz kid!" laughed Simor, who rapidly threw the ball to her, whereupon she walked, self-satisfied, back to the castle tree with the ball under her arm. "Will you make still more anti-Simor dissolution powder today?" Simor joked, following his sister.

"No," Albana answered categorically. "That trick you already know now. Therefore, I must invent something else."

"Shall we throw stones? He who throws them farthest has won," proposed Simor.

"O.K.," said Albana mercifully. "Not a long time ago, I have found a couple of nice stones."

I saw the two children walk again to the castle tree and looked back on the Markese travel report.

Each being that Landa's father had encountered was accused of having a more or less noble soul than the Markese. Few found mercy in his eyes, except the "Intangible Pig-Eye-Likes," who had refused to submit themselves to his research and judgment. Landa's father wondered whether this was because they were so ugly or because they had noble haughtiness. As I got to the chapter "Of the Endless Plain Animals," Simor and Albana reappeared on the lawn.

Simor carried a large bag of stones, which he let drop on the grass. "You may throw first," Albana offered. Simor grabbed a stone from the bag and threw it with all his strength. "No, that doesn't count," called Albana. "Your arm was not right. You are not allowed to stretch it; you must keep it close to you and only throw the stone with a flick." Simor tried to do it again in the suggested manner, whereupon his stone fell just close to his feet.

"That's good," said Albana. "Now it's my turn." She also grabbed a stone from the bag and threw it very far away with a stretched arm.

"But you didn't do it according to the rules!" protested Simor, who had lost.

"According to the rules which apply to you," stated Albana. "I have my own rules since you didn't say how I should do it. That, you could have understood, couldn't you?" I saw Simor breathing deeply for a moment, and the game was resumed.

"The endless plain animals are useful for the Markese," I read further, "because they never contradict and always accept their destiny. One must, however, pay attention not to look them straight in the eyes because they consider that an insult, and one gets a sentence of ..."

I was startled abruptly by a loud yell coming from outside. "Aah!" The sound, to my horror, was like a voice that I had known all but too well in former days. "That you are doing quite wrong!" called the voice. I looked from the window and saw a plump yellow bird with spread-out wings landing at the astonished children's feet. "That game must be played differently," continued Espra, grabbing the stone from Simor's hand.

Simor looked at the yellow bird, totally astonished, whereas Albana looked severely at the game-disturbing bird and said, "Who do you think you are?"

"A king's daughter!" answered Espra with her nose in the air.

"I am the only king's daughter here, aren't I, Simor?" said Albana, as she flipped her long red hair backward with one hand.

Espra had the intention of making a big discussion point of this when I hastily opened the window and, with waving arms, called down, "Espra! What a nice surprise after so many years to see you again! I will come down."

Espra waved back and leaped up. "Daddy!" she called delighted. "Come quickly!"

Simor and Albana looked at each other, dismayed, until Albana got a small light in her eyes and concluded, "That must be that crazy bird that we have heard of sometimes."

"What crazy bird?" asked Espra, turning to Albana with a jolt.

I did not wait for the result, but put down my book, hurried along the staircase and the corridors, and joined the trio on the lawn. Espra firmly embraced me under Simor and Albana's disapproving eyes.

"How happy you must be to see me!" she exclaimed. "I have forgiven your errors and have come to support you forever. Your only daughter will no longer leave you, but ..." Espra patted me comforting on the back because I had a small "*gulp*," which she took to be a swallowed tear.

"Eh," I said when Espra had released me from her embrace, "you aren't my only daughter." I pointed at Albana and Simor, who had followed this discussion. "This is Albana, my daughter, and Simor, my son," I said and presented them.

Espra was quiet for a moment but then jumped, full of joy, towards the children, clasping them at the same time, almost choking them in her arms. "But that is terrific!" she exclaimed. "Sister Albana and Brother Simor! So, you eventually listened to me! You have married Landa!"

"No, not at all," I objected. "I have married Toodle."

"That suspicious elf?!" called Espra, full of disbelief, letting go of the children with a bump. "But you nevertheless kidnapped Landa from Marka? They are still offended about it."

"Landa has married Frint," I explained patiently, wondering how she could know of the mood in Marka.

"Frint! That weeping willow?!" said Espra, equally incensed. "What has my mother to do with that?"

"You must visit Landa at the Solvetower," I proposed. "She

would really enjoy that." Espra looked flattered a moment but soon made a face as if she had expected nothing else.

"Where have you been all the time?" I asked curiously. "You have not changed, and where are Kroo and Kra?"

"Of course, I haven't changed," she laughed. "I the old king's wish, so I haven't the right to change; otherwise, I would no longer correspond to the wish. Kroo and Kra haven't changed either. They are in Marka in the birdcage." She played with the stone she had taken away from Simor and continued, saying, "After I had flown away from the Solvetower and had done some flying around, I went to Marka where I once had the pleasure of finding Landa. Everything was upset at my arrival. Landa's brothers continued to disapprove of your behavior. They never explained why you did that. The insult was too much to be talked about. I looked for a spot where we could live safely, far away from your abuses, and where everyone could support my plan for a peaceful life. The Markese agreed after your unforgivable intervention; thus, I took over the management of the birdcage and explained what an honor it was for them to have a king's daughter among them. That attracted them; they had hoped so much that Landa would marry a king."

Albana and Simor wanted to take another stone from the bag, but Espra rapidly took everything away from them. "Listen first," she ordered them, whereupon the children sat down in the grass, sighing. "I rapidly took over the management of the birdcage," Espra continued proudly. "It has become a real paradise there, and now not only birds are coming but also people and other beings, except elves. I have already had enough of them." Espra looked reproachfully at me for a moment. "But my higher tasks were calling," she continued with a finger in the air. "It was high time that I came again to you with advice and action. You are becoming older and will certainly want to leave a couple of things to me. Therefore, here I am!" She spread her arms out broadly.

"Oof, fine ..." I stammered.

"I will sacrifice myself again once more. I have left the birdcage permanently, in spite of Landa's family's constant appeals. Kroo and Kra can manage there very well," said Espra.

"I'll see what you can do ..." I said hesitatingly, my finger brushing over my chin.

"I will first re-educate these rascals." Espra proposed this idea to herself already. "That's obviously very necessary. They even don't know how to play the stone-throwing game properly! Come on! Sister Espra will teach you that."

Simor and Albana stood up. I remained standing with them, reflecting that I didn't want to leave them with Espra. The news that Espra would now live in the castle tree had certainly not delighted me.

The recent years had been very sociable and quiet, and something in me said that Espra's arrival would radically change that. I wanted to go to the castle tree to tell Toodle everything, but 1 watched for a moment to see how Espra would treat our children. I saw Espra disappearing between the trees, looking around on the ground, and then drawing forth with twisting movements a large, heavy package that was entirely covered with leaves.

"What's that?" asked Simor coming nearer.

"That's what's missing in the game," explained Espra, as she required all strength to draw the package over the grass. "This will serve as a target. You don't have to throw a stone as far as possible, but you must throw it exactly on this target which is slightly more difficult." Here Simor and Albana agreed enthusiastically. Espra wiped off the leaves of her object.

"Hey, it's a present!" called Albana, who was always terribly good at recognizing a present if she saw one.

"I say, yes!" Espra said. "I hadn't seen that." The two children removed the paper that had become all green and examined the heavy object inside.

"Look, daddy!" called Albana to me. "It's a colored stone."

I examined the stone Espra had found. It was a grey stone with metallic grey veins running through it. "That's a strong, armed stone!" I said, surprised. I cleaned the surface with my hand so that the characters became visible. Painted on it was: "For Toodle and Ody. That your alliance will be as solid as this stone." I reflected on where this armed stone could have come from and how it remained in the thicket for so long.

"That must be Steno's present or Block's or from one of their men for our Unbreakable Alliance Festival," I assumed. "They certainly had hidden this present and not found it again that night."

"Well," said Espra, "it will now be our target. Come, sister and brother; we must go far away and then throw the stones." Simor and Albana stepped back, whereupon Espra gave each a stone from the bag and explained how to throw them.

"Miss!" Albana said when Simor had thrown far beyond the armed stone.

"An even bigger flop!" called Simor, laughing, after Albana had thrown her stone at the target.

"I will show you," Espra sighed and grabbed a beautiful large stone from the bag. She clasped the stone in her fist and made a firm, swaying movement with her arm. I was only half paying attention because Espra was being kind, and I let my thoughts dwell on which harmless tasks I could entrust to Espra and where she couldn't do much wrong.

Suddenly my heart almost stopped beating from fright when my regard fell on Espra's fist. Between her fingers, I saw the stone that she clenched. It was a harsh yet sparkling grey stone, which she swung rapidly back and forth.

'The philosopher's stone! No! Don't throw it!' I shouted

with full strength, but it was already too late. As in slow motion, the stone shot from Espra's hand through the air. It made a high arc in the direction of the armed stone. I still jumped in the direction of the philosopher's stone in the hope of catching it in the air, but I fell on the grass as the stone continued its course and smashed with a *clap* into the middle of the armed stone, breaking into a thousand pieces.

"Yippee!" yelled Simor and Albana, leaping. "Terrific shot!" Espra looked at the children proudly. I lay face down in the grass for a while, fooling myself this that had not really happened.

"Daddy," said Simor, "you lie in our line of action." I stood up slowly and dusted down the grass and earth from my clothes. With a slow step, I walked straight to Espra, who looked at me delightedly.

"What were you doing there in the grass?" asked Espra.

"Now it's over, once and for all," I spoke in a voice that caused nobody to dare to doubt my seriousness. "You don't even know what you have done," I continued when I was right in front of Espra. "You have just, in one nonchalant movement, crushed and pulverized the philosopher's stone."

Espra speechlessly looked at me with large eyes.

"That there," I said, pointing at the armed stone, "is an armed stone, which is so hard that any stone will crumble at the slightest contact with it, and on a quiet afternoon in the middle of a child's game, you just threw the philosopher's stone at an armed stone!"

"But I didn't know that!" Espra defended herself while her eyes searched for a way out.

"No, you couldn't know that," I sighed. "But in one way or another, you always succeed in causing disaster."

"Disaster?!" exclaimed Espra, who started to get angry. "You claim I sometimes bring disaster?" Simor and Albana held onto each other, frightened by this outrageous exchange.

"Leave it at that," I said calmly. "There is nothing more to be done; the philosopher's stone is lost for eternity."

"I won't leave it like that," persisted Espra, who was in a fine form now. "I came here to help you teach those elf-like, good-for-nothing children an intelligent game, and I am immediately accused of bringing disasters! You haven't changed a bit, Father! It is time that you realize that you yourself are the real culprit. Who was given this armed stone, which he then lost in the forest? Who leaves the philosopher's stone lying around to be freely seized by anybody? If that's not bad management, then what is it?" Espra was deeply shocked, and I couldn't blame her. I had no imaginable idea how the philosopher's stone had gotten into the children's bag of stones. Indeed, I had not paid enough attention.

"You're right," I said in an attempt to soothe Espra. "It was not your fault. Come inside; we will find a solution for the broken philosopher's stone."

"Forget it, Father!" Espra yelled without calming down. "I no longer wish to be addressed in this way by you. Ungrateful, that's what you are. I was stupid to have some hope for you after all those years. I get nothing but ingratitude and false charges. Goodbye! I've my own world where you don't deserve a place." Espra jumped high in the sky and soon quickly flapped above our heads. Without looking back at us, she flew away, high above the trees. We heard her words still reverberate in the air: "Ingratitude! Nothing but ingratitude!"

The yellow bird disappeared from my sight, and a huge feeling of compassion arose in me. This feeling disappeared slowly when I considered that Marka was the place where Espra could truly be really happy and where she could be appreciated as a king's daughter. After this day, we would never see Espra again. Landa met her sometimes because Espra came to Landa's home when it was certain that I wouldn't be in the neighborhood. From Landa, we heard that Espra was very happy and satisfied and was soon chosen as chief governor of the entire Markese people. Kroo and Kra continued to adore their mother and were shortly appointed as aides for the Markese top governing board. Espra's presence in Marka had led to the fact that absolutely no invader had ever penetrated the Kingdom of Existence. Bandits and other violent persons made a big detour around Marka.

"Sorry about my stone," sighed Albana, whereas she ran to the armed stone and collected the rest of the philosopher's stone.

"Your stone?" I asked her. "Where did you get him from? I had hidden it very well."

"I have had it in my possession a while," explained Albana brightly. "I found it in a beautiful box hidden behind books on the upper shelf of the library when I looked for a new formula for my anti-Simor take-away powder."

"But it's not yours," I sputtered. "It is the philosopher's stone. You can only have it if you are wise enough; otherwise, strange things will happen to you!" I looked at my daughter questioningly.

She lifted her large blue eyes to my face and said, "Nothing strange has happened to me."

"But ... so, you can already handle the philosopher's stone!" I said slowly and bewildered. I had never underestimated the wisdom of my daughter but had not expected that she could be so young and already have the philosopher's stone in her possession without disadvantageous side effects. "That is terrific," I said softly.

"As a matter of fact," Albana said and laughed, as she picked up the bits of the philosopher's stone and laid them in her skirt. "I had thrown my newest anti-Simor take-away powder on this stone, and it worked. It could never take away this stone!" Simor started to growl gently.

"What are you now going to do with the rest of the

philosopher's stone?" I asked, trying to find out how much my daughter had understood of the possession of the philosopher's stone.

"Distribute it," she said and then looked up at the sky. "Hasn't each piece of the stone as much value as the entire stone?"

I reflected a moment. "Probably," I answered. "The stone stores knowledge. It can register an infinite amount. This means that also a small piece of the stone can accumulate a lot of knowledge. It's a kind of growing stone, after all."

"Well," Albana said as she kept her skirt together with a hand in order not to let the pieces of stone fall on the ground. "Then I give you a piece"—she handed me a small piece of the philosopher's stone—"and you a piece." Simor caught a small part of the old philosopher's stone. "You are lucky that no more anti-Simor powder is on it, so you can keep it," Albana said with laughter in her eyes. "The rest I will keep myself," she continued, walking to the castle tree. "I can distribute it later when I find enough wise men. In the meantime, I will treat the rest with anti-nitwit powder, and then it will all remain well protected." Simor looked happily at the piece of stone his sister had condescendingly given him.

"Son," I spoke, laying my arm on his shoulder. "Times will change. Wisdom is approaching." Laughing, we followed Albana.

Toodle and I now had only a small bit of the philosopher's stone, but nevertheless, it was able to store all our knowledge. It was now Albana's task to find many wise men to whom she could give bits of the philosopher's stone.

With the passing of many more years, it became more and more peaceful in the kingdom. Problems had been removed or prohibited. Simor and Albana grew up successfully and enjoyed bright and wise lives. Albana invented many skillful new formulas, and Simor couldn't long be away from his sister's company. Toodle and I still felt as happy as during the time of the Large Line solution. We had the satisfying feeling of having made the correct choice. However, there was one thing about which I worried: Toodle had eternal life, and I did not, and I never wanted to lose her for eternity. But when I was in my Solvetower, I eventually found a solution to the problem. After all, I knew still the Wisest Advisor, who could change me into a child so that I could always start my life again. And this Wisest Advisor had an eternal life too. How often had I already been to her?

About Atmosphere Press

Atmosphere Press is an independent, full-service publisher for excellent books in all genres and for all audiences. Learn more about what we do at atmospherepress.com.

We encourage you to check out some of Atmosphere's latest releases, which are available at Amazon.com and via order from your local bookstore:

Dancing with David, a novel by Siegfried Johnson
The Friendship Quilts, a novel by June Calender
My Significant Nobody, a novel by Stevie D. Parker
Nine Days, a novel by Judy Lannon
Shining New Testament: The Cloning of Jay Christ, a novel by Cliff Williamson
Shadows of Robyst, a novel by K. E. Maroudas
Home Within a Landscape, a novel by Alexey L. Kovalev
Motherhood, a novel by Siamak Vakili
Death, The Pharmacist, a novel by D. Ike Horst
Mystery of the Lost Years, a novel by Bobby J. Bixler
Bone Deep Bonds, a novel by B. G. Arnold
Terriers in the Jungle, a novel by Georja Umano
Into the Emerald Dream, a novel by Autumn Allen
His Name Was Ellis, a novel by Joseph Libonati
The Cup, a novel by D. P. Hardwick
The Empathy Academy, a novel by Dustin Grinnell
Tholocco's Wake, a novel by W. W. VanOverbeke
Dying to Live, a novel by Barbara Macpherson Reyelts
Looking for Lawson, a novel by Mark Kirby

Author's Note

The *ODY* trilogy was written by a girl, starting at the age of 13, over a period of six years. With fantasy and wisdom, Ody, after experiencing a kind of Odyssey, becomes, to his surprise, the King of Existence (first book, *Ody*), upon which he has to solve many problems in the world of four existences (above-existence, below-existence, existence, and non-existence) (second book, *King Ody*), and later solving the problems of existence by building a solve-tower, (third book, *Ody's Daughter*), helped by the elf Toodle and troubled by his so-called daughter Espra. This complete fairy-tale trilogy, full of symbolism and humour, of 64 chapters, can be read to children one chapter each evening, thus stimulating their imagination and helping the parents to better understand their world of fantasy. The experiences with the Dutch edition are that children understand immediately the symbolisms and humour ("If it depended on me, I would call it right away the best, best children book of the whole world," wrote a girl of 9 years old), which is more difficult for most of the adult readers. Of the first book exists a Korean, Catalan and Spanish edition, the Korean one was selected for a series of children books of different countries, with for France "Le Petit Prince" of Saint Exupéry. These four editions were directly translated from the Dutch edition, which were published under the pseudonym of Jony Dubosch. At present a complete Russian translation is also available as e-book with XinXii ebooks.

Milton Keynes UK
Ingram Content Group UK Ltd.
UKHW021021181023
430828UK00010B/89